Get an exclusive bonus chapter to

Sign up for the no-spam newsletter and r

free

You can discover details at the end of t   ...verse

CW00507645

End of the Universe

Mastery of the Stars, Volume 3

M J Dees

Published by M J Dees, 2023.

END OF THE UNIVERSE

First edition. June 25, 2023.

ISBN: 979-8223440703

Written by M J Dees.

The Story so far...

Sevan's life on The Doomed Planet was turned upside down when he became embroiled in a resistance plot to steal a Corporation freighter, The Mastery of the Stars, together with Ay-ttho, and her friend Tori. They foiled a Corporation attack on the Republic, were arrested on Daphnis then freed only to return to The Doomed Planet to discover it had vanished.

Looking for Barnes, the head of the Republic, they returned to Daphnis but discovered that it had gone missing as well and then found both of them inexplicably in orbit around Nereid, where Republic Fighters attacked them. They took refuge in the same place as the President's nephew, Ozli, and worked together to get off the planet.

Ay-ttho intended to kill Barnes, but she ended up agreeing to take Ozli to Atlas to negotiate a truce between the Republic and the Corporation. No sooner had they reach Atlas than Barnes folded space to send the planet to a distant part of the universe. They only escaped by following President Man's convoy to the capital planet Future.

On Future, Ozli discovered that President Man had murdered his father and was intending to kill him. Ozli planned his revenge but died, not without taking President Man with him. Man's successor, Akpom Chuba, accused Sevan, Ay-ttho and Tori of the murders, but Kirkland overthrew him when the Trial proved that Chuba was in cahoots with Man. Unfortunately, President Kirkland forgot to pardon them and they became fugitives.

They visited Saturnian High Priest Brabin to get fake identities, which served little use when Ay-ttho was recognised on the nearby planet of Sicheoyama while trying to rescue the orphan Nadio. They tried hiding on Angetenar, where Nadio fell in Love with the revolutionary Scotmax. Then, when an asteroid storm made Angetenar uninhabitable, they fled to Scotmax's home planet, Herse, where President Kirkland had sent his offspring, Matthews, to be safe from the Republic's war with Zistreotov.

President Kirkland's partner murdered him on his victorious return, so Scotmax, eager for an opportunity for a new Republic, agreed to accompany Matthews to avenge her begetter's murder. Sevan reluctantly agreed to go as well to make his disguise as a bounty Hunter seem realistic.

Having succeeded in their mission, Scotmax and the others who helped President Matthews waited for her to come good on her promises. But they fled from her newly formed army. Sevan, Ay-ttho and Tori fled as far as Herse to rescue Nadio, before being surrounded by Matthews' troops. They escaped through a tunnel and fled to the tourist planet of Pallene.

CHAPTER 1: INSPIRED MADNESS

Matthews and Barnes sat in the Channeatune Room, the most expensive restaurant in the explored regions of the universe.

"I appreciate your desire to meet in neutral territory," said Barnes. "But was it really necessary to reserve the entire restaurant?"

"Don't worry," said Matthews. "This one is on me."

She took a sip of Spiced Eclipse Pish, the most expensive pish in the Republic.

"So, what's new, Barnes?"

"You asked me here for a chat?"

"You keep your eye on things. I can do with the benefit of your intelligence."

"What do you need?."

"The whereabouts of a Hersean called Scotmax and a Corporation mining clone called Sevan."

Barnes laughed.

"Now why would you be interested in a corporation mining clone?" he asked.

"This corporation mining clone is a rebel."

"I can't help you with your Hersean, but I know where your mining clone is. He also interests me."

"Where is he?"

"Not so fast. This mining clone, in whom you are so interested, travels with an ex-corporation security clone and an ex-Republic military clone. They have become somewhat of a pet project of mine."

"So, what do you propose?"

"A game, of sorts. I would like to see how resilient one of my mining clones really is. Let us play with him and see how strong he is."

"I heard your mining clones are indestructible."

"Oh no, they are destructible. We can easily kill them. I simply overcame the biological constraints so they don't age, but we can easily kill them, either deliberately or accidentally."

*

On the Planet of Pallene, Sevan sat in the bar where Ay-ttho and Tori had told them they would meet him, but Nadio entered alone and rushed up to him.

"What is it?" Sevan asked, seeing Nadio was too out of breath to speak.

"It's Tori and Ay-ttho," he said, once he had recovered himself enough. "They have taken them."

"What? Who?"

"I don't know. They could have been bounty hunters."

"Where was this?"

"They were brawl boarding, and they were waiting for them on the beach. I escaped without being seen."

"Let's get back to the ship."

Nadio followed Sevan to the Mastery of the Stars, but when they arrived where they had left the ship, it was not there.

"They must have taken it," said Sevan, staring at the space where the ship used to be.

He realised they were alone on this strange planet and, apart from the small amount in his suit, he had no credits.

"Do you have any credits?" he asked Nadio.

"No."

"Great."

"What do we do?" Nadio was panicking.

"We need to get a job."

"I can clean."

Nadio hadn't worked since he was a young thug when he had worked in the bar of the thug that was meant to be looking after him. Sevan hadn't worked since he had been the Chief Council Member on The Doomed Planet, but he doubted there were any mining colonies on Pallene.

They wandered back to the bar where Sevan had been waiting.

"We need jobs and accommodation," Sevan explained to the bar owner.

"Good luck with that."

Sevan looked at the tall armoured, long-snouted, small-eared bar owner with his eight legs and claws, which he used to hold and wipe several glasses simultaneously.

"He used to work in a bar," Sevan said, pointing to Nadio.

"And what did you do?"

"I worked in a mining colony."

"Used to heavy lifting, eh?"

"Erm," Sevan thought it might be best not to mention that he worked on the administration side of the concession.

"There are some barrels out the back that need taking down to the cellar. You can start with those," the bar owner turned his attention to Nadio. "You can start cleaning."

The barrels were too heavy for Sevan, so Nadio had to help him. In return, Sevan helped Nadio with the cleaning, though Nadio had to supervise a lot as Sevan was fairly unknowledgeable about the art of cleaning.

When the bar closed, the owner gave them a bowl each filled with some not quite dead marine creature and a mug of cloudy liquid which Sevan knew they made from Ocrex ink.

He did his best to eat and drink it all and had to defend it from Nadio, who had wolfed his down and was looking for leftovers. Sevan wondered why, of all the planets, he could have been marooned on, why had the gods chosen one where there was no pish or fushy to drink and the food was not quite dead.

'Nevermarble,' he thought. 'I just have to make the most of it.'

*

"Has our experiment on Pallene begun well?" Matthews asked Barnes via a tachyon transmission.

"We have removed all his colleagues but one, but he seems far from being crushed."

"Then we must increase the pressure until he breaks."

"Agreed. I will implement the next phase of the plan."

*

Sevan and Nadio slept on the floor of the bar.

"What in the worst place happened to you?" said the bar owner when he came to wake them.

"What do you mean?" asked Sevan, itching himself.

"In the name of Vyysus, God Of Magic!" Nadio exclaimed, moving away from Sevan.

"What?" Sevan looked at his arms and saw that it was covered so completely in yellow boils he could not see his turquoise skin.

"It's Scophumen Pernilica," said the owner.

"What's that?"

"It's normally caused by gendrid or iq'oik bites. I'll get you a healing staff."

"Why hasn't he got it?" Sevan asked, pointing to Nadio.

"They don't like thugs. Here you go."

"What's that?"

"A healing staff," said the owner, handing Sevan what looked like a broken piece of pot.

"It looks like a broken piece of pot."

"Your broken piece of pot is someone else's healing staff. Do you want it or not?"

"What am I supposed to do?"

"Burst every scophumen, otherwise they will swell until you explode."

"Every one?"

"Every one. And go out the back to do it. I don't want my floor covered in scophumen puss."

Sevan went out the back and began piercing the scophumen boils. Each one exploded spectacularly, sending green puss showering everywhere. As the boils he burst became smaller, the effect of their bursting became relatively less spectacular and he relied on Nadio to help him locate ones in difficult to reach areas.

However, no sooner had he thought he had lanced the last boil than more emerged and it was like the old fable of having to paint the Gaia Station, it was so huge that, no sooner had they finished painting than they had to start again.

"Why didn't they make it out of something they didn't need to paint?" Sevan mused.

"What?" asked Nadio.

"The Gaia Station."

"What's the Gaia Station?"

"It's a huge space station, the biggest. I wouldn't be surprised if it was bigger than the Tomorrow space station."

"What about it?"

"Why didn't they make it out of something that didn't need painting?"

"Why would they?"

"Do you not know the story? They take so long to paint it that, by the time they finish, they have to start again."

"At least it gives someone a job."

"I suppose so."

Nadio thought about it for a moment.

"Of course, if they used more painters, they would paint it quicker and then they could all have a holirotation."

"You are a genius," Sevan said as sarcastically as possible.

Working together, they kept the boils more or less under control, but by this time they were both covered with, and sat in a puddle of, putrid scophumen boil puss.

"Get this cleaned up," the bar owner said when he saw the mess. "Then there're more barrels to shift. Then you need to clean the inside of the bar."

Nadio helped to shift the barrels and, as they worked, new boils would grow and burst whenever they were pressed against a barrel or any other surface.

When they had finished moving the barrels, they had to clean the scophumen boil puss off various surfaces, then Nadio cleaned the bar. He didn't want Sevan spreading his puss around, as that would have meant having to clean the bar twice.

When the bar had closed, the owner gave them the same food and drink as the previous night and then told them they could sleep on the floor.

"But won't I get more bites?" asked Sevan.

"It doesn't matter. Once you've got scophumen pernilica, you're immune. On second thoughts, sleep out the back. I don't want puss on my floor."

Sevan lay down in the dirt outside, which seemed to soothe his sores. Nadio, in a sign of solidarity, followed Sevan outside and lay in the dirt next to him.

"Don't you ever feel like giving up?" Nadio asked.

"Why?" said Sevan. "I can't do anything about any of this, so why worry?"

"Do you never feel like it's all too much?"

"I always feel like it's all too much. It's a sensation I've become accustomed to living with from moment to moment. Why did Barnes create us so that we never get old?"

"You can't die?"

"I can die if someone kills me or I have a fatal accident or a disease. But one thing is sure, I won't die of old age. He removed the ageing process from our genetic makeup."

"Wow, that's cool," it impressed Nadio.

"Why? What's wrong with growing old?"

They lay in the dirt and stared up into the night sky.

"What's that bright star there?" Nadio asked.

"No idea," said Sevan. "Maybe it's not a star. Maybe it's a satellite or a space station."

"Or a comet?"

"Or a comet, heading straight for us so we can't see its tail."

During the night Sevan's boils grew and in the morning Nadio helped him burst them with the usual resultant explosions of putrid puss juice.

However, one boil on Sevan's back proved stubborn and would not burst.

"What do you think?" he asked the bar owner when he arrived to complain about the mess.

"Have you been using the healing staff?"

"If you mean the broken piece of pot, then yes."

"Well, if the healing staff won't burst it, then it must be a scophumen stubornus."

"What is one of those when it's at home?"

"A scophumen that won't burst."

"What happens if it doesn't burst?"

"It just gets bigger until your whole body explodes."

"I'd rather avoid that. Is there nothing I can do apart from poking it with a broken piece of pot?"

"There is a healer who lives outside the settlement, but it will take you all day to get there, and I'm not paying you if you don't work this rotation."

"You don't pay us, anyway."

"Well, don't come rushing back expecting food and drink and a nice floor to sleep on. Actually, judging by the size of that scophumen, you'll be lucky to make it to the healer. It'll probably explode before you get there."

"Would you at least tell us which direction?"

The owner extended a claw and Sevan and Nadio headed off in the general direction.

CHAPTER 2: A STAR IS GONE

Sevan and Nadio wandered in the rough direction of where the bar owner had waved his claw. All the way, Sevan wondered why Barnes had created him. His entire life, he had encountered nothing but problems. Even on The Doomed Planet they had bullied him at work.

Just when things looked up for him and they had chosen him as the workers' council representative, it transpired they had chosen him for his apparent lack of qualifications and the perception of others that he would be incapable of doing the job.

He would have been happy with that. The food and accommodation were excellent, not to mention the quality of the pish. But even his cushy job at the concession had to be spoiled when the resistance kidnapped him.

Sevan had wanted none of it. His aunt had always warned him about getting involved with anything too exciting.

"Don't get involved in anything too exciting, Sevan," she used to say. "Only bad things can come from excitement."

Sevan knew he should have listened to her, but it wasn't as if he'd chosen to do anything exciting. He hadn't chosen to join the battle of Genzuihines; he hadn't chosen to be imprisoned on Aitne, or stranded on Nereid. It wasn't his fault that his friend, Ozli and Ozli's begetter had killed each other, or that the President had blamed the murders on Sevan and his friends. And it hadn't been his idea to help President Matthews to kill President Ydna, or that they were constantly running from the Republic. It had always been his desire to return to The Doomed Planet, not go to Pallene to get stranded there as well.

Sevan looked at Nadio, leading him along the street. At least Nadio had wanted to leave Sicheoyama. He had sympathy that Nadio has lost his co-begetter, and that his partner, Scotmax, was missing, but at least Nadio wasn't covered from antennae to claws in festering boils. He could feel the pressure of the scophumen stubornus on his back increasing.

"Where are we going, Nadio?" he asked. "The pressure on my back is building."

"Let me ask someone."

Nadio approached a creature that looked strange to Sevan. Instead of antennae, its head was topped with thin fur but, unlike Nadio, that was the only fur it had, the rest of its dark brown body it had covered with rags, it only had one row of teeth and had stumps where its claws should have been.

"Do you know where we can find the healer?" Nadio asked in Republic Standard.

"Whoa, are those that scophumen? You are covered, mate."

"Yes, I know," said Sevan. "Do you know where the healer is?"

"What do you want the healer for? Just burst them."

"He has scophumen stubbornus," said Nadio.

"Oh bloody hell, you'd better hurry before you explode. The healer is that way," the creature pointed a stubby hand in the direction they had been heading.

"Thank you," said Seven, walking away as quickly as he could manage.

The enormous boil on his back was impeding his ability to both walk and breathe. Nadio tried to help him as best he could.

"He was an odd creature, wasn't he?" Sevan commented.

"Strange," Nadio agreed. "I've never seen a creature like it and such a funny way of speaking. Strange use of Republic Standard."

"Where is the healer?" Nadio asked every creature they passed. Some hadn't heard of a healer, but those that had all pointed him in the same direction.

"How far?" he would ask each of them, confirming they were getting closer and closer. The buildings became less numerous until they were in the countryside and then the vegetation became more sparse until the desert surrounded them.

Eventually Sevan could walk no further and lay in the road like a large green, blue, yellow balloon.

Nadio ran ahead and found that the healer's home was a tent on the crossroads of two tracks, seemingly in the middle of the desert.

"Are you the healer?" Nadio shouted into the tent.

"They seek healing?" a voice emerged from the darkness.

"My friend has stubborn scophumen. Please, would you help him?" said Nadio, searching for the source of the voice.

"Where is the physical manifestation of this illness?"

"He collapsed on the road here. I'll take you to him."

Nadio still couldn't see the healer. He stepped back from the tent.

A tiny figure emerged, carrying what looked like a huge blaster which was four or five times larger than the tiny figure but didn't seem to bother it.

"Would you like help with that?" asked Nadio.

"Show me where the illness is."

Nadio led the diminutive healer to the place where he had left Sevan. They found a large ball with roughly Sevan-like features on the surface.

"There may be an explosion," said the healer. "Take this if you see it."

It handed Nadio the blaster looking tool and removed a small rectangle from its robe, then unfolded the rectangle until it was as large as the healer. This, the healer stuck to the surface of the spherical Sevan before taking the blaster tool back off Nadio.

The healer plunged the end of the blaster into the centre of the rectangle, piercing Sevan's sphere. The healer pulled the trigger on the blaster and it sucked the scophumen puss out of the boil and jettisoned it across a wide area of desert.

Slowly the balloon shrank and Sevan's features became more discernible until he was almost his usual size, loose flaps of boil casing hanging off him. The healer removed the tool and sprayed Sevan with a misty vapour.

"Ouch, that stings," Sevan complained.

"Explosion is preferred?" asked the healer.

"Thank you," said Nadio.

"No, problem. That'll be three hundred credits."

"What? Oh... I... er."

"Have you abandoned the concept of money?"

"Er... not exactly."

"They always say: get the credits up front, but does that appear to happen?"

"No?"

"Oh well, all this stuff should go back in then."

The healer picked up the tool, fiddled with some controls, and a large sack emerged from the back. He began using the tool to suck up the puddle of puss, which filled the sack.

"No, wait," said Nadio. "There must be a way."

"Why? There is a way to get three hundred credits in the next nano unit?"

"No, but..."

"So, all this stuff should go back in before it seeds."

"Seeds?" asked Sevan. "What do you mean?"

"It appears to seed. That's how it appears to reproduce. It'll never fit in your boil sack if it seeds first."

"And if it seeds after?"

"Hmmm," the healer contemplated this possibility.

"Wait," said Nadio. "Maybe we can come to some kind of arrangement."

"Is it an arrangement that involves three hundred credits?"

"Well..."

"This won't take long," the healer carried the tool over to Sevan. "Now, there was a hole."

"No, please. Don't put that stuff back in me."

"There must be some other way," Nadio pleaded.

"Such as?"

"Maybe we could work for you?"

The healer laughed so much he dropped the tool and the collection bag burst, sending a river of puss flowing back out onto the desert sand.

"Oh well," he cursed.

A moment later, every lump in the puddle of puss burst into several small spheres which sprouted in all directions. Some tendrils rooted themselves into the desert ground while others reached up towards the sky until, within moments, the puddle had transformed itself into a small coppice of slimy tendrils swaying slowly in the light desert breeze.

"Oh, well," said the healer again.

Resigned to the fact that nothing more could be done, the healer took his equipment back towards his tent. Nadio and Sevan followed him.

"Still here?" the healer asked when he reached the tent.

"There must be something we can do," said Nadio.

"There is a river between here and the settlement. Take this and wash it."

The healer dropped his equipment at their feet.

"Of course," said Nadio.

He and Sevan took the equipment, then found the river and washed everything thoroughly, being careful not to damage anything. When they had finished, they took the equipment back and presented it to the healer.

"Hmm, not bad," he conceded. "There is some food. Please come and sit by the fire."

Sevan and Nadio sat where the healer had gestured and waited while he brought them a bowl of not quite dead marine creature, and a mug of cloudy Ocrex ink each. Sevan didn't complain. He was glad to have any food at all.

The healer gave them blankets to lie on and cover themselves with and retired to his tent, leaving them beneath the stars.

"That's odd," said Nadio after a while.

"What is?"

"That star we saw last night, it's gone."

Sevan looked and saw Nadio was right.

"Maybe it was a space station?" Nadio mused.

"The Gaia station?"

"Who knows? Or Tomorrow."

"I hope not."

"Why not?"

"Because if it's the Tomorrow station, then Barnes might be there."

"Barnes of the Corporation?"

"The same."

"Why would that be a problem?"

"He keeps trying to kill me, or not, depending on his mood."

"Kill you? Why would the head of the Corporation want to kill you?"

"Yeah, laugh it up, thug. I used to work on the Corporation's concession on The Doomed Planet. Barnes selected me to be the workers' representative on the council because he thought they could easily manipulate me."

"And?"

"The resistance kidnapped me."

"None of this makes any sense, Sevan."

"Do you think? None of it makes any sense to me either, Nadio."

"If you don't want to meet Barnes again, then it's a good thing that the space station has gone, isn't it?"

"I suppose."

"Are you afraid of dying?" Nadio asked.

Sevan thought about it for a moment.

"I don't particularly want to die, but if Barnes hadn't created me, I wouldn't be suffering now. At least when we die we can rest and criminals no longer commit crimes. The prisoners are free and the servants no longer serve."

"So, you believe in the better place?"

"I used to believe in the Giant Cup until I discovered it was just a moon. Maybe that's why I don't want to die because if the Giant Cup doesn't exist, then why should the Better Place exist?"

"But you must know, Sevan, that those who do good deeds will be rewarded by Ruthos, god of hope and evildoers will be punished by Tomos, god of revenge. And even if you have been naughty, Sevan, there is always Roraldir, god of forgiveness."

"You really believe in all these gods?"

"When I was on Herse, waiting for you all. I never lost faith because I knew the gods would protect me."

"Blah, blah, blah," the healer's voice came through the walls of the tent. "There is a god for everything. Ppark, the god of doing a poo."

"That's not a god."

"It may as well be. No idea of what is going on in the universe." He seemed to talk to himself.

"We are all entitled you our own beliefs."

"Even when those beliefs are wrong?"

"That's just your opinion."

"That's as may be, but it's also true."

"What do you believe in, then?" asked Sevan.

"The universe is a single entity. We are all one. You, me, god lover and Barnes are all the same."

"How long have you been listening to us?"

"We appear to be separated by a sheet of strun hide. It's hardly sound proof."

"How are we all the same thing?" asked Nadio.

"Think of the universe as a giant cosmic soup, with lumps floating within it."

"Okay, but in a bowl of treguns bio-algae, for example, the individual lumps of algae are all separate."

"No, they are not. Your mind just tells you they are, but your mind is an illusion. Everyone is nothing more than a group of stellar fibre vibrating at different frequencies."

Nadio fell silent.

Sevan couldn't get his marbles around the concept so he just did what he did with everything else he didn't understand, ignore it and go to sleep, hoping that in the morning it would have gone away.

CHAPTER 3: DESPERATE ALLIANCE

In the morning, the healer brought them more bowls of not quite dead marine creature, and mugs of cloudy ocrex ink.

"Oh, that ocrex ink is strong," Sevan winced.

"What is the plan?" asked the healer. "Call on the gods and ask them to help? Be careful, because wrath kills the foolish, and envy slays the silly."

The healer chewed on a piece of not quite dead marine creature.

"The foolish try to settle here," he continued. "Their camps are cursed. They bring offspring far from safety and are crushed at the gate of the settlement. No-one helps them."

"Why do they come here?" asked Sevan.

"The hungry have eaten their harvest. They even pick the stray crops that have been growing within the thorny red thimbleberry bushes. The thieves take everything. Evil does not come out of the soil, nor trouble. We birth creatures into trouble, as sure as the sparks fly upward."

The healer gestured to the fire.

"I would look to the gods," said Nadio. "They give us everything, the goodness we need to grow food, the water we drink, and when we pass, they take us to the Better Place. The gods confound evil creatures so that they cannot execute their malevolent plans. They bless the wise and ignore the awkward. They provide us with light on every rotation and save the poor from murderers."

"Where is all this learned?" asked the healer.

"We should be happy when the gods correct us," Nadio continued. "So don't complain about them because they heal us."

"They don't. Who healed your friend?. His boil sacks should refill."

"It is written," Nadio persisted. "That the gods will give us six trials and on the seventh we shall be free to enjoy the greatest halls of the Better Place."

"And you believe that."

"The gods will save us from famine, war, defamation, destruction, beasts, and land."

"I saved you from famine by the food you have now. Perhaps the gods should feed you."

"We appreciate your help," said Sevan. "Nadio is just very passionate about his beliefs. But what about the Star Masters? I've seen them."

"They aren't gods, they are just very ancient beings who predate all of us, especially the Republic."

"But the drirkel straalkets said they did the work of the gods."

"That doesn't mean the gods exist."

Sevan and Nadio slipped into silent contemplation of the healer's words. Nadio trying to think of other arguments to disprove the healer's assertions.

"Life is suffering," said the healer. "It is no good blaming others for woes or expecting deliverance. It happens and has to be dealt with it as best possible. Talk until you are pink in the face, but you must deal with it. Suffering occurs whether it is deserved and it will always be a problem. "

"I beg to differ," said Nadio.

"Understand the truth of suffering, the truth of the cause of suffering, the truth of the end of suffering, and the truth of the path that leads to the end of suffering."

"And you know the truth, do you?"

"Suffering exists; it has a cause; it has an end; and it has a cause to bring about its end. In the end, only aging, sickness, and death are certain and unavoidable. "

"But I don't age," said Sevan. "I'm a Corporation mining clone. I'm genetically engineered not to age."

"But you get sick and you can die."

"Of course. What causes our suffering?"

"Desire and ignorance lie at the root of suffering. What do you desire?"

"I want to go home to The Doomed Planet and see my aunt."

"Can you?"

"No, I'm stuck here."

"And so you suffer?"

"Yes, I suppose."

"And what do you desire?" the healer asked Nadio.

"I want to be with my partner, Scotmax."

"Can you?"

"No, I'm stuck here and even if I wasn't, I don't know where she is."

"And are you suffering?"

"Yes, I am."

"Because you have wants that cannot be satisfied, desiring them brings you suffering."

"You said desire and ignorance," said Sevan.

"Yes, ignorance relates to not seeing the universe as it actually is. Without the capacity for mental concentration and insight, they leave marbles undeveloped, unable to grasp the true nature of things. Vices, such as greed, envy, hatred and anger, derive from this ignorance."

"Whereas you know everything, I suppose," said Nadio.

"So, you know how to end this suffering, do you?" asked Sevan, ignoring Nadio.

"Reach a transcendent state free from suffering and our universal cycle of birth and rebirth."

"And how do I do that?"

"Understand, think, speak, act, live, try, exist and concentrate in the correct way."

"Sounds complicated."

"It is. By the way," said the healer. "That star you were discussing last night. It was the Tomorrow space station."

"How do you know?"

"For many solar orbits, this sky appears unchanged. Like the back of my paw."

"What would the Corporation be doing here?"

"Don't forget, the Corporation and the Republic have a long history of alliances, always supporting each other."

"What about the Battle of Genzuihines?" asked Nadio.

"The Battle of Genzuihines, a joint operation between the Republic and the Corporation. President Mann needs an enemy to distract the citizens from the failures of the Republic and so Barnes agrees to be the baddy."

"That doesn't explain the Corporation's interest in Pallene."

"Have you not heard? President Matthews has annexed a sizeable chunk of the outer worlds. Pallene is a frontier world."

"Are you not worried?"

"Worried? Presidents come and go. It doesn't really matter who thinks they rule the galaxy. It doesn't change the truth about reality."

"Which is?"

"That the universe is a giant soup with lumps in it. Anything else is just an illusion. There's someone coming."

Sevan and Nadio looked around but could see no-one.

"I can't see anyone," said Nadio. "How do you know?"

"My eye pits sense their heat," the healer explained.

Sevan looked but couldn't see anything under his dark, round eyes.

Sure enough, a group of creatures appeared from the direction of the settlement. The healer watched them carefully as they approached, but they appeared to be in no mood to stop.

"Where are you going?" the healer asked.

"Anywhere far away from the settlement," one of them replied. "Republic troops have just landed."

Sevan and Nadio immediately panicked.

"We should follow them," said Nadio.

"Why?" asked the healer.

"The Republic is coming. The Republic can't catch us."

"Where are you going to go?"

"We'll follow them," said Nadio, gesticulating towards the travellers who were already disappearing into the desert.

"To where?"

"I don't know. They must know where they're going."

"What makes you so sure?"

Nadio thought about it.

"Don't they?" he asked after a moment.

"They are walking towards the sodium lake. There is nothing but death where they are heading."

"Why didn't you tell them?"

"They didn't ask me. Everyone handles their own destiny."

"What are we going to do, Sevan?"

Sevan shrugged.

"Why are you so afraid of the Republic?" asked the healer.

"They are looking for us," said Nadio. "My partner is a resistance leader and Sevan was part of the force that helped Matthews take the presidency."

"It sounds like she should thank him then."

"Matthews made promises to those who helped her take power, but as soon as she had power, she went back on her promises."

"And what did she promise you, Sevan?"

"I have a criminal record. She promised a pardon."

"Of course she did."

"I'm innocent."

"Of course you are."

"What are we going to do, Sevan?" Nadio repeated.

Sevan shrugged again.

"What is the suggestion?" he asked the healer. "Desire for freedom is causing you suffering. Accept the present situation and it is easier to achieve peace."

"So, you're saying we should just wait for them to come for us?" asked Nadio.

"We cannot change the future any more than the past. All that can be controlled is the present. If there is something you can do, then do it. If there is nothing you can do, then don't worry about it."

"What can we do?" asked Sevan.

"We can leave?" said Nadio

"And go where?"

Sevan looked at the healer.

"Will you help us?" he asked.

The healer thought about it for a while.

"There is a tribe beyond the sodium lake. A visit to them is long overdue. They hate the Republic. You need to help me pack my things."

They gradually folded, dismantled, arranged, and tied into one large bundle, the healer's tent and all of its contents were which was at least ten times the size of the healer himself.

With ease, he hoisted the pack onto his back.

"Right, let's go," he said to Sevan and Nadio, who both stared with incredulity at the strength of the tiny healer.

He led them away. Not toward the salt lake but towards the mountains, which seemed to border the lake itself.

"Who is this tribe?" asked Sevan.

"They are the original inhabitants of Pallene, here long before the colonists arrived to build their leisure resorts. They used to live by the oceans, but when the colonists tried to exterminate them, they fled inland."

"Exterminate them? Why?"

"They wanted the colonists to compensate them for the land they had stolen."

"Sounds reasonable."

"The colonists didn't think so. They gathered in a line along the coast and moved inland, killing every gherceid they encountered."

"Gherceid?" that's the name the colonists gave their species.

"What is their real name?"

"No-one knows. They won't tell anyone. They say that if no-one bothered to ask them when the colonists first arrived, why should they go to the trouble of explaining who they are now?"

"Seems reasonable."

"I must warn you, though. They are a most hideous looking creature. They have no fur, except for a few tufts on their heads, and they are so ashamed of the purulent nature of their skin that they attempt to cover most of it with putrid rags."

"Sounds a bit like the drirkel straalkets," Sevan mused.

"Not a bit like them. Far more hideous. They have these little stubs instead of claws, not an antenna in sight. I don't know where they keep their marbles, and they come in hideous shades from light pink to dark brown."

"Sounds horrible."

"It takes all sorts to make a universe."

The healer seemed to have no problems walking with a pack ten times his size, whereas Sevan and Nadio were already out of breath following him along the track which led to the foothills of the mountains which surrounded the lake.

"How are is it?" Sevan asked.

"You are very impatient, aren't you? Don't think about the future, think about the now."

Sevan thought about the now. He thought about how tired he was already. He thought about how nice it would be to stop for a rest.

"Desire causes suffering," said the healer as if he could read his thoughts.

Eventually they did rest, but instead of enjoying the rest, Sevan worried about how long it would be before the healer would make them start again.

"When will we get there?" Sevan asked.

"We will get there when we arrive."

"When is that?"

"It is when it is."

CHAPTER 4: FORGOTTEN ALLIANCE

"It is when it is," Nadio grumbled. "The gods have a time for everything."

"This desire for order causes suffering," the healer told Nadio. "Our time in this universe is brief. Do not wish it away."

"There is the better place."

"Nadio, do you see that cloud over there?"

"No," said Nadio, observing the clear sky.

"Exactly. Our lives are as brief and as significant as collections of moisture in the atmosphere. We come together for a moment and then we dissipate."

"You shouldn't speak like that. You will upset the gods."

"I'm not afraid of what will happen to me once this illusion ends and I return to my place in the cosmic soup."

Sevan was hungry. The sound of cosmic soup appealed to him.

"What is going to happen when we find this tribe?" Sevan asked.

"Why do you insist on living in the future? You will find out when you get there. Live in the present. Watch where you walk, what you pass, how you feel, what sounds you hear, the photons heating your skin, the wind cooling you."

Sevan tried to do what the healer had suggested. He looked at the dusty track in front of him, the mountains which towered above on one side and the desert which stretched out on the other. Sevan could feel the heat of the day but also a light breeze, which came and went. He could hear their steps on the track, some distant tronqaks, and the rustle of leaves in the breeze.

They had climbed high into the mountains and Sevan could see they were skirting the salt lake, already some way around it, but he could still see the shimmer of the ocean in the distance.

They climbed further and then crossed a ridge and descended momentarily before the land flattened out into a vast plateau stretching out into the distance.

The plateau was dusty and barren but soon the sparse vegetation appeared and then became more plentiful and before Sevan realised; they were passing cultivated field and then fenced off areas enclosing bizarre looking animals.

Ahead, Sevan could see a hill standing in the centre of the plateau. As they drew closer, it became clear it was not a hill, but a construction fashioned out of dirt. There were ladders at regular intervals along the walls, and then Sevan noticed some of the hideous creatures the healer had spoken of. They were not dissimilar to the bizarre being Sevan had seen in the settlement by the ocean.

They wore rags as the healer had described and stopped their work to watch with suspicion as Sevan and the others passed.

There were shouts up ahead and Sevan saw several of the beings emerge from the top of the pile of mud and descend the ladders.

The beings waited for the group at the foot of the ladder and the healer took off his enormous pack without the slightest sign of fatigue. Nadio and Sevan sat on it to recover his breath.

"Why do you shatter the peace of the Çatalhöyükans?" one being asked.

"Forgive us," said the healer. "We did not intend to disturb you. We have travelled far from the settlement by the ocean to bring you terrible news of great concern."

"You are a trusted acquaintance of the Çatalhöyükans. Many a time you have assisted in the healing of our people. When you speak, we listen. What is this news of great concern of which you speak?"

"We believe the Republic has arrived in the settlement."

"Did you recognise them with your own marbles?"

"No, but we witnessed many unfortunates fleeing into the salt lake."

"You did not save them, did you?"

"Of course not. To have done so would have endangered the peace of your community."

"Thank you Notseldduh."

Sevan exchanged a glance with Nadio at the discovery of the healer's name.

"But how can you be sure it is the Republic?" The being asked.

"My colleagues here are fugitives from the Republic. They fear they are being hunted."

"And yet, you bring them here to bring the threat to our door."

"Llahsram, President Matthews has annexed all the systems in the outer regions between here and Future. It was only a matter of time before they came. Nadio here is a thug."

"A thug? Our elders still remember the days when thug and çatalhöyükan joined forces to oppose the Republic. We are co-begottons in weapons. But, Notseldduh, in those days, both the thugs and the çatalhöyükans had mighty armies. Now we are but a few and ill-equipped to face the technology the Republic has developed."

"Not just the Republic but the Corporation as well," another çatalhöyükan chipped in. "The Corporation was one of the first to arrive and steal our resources. They have built impressive machines which have scoured Pallene and robbed its treasure."

Llahsram nodded in agreement.

"My other colleague here is a fugitive corporation mining clone."

"Then he is the enemy!" the çatalhöyükan shouted.

"He is as much an enemy of the Republic and Corporation as you and I," Notseldduh reassured him.

"That's as may be," said Llahsram. "But it doesn't change the fact that bringing them here has put our community in danger. You must leave immediately."

Notseldduh moved closer to Llahsram and lowered his voice to a whisper.

"Think of this as an opportunity," he said. "You have something the Republic wants. Use it to your advantage."

"You may stay tonight," Llahsram spoke loud enough for all to hear. "We will discuss this together in my abode this evening and, at the beginning of the next rotation, I will make my decision."

The çatalhöyükans led them up the ladders onto the roof of the mud structure. Sevan realised it wasn't one structure but a series of smaller structures, all built against each other, with individual entrances on the roofs. The rooftops resembled a street with the doorways in the pavement. Smoke was emerging from many of the entrances.

Llahsram led Notseldduh into one entrance, but it ushered Nadio and Sevan to a different entrance. They climbed down a ladder into a small dwelling with a fire in the centre. The light which entered through the door cast a beam of light through the smoke. On the fire, a pot was bubbling. Sevan noticed what looked like the leg of some unfortunate small beast, together with grain and some plant matter.

Healthy portions of the mixture were heaped into bowls and given to Nadio and Sevan, who quickly devoured the meal. They had been exhausted and hungry and any meal was very welcome.

As he ate, Sevan noticed that the walls of the dwelling had been painted. The stubby appendages the çatalhöyükans had instead of claws had clearly made some marks. Other pictures depicted beasts, presumably the ones they were eating, while others were patterns of a much more abstract nature.

When Nadio and Sevan had finished eating, their hosts gave them a cloudy drink poured from large jugs into glazed mud cups. Sevan soon realised that the strange tasting liquid was just as potent as pish or fushy and it went straight to his marbles.

Their hosts perceived they were struggling to stay awake and prepared beds for them on the mud benches they had been using as seats. Sevan settled down on and under some of the softest blankets he had ever encountered and soon fell asleep. The scabs from his boils no longer bothered him and he submersed into a deep sleep

Sevan had a terrible dream. He dreamt about the healer who seemed to attack him in his bed. Sevan wanted to fight off the healer, but inexplicably couldn't move his limbs.

When he awoke, he was perspiring profusely, and the healer was sitting beside him.

"I dreamt about you," said Sevan. "You were attacking me, but I couldn't move."

"What is I, Sevan? We are all I."

"What are you talking about?"

"That wasn't a dream. You were feverish, your wounds have become infected. They have been treated, but it will take time for the remedy to work."

"But I couldn't move."

"You mean the illusion of your physical self could not."

"That doesn't make sense."

"You had to be held down because you were delirious."

"Where am I?"

"That is a good Question. What is I, who is I, why is I and how is I and when is I are equally valid."

"Just answer the question."

"What you perceive around you is known as the city of the çatalhöyükans."

"What about the Republic?"

"Llahsram is making preparations for their inevitable arrival. There is nothing now but rest."

"Where is Nadio?

"The one you call Nadio is being looked after at another house. You'll undoubtedly see him soon."

*

"The alliance between our societies goes back many solar cycles," Llahsram told Nadio. "Long before either of us was birthed. Long before the Republic or the Corporation existed. There have been many changes since then. The Republic and the Corporation have both grown large and powerful. Our people can no longer combat such a threat."

"What are you saying?"

"If the Republic is coming, as we think they are, then it will be almost impossible to defend our city. We will almost certainly be destroyed. I have a responsibility to my people, over and above the debt we share with the Thug."

"You are going to give us up, aren't you? Where is Sevan? We need to leave."

"Sevan is not in a position to travel at the moment. Notseldduh is taking care of him."

Nadio panicked.

"What I mean is that Notseldduh is looking after him. His wounds are infected, he is being treated."

"This is outrageous. We won't be part of your plan."

"It is you who brought the Republic here."

"I wish to be taken to Sevan immediately."

"Very well."

*

"Sevan! They are going to give us up to the Republic," said Nadio, as he descended the ladder into the home where Sevan was being treated. "We need to go before they get here."

He looked at Sevan and realised his friend was in no state to travel.

"What's wrong with him?"

"The body is infected. It is healing," said Notseldduh.

"You go," said Sevan. "I'll take my chances."

"I'm not leaving without you."

"There's no point in us both being captured. You find Scotmax."

"What use am I going to be in this desert all alone?"

"It's not all desert. I heard that beyond the mountains, there is a forest."

"Where the megadons eat creatures like you," said Notseldduh.

"See," said Nadio.

"What happened to this great alliance between these people and the thugs they were talking about?"

"It seems to have been forgotten."

"We have not forgotten," Llahsram interrupted. "We are, even now, praying over the graves of our ancestors to bring your friend good health. He gestured to two çatalhöyükans, huddled under the table praying to the floor."

"You bury your ancestors under the table in your own homes?" asked Sevan.

"Of course. Where do you bury yours?"

Nadio and Sevan stared at Llahsram with incredulity.

"It comforts us to know that our loved ones are still with us in our homes," Llahsram continued.

"They are coming!" a çatalhöyükan shouted down through the entrance.

"Please excuse me," said Llahsram. "I must prepare to greet our visitors."

CHAPTER 5: BATTLE LINES

When Nadio emerged from the entrance of the roof of the dwelling, he saw the çatalhöyükans had assembled a defence force which stood in lines across the rooftops facing in the settlement's direction. He imagined some kind of Republic force must be approaching.

He tried to approach the lines of çatalhöyükan defenders, but was stopped by Notseldduh.

"Back inside," said the healer. "It isn't safe here."

"If you trusted in the gods, you wouldn't be so afraid," said Nadio.

"We are the same," said Notseldduh. "We both believe that life is suffering. The only difference is that, for me, desire causes suffering and to free myself from desire will bring me true contentment in this life. You have been told by those who wish you to suffer on their behalf that, if you suffer for them in this life, you will reap your rewards in the better place, but if there is no better place then you have slaved for others for nothing, whereas if you find true happiness in this life, a better place would be a bonus."

"But we have to suffer in this life in order to reach the Better Place."

"And who told you this? Those who wish to keep you on slavery and penury in order to generate wealth for them."

"You expect us to find happiness in this life by handing us over to the Republic?"

"You suffer because you desire to be free of the Republic. Embrace your captivity and you will find the path to happiness."

"It is the gods who tell us these things?"

"Is it?"

"Of course, they created us."

"Did they?"

"Yes, we came from the gods and we will go back to the gods."

"We are and always will be part of the universe."

Notseldduh led Nadio into the dwelling where Sevan was recovering.

"The Republic is here," said Nadio as he was descending the ladder. "They are going to hand us over."

"They have no choice," said Notseldduh. "They have a responsibility to their own community first. Besides, nothing has been decided. The çatalhöyükans have formed a defensive line and are preparing to negotiate. It is to be hoped that the Republic is minded towards a discussion. By the way, you may be interested to know that your star returned last night. If it is the Tomorrow station, then Barnes could coordinate the operation personally. You must be a very important clone."

"I hope he is," said Sevan. "I will ask him why he created me the way he did and why he is so insistent on tormenting us. I think it is because we remind him of his own imperfections."

"So, you are happy to go?"

"I'm not happy, but there is very little we can do about it, so why "

"Now you are getting the idea," said Notseldduh.

"Not really," said Sevan. "I have serious doubts about going. I don't want to go, but there is not much I can do about it."

"How do you feel?"

"Scared. I don't know if I can face Barnes. Do I have what it takes? Should I go at all or should we try to escape?"

"Yes, let's escape," Nadio urged.

"Llahsram is negotiating with them. Let's see what he has to say."

The time units dragged by slower than ever as they waited in the gloomy dwelling for news of the meeting between the Republic and the çatalhöyükans.

Eventually, Llahsram descended the ladder.

"They have clarified that they have come for you both," he said. "They want us to hand you over and were very detailed in their account of the repercussions on our community if we don't. I have a duty to protect our community, but I also have a duty to respect the ancient alliance between the çatalhöyükans and the thugs. Therefore, we have allowed you to choose. If you choose to go peaceably with the Republic, we have their assurances that they will treat you with the utmost respect, however, should you not wish to go then we are prepared to fight the Republic to prevent them from taking you, whatever the cost."

"Well, that's settled then," said Nadio. "We fight."

"No," said Sevan. "It is very kind of you to offer to sacrifice your community on our behalf, Llahsram. But this is too great a price to pay."

"What are you talking about?" Nadio was dumbfounded.

"Nadio, you also have a duty to maintain the alliance between the thugs and çatalhöyükans, and that alliance does not allow for the sacrifice of an entire community to protect one. You understand that?"

Nadio was silent.

"Tell the Republic we will go," said Sevan. "You have been very kind to us and we hope that someday we can repay your kindness."

"You already have," said Llahsram.

They made their preparations to leave, thanked the owners of the dwelling and followed Llahsram to the rooftop where, beyond the lines of çatalhöyükans, they could see Republic forces stretching out across the mountains and down to the sodium lake below.

"They must consider you to be very important," said Llahsram.

"Apparently they do," Sevan agreed. "But I can't imagine why."

They passed through the ranks of relieved looking çatalhöyükan troops and descended the ladder to the foot of the settlement where Republic officers were waiting.

"Sevan Thowsandantwentee For?" one officer asked.

"That's me," said Sevan.

"That's your full name?" asked Nadio, barely able to stifle a giggle.

"Nadio, offspring of Nosliw, partner of Scotmax?" that's me, said Nadio.

"That's your full name?" Sevan asked sarcastically.

"It's not as bad as yours."

"You are both to come with us," the officer continued. "You are to come peacefully. If you offer any resistance, we will deal with you by force."

The Republic officers led them down the mountain to a shuttle that was waiting on the edge of the sodium lake. Once inside, they took Sevan and Nadio to a cell and locked inside.

"Purely for your own safety," an officer reassured them.

From his experience, Sevan knew Republic shuttles carried some of the best pish in the galaxy, but he doubted very much that he would sample any on this trip.

For a long time, the shuttle remained where it was and Sevan could hear much activity from outside the cell block. Eventually it took off, but as the cell block contained no observation windows, Sevan could not work out which direction they were heading.

It couldn't have been very far, because, in a relatively short amount of time, the shuttle docked with something.

After another wait, guards arrived to take Sevan and Nadio from their cells. The guards escorted them off the shuttle and onto a large space station which Sevan thought could have been the Tomorrow station which he had visited before.

It was a long walk to their new cell, which was even less comfortable than the one they had shared on the shuttle.

"Why did we have to come here?" Nadio complained.

"If we hadn't, they would have probably wiped out the çatalhöyükans."

"They probably will anyway."

That thought hadn't occurred to Sevan, and he was now worried about Notseldduh, Llahsram, and the rest of the çatalhöyükans.

"What do you think they will do with us?" asked Nadio.

"I'm not sure, but I hope they take us to see Barnes. I would like to give him a piece of my mind. What's he playing at?"

"And if he's not here?"

"I'll search the universe if I have to."

"It's a gigantic place. Prepare your hearts for the gods. Reach out to them, they will help you forget all your troubles. They will keep you safe."

"They haven't done a wonderful job so far. Maybe Notseldduh is right? Maybe we are simply lumps in a soup of vibrating strings."

"That's just primitive superstition. You need to put your faith in science, which was created by the gods to help us understand their will."

"I wish your gods could get us out of our predicament, but I have been thinking about what Notseldduh said about desire causing suffering and suffering causing pain. We are only unhappy because we don't want to be in this cell. As soon as we accept being in this cell, it ceases to be a problem."

"Why would we accept being in this cell?"

"To end our suffering."

Nadio tried to contemplate Sevan's argument, but it hurt his marbles.

"Are you turning into a healer?" Nadio asked, when he had given up trying to understand Sevan's argument.

"Would that be a bad thing?"

"Of all the ustrtors' rat flakes in the universe, I have to be stuck in here with you."

"Accept it, Nadio, and your suffering will end."

Nadio grumbled inaudibly.

"There is nothing we can do about our situation, so why worry about it?" Sevan continued.

His words only made Nadio more grumpy.

"If you asked a tronqak what time it is, what would they say?" Sevan foolishly continued to explain.

"Nothing, tronqaks can't speak Republic standard."

"No, but if they could speak, what would they say?"

"If a tronqak spoke to me, I wouldn't be asking it what the time was. I'd be asking it how it learned to speak."

"Forget about its ability to speak. Just think about the question. If you asked a tronqak what the time was..."

"Where would a tronqak keep its timepiece? On its wing? It wouldn't be able to fly with a timepiece attached to its wing."

"No, it wouldn't have a timepiece..."

"Of course not, it's a tronqak."

"What I mean is, if you asked a tronqak what the time is, it would say: 'Now'. Tronqaks don't have any concept of time."

"Of course not, it's a tronqak. If you asked it what time it was, it would probably just bite your head off."

"Exactly, because they don't worry about the past or the future, they just think about now."

"You don't half talk some uxclod sometimes, Sevan."

A guard interrupted their philosophical meanderings.

"Follow me," she said after she had opened the cell.

Sevan couldn't help marvel at how similar she looked to Ay-ttho until he realised she was probably a Corporation Clone and therefore would look similar to Ay-ttho. Then the realisation hit him. Although they had been picked up on Pallene by Republic troops, they had taken them to a

Corporation station, perhaps Tomorrow or even Gaia, the largest station of them all. Sevan had thought the surroundings had looked familiar. He had been on Tomorrow before and now he was sure this was the same station.

"What does the Corporation want with us?" Sevan asked the clone.

"Shut up and keep walking," came the curt reply.

The guard led them into a large chamber and placed into a booth. Sevan had the sensation of being watched, but black reflective material surrounded them so all they could see were dark shadows of themselves.

"Sevan Thowsandantwentee For," a voice echoed around the chamber.

He looked around, but he couldn't see who owned the voice.

"We have found you guilty of crimes to both the Corporation and the Republic," the voice continued. "We sentence you to a life of penal servitude in The Dark City."

"Nadio, offspring of Nosliw, partner of Scotmax?"

"Yes?" Nadio acknowledged nervously.

"We have found you guilty of treason in the Republic. You are sentenced to death. We will carry out the sentence immediately."

CHAPTER 6: MEETING IN SPACE

"Hold on one unit," Sevan pleaded. "I haven't had a trial."

"Your trial has just concluded."

"We didn't defend ourselves."

"You have no defence."

"I will be his defence," said Nadio. "With what crimes are you charging him?"

"We have found you guilty of the following crimes. Using a guard's seat on a Corporation shuttle."

"Really? That's it?" asked Nadio.

"Taking unnecessarily long shuttle routes to your place of work."

"Only to get a seat," said Sevan

"Failure to meet targets on The Doomed Planet mining concession."

"Tsk tsk," said Nadio

"Hardly a crime," Sevan complained

"Consorting with members of the 'so called' resistance in your workplace."

"Who?"

"Fore."

"Fore! He was as pro-corporation as they come, wasn't he?"

"Assisting the resistance to infiltrate the council."

"Who?"

"Thertee."

"Okay, he might have been a member of the resistance, but I didn't know."

"Consuming illegal drugs?"

"When?" Nadio's eyes widened

"In Thertee's apartment."

"The pill he gave me? How was I to know?"

"Ignorance is no defence in the marbles of the law," said Nadio.

"You are my defence," Sevan grumbled.

"Oh yes, sorry. I was getting carried away."

All this talk of Sevan's life on the Doomed Planet made him think about his life there. He missed his entertainment implant and wondered what was happening in 'Where the Hills Shine Most', his favourite show.

"Watching illegal films."

This jolted Sevan from his rotation dream.

"Where the Hills Shine Most?"

"No, History Lesson."

"But an important council member gave that to me."

"We found it hidden in your living quarters. You stole a Corporation freighter, for which they gave you the automatic penalty of immediate termination."

"Why am I still here, then?"

"We haven't finished yet. You attempted to assassinate President Man at the Genzuihines diplomatic conference."

"You didn't?" It impressed Nadio.

"I did not," Sevan protested. "It was the Corporation spies that attempted to kill him."

"You stole the presidential cruiser."

"You are naughty."

"Shut up Nadio. The president told us to fly it."

"You scuttled the ship and fled in an escape pod."

"That bit is true."

Nadio made notes.

"Stealing food and damaging property in a Genzuihines property."

"Wait. How do you know all this? And, anyway, they tried to help me before they were murdered."

"Sabotage of an alliance shuttle."

"Uxclod! Stray fire hit it."

"My client is sorry for their language," Nadio apologised

"The murder of three Alliance guards."

Nadio looked shocked.

"They were torturing me and would have killed me."

"Vandalism of an Alliance ship."

"Well, technically, that wasn't me."

"We have footage of you blasting the control room entry controls."

"Okay, yes, technically, that was me."

Nadio shook his head and made more notes.

"You sabotaged the space station Tomorrow."

"Impressive," Nadio whistled.

"I only distracted Barnes while the Republic was attacking."

"You also destroyed part of the Hygeia community on the Doomed Planet."

"That wasn't me."

"Who was it then?" asked Nadio.

"And started fires in several communities. Where you had been witnessed behaving drunk and disorderly."

"That definitely wasn't me. I was taking Ay-ttho to the Tomorrow space station. The drunk bit might be true, but...."

"You gave the orders."

"Did you?"

"I did not."

"And you fixed the election to re-elect your friends."

"They are not, and have never been, my friends."

"Who?"

"You also ordered the murders of a Corporation Security patrol."

"When?"

"You had Ay-ttho carry out the act in the Mastery if the Stars."

"Oh, that. They just woke her up too early, that was all."

"I can feel that," Nadio empathised.

"Stealing a Corporation shuttle."

"Hang on, we've already had that one," Nadio interjected.

"No, that was a freighter, this was a shuttle."

"My mistake," said Nadio, consulting his notes. "Carry on."

"And a fighter."

"A fighter as well," Nadio shook his head.

"Hang on," said Sevan. "It was technically Tori who stole the shuttle and the fighter."

"But you did not stop him."

"You didn't?"

Sevan gave Nadio a hard stare. Nadio buried his head in his notes.

"And you damaged all vehicles beyond repair. You also associated with the traitor known as the professor."

"Oh, for fushy's sake, you're really digging deep, aren't you?"

"And you murdered a dozen Corporation guards."

"Where?"

"On Daphnis."

"They shot each other?"

"Why would they shoot each other?" asked Nadio.

"Are you sure you're not on their side?" Sevan complained. "And the Corporation sent me to Aitne following that precise incident."

"What is Aitne?" asked Nadio.

"It's a prison asteroid. You really don't want to go there."

"It was on Aitne that you attempted to attack President Mann."

"You attacked the President?"

"I didn't attack the President. In fact, he thanked me for my service in the battle of Genzuihines and for my service on the Doomed Planet."

"Do you have proof of this?" asked the voice.

"No, but..."

"You stole a presidential escape pod, damaging two buildings on Future, and conspired with the traitors Daxu, Pelou Furle, D'Heli and Alyr..."

"Traitors?" Sevan was confused.

"You have been naughty," said Nadio

"... to cause an exodus on Future and kidnap the leader of the Corporation."

"Barnes thanked us for the exodus," Sevan protested. "And we didn't kidnap him. We should have done."

"You took part in illegal gambling and fighting on Pandoria...."

"How could you possibly know all this?"

"They've got you good."

"... destroyed Corporation and Republic fleets and then stole another Corporation ship which you took to Nereid. And then there is consorting with Tenuils pirates."

"Hardly consorting. They tried to kill us."

"Then you forged a message from the President to engineer the deaths of his messengers."

"It was Ozli who did that."

"Convenient that you blame someone who cannot defend himself."

"They've got a point," said Nadio.

"Shut up," said Sevan.

"If you were innocent, you would not have fled," said the voice.

"Kirkland told us to go."

"More claims that cannot be substantiated. You also smuggled illegal aliens."

Sevan looked confused.

"Over a hundred Arint."

"We didn't smuggle them. We saved them."

"You conspired with President Kirkland in the overthrow and execution of President Chuba."

"How could we have done that? We were on Sirius."

"The perfect alibi, almost. How do you explain away the theft of the matter-antimatter?"

"That wasn't me."

"Then who was it?"

Sevan did not want to get Ay-ttho into trouble, so he said nothing.

"I thought so," said the voice, smugly. "Would that have anything to do with the fugitive you helped to escape from, Aitne?"

Sevan remained silent.

"Destruction of a hotel room on Angetenar," the voice continued.

"Again, not me," said Sevan. "But I think it hardly matters, seeing as though Angetenar was virtually destroyed and we were the only ones to rescue anyone who couldn't afford their own transport."

"And conspired with the Swordsmen of Angetenar, a well-known terrorist group, some of whom you smuggled off the planet. You conspired to murder President Ydna Kirkland and her partner."

"Who am I being prosecuted by?" asked Sevan. "The Corporation or the Republic?"

"Both parties have an interest, but Matthews is also busy annexing the Rechinia system."

"That's the other side of the system."

"Exactly, and that's why he has entrusted your incarceration to the Corporation."

"Incarceration?"

"Correct."

"Why?"

"Don't make me go through the list again."

"Where? Aitne?"

"No, we consider transportation to Aitne too expensive. The Corporation and Republic are now subcontracting all penal services to a third-party supplier."

"So, where are you taking us?"

"We will take you to the penal colony on Ogenus."

"Ogenus? Never heard of it."

"Me neither."

"You wouldn't have. It is a secret facility. Once on Ogenus, no-one leaves."

"They said that about Aitne," Sevan whispered to Nadio.

"No-one leaves Ogenus, because nothing ever lands," explained the voice.

"But at the beginning of this session, you said we were being sentenced to death," asked Nadio.

"You are. Life on Ogenus is a death sentence."

"Hang on a nano-unit," Sevan interrupted. "If no-one ever lands Ogenus, how do you plan to leave us there?"

At that moment, the floor of the chamber began to open and Sevan could see the surface of a planet passing quickly below. They both struggled to stay on the retracting floor, but as it disappeared beneath them, they both fell out of the bottom of the ship and tumbled across the dusty surface.

As a Sevan came to a halt, he could see the ship rising into the atmosphere, dropping bundles from its cargo bay doors, before it disappeared into the clouds.

"Are you okay?" He asked Nadio, who hadn't moved since he had come to a halt.

Nadio didn't move. Sevan rushed over to see if he was okay.

"Nadio? Speak to me," he said, shaking the Thug's body.

Nadio rolled over onto his back and Sevan could see he was badly bruised, cut and bleeding. One advantage of being a Corporation mining clone was that they had designed Sevan to be hard wearing.

A noise on the horizon caught Sevan's attention. He looked up and saw dust rising.

"Come on," Sevan urged Nadio. "Try to sit up."

He did his best to help the thug into a seated position but realised the nearest place to hide was too far for Nadio to reach before whoever was approaching arrived.

As he looked towards the horizon, he saw large sails heading his way and, as they got closer, he saw the sails were propelling some kinds of frames on which creatures were riding. They were too far away for him to identify a species, but whatever the species, Sevan assumed they would not be friendly.

"Come on," he encouraged Nadio to move, but Nadio simply winced in pain.

Sevan did his best to get Nadio to his feet, all the time watching the sailing vessels getting closer. They appeared to be skimming the surface of the dust, sending large plumes into the air. The passengers seemed to be wrapped from head to foot in cloth and wore hats and goggles.

He helped Nadio to move as fast as he could, but it was clear they would not make it to the rocky hillside which bordered the dusty plain.

As the vessels approached, Sevan and Nadio stopped and turned to face the arrivals. As they approached, the creatures adjusted the sails and brought the vehicles skidding to a halt in front of Sevan and Nadio.

On board were some of the ugliest, most vicious looking creatures Sevan had ever had the misfortune to lay eyes upon.

"My friend is injured. We need help," he ventured optimistically.

The creatures were silent. They surrounded Sevan and Nadio and then helped them to climb up onto the vehicle.

"Thank you, thank you," Sevan blathered.

Once on the vehicle, the creatures showed Sevan and Nadio where to sit and then strapped them to a post.

"Safety first," said Sevan.

When the creatures had bound Sevan and Nadio securely, they then secured their arms and gagged their mouths. It was at this point that Sevan realised the creatures' intentions might not be as friendly as he imagined.

All the creatures jumped on board and unfurled the sails. The vehicle immediately shot off across the plain in the direction where the Corporation craft had dropped its bundles.

In the distance, Sevan could see movement. Figures were gathering something from the ground. As they drew closer, Sevan realised they must be gathering the bundles dropped by the craft.

When the gatherers saw the vehicle approaching, they grabbed what they could and ran off in all directions. By the time the vehicle skidded to a halt, the site was deserted apart from piles of discarded bundles which the creatures busied themselves loading onto the vehicle. Sevan realised Nadio, and he had been captured by creatures who scared the other inhabitants of the planet silly.

Sevan had an ominous feeling about his future and wondered how things could get worse.

CHAPTER 7: A PRISONER'S LIFE

As they rode on the vehicle, Seven had plenty of time to consider the eternal problem of unmerited suffering and could reflect on the healer's words about desire causing suffering and suffering causing pain. He realised that his current suffering was because of the desire to not be kidnapped by a band of ugly creatures and that if he could only accept his current situation, he would suffer much less. He shared his thoughts with Nadio.

"Do you remember what the healer said?" he mumbled under his gag. "If we could only accept our current situation, we would not suffer."

"I saw, heard and understood him," mumbled Nadio, still very sore from his fall. "I know the same as you. I am not inferior. I can speak and reason with the gods. But you are a liar, a useless healer."

Sevan imagined Nadio must have suffered a blow to the cranium during the fall.

"You should be quiet," Nadio continued to shout from beneath his gag. "That would be your wisdom. Listen to me. You speak badly of the gods, lie about them. Will you confront them? They should seek you out. You mock them and they should come and get you. Does the awe of their might not frighten you? Your memories are ashes and your body earth."

"But Nadio..." Sevan mumbled to reason with him.

"Be silent! Let me speak. I trust in the gods. Even if they decide I must die, I trust them. They are my salvation and I will not be a hypocrite, but stick to my ways. Hear my declaration. I know I am justified. If I remain silent in the face of your lies, I will have already given up. I ask the gods not to desert me and not to let their wrath frighten me. If they call me, I will answer. How plentiful are my transgressions? May the gods reveal to me the true extent of my sin?"

Sevan rested his head in his bound palms.

"Hide your face, consider me your enemy," Nadio continued to rave almost inaudibly. "You fill my head with foolishness as if I were still a youngling and imprison me and eat away at my soul."

"I haven't imprisoned you," Sevan mumbled. "These creatures have kidnapped us."

"Thug that is born of co-begetter is few of days and full of trouble," Nadio ignored him. "The thug emerges like a flower and is cut down, disappearing like a shadow. Open your eyes to the ones who will bring judgement on me. Who can clean the unclean? No-one. The gods have marked the day which the thug shall not pass. But there is hope that when a deadly thimbleberry is cut down, it should sprout again. Though the old plant dies in the soil, they bring new life forth. But not so with thugs. Their bodies rot in the ground and they bring no new thug forth. Oh Gods, that you would not forget me in a soil but remember me when the time comes and raise me up for the end of the better place. You will call, and I will answer you. You observe my transgressions, and just as water wears the stones, you erode my hope. The thugs praise and worship you, but they are filled with pain and their souls mourn."

Sevan thought Nadio had lost his marbles and was glad to see that the vehicle was approaching a settlement. They had transformed the dusty plain into fields of crops filled with workers who did not seem to notice or to care that the vehicle was passing.

Some creatures began covering Sevan and Nadio in some kind of oil, which made them seem to shine.

Soon, the fields gave way to buildings and eventually the vehicle skidded to a halt in the middle of a square, surrounded by buildings and other creatures of all shapes and sizes who quickly approached the vehicle and began bargaining with the creatures for the products contained within the bundles they had collected on the plain.

The creatures also untied Sevan and Nadio from the post, although their hands remained bound and their mouths gagged. They were led off the vehicle and led to a cage in which they were locked, and soon a crowd had gathered to inspect them. Sevan assumed the purpose of the oil had been to make them look better.

They were poked, prodded, and their gags were removed so that they could inspect their mouths.

In a language neither Sevan nor Nadio understood, the creatures began what sounded to Sevan like an auction and he soon realised that the crowd was bidding on Nadio and himself.

To Sevan's disappointment, the crowd didn't seem enthusiastic about the offer with which they had been presented. One by one, the crowd dwindled until only one bidder remained, a decrepit creature.

At the same moment, the wind picked up, and rain fell. The few creatures that occupied the square soon left to find shelter. They left Sevan and Nadio in the pen to get wet and cold.

Even the decrepit creature had retired to an adjacent hostelry with the traders, presumably to negotiate, and soon returned wearing a rain cover with a trader who unlocked the pen and handed Sevan and Nadio over to their new owner.

They were led, with the use of an electrical prod, to a smaller vehicle, similarly equipped with sails, on which they forced them into a smaller cage in which the two could barely crouch. Their new owner lost no time in preparing the vehicle and soon they were speeding through the streets of the town back towards the fields Sevan had noticed on their way in.

Soon, the vehicle turned off the main road and down a narrow track in between fields. The fields seemed to stretch on forever but, eventually, a group of buildings appeared and, before long, the vehicle had skidded to a halt in a space in the middle of them.

Their new owner unlocked their cage and, using the electric prod, steered them towards a long building. The door opened as they approached. He pushed them through the opening and heard the door shut behind as they lay face first in the dirt.

It took a few moments before Sevan's eyes adjusted to the dim light, but when they did, he realised the sorriest looking group of assorted creatures he had ever seen surrounded them. Some were watching them with curiosity, some with fear, and others looked as if they bore malice for the newcomers.

An unseen creature untied their limbs, and they turned to see a viscous looking creature hovering over them.

"Show them to their corner," the creature growled, and some of the more malicious looking creatures dragged Sevan and Nadio to a corner where they unceremoniously dumped them roughly.

"My friend is hurt," said Sevan.

"Shut up!" came the abrupt reply.

Sevan knew better than to argue. He could see through the various holes which decorated the walls that outside it was becoming dark.

"I'm hungry," he confessed to Nadio.

"Why don't you call room service? I'm sure they'll oblige."

"How are you feeling?" Sevan changed the subject.

"Pretty rough, but I think I'll live."

"Let's hope so."

Sevan realised they were being stared at and that there appeared to be a great deal of gossiping among the other inhabitants of the building which Sevan accredited to his and Nadio's recent arrival.

Before long, almost complete darkness enveloped the dim interior, with only the light of some rising moons casting long silvery beams through the plethora of holes in the walls.

In this light, Sevan perceived a dark figure edging towards them. The figure stopped within a few steps of their corner.

"Who are you?" it asked in deep, rasping tones.

"I'm Sevan and this is Nadio."

"The Sevan who murdered Co-Presidents Ydna and Kcokaep?"

"I didn't murder them."

"There's plenty to say you did. That's why you're here, they say."

"And who are you?"

"Never mind who I am. There's them that will pay handsomely for the knowledge of your whereabouts."

The figure slunk back into the darkness.

Sevan and Nadio could not sleep during the night. Sevan through fear that someone would murder them in their sleep and Nadio, partly for the same reason but also because his body ached all over from the fall from the ship.

Eventually, the light of the next rotation poked its solar rays through the holes in the walls and, soon after, the doors were opened, bathing everyone in bright light.

In the solar rays, the inhabitants didn't appear as threatening as Sevan had imagined them, but he knew appearances were often deceiving.

An ugly creature approached them and gestured for them to follow. It gave Sevan a large receptacle and directed towards a river where he was expected to fill it with water. It directed Nadio to a nearby coppice of woodland where he was to collect firewood.

When they returned, they were each given long metallic implements and told to follow a group which led them to a field filled with long, thin plants. Copying the other workers in the group, they realised their task was to hoe the earth between the plants.

The triple suns were already high in the sky before they could stop and rest. They were each given a small brown disk which they ate. Sevan liked the taste and only wished there was more and that their brief rest was longer, but their supervisors soon had them back weeding between the plants.

Sevan was tired of the work long before they were told to stop. He hoped they were having another rest, but the supervisors led them to a wagon loaded with heavy sacks, which they were told to unload. No sooner had they completed the task than they were told to reload the wagon with sacks from an adjacent pile.

To Sevan's relief, once they had finished loading the wagon, they were each given a bowl of brown liquid containing lumps of a variety of colours. It didn't taste of anything but he was still glad to eat and rest a little.

A supervisor interrupted their rest to order Sevan to join a work party to a nearby swamp where he was ordered to dig up the roots of strange looking trees which grew there.

Another supervisor took Nadio and told him to feed the menagerie of animals in various pounds. There were four large cateveexea, ten smaller critadeo, fifty-two sereosleodo which had already been milked that morning, five mongeaddeomo offspring, but Nadio couldn't tell their gender so wasn't sure whether they would be eaten now or allowed to grow to maturity, sixty-five driparak which were obviously the source of the warm coats the other workers were wearing. There were also eight praapoose which Nadio hoped would not be eaten but could grow to maturity.

As the shadows from the solar rays grew longer, they led Sevan and Nadio back to the building where they had spent the night. The guards gave them another brown disk, and a fried neaxhawk, which Sevan assumed must have come from the river.

They were both covered in mud and filth and tried to clean themselves as best they could. Less concerned about the potential threat from their fellow residents, Sevan and Nadio lay down in the dirt and soon fell asleep.

In the middle of the night, Sevan woken with a sharp implement at his neck and a clawed paw covering his mouth.

It was too dark to see his assailant, but he knew well enough to do exactly what the stranger wanted.

CHAPTER 8: THE DARK CITY

The assailant led Sevan out of the building through a large hole at the back that he hadn't noticed before, presumably because they had hidden it by large objects which they had now removed.

Silver moonlight reflected off the fields, but they soon left these behind for the dust of the plain, which appeared to sparkle.

He led Sevan around one of the rocky hills and, as the triple suns rose above the horizon, they arrived at a small valley in which was a very large tent. Inside the tent it was furnished luxuriously and, on two chairs, sat two individuals whom Sevan couldn't help think looked familiar.

"So this is him?" said one individual in disbelief.

"Yes, my Lord," Sevan's assailant said as he dropped Sevan at their feet.

"This is the clone who is supposed to have murdered our begetter."

"Now wait for one unit..." Sevan began.

"Silence!" shouted the assailant as he hit Sevan with the butt of his weapon.

"Your name is Sevan?"

Sevan nodded as he rubbed where he had been hit.

"You masqueraded as Edicla, the bounty hunter?"

Sevan nodded again.

"I can't believe it. This scrawny clone couldn't possibly have killed our begetter."

"May I speak?" Sevan asked while keeping a wary eye on the assailant who was raising his weapon to strike again.

"You may," said the first individual.

"Who was your begetter?"

"Our begetter was President Kcocaep."

"Then you are correct. I did not kill your begetter. President Matthews killed your begetter."

"He said you would say that."

"Who?"

"President Matthews. He said you would blame him. Why would he kill his own co-begetter?"

"That's an excellent question. I think he was deranged."

"That's as maybe, but the Lenguicarreans cleared him in a court convened by the Star Masters."

"Only because his co-begetter killed her own partner. And the jury was undecided. It was Chronos himself who cast the deciding vote."

"If Chronos deems President Matthews innocent, who are we to argue?"

"But he killed your begetter."

"How do you know?"

"Because I was there."

"So you admit it."

"I admit to being there. I don't admit to killing your begetter because I didn't."

"Well, that's your word against President Matthews, and who are we going to trust? The President of the Republic or a common criminal who has been sent to end his days here on Ogenus."

"What are you doing here?"

"The President, in his goodness, has sent us here for our own protection."

Sevan laughed.

"How dare you laugh at us, scum?"

Sevan received another blow from the assailant's weapon.

"You really think the President sent you here for your own protection?"

"Of course. There are many in the Republic who still hold a grudge that our begetter conspired in the murder of President Kirkland. Although we had nothing to do with it. There are those who wish to eradicate the entire line of our begetter, therefore we are safer here."

"And you believe that?"

"Why would a wise man utter lies and fill his belly with the wind? Why would he reason with unprofitable talk, or with speeches wherewith he can do no good? We do not fear him, we have faith in the gods."

"You sound like my friend."

"What friend?"

"Nevermind. It is not unprofitable for President Matthews, is it? When your begetter was President, you were next in line for the throne, his opponents might use you as a beacon of hope for those who oppose his regime."

"Your lies betray you as the untrustworthy criminal you are."

"Were you born in the last rotation?"

"We were born to be righteous, to put our trust in the gods and their representatives they have sent to our universe to keep us safe."

"You surely don't mean Matthews."

"Do you not walk with the gods? Surely you know Matthews is their chosen representative, sent to guide us through these difficult times."

"But he killed your begetter."

"So you say. You have turned from the gods and love wickedness. Long will be the rotations of your pain. You will live in the darkness, praying for the end, wander searching for food but not find it, live in desolated cities and have no wealth."

"Is this your prediction? I could make some predictions for you. I have already suffered much, lost my home, been chased around the galaxy, imprisoned and escaped. If the gods are responsible for this, then what is their purpose? One rotation, I will return to my home, I will return to The Doomed Planet. That is my prediction for you."

"We were not making predictions, simply stating the facts as we see them. Our prediction is this. You will travel with us to The Dark City and there you will understand these things of which we speak."

"Suit yourself."

"Prepare him for the journey," the first individual ordered.

A guard dragged Sevan off.

"Who in the worst place do they think they are?" Sevan complained as they dragged him outside.

"They are Llessur and Enyaw, true heirs to the Presidency of the Republic," said the guard.

"I wasn't really asking. It was more of a rhetorical question."

"I don't care what kind of question it was. That's who they are, got it?"

"Got it."

The guard dragged Sevan to a cage made from the stalks of what Sevan assumed must be some kind of native plant.

From the cage, Sevan could see various attendants working to dismantle the camp. In an astonishingly short amount of time, they had transformed the camp from luxury tent accommodation to a wagon train pulled by large cateveexea beasts that had been grazing further up the valley.

Sevan's cage was lifted onto the back of a wagon pulled by another enormous cateveexea and the train trundled off up the valley towards, he imagined, the Dark City, whatever that was. He wondered what had happened to Nadio and hoped the thug was managing without him.

The journey was boiling hot, and they didn't give Sevan any food or drink. Eventually the sky darkened, not because the suns were setting but because they were entering an area of intense cloud cover.

Sevan thought the dark grey clouds were incongruous with the bright sunshine of the area they were leaving. It became so dark that it felt like they were travelling at night and the guards lit lights along the length of the train, including the side of the wagon carrying Sevan's cage. He imagined they probably made the lights of ghiqans wax or the oil of a bleak fern.

Soon it was so dark that all he could see was a line of twinkling lights, and then, in the distance, Sevan could make out the dim twinkling of lights in the distance.

As the train drew closer, he could see that the lights they were approaching were large versions of the lights on the wagons, marking the way to which Sevan soon realised was a city comprising ramshackle buildings constructed from the same material as the cage which imprisoned him.

Something dimly illuminated each dwelling, but the overall aspect of the city was gloomy.

Sevan assumed they were travelling towards the centre as the dwellings became more tightly packed together and contained more storeys.

Eventually the tightly packed dwellings gave way to a large square, at one end of which was a huge dwelling, far more grand than any of the other properties to the extent that it appeared to be some kind of palace, complete with fenced off courtyard.

As the train approached, guards opened the enormous gates of the courtyard to allow it to pass through. As it did, Sevan noticed bizarre creatures which he imagined were observing him with suspicion, but he had no evidence for that as they possessed no eyes, or even faces. They were just formless clouds of an indeterminate substance with a yellow, orange light within which occasionally became visible, giving the illusion of a face or even eyes.

The train crossed the courtyard and passed beneath an arch into another central courtyard surrounded by impressive structures.

In the centre of the courtyard, the train halted, and the passengers dismounted and unloaded the belongings.

Sevan saw Llessur and Enyaw descend from a covered wagon and cross the courtyard, disappearing into one of the surrounding structures. The guards mostly ignored Sevan until almost all the possessions had been unloaded from the wagons. Only then did they remove Sevan's cage from its transport. No sooner had this been achieved than guards arrived and took Sevan into a structure on the opposite side of the courtyard to the one Llessur and Enyaw had entered.

They led him into the structure and down a set of stairs that had been dug into the solid earth. In the basement, there were rows of cells into one of which Sevan was slung. There were lights, sparsely arranged in the corridor, that provided the minimum of illumination. It was so dark that it was a while before Sevan realised he was not alone in the cell.

Two figures lay slumped against the wall opposite the bars.

"What took you so long?" asked a familiar voice.

"Ay-ttho?" Sevan peered into the darkness. "And Tori! Is that you?"

He moved closer and could make out, through the darkness, the very sorry-looking figures of Ay-ttho and Tori.

"What happened to you?"

"We were brawl boarding," Ay-ttho explained. "They were waiting for us on the beach."

"Who were?"

"Bounty hunters. I don't know what happened to Nadio. Scotmax will kill me."

"Nadio is here."

"Here? Where?"

"Well, not here, here. But he is on the planet. They set us to work in some fields. Hopefully, he's still there."

"We were taken there as well," said Tori. "But Ay-ttho didn't take well to being woken up and... well... you can imagine what happened."

Sevan wondered whether the holes in the building where they slept had been there before Ay-ttho's visit.

"How did you end up here?" Sevan asked.

"It seems somebody knew we would be sent to this planet," said Ay-ttho. "We were taken from the farm and brought straight here, we are supposed to see someone at some point but so far we have just been left to rot in this cell."

"I met Llessur and Enyaw," said Sevan. "They are the offspring of Kcokaep. They accused me of killing him."

"What did you say?"

"I told them it was Matthews, but they didn't believe me. They seemed to think they had been sent here for their own protection."

"Didn't they tell you what this place is?"

"No, they just told me they were bringing me to the Dark City and that I would understand everything here."

"And do you?"

"No-one has explained anything to me. They just said I would be in pain, live in the darkness, be hungry, live in desolated cities, be poor."

"Well, that seems to be true."

"But the entire planet is a prison. Why lock us in a prison in a prison?"

"I don't know, but I know I don't intend to stay here. Tori and I have been planning an escape."

"That's all very well," said Sevan. "But even if we can get out of this cell, or out of this city, we still can't get off the planet."

"Why not?"

"Nobody has escaped from Ogenus. It's impossible to leave because no ships ever land."

"Leave that to us."

A guard cut their conversation short by opening the cell door.

"Akpom Chuba will see you now."

"Akpom Chuba?" they said in unison. "But he's dead."

CHAPTER 9: THE ENEMY'S CHOICE

Ay-ttho, Tori and Sevan were led out of the basement, across a courtyard and into a large hall. Sevan immediately recognised Llessur and Enyaw at the far end. They led them to the middle. Next to Llessur and Enyaw, Sevan could see a machine containing the same type of formless cloud of indeterminate substance with a yellow, orange light that he had witnessed outside the palace.

"Welcome to my humble abode," a voice emanated from the machine. "You don't recognise me. I have changed a great deal since our last meeting."

"You will kneel when addressed by the great Akpom Chuba!" shouted a guard, hitting them in the back.

They fell to their knees.

"Yes, that's right," said the voice. "What you see is the remains of the great Akpom Chuba of the Cheng-Huang colony."

"I thought you were dead," said Ay-ttho.

"Everyone did. In fact, you might say that I was. If it wasn't for my followers using a particle preserver, I would have been. Unfortunately, as you can see, the process is far from perfected and, as a result, I am trapped in this form until we can straighten out a few technical problems."

"Why did you say that we killed President Man?" asked Tori.

"Ah, yes. That was necessary, I'm afraid. Unfortunately, the situation did not work out quite as I had planned and, instead of you being exiled on Aitne and me enjoying the presidential palace on Future, we are all here in this starless place."

"You haven't answered my question," Tori protested.

"Silence!" the guard delivered another blow to the back of Tori's head.

"What do you want with us?" asked Ay-ttho, in defiance of the guard.

"For hundreds of standard solar cycles, there has been a struggle for power in the Republic," Chuba explained. "For a long time, the Man dynasty was successful. They usurped my ancestors, and I thought I had brought their reign to an end. Unfortunately, Kirkland got in the way. My offspring dealt with him, but then you helped Matthews to regain the presidency. You owe me."

"How so?" asked Ay-ttho.

"You helped steal the presidency from my family. Now you must help to restore it."

"How do you expect us to do that?"

"You will assassinate Matthews."

Ay-ttho, Tori, and Sevan looked at each other in disbelief.

"That's difficult when we are stranded here."

"You will leave Ogenus, find Matthews, and kill him. You will then return here with a fleet of ships to take us to our rightful place on Future."

"Impossible," said Tori.

"And why should we help you?" asked Ay-ttho. "Even if we could leave the planet, the last thing we would do is track down and assassinate the president."

"Oh, but you will."

A guard brought in another prisoner, Nadio.

"And I have some help for you," Chuba continued.

Another two guards brought in Scotmax and Yor. They took Yor to Nadio, and they dumped Scotmax next to the others.

"Nadio! Thank the gods you are safe," said Scotmax.

"Scotmax, my love. Oh, how I've missed you."

"This is so touching," said Chuba. "Scotmax is going to help you with your mission. If you fail, I will execute Nadio and Yor."

"You fushing uxclod!"

"Such strong language. You really should wash your mouth out, Scotmax. You have 100 mega units to complete your task or Nadio and Yor die. Show them out."

Guards dragged Scotmax, Ay-ttho, Tori and Sevan out of the hall, across the courtyard and through the gates, leaving them in the square outside the palace.

"Now what?" asked Sevan

"Now we have 100 mega units to kill Matthews and get back here will a fleet or they die," said Scotmax

"Are we really going to try?"

"I have no problem killing Matthews. In fact, I would probably have tried it, anyway. I don't like the idea of helping Chuba, but I don't see that we have any choice."

"Scotmax is right," said Ay-ttho. "We ensure the safety of Nadio and Yor, and then we deal with Chuba."

"We could just try to release Nadio and Yor," Tori suggested.

"Too risky," said Scotmax.

"More risky than attempting to assassinate the president of the Republic?"

"I'd rather risk my own life murdering Matthews than risk Nadio's life trying to rescue him."

"I agree with Scotmax," said Ay-ttho.

"So how do we get off this planet, then?" asked Tori.

"No ships land," said Ay-ttho. "But they fly low to drop off prisoners and supplies. All we need to do is to get ourselves on a ship when it flies in to drop off its cargo."

"Simple," Sevan said.

"Nice to see you being positive for a change," said Tori, completely missing Sevan's sarcasm.

"First things first then," said Ay-ttho. "Let's get out of this city and back to the plain. If we can steal one of those sail boards, we might modify it to get it to fly."

"Fly?" Sevan felt woozy. "You want to use one of those things to fly into the back of a cargo ship?"

"Sevan has a point," said Tori.

"I do?"

"We won't match the velocity of a cargo ship. We either need to shoot it down, which might render it inoperable, or we go in through the front."

"Forget I said anything," Sevan urged.

"When you say the front, you mean the observation windows," Ay-ttho clarified.

"Do you have a better idea? Come on."

Tori led them along the dark street. On the horizon, Sevan could see a light where he imagined the clouds which shrouded the city must end.

"What's with the clouds?" he asked.

"I think it's something to do with Chuba's experiments to regenerate himself," said Scotmax.

This did nothing to clarify the situation for Sevan, but he dropped the subject for the present.

"Does anyone else consider it odd that Chuba would choose us for this mission?" Tori asked as they walked.

"Not really," said Ay-ttho. "Trying to assassinate Matthews is practically a suicide mission. He needed someone he could blackmail. With Nadio and Yor he knew that Scotmax and I could not say no."

"How did you end up here, Scotmax?" Sevan asked.

"Matthews' special forces caught Yor and me. They sentenced us to life here without trial."

"Republic forces picked Nadio and me up on Pallene," said Sevan. "But I'm sure the Corporation brought here us."

"The Corporation runs all the Republic penal colonies," said Tori.

Gradually the sky brightened as the clouds thinned and the dwellings became less numerous until only hills surrounded them once more on their way to the dusty plain.

The hills delivered a stunning panorama of the plain and it wasn't long before Ay-ttho spotted a sail board vehicle skipping across the dust in the distance.

"The dust makes them easy to spot," Tori commented.

"Sure does," said Ay-ttho. "The question now is how do we get our hands on one and how do we know where and when the cargo ship will make its next drop?"

"The creatures seem to know," said Sevan.

"They probably just watch the skies. I still have my communicator. It tells me where the Mastery of the Stars is. With some modifications, it might track a cargo ship."

"You know where the Mastery of the Stars is?" Scotmax was excited.

"Yes, it's still on Pallene."

"I checked when you were taken," said Sevan. "It had gone."

"No, I simply told Ron to park somewhere safe."

"Why didn't they take your communicator?"

"I guess they assumed it was no use without the ship."

"So all we need to do is get back to Pallene," said Scotmax.

"Yes, that's all," Sevan laughed, ironically.

The group carried on along the ridgeline of the hills so they could maintain their excellent view of the plain and the creatures on their sailboard.

"They're swinging around," Ay-ttho observed.

"Look!" said Tori, pointing to the sky. "A cargo ship."

Ay-ttho took the communicator and fiddled with it as she pointed it towards the ship.

"Come on, come on," she mumbled to herself as the ship made its approach.

"They must come every other rotation," Sevan surmised.

"We can't be sure of that," said Tori.

As the ship flew low over the plain, the creatures on their sailboard raced towards it.

"Are they going to try what I think they're going to try?" Tori mused.

When the ship had reached its lowest point, bundles of cargo tumbled out of the back. It climbed, but the creatures racing towards it had picked up speed and they, too, were lifting into the air. They gained enough height to slam their vehicle into the front of the cargo ship but, instead of crashing through the observation windows as Ay-ttho had theorised, their vehicle simply shattered into a plethora of fragments which scattered across the dusty plain as the ship ascended into the sky and disappeared from sight.

"Got it," said Ay-ttho, triumphantly.

"Well, that blows that idea," said Sevan.

"Yeah," said Tori. "I don't think we can go in through the front."

"We might not need to," said Ay-ttho. "I could access their call sign and tracking systems easily. Terrible security. Ron can track them for us and let me know when they return."

"So, what now?" asked Scotmax.

"We find something to eat, somewhere to sleep, and wait."

"I know somewhere," said Sevan.

*

The group crouched on the edge of the settlement, waiting for darkness. Both Scotmax and Tori had recognised the crops in the fields, so it was only a matter of waiting until the coast was clear before harvesting what they wanted.

In a clearing in the woodland, Tori dug a fire pit and cooked the produce, which Sevan decided was delicious.

They slept on a blanket of leaves and Sevan thanked the Giant Cup that it was a mild night, even though he knew the Giant Cup didn't exist.

"You know the Giant Cup doesn't exist," said Scotmax.

"I know," said Sevan.

"Do you know why they tell you there is a Better Place?"

"No, tell me."

"They tell you there is a Better Place so that you don't mind suffering in this life. You don't rise against your oppressors because they tell you that you will receive your reward in the next life. The more you suffer now, the better your life will be in paradise. It's just a scam so they can exploit you."

"You're probably right."

"I am right."

Eventually, after no-one responded to Scotmax's revolutionary diatribe, he gave up and went to sleep and so did everyone else.

*

"How are we going to get on a ship?" asked Tori, as they ate the cold leftovers of the evening meal for breakfast.

"There are two options," said Ay-ttho. "One of them is a long shot and the other might not be possible at all."

"Okay, let us have it."

"The first option is that we create some kind of sling which we hook onto the ship as it passes, which then drags us up into the air along with it."

"And the second option?" asked Sevan, clearly convinced the first option would fail.

"It's possible that I retrieved enough data from the cargo ship for Ron to hack their navigation computer. If he can do that, and it's a big if, then he might take over the controls and land the ship."

"Well, it's obvious. We go for the second option then."

"The second option might not be possible, Sevan."

"Yes, but it has to be better than option one, doesn't it?"

"Let's try both."

Sevan felt woozy again.

CHAPTER 10: TREACHERY

Sevan helped the others search for materials they could use for a giant sling. It was no simple task because they were constantly attempting to avoid detection while rifling through the farm buildings.

He was feeling very sorry for himself.

"Do you believe in the gods?" he asked Scotmax.

"No. My begetter does."

"Yes, I know Yor believes in the gods. If you don't believe in the gods, what do you believe in?"

"Why do you have to believe in anything?" Ay-ttho, who had overheard, interrupted.

"I believe we are all part of the universe," said Scotmax, ignoring Ay-ttho. "We are all made of the same stuff as the stars and the planets and when we die, we simply become something else, like a rock or a tree."

"But where did the stars and the planets come from?"

"They came from the birth of the universe."

"But where did the universe come from?"

"It didn't come from anywhere."

"How is that possible?"

"To have something, or even nothing, you must have space. Since space only came into existence with the universe, then not even nothing could have existed before the universe."

"So, how did the universe come into being?"

"It just did."

"But how?"

"Sevan, it is pointless wasting your time asking questions that cannot be answered. You are much better off simply accepting that things are the way they are and doing the best you can."

"But you don't accept things the way they are."

"There is a difference between accepting there is no purpose to the universe and accepting the terrible things that are done in the universe. The Swordsmen of Angetenar believe we are all one with the universe and that if anyone does anything to harm any part of the universe, then they are harming all of us. We fight for a better society because if there is suffering, we suffer too, so we must take measures against those causing the suffering."

"That is why you helped Matthews."

"Yes, and why I must now stop Matthews."

"Nadio believes in the gods."

"I know. And that is the only source of arguments between us."

"It is difficult to accept there is no purpose to the universe when, all your life, you have been indoctrinated."

"I don't think Nadio has been indoctrinated."

"Are you kidding," said Ay-ttho. "I imagine that the partner of D'Auria filled her head with all kinds of rubbish."

"Nadio's begetter believed in the gods," said Tori. "He told me. I believe in the gods, too."

"What?" Ay-ttho was genuinely surprised. "You never told me that."

"Why would I? Faith is a personal thing."

"And it's blind," Ay-ttho muttered.

"I believe the scriptures when they say that the gods shall put the light of the wicked out, and the spark of their fire shall not shine."

"They are only promising you an afterlife so they can exploit you in this one," Scotmax warned Tori.

"I am not being exploited," said Tori.

"Then why do we suffer?" asked Sevan.

"The gods might have fenced up my way that I cannot pass, and set darkness in my paths," Tori explained. "But I know that my redeemer liveth, and that he shall enter at the latter rotation into the universe, and though after my skin greluts destroy this body, yet in my flesh shall I see the gods."

"You can quote the scriptures as much as you want," said Scotmax. "But it doesn't make them true."

"Look here," said Tori, revealing a pile of sheets he had discovered in a wooden chest. "We could tie these together."

They all took as many sheets as could carry and sneaked out of the settlement and headed back towards the hills which overlooked the plain

"Any sign of the cargo ship?" asked Scotmax

"Nothing," said Ay-ttho, checking her communicator.

They continued until they found an area they could rest, which overlooked the plain. They hadn't rested for long before Tori spotted a cargo ship approaching.

"I thought you said they weren't coming," said Scotmax.

"They're not, according to this," she said, checking her communicator again. "They must use more than one ship."

"In which case, we could wait a long time for the other ship to arrive."

"Can you hack the system of this ship too?" asked Tori

"I'll try," said Ay-ttho, pointing her communicator towards the ship.

The ship descended, levelled out and then dropped its cargo. The first load, clearly the convicted, landed in a way that made Sevan wince. As it began its ascent, the ship unloaded the rest of its cargo before disappearing into the sky.

"Any luck?" Scotmax asked Ay-ttho.

"Nope, nothing."

"Then we just have to wait."

The group watched the ship disappear and then observed as one sailboard entered the plain and headed towards the new arrivals, who had not risen from the ground.

The sailboard skidded to a halt next to the bodies, and the creatures dismounted to inspect the new arrivals. To Sevan's horror, the creatures began beating the bodies until Sevan was sure they must be dead. They dragged the corpses onto the board and then sailed away to where the rest of the ship's cargo had landed.

"If we can get a ship to land, we are going to have to be prepared for those creatures," said Tori.

.

"There's nothing we can do until tomorrow," said Ay-ttho. "Let's make a camp and get ready for tomorrow."

The group set about creating a camp to shelter them for the night and Scotmax began tying the sheets together.

"I can't see how this is going to work," he mused.

"Me too," said Tori. I can't imagine how it is going to get us on the ship without killing us.

"Okay, so let's try Plan B first," Ay-ttho agreed. "If Ron can't land the ship, then we will have to bring it down."

By the time the stars were low on the horizon, they had created a sheltered encampment and camouflaged it as best they could.

"All we can do now is wait," said Ay-ttho.

"I'm hungry," said Sevan.

"Is that all you can think about? Your stomachs?"

"We haven't eaten in a while."

"He's right," said Scotmax. "I'll go out and see what I can find."

She soon returned with three ulqen, small furry creatures with huge ears which Sevan felt looked far too cute to eat, but he set his qualms aside as Scotmax skinned the animals and Tori prepared a fire.

Sevan tried to forget how cute the creatures had been as he shared the meat with the others. His three rows of teeth made quick work of the tough flesh. The night was chilly and Sevan did his best to stay warm beneath a seat next to the dying embers.

As the stars rose at the beginning of the next rotation, the group prepared for the next cargo ship, hoping it was the ship that Ron had hacked. They hid the camp as best they could, aware that they might have to use it again that night.

Scotmax had disappeared early and returned with a handful of zorguks.

"They slip into a torpor overnight," she said. "If you get up early enough, you can just pick them out of the bushes."

She and Tori plucked them in what seemed like nano-units and Ay-ttho soon had a fire ready on which to roast them. Compared to the ulqen, the zorguks had very little meat, though Sevan appreciated the opportunity to eat.

He felt that the rotation dragged by slowly and it seemed forever until Ay-ttho suddenly became very excited.

"The ship is on its way," she said. "Ron is tracking it on its way here."

"Can he land it?" asked Scotmax.

"That is what we are about to find out."

Ay-ttho looked up at the sky in expectation. The others followed her gaze with the same hope that Ron could control the ship.

"There it is," said Tori, pointing to a distant speck.

Ay-ttho alternated glances between the approaching ship and her communicator.

"How does it look?" asked Tori.

"Difficult to tell. I keep losing contact with Ron. I just hope he has a clear signal with the ship."

They watched as the ship drew closer, levelling out over the plain as it usually did. They watched as two convict passengers fell to the ground and tumbled to a halt.

"Come on, Ron. Come on," Ay-ttho urged as she watched the ship continuing its usual flight path.

As it climbed, it dropped the usual cargo, and the group assumed the plan had failed until, suddenly, it lost altitude and almost skimmed the surface of the plain. Then it jolted up again as if two parties were wrestling with the controls.

"Come on," said Ay-ttho, getting up and rushing down the hill.

The rest of the group followed her, trying to watch their footing and the trajectory of the ship which appeared to be losing its battle to ascend and within moments and skidded to a halt in a cloud of dust.

The group sprinted across the plain towards the ship, which was beginning to re-emerge from the dust.

"We have to get there before the creatures appear," Scotmax shouted.

"Have you considered how we are going to overcome the ship's crew?" Sevan shouted from behind where he was lagging.

"That's where the creatures come in," Ay-ttho shouted back.

When they reached the ship, it seemed relatively undamaged.

"How do we get in?" asked Sevan.

"We ring the bell," said Ay-ttho.

She walked up to the entrance of the ship and pressed the entrance intercom.

"We are armed," said a voice.

"I'm sure you are," said Ay-ttho. "We are not, but what you must understand is that I am the Captain of the Mastery of the Stars, a corporation class 2 freighter and my navigational computer has hacked into your systems. You cannot leave unless I give the command to unlock your systems."

"What do you want?"

"Let us on board."

"Why would we do that?"

"In a moment, a sailboard will appear over the horizon. The creatures riding that board will tear this ship apart and sell it for scrap. Then they will sell you into slavery, as long as they don't eat you first."

"Look," said Tori

Just as Ay-ttho had predicted, a sailboard arrived on the horizon.

"If you let us in, we will unblock your systems and you will be free to leave."

Sevan watched as the creature's sailboard came closer.

"Hurry," said Scotmax.

"I'm trying," said Ay-ttho, pressing the intercom again. "Look, if these creatures get us, you won't be able to regain control of your systems and they will get you, eventually. We are unarmed. If you let us in and we don't do what we say, you can just shoot us."

"Oh, great," said Sevan.

The creatures' sailboard was almost upon them when the entrance slid open. They all leapt aboard just as the sailboard rounded the rear of the ship. As the entrance door closed, some creatures attempted to leap from the sailboard into the entrance and the closing doors crushed one of them.

Relieved to be safely aboard the ship, the group found themselves faced with a group of Corporation security clones pointing weapons at them. To Sevan it was like staring at a group of angry Ay-ttho's all only slightly different in the tiniest details or hues.

"What are you doing here?" one of them asked Ay-ttho, observing her similarity to themselves.

"That's a good question," she said. "But right now, we need to get this ship out of here before those creatures rip it apart."

They could hear the creatures banging on the entrance and attempting to tear off the panels.

"Ron, get us out of there."

The ship lurched and several of the corporation clones fell over as Ron lifted the ship off the surface in a steep ascent. When it had exited the atmosphere and levelled off, the group picked themselves up to find the clones, still pointing their weapons at them.

"Return the control of the ship to us," a clone demanded.

"There's something we have to do first," said Ay-ttho.

"Return control now."

"The ship will first drop us on Pallene. We will then return control to you and you can do what you wish."

"Return control now, or we will shoot you."

"If you shoot us, the ship will still continue to Pallene, but we will not return control to you. How do you plan to explain to the Corporation that we stranded you on Pallene where we observed many Republic troops?"

The clones glanced at each other nervously.

"How can we trust you?" one of them said.

"You can't."

The clones ushered the group into the brig, where they were guarded until the ship landed on Pallene, then they escorted them back to the entrance.

"Now return control to us."

"As soon as we are safe on our ship."

Reluctantly, they opened the doors and Sevan recognised the environment of Pallene and the familiar form of the Mastery of the Stars in the distance.

Immediately, Scotmax ran towards the freighter and, as soon as they were convinced the clones would not shoot them, the others followed. Before they had reached the Mastery of the Stars, Scotmax had already entered and as they approached, the entrance doors closed.

"Ron! Open the doors!" Ay-ttho shouted, but the group had no option than to watch in horror as the Mastery of the Stars took off without them.

They turned on their heels and rams back towards the Corporation cargo ship.

"Ron! Ron!" Ay-ttho shouted into her communicator, but there was no response.

They were barely halfway back to the Corporation ship as it closed its doors and lifted into the sky, leaving them prisoners of Pallene once more.

CHAPTER 11: THE KILLER

"What have we done to deserve this?" Sevan lamented. "Why are the gods punishing us? Am I so bad?"

"Do you think the gods are bothered whether you are good or bad?" asked Ay-ttho. "And what good have you ever done? Have you fed the hungry? Helped the poor? Even if there were gods, they're hardly going to single you out for special treatment."

"Then what is the point of anything?"

"There is no point, Sevan."

"Then why bother?"

"We bother because we are all part of the universe and if we harm any part of the universe, we are harming ourselves."

"Since when did you become so profound?"

"There's a lot you don't know about me, Sevan."

"So what are we going to do, then?"

"What can we do? Our ship has gone. Ron is not responding. There's not much we can do except wait and hope we regain contact with Ron. But we can't have more than forty mega units to save Nadio."

"How long is that?" asked Sevan.

Ay-ttho sighed with impatience.

"On Pallene, it's about two rotations," said Tori.

"Everything we do just seems to make matters worse," Sevan complained.

"And what do you want, Sevan?" Ay-ttho lost her patience.

"I want to go home."

"And where is that?"

"Home! The Doomed Planet. Where my aunt is."

"Fine. As soon as we've got off this planet, find and kill Matthews in the next two rotations to save Nadio's life, then we'll get you back to the Doomed Planet."

"You've been saying that ever since Nereid."

Ay-ttho sighed again.

"Why would Scotmax abandon us like that?" Tori mused.

"I don't know," said Sevan. "Perhaps he just wanted to take the risk of killing Matthews by himself."

"Or perhaps he's in league with Akpom Chuba?" said Ay-ttho. "He was there in the Dark City. We don't know how long he was there or whether he was a prisoner or a guest."

"You are so cynical," said Tori.

"Maybe I am, maybe I'm not, but I can't just sit around here for 40 mega units waiting to see whether Scotmax comes back. The communicator still tells me the location of the Mastery of the Stars. If we can find a ship, we can go after him."

"Pallene is a tourist hub. There must be loads of ships we can borrow."

"Borrow?" asked Sevan.

"Just be quiet," said Ay-ttho. "Follow us."

Sevan did as he was told and followed them into the tourist centre, where they themselves had enjoyed many water sports when they had first arrived on the planet.

"Look," said Ay-ttho, pointing to a cruiser that seemed unattended. They could see the pilot some distance away, chatting to the landing crew, and the ship's entrance was wide open.

"Who leaves a ship open and unattended like that?" asked Tori.

"I don't know. Let's not hang around to find out. Come on."

Ay-ttho led them onto the ship, which appeared deserted. They headed straight for the bridge, which was also empty, and Ay-ttho immediately set to work, overriding the security protocols.

"Got it," she said at last, and the entrance doors closed.

Ay-ttho leapt into the pilot's seat and fired up the engines which sent the already confused genuine pilot on the landing pad into a panic but before he could sprint back to the ship, Ay-ttho had lifted the cruiser into the air and was already leaving the spaceport.

"SC Desire?" a voice echoed from the communications panel. "We do not clear you for takeoff."

"What are they going to do? Shoot us down?" Ay-ttho kept the ship on a course to leave the atmosphere.

"SC Desire? Please respond."

Ay-ttho ignored the voice.

"SC Desire? We are deploying BS Baldrin to intercept."

"A battleship?" Sevan exclaimed.

*

Scotmax knew that trying to kill the President was virtually a suicide mission, and he knew also that it couldn't be, because just killing Matthews was not enough. She would have to return to the Dark City with the fleet Chuba had requested.

She also knew that killing Matthews and surviving was possible. After all, she had helped Matthews kill her co-begetter when she had been the president and they had survived.

Scotmax navigated the Mastery of the Stars to the location Chuba had told her that Matthews would be. She didn't question where Chuba had got his intelligence, she just hoped it was correct.

Matthews' location didn't intimidate Scotmax. That it was the most heavily fortified space station in the known galaxy wouldn't prevent her from getting in. It would be getting out that would be the challenge.

Scotmax watched as the Tomorrow space station loomed closer. It was the perfect choice of location for Matthews; close to her Corporation ally, Barnes, with easy access to the capital system, Future, via the catapult system, a portal that permanently linked Tomorrow and Future, no matter where the space station was located.

She felt like the blind spaceman of the legends who hid and discovered the truth, devoid of emotion, just like the blind spaceman when they woke him for battle. The problem was that in the fable of the blind spacemen; he spied on his enemies only to meet his own death.

The huge space station took control of the ship's navigation system and Scotmax waited as she let them capture her.

*

Ay-ttho lifted the cruiser high into the atmosphere.

"Ship approaching," said Tori, pointing to a Republic battleship on the monitors.

"SC Desire? This is BS Baldrin. We do not clear you for takeoff. Please return to the spaceport."

"This is the SC Desire," said Ay-ttho. "We acknowledge your message and will return to the spaceport."

"What?" Tori exclaimed.

Ay-ttho began a large turning procedure but instead of completing the turn, she accelerated the ship towards the Sonvaenope portal. The acceleration was so sudden, and so great, that it threw both Tori and Sevan from their seats.

"What are you doing?" asked Sevan.

"You didn't think we were going back to Pallene, did you?"

"Where are we going?"

"We are following the Mastery of the Stars."

"Where to?"

"You'll see."

The battleship was giving chase towards the Sonvaenope portal but suddenly, Ay-ttho veered the ship around and headed towards the Ogenus portal.

"This ship can really move for a cruiser," she said.

The battleship, larger and less manoeuvrable, had a much larger turning circle and lost ground on the cruiser.

"Why are we going back to Ogenus?" asked Tori.

"We're not."

"But..."

"The Mastery of the Stars went through this portal and then through another. If the data on the communicator is correct, then it has just docked with the Tomorrow space station."

Both Sevan and Tori turned paler shades of their respective hues.

"Why would Scotmax go there?" asked Tori

"Presumably because Matthews is there."

"With Barnes?"

"Why not?"

"But the Tomorrow station has enough firepower to destroy a planet."

"We survived it before, and can survive it again."

"We ended up on the Aitne penal colony."

"From where Barnes rescued us."

"Before he stole Sevan's home planet. And don't forget, he tried to kill us on Atlas."

"He was trying to kill President Man."

"He knew we were there."

"Look, you can complain all you want. We're going to Tomorrow. Scotmax needs us."

"You still trust him."

"Why shouldn't I?"

"He stole our ship."

"To protect us."

"You don't know that."

Ay-ttho turned to Sevan as they entered the Ogenus portal.

"If it's any consolation, we are heading toward Nereid."

Ay-ttho didn't have to explain to Sevan that they had moved his home planet there.

The door to the bridge opened, and a steward entered. At first, he did a double take at the unexpected occupants but then composed himself.

"I'm sorry to disturb you, Captain," he said. "But the passengers are enquiring as to the reason we have taken off and why the ship is making such extreme manoeuvres."

"Passengers?" Sevan exclaimed.

"Yes, sir," the steward continued unabashedly.

"We have around 250 that either didn't want to do the tour of the port or had returned early. What should I tell them?"

"Tell them we are going to see the second largest space station in the galaxy."

"Very well sir... er... ma'am," said the steward, before turning and leaving.

*

They led Scotmax from the Mastery of the Stars and along some corridors before dumping her in a holding cell. She was glad that, so far, everything was going to plan.

*

"We have 250 passengers!" said Sevan.

"And they are going to get a much better tour than whatever they paid for."

"And how do you know that, Ay-ttho?"

"Because you are going to be the tour guide, Sevan."

*

Scotmax waited in the cell with patience. Eventually, the door opened, and a guard led her to a room where they secured to a seat. After a while, Matthews entered with a group of Corporation security clones.

"I knew you couldn't resist seeing me," said Scotmax.

"I knew you would come to find me and I'm glad you did, because I now have the opportunity to kill you personally."

"It is you who will be killed."

"How do you expect to do that?" Matthews laughed. "You are bound in a chair. Do you plan to talk me to death?"

"No, I won't need to."

At that moment, the diminutive robed figure of Barnes entered, followed by more corporation security clones.

"My dear Barnes," said Matthews. "Have you come to see me execute this rebel?"

"No," Barnes told Matthews, without even glancing at Scotmax.

*

"We will soon approach Tomorrow," Sevan addressed a gathering of easily entertained tourists who looked as though they had mainly travelled from Future on a package deal that hadn't involved a visit to the second largest space station in the known galaxy and they were now very pleased with the unexpected addition to their itinerary. "Though not the largest space station, it was the most expensive to build, largely because of its unparalleled weapons system."

The tourists nodded appreciatively.

"As we approach," Sevan continued. "You will notice some ships approaching. These are Corporation fighters which I imagine will escort us, which is very nice, isn't it?"

The tourists nodded again in agreement.

"As I thought, the fighters are escorting us to the station and, with a bit of luck, they will allow us to dock."

A ripple of excitement passed through the crowd of tourists and when the sound of the locking mechanism gripping onto the hull echoed through the cruiser, the tourists burst into cheers.

Moments later, Corporation security clones burst into the cruiser, pointing their weapons at everyone, at which point the tourists exploded into rapturous applause.

*

Barnes pulled a weapon from his robes and shot Matthews in the head.

*

Corporation security clones led Ay-ttho, Tori, Sevan, 250 tourists and a steward off the ship and through the corridors to the detention centre. The tourists were bristling with excitement, gazing all around, pointing out every door, notice or control panel.

Even when they were locked in a large holding cell, the tourists were thrilled, as if taking part in an immersive theatrical experience.

Corporation security clones searched the entire party, including the tourists, who were ecstatic with joy at the whole procedure. Before long, they escorted the group to a large hall and told them to wait.

Suddenly, hundreds of Corporation Security clones entered and lined the perimeter of the hall.

A moment later, Barnes entered.

"President Matthews is dead," he announced.

CHAPTER 12: REBELLION AT HOME

There was a collective gasp among the tourists and a great deal of doubt whether the news was true or just part of the fantastical theatrical experience.

"We came for Scotmax," said Ay-ttho.

"I know you did," said Barnes.

He gestured to a guard who left the room briefly, returning with Scotmax.

"As you can see," said Barnes. "She is in good health."

"Then, if you will excuse us, we will take her. We have very little time."

"To return to Akpom Chuba, I know."

Sevan imagined Barnes smiling a knowing smile beneath his robes.

"Scotmax told me that Chuba requested a fleet," Barnes continued.

"Yes, but we have very little time to return. Our friends are in danger."

"Ah yes, Scotmax's partner, Nadio and his begetter's begetter, Yor. Yor fought against me at the battle of Penrewei. Did you know that?"

"I did not know. But he is old and..."

"Don't get me wrong. I don't consider him a threat and doubt he would align himself with Chuba. I am minded to provide you with a fleet, but I require you to do something for me first."

"We have very few mega units in which to accomplish our task."

"Of this I am aware. If you wish me to do something for you, you must first do something for me."

"I am listening."

"You are all familiar with The Doomed Planet."

Sevan's antennae perked up at the mention of his home planet.

"There has been continued unrest there since you left. You have become somewhat iconic with the struggle. I think if you could go there, you might calm the situation a great deal and then I would be happy to supply you with the fleet you need for Chuba."

"Why are you so keen to help Chuba?"

"Chuba and I go way back. We were old allies, back to the days before President Man."

"So why didn't you just help him yourself?"

"Because now I have an opportunity for you to help me."

Sevan felt very used, but he knew he would have to go along with it.

*

"Why did you leave us on Pallene?" Ay-ttho asked Scotmax on their way to the Mastery of the Stars.

"I didn't want to get you involved?"

"How did you let her take the ship?" she asked Ron as she entered the Mastery of the Stars.

"She explained she was keeping you safe. I thought I was doing the right thing," Ron explained.

"Why didn't you contact me on the communicator?"

"She told me you would try to talk me out of it."

"Of course I would. Set a course for the Doomed Planet, Ron."

"Are we going home?"

"Kind of. Plot a course please, Ron."

"Shouldn't take long. We are close now that it moved to Nereid."

"Good, we have little time."

Sevan was excited to be going back to his home planet finally, but he was also annoyed with himself that he had been in the presence of his creator, Barnes, again and missed the opportunity to ask all the questions that had been irritating him. Why had Barnes created them in the way he had? Why did he allow suffering to continue?

It also intrigued him what was happening at home and hoped that his aunt was safe. The last time he had been on the Doomed Planet, the population had booed him and, in the election, they had opted to return to the previous regime. He found it difficult to believe that they would now welcome them with open antennae.

They only had to traverse a couple of portals to arrive in the Nereid system and Sevan wondered why, if it was so close, they had not visited earlier and then the reason became clear. At the last portal before Nereid, on the old frontier of the Republic, was a large checkpoint policed by a fleet of Republic ships.

"How are we going to get past them?" he asked.

"Barnes has given us a pass," said Ay-ttho.

"But what about Matthews?"

"Barnes has just as much influence in this part of the galaxy as Matthews."

"No, what I mean is, will they know Matthew is dead?"

"I doubt it. Barnes will keep that quiet for a while until Chuba is ready to assume the presidency."

"Why?"

"The death of the president creates a vacuum and often a power struggle ensues."

"But Matthews left no obvious successor."

"Of course he did. Xocliw, his co-begotton."

Sevan was tired of all these power struggles. He had known Matthews, not as a president but as a colleague on a journey and admittedly for a while, as a matricidal maniac. But Sevan had cared for Matthews on the journey and it upset him to hear of her death, even if it provided them with the opportunity to return home.

"I have transmitted our security credentials," said Ron. "Just waiting for authorisation."

They had barely approached the outer limits of the checkpoint when they received the authorisation and could proceed, without stopping, towards the portal.

Sevan breathed a sigh of relief and sat back in the spare chair, to relax as much as he could for the journey to Nereid.

Nereid did not bring happy memories. It was where he had met his friend Ozli, but the friendship was short-lived and now the only positivity Sevan could muster was the possibility of returning to the Doomed Planet.

The grey planet Nereid came into view first, and Sevan tried not to remember the trauma of his days there. He looked to see when his home planet would come into view and as they orbited Nereid, the immense sphere that contained both the Doomed Planet and Daphnis rose above the horizon.

Sevan sat forward in his chair, ready to catch his first glimpse of his home for what seemed a very long time.

As the sphere came into view, it was the red Daphnis that appeared first. Then, slowly but surely, the blue green sphere of the Doomed Planet appeared and Sevan felt a shiver travel from his marbles, down his antennae.

The Mastery of the Stars passed through the gaps between the solar array and the sphere's defence systems. As it did, Sevan glimpsed the Giant Cup, the Doomed Planet's moon.

They descended through the atmosphere and headed towards the concession, which served as the planet's administrative capital. It looked to Sevan as if nothing had changed and they passed the busy shuttle terminals and headed towards the centre where the enormous tower of the council building came into view. It reminded Sevan of his friend, Thertee, who had fallen to his death from that very observation platform.

The tower gave Ron authorisation to land in the council building's own hangar and, in their approach, Sevan could see the familiar movements in the streets not that far below.

"Here we are then," said Ay-ttho, and Ron landed the ship.

"It feels good to be back," said Sevan

"Let's see," said Tori, who looked uncomfortable.

Ay-ttho gave him a quizzical look.

"Something doesn't feel right," he said, pointing to the streets. "Does that look like a concession in rebellion to you?"

"Looks can be deceiving."

As they descended from the ship, a platoon of armed guards met them. Sevan assumed the high level of security must have been a symptom of the rebellion.

They escorted them directly to the council chamber where a full council was in session. They were told to stand in the witness box, which was normally only used when the council conducted a trial or passed judgement.

They asked them to swear on the scriptures of the Giant Cup to tell the truth. Sevan felt this was pointless as they weren't on trial

The Chief Council Member cleared his throat.

"You are standing trial for treachery to the concession and collusion with an enemy of the republic.

"Wait, a nano-unit," Ay-ttho exclaimed. "We are what?"

"You are on trial for treachery to the concession and collusion with an enemy of the republic."

"I thought that's what you said."

"You are to be sentenced to life imprisonment in the penal colony on Ogenus."

"We just came from there."

"You are about to go back."

"How can we be on trial if you have already sentenced us?" asked Sevan

"We had the trial while you were on your way."

"Don't we get to defend ourselves?"

"No."

"Why does this keep happening to us?"

"Barnes has tricked us again?" said Ay-ttho.

"Why do we keep listening to him?" grumbled Tori.

"We have to get out of here," said Scotmax. "I have to get back to Ogenus."

"They are going to take us to Ogenus," said Ay-ttho.

"That gives me an idea."

"Silence!" the Chief Council Member ordered. "We have found you guilty of collaborating with President Man in his illegal coup in the concession and of fleeing justice in a stolen shuttle. We will now take you to Ogenus, where you will spend the rest of your lives. Scotmax, offspring of Yor's offspring, you have been found guilty of collaborating with these traitors and therefore you are also sentenced to life imprisonment on the Ogenus penal colony."

They led the group away and secured them into individual cells in a convict transporter. The cells were completely dark and, although they were far from comfortable, the group soon fell asleep in their respective cells.

They rudely awoke Sevan when they opened the door and light rushed in. He assumed they must be approaching Ogenus. A guard led him into the corridor where he saw Scotmax and Tori standing outside their respective cells. Tori gave Sevan a knowing wink. At first he didn't understand what Tori was trying to tell him and then he realised Tori and Scotmax were both looking past him towards the next cell where the guards were trying to wake Ay-ttho.

"Get down!" shouted Tori and the three prisoners leapt back into their cells just as the first guard flew out of Ay-ttho's cell and crashed into the wall opposite the door.

CHAPTER 13: THE SPACEMAN'S DESPERATION

Sevan waited until the sounds of violence and destruction had died down before lifting his head.

"What are you hiding in there?" Ay-ttho was standing in the doorway surrounded by the bodies of guards.

He followed her into the corridor where Scotmax and Tori were emerging from their cells. Scotmax was collecting weapons from the fallen guards.

"Come on," he said. "We need to take the bridge."

As an ex-corporation security clone, Ay-ttho was almost indistinguishable from the guards, once she donned one of their uniforms and a respirator mask. Two weapons each, the others hid from the view of the security camera while Ay-ttho buzzed the intercom to the bridge.

"We do not permit it you to open the door to the bridge while transporting convicts," the Captain denied her request.

"We have had an air failure. The rest of the guards and the prisoners are dead. Check the camera."

The captain checked the camera and saw the bodies of the guards behind Ay-ttho.

"My mask is faulty," Ay-ttho wheezed.

The door slid open and Ay-ttho burst in, followed by Tori, Scotmax and Sevan.

"Move away from the consoles," Ay-ttho ordered.

Faced with eight weapons pointing at them, the bridge crew followed Ay-ttho's instructions to go to the cells and were locked in.

"We have little time," said Scotmax, jumping into the pilot seat.

He navigated the ship across the plain of Ogenus where they could see the sailboards hovering below. He steered the vessel towards the hills and headed towards the clouds which enveloped the Dark City.

At the palace, Scotmax landed the convict transporter in the courtyard. Guards instantly surrounded the ship.

"I have come to see Chuba," Scotmax shouted to the guards as he opened the entrance. "Tell him I have done as he asked and have brought him a ship to leave this planet. I demand to see Nadio and Yor."

Some guards entered the palace, and moments later, Llessur and Enyaw emerged.

"So, this is what you call a fleet?" asked Llessur.

"It is a ship that will get you and your begetter off this planet. That's more than you have now. Matthews is dead. Return Nadio and Yor."

"The deal was to return with a fleet. It was all arranged with Barnes."

"Barnes betrayed you all. He had no intention of sending you a fleet. He wanted us returned here as convicts."

"And what are we supposed to do with this?" asked Enyaw.

"Leave this planet. It will get you to the Cheng-Huang colony or to another sympathetic planet where you can build an alliance."

"We need no alliance. Matthews is dead. The presidency belongs to the Chubas. Our dynasty is about to recommence."

"Have you forgotten about Xocliw?"

"Who in the worse place is Xocliw?"

"Matthews' co-begotton. She is on Future now. As soon as word reaches there that Matthews is dead, they will inaugurate her as President."

Llessur and Enyaw seemed concerned about this and immediately disappeared into the palace. The courtyard was filling with guards.

"I've got a bad feeling about this as well," said Tori.

"You have a bad feeling about everything," said Ay-ttho.

"Yes, and I'm usually right. Have your weapons ready."

After a while, only Llessur appeared in the doorway.

"You are too late," he said. "I have already executed Nadio and Yor. Kill them!"

As the guards opened fire, Scotmax closed the doors and rushed back to the bridge. Portable weapons fire pinged off the hull as she lifted the convict transporter off the ground.

"Let's get out of here," said Tori.

"I can't," said Scotmax. "Nadio and Tori might still be alive. I can't leave until I know for sure."

"What's your plan?"

Scotmax set the ship down far enough outside the Dark City for it not to be spotted. They left Sevan with the ship and told him to contact them with his communicator if he was discovered. As soon as they had left, he locked the doors.

Scotmax, Ay-ttho and Tori crept back into the city, trying their best not to be spotted so as not to raise the alarm.

They got as far as the palace compound without being spotted and circled the site to see whether any sides were less guarded than the others.

"What I don't understand," said Tori. "Is that everything on this planet has been built from whatever materials the convicts could find, right?"

"Yes," Ay-ttho agreed. "What's your point?"

"Where did the guards get all their weapons from? And what technology is keeping Chuba alive? Where did that come from?"

"That's a good point. I doubt the Corporation would drop any cargo that would allow them to make weapons."

"Unless Barnes is secretly equipping them," said Scotmax.

"Then why didn't he just give us the fleet we asked for?"

"Maybe he can't be seen to be helping Chuba. You heard what he said about them going back a long way."

"I believe nothing Barnes says anymore. And anyway, how does he expect Chuba to get off the planet if he doesn't give them a ship?"

"He probably expected us to hijack the convict transporter and bring it here."

"If he did, then we've messed up his plans."

"I feel like the Blind Spaceman again, spying on his enemies."

"But you keep forgetting. The blind spaceman dies at the end of the story. You and Nadio are going to have a happy ending."

"You are so romantic, Ay-ttho," taunted Tori. "Now, would you two like to be quiet before you attract the attention of all the palace guards?"

The rear of the palace seemed the most vulnerable, and there were places they could approach the wall of the building itself without being observed. Chuba obviously hadn't considered a land attack to be much of a threat, given the superior firepower of his guards. Ay-ttho, Scotmax and Tori were armed with two weapons each, although they were hopelessly outnumbered.

"Let's go," said Scotmax.

"Where?" asked Tori.

"In there."

"Calm down, we need to formulate a plan first."

"We don't have time to plan. Nadio's and Yor's lives are at stake. I spent some time in the palace before you arrived, and I'm fairly sure the location of the cell blocks is on this corner here."

Scotmax pointed her weapons at the corner of the building and, before any of the others could say anything, she had blown the corner of the building to smithereens and was charging towards the hole.

With little option, Ay-ttho and Tori followed her, firing at the startled guards who were trying to get back to their feet amongst the debris inside.

As they entered the building, Ay-ttho and Tori could see that Scotmax had been right in her estimation of where the cell block was located.

Scotmax was already halfway along the corridor, blasting guards as she went with Ay-ttho and Tori struggling to keep up, when she stopped at a cell.

"Cover me!" she shouted before blasting the door open.

Tori and Ay-ttho crouched by the entrance, shooting at any guards that appeared at either end of the corridor. Inside the cell, they could see the huddled figures of Nadio and Yor.

Scotmax helped them to shuffle close to the entrance.

"Now we just need to fight our way back through that hole," she said.

"That won't be easy," said Tori

"I don't think we have any choice," said Ay-ttho. "You cover our backs, I'll take the front. Scotmax, you help them."

She nodded at Nadio and Yor, who looked in no fit state to walk anywhere, let alone through a gunfight.

Ay-ttho began firing as rapidly as she could towards the corner where Scotmax had blown a hole in the wall. Tori did the same to the rear to dissuade any guards from following them, and Scotmax helped Nadio and Yor to move as fast as they could manage.

In this way, they made slow progress towards the hole. They had provided the guards with weapons, but it didn't appear that they had trained them on how to use them.

Once Scotmax had helped Nadio and Yor through the hole, both Ay-ttho and Tori covered their rear as they escaped into the darkness of the city.

They hid as best they could as they skulked along the dark streets. But progress was very slow and they could hear the guards that had left the palace to search for them.

"Help me," said Scotmax, lifting Nadio onto her back.

Taking her lead, Tori lifted Yor onto his and, this way, they could make quicker progress than before, with Ay-ttho constantly guarding the rear.

By retracing the route by which they had entered the city, they could avoid detection, and soon found themselves back at the convict transporter, though it took a while to convince Sevan to open the door.

"What now?" asked Tori, once they had made Nadio and Yor as comfortable as possible.

"We go back for the Mastery of the Stars," said Ay-ttho.

"In this?" asked Scotmax. "Have you lost your marbles?"

"Do you have any better ideas?"

"Yes, you drop me, Nadio and Yor somewhere safe first."

"Listen," Ay-ttho could barely contain her rage. "We lost our ship helping you get them back. Now you are going to help us get our ship back."

"Wait," said Tori, trying to calm the situation. "Ron can fly the ship. Why don't you just contact him and have him meet us somewhere?"

"Because all Corporation facilities have jammers which block navigational computers from taking ships out of hangars for this very reason. We have no choice. We have to go back to The Doomed Planet."

"Well, I'm piloting this ship and I say where we go."

"And I am pointing this blaster at your head," said Ay-ttho. "So you go where I say."

Reluctantly, Scotmax left the pilot's chair and Ay-ttho replaced her.

"So, what's the plan?" asked Tori.

"We could fly straight into the council building. We just pretend we are returning from Ogenus. They will expect us."

"And then what?"

"Ron opens the cargo doors and we fly directly inside the Mastery of the Stars."

"Not a bad plan. Let's do it."

Sevan felt unwell as they approached the cargo building.

"Convict Carrier x9 requesting landing clearance," Ay-ttho spoke into the communicator.

"You are not scheduled, Convict carrier x9."

"We have just returned from Ogenus."

"According to the manifest, you were to proceed to Aitne. What is your reason for returning?"

"Er... we had a malfunction and require maintenance."

"Then you should have proceeded to the maintenance centre on Future."

"Fushy this!" Ay-ttho had had enough. "Ron, open the doors."

Ay-ttho sped up towards the hangar entrance. The gun emplacements opened fire and several blasts glanced off the sides of the carrier. The ship entered the hangar at speed. Sevan could see the cargo doors on the Mastery of the Stars slowly opening. The ship bounced off the hangar floor before sliding into the mastery of the star's cargo bay. As the doors slowly closed, guards fired their blasters through the gaps.

When the ship doors closed, Ay-ttho jumped out of the carrier and rushed towards the bridge of the freighter. The guards began closing the hangar doors.

Ay-ttho lifted the Mastery of the Stars off the hangar floor and propelled it towards the closing hangar doors. She banked sharply and squeezed the freighter through the gap, only losing two of the ship's antennae.

As the freighter ascended into the atmosphere, the concession scrambled half a dozen fighters but the local pilot's were not as organised as those who flew for the Republic or the Corporation's central security forces and their slowness enabled the Mastery of the Stars to escape.

"What now?" asked Tori.

"Does this mean we can't return to the Doomed Planet?" asked Sevan.

"Nadio and Yor need help," said Scotmax.

"I am as eager to get back to The Doomed Planet as you," Ay-ttho told Sevan. "But that won't be possible as long as Barnes has an arrest warrant out for us. We need to make minor advances, taking one step at a time and the first step we need is to get help for Nadio and Yor."

"Thank you," said Scotmax.

"Where is the nearest independent system where we can find help?"

"The nearest independent system is Pallene," said Ron.

Nobody was happy with his suggestion.

"I know a healer on Pallene," said Sevan. "Notseldduh."

"Okay, let's go."

CHAPTER 14: MINOR ADVANCES

Sevan told them the story of his boils and the journey they had taken to meet Notseldduh, so Ay-ttho attempted to set the Mastery of the Stars down as close to the location Sevan had described as possible but there was no sign of Notseldduh or his encampment.

Then Sevan described the journey they had taken to the Çatalhöyükans, so they took off again and Ay-ttho bordered the sodium lake until they found the Çatalhöyükan settlement.

When they arrived, smoke was emerging from many of the homes, but otherwise it appeared deserted. They landed and no-one arrived to greet them.

On closer inspection, they found each dwelling contained the charred remains of its occupants. Someone had apparently wiped out the entire community.

"You shouldn't blame yourself."

Sevan turned and saw Notseldduh.

"What happened?" he asked.

"Shortly after you left, the Republic exterminated the Çatalhöyükans."

"How did you escape?"

"I left as soon as you were taken. Fortunately for me, I was out of sight of the settlement before the slaughter began. As soon as I saw the smoke, I returned, but by that time it was too late."

"Did no-one survive?"

"No-one, they were very systematic."

"Such a tragedy," said Tori

"They have simply returned to the universe whence they came," said Notseldduh. "It has released them from the torment of the illusion of life."

"What is he talking about?" Tori asked Sevan.

"He doesn't believe in the gods."

"Not believe in the gods? That's ridiculous."

"Is it? Where were they when we needed them?"

"How do you know they weren't? We're still here, aren't we? They created us for their own purposes and they use us for their own purposes. Who are we to question them?"

"You really talk a load of uxclod sometimes, Tori," said Scotmax.

"What do you mean? Look at the clouds. They are greater than you."

"They are you," said Notseldduh.

It rained, and the group took shelter underneath the Mastery of the Stars.

"You are about to witness a rare spectacle of the galaxy," said Notseldduh.

As they watched the rain outside, it became heavier and soon there were torrents of water rushing over the parched earth.

Sevan couldn't believe his marbles as small seedlings appeared immediately and began growing at a fantastic rate. Before long, a blanket of plant life covered the entire hillside.

They were still marvelling at the incredible beauty of the fresh shoots when the ground shook.

"Look over there," said Notseldduh, pointing to a ridge on the horizon.

A herd of colossal beasts came into view. They were large, hairy, four-legged creatures with a large horn protruding from each of their foreheads. Sevan watched with amazement as they galloped along the brow of the ridge.

"Down there," Notseldduh whispered, pointing to a newly vegetated knoll much closer.

Sevan looked and couldn't see any at first, but then noticed there was something tiny and very fluffy emerging from a hole. It was looking around nervously. Then it darted out and grabbed a bunch of the new vegetation before turning and rushing back down the hole.

"This is all very nice," said Scotmax. "But my partner and begetter's begetter need help. We were told you might help them."

"Maybe, maybe not," said Notseldduh. "Lead me to them."

"They simply need nourishment and rest," he said after examining them. "I don't think space travel is a good idea. You should find somewhere you can stay for a while until they recover."

"We need to clear our names," said Ay-ttho. "We can't live as fugitives forever. We need to get back to the Doomed Planet without fear of being arrested."

"What do you suggest?" asked Tori.

"It's hopeless talking to Barnes. We need to get an audience with President Xocliw."

"But she is Matthews' co-begotton."

"Yes?"

"Well, it was Matthews who betrayed us and exiled us."

"Was it? Or was it Barnes?"

"I don't understand."

"We fled Future of our own accord."

"Have you forgotten that they hunted us down at Yor's house? They used Nadio as bait."

"I hadn't forgotten that, but we can't be sure that it was Matthews who ordered it."

"Come on, Ay-ttho. Matthews had lost his marbles."

"Anyway," Scotmax interrupted. "I understand that you have things you need to do. I am happy to stay here with Nadio and Yor until they recover."

"And when they do, how are you going to get off the planet?"

"We'll hitch a ride."

"We'll come back for you," said Sevan.

"Don't worry about us. We'll be fine."

"You say that now," said Tori.

"We'll manage."

"Come with me," said Notseldduh. "I will show you somewhere in the tourist settlement where you can stay and will be safe."

"Can we give you a lift?" asked Ay-ttho.

"That would be very kind, thank you."

*

Ay-ttho, Tori and Sevan said their goodbyes to Scotmax, Notseldduh as well as Nadio and Yor, who were still too delirious really to know what was happening. Then they boarded the Mastery if the Stars again and Ron lifted the ship out of Pallene's atmosphere.

"I assume you have a plan," said Tori

"Not really," said Ay-ttho. "We only hope to visit President Xocliw and convince her to repeal our sentences. That Sevan assisted Matthews in his mission to kill his begetter should help."

"Yes, I met her," Sevan admitted. "But they introduced me as Edicla, the bounty hunter."

"Then you shall become Edicla, the bounty hunter again. We shall all assume our alternative identities and then we should be able to enter the Republic without being arrested."

"I will not be the cleaner again," Tori complained.

"I thought we were a team," said Ay-ttho. "You think I enjoy being a Saturnian missionary?"

"It's better than being a cleaner. I should swap identities with Sevan. I look more like a bounty hunter and he looks more like a cleaner."

"You forget, Xocliw has already met him."

Tori descended into a sulk.

Every portal they passed had Republic security checkpoints. Since Matthews had annexed this sector of the outer regions, they had stepped up security against insurgents and there were long queues of ships at every portal.

Enterprising locals were taking advantage and had set up small space ports to provide refreshments, entertainment and sell various goods from the tourist trinkets of Pallene to components for hyper-drives.

The impromptu service areas were, of course, illegal, but a sufficient percentage donated to the Republic guard benevolent fund ensured that the officials in charge of the checkpoints turned a blind eye.

The Sonvaenope and Angetanar services were fairly paltry affairs, but the station at Sicheoyama was huge and Sevan marvelled at the station called the Sicheoyama Pleasuredome, which boasted pleasure hosts from every species in the known galaxy.

They didn't hang around the sample any of the delights. So far, they had passed unchallenged through two portals and they didn't want to chance their luck at the third.

If they successfully navigated this checkpoint, there should only be two more, one at Inic B'Campa and then the final portal to Future.

Ron brought the ship to a halt in the inspection bay and transmitted the documentation.

"What are a bounty hunter, a missionary and a cleaner doing going to Future together?" asked the Republic guard.

"The cleaner comes with the ship," said Ay-ttho. "Edicla and I met on Lenguicarro. We are going to Future to see the sights."

"In a freighter?"

"It was the only ship we could hire. Besides, I am fond of shopping."

"But you are not coming from Lenguicarro, you came from Angetanar."

"Yes, we went to Pallene first. We both like water sports and we thought we would make a trip of it."

"Vaccination certificates?"

"What?"

"There have been outbreaks of Vermis Hirudo and Scophumen Pernilica on Pallene. If you don't have a vaccination certificate, you will need to be dewormed, fumigated and the quarantine for ten units."

"But the other checkpoints didn't ask for certificates."

"Sonvaenope and Angetanar are desperate for settlers they can't afford to turn anyone away but sicheo... hang on a moment. Your navigation computer has just transmitted the certificates to me. You are free to go."

"How did you manage that?" Ay-ttho asked Ron once they had cleared the portal.

"Us navigation computers all talk to each other. One of them sent me a genuine certificate, so I just used it to forge versions for you."

"You are the best, Ron. Have I ever told you that?"

"Not often enough."

There was very little in the way of activities at the Inic B'Campa and Future portals and, although security was tighter and the queues longer, the fake identity documents that High Priest Brabin had given them on Lenguicarro in what seemed like an eternity ago seemed to be still working.

"Well, that was easy," said Ay-ttho.

"A little too easy, don't you think?" said Tori, displaying his customary caution.

"Not another trap," said Sevan. "I don't think I can take another trap."

Ron steered the Mastery of the Stars into the long queues for the tourist hangars.

"Freighter Flavia?" a traffic coordinator's voice came from the communications panel.

"That's the false identify for the ship, right?" said Sevan.

"No, qheqeils on you, Sevan," Ay-ttho said sarcastically.

"This is Flavia," Ron replied.

"Please follow the pilot shuttle."

"Uxlod!" said Ay-ttho.

Sure enough, next to the queue was a pilot shuttle waiting to escort them to what turned out to be the Presidential hangar.

"We are in deep uxclod," said Tori.

"Hold your scrivvoixes. It might not be that bad."

"It's going to be that bad," said Sevan. "We are going to end up in another cell, so I am bringing a pillow and a hidden bottle of pish."

"Where did you get the pish from?"

"I had it delivered at the station at the Sicheoyama checkpoint."

"Where did you get the credits?"

"It just swapped them for some parts from the engine room."

"Sevan!" Tori exclaimed.

"What if we need those parts?"

"The ship seems to work fine. It's all part of my new policy of not worrying about things."

Ron landed the Mastery of the Stars in the presidential hangar and opened the doors. A platoon of presidential guards greeted them.

CHAPTER 15: SHADOW OF DEATH

President Xocliw and Barnes sat in The Channeatune Room, the most expensive restaurant in the explored regions of the universe.

"I appreciate your desire to meet in neutral territory," said Xocliw. "But was it really necessary to reserve the entire restaurant?"

"Don't worry," said Barnes. "This one is on me."

He took a sip of Spiced Eclipse Pish, the most expensive pish in the Republic.

"So, what's new, Xocliw?"

"You asked me here for a chat?"

"You know I keep your eye on things. You can do with the benefit of my intelligence."

"I have been monitoring matters. I am particularly interested in President Matthews' death. There are some who say you were involved."

Barnes laughed.

"Now why would you think I would be involved in the murder of your co-begotton?" he asked.

"There are some that say that Akpom Chuba is still alive and that you support his return to the presidency."

"I see. Well, not only is Chuba dead, but his offspring are currently serving life sentences on the Ogenus penal colony. No-one has ever escaped from Ogenus."

"That's interesting because there are others who say that a group has done exactly that. Three clones of yours. They were seen on the Doomed Planet, twice, despite having been sentenced to life imprisonment on Ogenus."

"I am aware of whom you speak. They have caused me problems before and have become somewhat of a pet project of mine. If what you say is true, then I think you need look no further to find Matthews' murderers."

"I heard your clones are indestructible."

"A common misconception, apparently. They are destructible. We can easily kill them. I simply overcame the biological constraints so they don't age, but we can easily kill them, either deliberately or accidentally."

"So, why did you ask me here?"

"I simply wanted to convey my personal condolences on the loss of your co-begotton, my congratulations on your inauguration as president and my assurances that the corporation will do everything in its power to maintain amicable relations with the administration of the Republic."

"If you really mean what you say, then prove it."

"And how would you like me to do that?"

"Find these rogue clones of yours and dispose of them."

"Consider it done."

*

Scotmax was sitting in a bar where she had spent the last of her credits on accommodation and food for Nadio and Yor.

She would have liked to have been brawl boarding, but she couldn't afford it.

The bar owner approached

"The rent of your friends' room is due," he said.

"Oh," said Scotmax, unsure of what to say. Nadio and Yor were still recovering and not yet fit to travel.

"Do you have any credits?" the bar owner asked.

"No."

"Great, you can move out the next rotation."

"I can't. My friends are not well enough to travel yet."

"Then you need to get a job."

Scotmax hadn't worked since she was young when he did chores for Yor. Since then she had lived off handouts from her begetter.

She looked at the tall armoured, long-snouted, small-eared bar owner with his eight legs and claws, which he used to hold and wipe several glasses simultaneously.

"I can work for you," she said.

"And what can you do?"

Scotmax was silent.

"There are some empty barrels down in the cellar that need taking out backs. You can start with those. Then you can start cleaning."

When the bar closed, the owner gave them a bowl each filled with some not quite dead marine creature and a mug of cloudy Ocrex ink.

They did his best to eat and drink it all.

*

"Do you have news for me?" Xocliw asked Barnes via a tachyon transmission.

"We have identified their last known location as Pallene. Their friends are still there."

"They might be useful."

"Agreed. I will maintain surveillance."

Xocliw ended the transmission.

"Where are they?" she asked the guard who had just entered the room.

"We have made them comfortable in the state apartments, as you requested."

"Good, it's clear Barnes does not know they are here. I'll let you know when I wish for them to be brought to me."

"Very good," said the guard before leaving.

*

Scotmax, Nadio and Yor could sleep on the floor of the bar and Nadio helped Scotmax with her chores

"What's wrong with him now?" said the bar owner when he came to wake them.

"What do you mean?" asked Scotmax.

She looked at Yor, who had sprouted blue, black, and red hairs.

"It's Vermis Hirudo," said the owner.

"What's that?"

"Leech worms. You usually get them from Gendrid or Iq'oik poo. I'll get you a healing staff."

"Why haven't we got it?" Scotmax asked.

"No idea. Here you go."

"What's that?"

"A healing staff," said the owner, handing Scotmax what looked like a broken piece of pot.

"It looks like a broken piece of pot."

"Your broken piece of pot is someone else's healing staff. Do you want it or not?"

"What am I supposed to do?"

"Scrape off the worms otherwise, they will burrow into the skin and lay their eggs."

"Every one?"

"Every one. And go out the back to do it. I don't want my floor covered in leech worms."

Scotmax and Nadio took Yor out the back and began scraping off the worms. Each one burst spectacularly, sending yellow entrails showering everywhere.

By the time they had finished, Scotmax and Nadio were both covered with, and sat in a puddle of leech worm entrails.

"Get this cleaned up," the bar owner said when he saw the mess. "Then there are more barrels to shift. Then you need to clean the inside of the bar."

Nadio helped Scotmax to shift the barrels and, as they worked, new boils would grow and then they had to clean the leech worm entrails off various surfaces, then they cleaned the bar.

When the bar had closed, the owner gave them the same food and drink as the previous night and then told them they could sleep on the floor.

"But won't he get bitten more?" asked Scotmax.

"Good point. You should sleep out the back. I don't want Leech worm entrails on my floor."

They lay down in the dirt outside.

"Don't you ever feel like giving up?" Nadio asked.

"Why?" said Scotmax. "I can't do anything about any of this, so why worry?"

"Do you never feel like it's all too much?"

"It is what it is."

They lay in the dirt and stared up into the night sky.

"What's that bright star there?" Nadio asked.

"No idea," said Scotmax. "Maybe it's not a star. Maybe it's a satellite or a space station."

"What do you think?" Scotmax asked the bar owner to look at Yor when he arrived to complain about the mess.

"Have you been using the healing staff?"

"If you mean the broken piece of pot, then yes."

"It looks bad."

"Is there nothing we can do apart from scrape them off with a broken piece of pot?"

"There is a healer who lives outside the settlement, but it will take you all day to get there, and I'm not paying you if you don't work this rotation."

"You don't pay us, anyway."

"Well, don't come rushing back expecting food and drink and a nice floor to sleep on."

Scotmax and Nadio decided not to risk it and borrowed an old door from the bar owner to use as a makeshift stretcher.

They set off to look for Notseldduh, the healer.

*

"Are you glad you brought your pillow?" Ay-ttho laughed as they surveyed their luxurious quarters.

She opened a cupboard packed solid with pish.

"Good job you brought those bottles, too."

"I still don't like the look of it," said Tori.

"You don't like the look of anything."

"I like the look of the pish," said Sevan. "I'm going to suspend judgement until I've tried a few bottles."

"Maybe it's poisoned," said Tori.

Ay-ttho rolled her marbles, which is what Corporation security clones did instead of rolling their eyes, but Tori knew exactly what she meant and ignored her.

"I'll join you in some pish," she said.

"Well, I won't," said Tori. "I want to stay sharp for when they spring the trap."

"Okay," said Ay-ttho, opening a bottle of pish. "Let us know when that happens."

There was a buzz at the door. Tori opened it. A Republic Presidential guard stood on the other side.

"President Xocliw will see you now," she said.

"But we didn't ask to see the president," said Tori.

"No, but she would like to see you."

*

"Ysteb, Edicla and Sirrah, so good to see you," said President Xocliw. "I have been expecting you."

"President Xocliw," Ay-ttho began. "We are not..."

"Ysteb, Edicla and Sirrah, yes I know."

Ay-ttho was speechless.

"But how..."

"Oh, I allowed you through the checkpoints. We picked you up as soon as you left Pallene. My co-begotton, President Matthews, told me all about you. He was very grateful to Sevan here and his friend Scotmax for helping him to murder our Co-begetter."

"But why, after he took power, did he turn against all those who helped him?"

"I think he felt he needed to assert his control, plus it was an excellent opportunity to continue the expansionist dreams of our begetter."

"His forces tried to kill us on Herse."

"That was unfortunate, yes. A symptom of relying too much on third parties to get things done. I think we share a mutual friend."

"Who?"

"Barnes."

"I'd hardly call him a friend."

"Well, the good news for you is that I don't think he knows you are here. The bad news is that he has your friends on Pallene under surveillance."

Ay-ttho allowed a moment of panic to influence her expression.

"Don't worry," President Xocliw continued. "I can have him bring them here."

"Barnes?"

"I'll have him treat them well and, at the moment, the catapult is the quickest route between Tomorrow and here."

"But..."

"Yes, I imagine you are not keen on meeting Barnes again."

"He sent us to the Doomed Planet to be arrested."

"I know, and that is part of the reason I wanted to see you. I know you went to Ogenus and I know you escaped."

Ay-ttho, Tori, and Sevan glanced at each other.

"What I am interested in knowing," said the president. "Is whether the rumours are true?"

"What rumours?"

"Is Akpom Chuba alive?"

"Alive is a very strong word," said Ay-ttho.

"Did you see him?"

"We saw something that claimed to be Akpom Chuba."

"Then the rumours are true. What else can you tell me?"

"Before we tell you anything," said Ay-ttho. "We want your assurances that you will repeal all our convictions and give us, and our friends, safe passage to the Doomed Planet."

"Before I give you anything, you need to convince me of something. How were you involved in the death of my co-begotton, President Matthews?"

Ay-ttho took a deep breath.

"The thing that called itself Akpom Chuba was holding our friends prisoner. He gave us 100 units to kill Matthews and return with a fleet to take him off the planet."

"We got off the planet..."

"So, it's true, you escaped Ogenus."

"Yes, but then Scotmax stole our ship and went to Tomorrow by himself. When we got there, he told us that Barnes had killed Matthews."

"And I'm supposed to believe you."

"You can believe what you want, but it's true."

"You know I could have you executed."

"So why don't you?"

"You will be of use to me still. In the meantime, you may enjoy the facilities in your quarters and I will send for your friends."

And so it was, that a corporation vessel took Scotmax, Nadio and Yor to Future where they were reunited with Ay-ttho, Sevan and Tori in the presidential residence. The sick bay on the corporation ship had treated Yor, who was more or less healed by the time he arrived.

"What does she want with us?" asked Scotmax.

"We don't know," said Ay-ttho. "We requested to return to The Doomed Planet, but she says she has some use for us. She knows about Akpom Chuba and we told her you saw Barnes kill Matthews."

"What did she say to that?"

"I don't know whether she believed us, but we're still here, for now."

"Does she know she will face constant rebellion while she continues to pursue the expansionist plans of her co-begotton?" asked Yor.

"I don't know. Why don't you ask her yourself? She wants to have dinner with us all once you have rested."

"That's something to look forward to," said Scotmax.

*

"My co-begotton has wronged you. You have been wronged by Barnes and Akpom Chuba has wronged you," President Xocliw began once everyone had been seated at the large table in the banqueting hall. "As far as I am aware, I have not wronged you. Please put me right if I am mistaken."

"President Xocliw?" Yor rose from his seat. "Your forces occupy Herse. As you know, we are very loyal to the Republic. However, we also cherish our autonomy and we did not invite your forces."

"I welcome your candid speech on this matter. As you know, it was my co-begotton, President Matthews, who ordered the occupation and I am in favour of a timely withdrawal, however, you will also know the great danger posed by terrorists and we must be sure that any cells of insurgents are routed out before our forces can safely withdraw."

"With respect, it is the forces which provoke the terrorists."

"I welcome your insights on these matters and therefore I would like you all to remain here for a while to assist me with the transition to what I envisage to be a new Republic."

"Do we have a choice?" asked Ay-ttho.

President Xocliw laughed.

"Of course you have a choice," she said. "But I might consider your refusal a slight on the presidency, and it would not be wise for me to allow a slight on the presidency to go unpunished."

"So, no, then."

"Can we stay in the rooms we have now?" asked Sevan.

"Of course."

"Looks like we are staying then," Tori grumbled.

CHAPTER 16: THE NEXT ASSASSINATION

"Akpom Chuba has left Ogenus," President Xocliw's adviser, Allecram, told her.

"What is the current situation?"

"His party has made contact. They wish to meet."

"Send Oiluj. He is a skilled diplomat. I trust him to represent us. Where do you suggest? Where are they?"

"The nearest neutral planet is Pallene. We were planning to annex it also, but it might be worth putting a hold on those plans until after the summit.".

"Very well, send Oiluj to Pallene."

*

When Oiluj arrived at Pallene, it was obvious where he would find Akpom Chuba. A large system of dark clouds was circulating over the sodium lake and, sure enough, that was where Oiluj found Chuba's encampment.

Oiluj's delegation landed nearby and soon established communications. By mutual consent, they set a camp up near the edge of the cloud system, where a summit could be convened.

When Oiluj entered the summit tent, he could see the amorphous figure of Chuba in a containment vessel at the far end, but that wasn't what caught his attention the most. Next to the containment vessel were two figures, almost identical, but not quite. They were both exquisite, but one was the most beautiful creature Oiluj had ever seen.

"Who is that?" she asked the presidential adviser, Allecram, who President Xocliw had requested to accompany Oiluj on the trip.

"Enyaw, heir to the Chuba dynasty along with his twin, Llessur."

"You must introduce me."

"Yes I must," an idea was already formulating in Allecram's mind.

"Akpom Chuba of the Cheng-Huang colony..." Allecram began.

"President Chuba, leader of the Republic," Chuba interrupted.

"It is for exactly this reason that it is essential we engage in a productive dialogue," Allecram tried to recover the situation.

"The only productive dialogue is one which returns the republic to my command. I am the logical successor of President Man. Kirkland's coup should be declared illegal."

"May I introduce you to Oiluj, offspring of President Xocliw," Allecram persisted.

"I do not recognise Xocliw's claim to the presidency, nor am I interested in descendants of that criminal, Kirkland."

"It occurred to me," Allecram was persistent. "That a union between these two great dynasties would be beneficial for both parties. President Xocliw appreciates that territory has been annexed that is very dear to you and your people and that if such a union was in place, it would be easier for him to justify a biumvirate in which you would administer the Republic together."

The silence which followed suggested that Chuba was contemplating the proposal.

"Tell me more about this proposal," he said at last.

"A union between President Xocliw's offspring, Oiluj and your own offspring's offspring, Enyaw, would be a perfect match."

Oiluj suddenly perked up at this suggestion and there seemed to be a reasonable amount of excitement among those who surrounded Enyaw as well.

"I accept your suggestion. Enyaw and her offspring shall become partners in return for an immediate biumvirate as a sign of goodwill on both sides."

They executed immediately the arrangements for the ceremony and partnered the couple the next rotation.

As soon as the ceremony had finished, Allecram set off for Future with Oiluj and his new partner Enyaw, and the Chuba delegation continued to the Cheng-Huang colonies where he would prepare to administer his share of the Republic.

However, the period of friendship following the agreement lasted barely as long as Oiluj and Enyaw's post union holirotation, commonly known as a moon of bloeux snail megaplums.

Chuba was demanding the demilitarisation of Xocliw's forces and, when Xocliw refused, Chuba issued a range of threats which gave Xocliw the excuse she needed to invade the Cheng-Huang colonies.

She commanded her fleet to the Zistreotovian portal, but did not enter it at first. She ordered the fleet to wait while she slept and contemplated the issue.

As she slept, she dreamt she was eating a banquet with some of the leading figures in the Republic. The conversation convinced her that crossing the portal was the correct course of action.

"The thermal homogeniser has been blended," said President Xocliw, repeating a popular phrase to mean that what has now been done cannot be reversed.

When Xocliw's fleet passed through the portal from Future to Zistreotov, Chuba considered it as a blatant disregard for their agreement and an invitation to war.

However, the size and speed of Xocliw's attack was such that Chuba decided it was better to abandon the Cheng-Huang colony with his own fleet in order to buy time to assemble a force that could challenge that of Xocliw's.

"We should attack Rechinia," President Xocliw told Allecram.

"Why?"

"Because, at the moment, that is the principal supply route for the Cheng-Huang colony via Zistreotov. If we occupy Rechinia, we cut off both systems."

Xocliw took a small fleet to what she imagined would be a simple task, leaving the rest of the fleet with Allecram, but they arrived in the Rechinia system to discover that Chuba had already second guessed their plans and was there with a fleet of his own, one strong enough to repel President Xocliw's attack.

She signalled for Allecram to join her and together they laid siege to the system. There, they remained in a deadlock for some time until a message arrived.

"It's from Rechinia," said Allecram. "Some occupants might betray Chuba."

"It could be a trap."

"They want us to send a delegation to meet with their representatives on Leda."

"But there's nothing on Leda."

"I think that's the point."

"Okay, I'll go. You stay here to manage the fleet."

No sooner had Xocliw emerged on the Leda side of the portal than she received a message from Allecram explaining that Chuba had launched a three-pronged attack on the blockade.

Allecram's forces put up a stiff resistance until Xocliw could return and relieve them. During the skirmish, some of Chuba's forces were cut off from the primary force and were pursued by Xocliw's ships for five units before they escaped.

"We inflicted many losses on them," Xocliw announced.

"Nevertheless," said Allecram. "It is difficult for us to maintain a blockade of such size. And I have worse news."

"What is it?"

"Two of your chief auxiliaries defected to Chuba during the skirmish."

"Uxclod! They could give Chuba information which would enable him to identify a weakness in our defence systems. We must expect an attack."

Sure enough, Chuba launched an attack at what proved to be the blockade's weakest point and broke through. They only held the position when Xocliw sent reinforcements. However, during the battle, Chuba's forces secured a position on one of the Rechinian moons.

Xocliw launched a hastily arranged attack, but in their haste the directions were confused and her forces suffered so many losses that it forced them to retreat.

Chuba's forces did not pursue.

"What's he doing?" asked Allecram.

"I do not know," said Xocliw. "But unbeknown to him, he might have just missed his opportunity for victory."

"I don't know why you say that," said Allecram. "Our position is substantially weakened: Chuba has captured one end of our fortified line and we cannot establish an even longer line to encircle his position."

"Then we will withdraw to the moon of Apollonia, leaving two divisions to deceive Chuba into thinking we are still present."

They executed their plan, but Chuba discovered it, and sent platoons in pursuit. They held them off in a skirmish with Xocliw's rear-guard.

"President Xocliw?" said Allecram. "The magistrates of Apollonia are refusing us permission to land."

"They think we are going to lose," Xocliw laughed. "And they don't want to upset Chuba. Sack the spaceport, be ruthless."

*

"Chase Xocliw down," Llessur urged Chuba. "Crush him."

"I urge caution," said Nala, who had joined Chuba with his legendary fighter because he desired revenge on Xocliw because her co-begotton, President Matthews, had broken his promise to Nala by colonising the Rechinia system. "Return to Future and retake the capital."

"I can't believe the great Nala is urging caution," Llessur laughed. "You have the most advanced fighter in the galaxy and you want to run away?"

"Committing to a pitched battle is both unwise and unnecessary," said Chuba. "We will be patient and wait for reinforcements from the Cheng-Huang colony. We will exploit Xocliw's weak supply lines."

"We should attack now," Llessur repeated. "Trust in your forces and your pilots."

Chuba thought about it.

"Very well," he said. "We will attack. Order the fleet to move close to Apollonia but do not attack. Wait for Xocliw's fleet to approach first."

*

Xocliw had to spread her forces thin to cover the same area of space that Chuba's fleet was covering.

She waited for Chuba's advance, but it never came, so instead, she ordered Allecram to advance with his ships.

This he did, but he stopped them before they came within range of Chuba's fighters. There was a tense moment as the two fleets faced each other, and then Allecram ordered the attack.

Chuba's ships held their ground and pushed Xocliw's fighters back. Then Xocliw revealed another platoon he had hidden behind Apollonia and they surprised Chuba's forces with the ferocity of their attack. His fighters retreated, leaving the rest of his fleet exposed.

"It is lost," he said as he watched his lines of fighters fall into disarray. "Retreat."

Chuba fled to Rechinia, leaving his remaining forces to fight Xocliw's fleet. At Rechinia, he transferred to his cruiser and fled the system, leaving his confused fleet behind.

Xocliw's fighters routed the remaining Chuban fleet and reclaimed Rechinia for the Xocliwian Republic.

Chuba passed through the Mytilene and then the Cilician system, where he held a council of war. The council broke up in disagreement and Chuba fled further to Ptolemy where, unbeknown to him, Xocliw had dispatched a troop of elite mechanical bowmen to assassinate him.

As he descended from his ship at Ptolemy, the bowmen were waiting. They unleashed a barrage of shots, killing Chuba instantly, then severed his head to ensure that his followers could not attempt to resurrect his life spirit again, and threw his remains into the Ptolemy ocean to be eaten by Ocrex.

On Rechinia, Chuba's surviving generals surrendered to Xocliw, who welcomed them.

"Let us return to Future," she announced.

CHAPTER 17: THE REAL TREASURE

"Explain to us again," Sevan asked Ay-ttho, as they walked in front of the Presidential palace. "What is our job? What are we supposed to do?"

"This is the last time, Sevan," Ay-ttho sighed with impatience. "We are representatives. You represent the mining colonies. I represent the corporation security clones and Tori is the representative for Republic security clones."

"But who chose us, and what are we supposed to do?"

"Xocliw chose us."

"Shouldn't those we represent choose us?"

"You are so naïve, Sevan. If you allowed clones to choose their own representatives, those wishing to be chosen would resort to popularist measures in order to get elected, rather than representing the best interests of the clones. It is much better to select individuals best suited for the task."

"How are we best suited?"

"Don't question things, Sevan. At the moment, we each inhabit luxurious apartments and have all we could need."

"As representative of the concession mining clones, does that mean I can visit the Doomed Planet?"

"I'm sure it does," said Ay-ttho. "We should organise such a trip right away."

"I heard Xocliw has made Nadio speaker of the Senate."

"That is true."

"And Scotmax a senator?"

"Also true."

"Oi, you lot!" Tori shouted at a group resting on a wall outside the front of the palace. "Don't you have homes to go to? Be off with you, loitering around here."

"He's taking his job seriously, isn't he?" Sevan whispered to Ay-ttho.

"I know. He's not even responsible for palace security."

"Are you on holiday?" Tori continued. "What are you doing hanging around here? You there? What is your job?"

"I construct the interiors for apartments," the shocked individual replied without questioning Tori's authority.

"Then where are your tools? What are you doing walking around here in your best clothes? You? What do you do?"

"I mend shoes," said the second individual.

"You mend shoes? Does that still happen here on Future?"

"It does."

"Then why aren't you doing it today? Why are you leading this lot around the streets?"

"To wear out their shoes and make more business for myself. No, seriously, we have come to the palace today to share in Xocliw's triumph."

"Xocliw's triumph?" Ay-ttho blurted out. "The population of Future turn out to celebrate Xocliw's triumph over Chuba and yet you were here celebrating Chuba's presidency following the death of President Man, weren't you? Any excuse for a holiday, Chuba's triumph, Xocliw's triumph, go back to your homes."

"Away with you!" shouted Tori.

The group went away without protest.

"You know it is Lupercalia," Ay-ttho warned Tori.

"Oh yes, any excuse to get drunk and fornicate."

"What's Lupercalia?" asked Sevan.

"It's a festival. They call it the festival of the real treasure, a bit like Binge on The Doomed Planet. It's an excuse for the population to get off their marbles on fushy and pish."

"Tell me more about this festival."

"No one knows the true origins, but they have celebrated it for 2,500 solar cycles, at least. According to legend, there was a President of another republic who ordered his co-begotton's offspring to be ejected into deep space."

"Why?"

"His co-begotton had promised not to reproduce."

"Why?"

"Do you want to hear the story or not?"

"Of course, sorry, go on."

"The guard charged with ejecting them into deep space felt sorry for them and placed them in a long-term hibernation unit which travelled across space until it landed here on Future. They created offspring, which were the first founders of the Republic."

"You mean they reproduced with each other?"

"They must have."

"But that's..."

"Exactly. Anyway, legend has it that the offspring developed the technology to return to the galaxy of their origins and kill the President that had ordered their deaths. They celebrate Lupercalia every year to mark the founding of the Republic."

"But wouldn't the President have already been dead by the time they made it back to the old galaxy?"

"I don't know. Maybe they discovered a wormhole or something. They partner the population of Future at random and attempt to reproduce."

"Random?"

"Yes."

"I'm so glad I'm asexual."

"Me too."

"I don't care whether it is Lupercalia," said Tori. "If I find any of them on the palace grounds, I'll drive them away. They use Xocliw's victory as an excuse to celebrate while we are all her prisoners."

"Shh, someone might hear you," said Sevan, looking around.

*

Xocliw was walking with her latest partner, Calpurnio. Allecram, her adviser, was trailing behind them with Scotmax and her partner Nadio, Scotmax's begetter, Yor, Xocliw's offspring Oiluj, his partner, Enyaw, and High Priest Callahan.

"Calpurnio!" Xocliw shouted.

"She speaks," Calpurnio mumbled to himself.

"Calpurnio!"

"Yes, Xocliw."

"Get out of the way, can't you see Allecram is trying to get through?"

"Yes, President?" asked Allecram, not aware that he was trying to get through.

"Touch Calpurnio as you pass, will you?" said Xocliw. "They say it will cure the sterile if they touch the fertile during Lupercalia."

"Your wish is my command," said Allecram.

"President?" called High Priest Callahan.

"Who is calling me? What is it?"

"President Xocliw, I must urge caution. Our intelligence suggests this is not a time to take risks."

"You and your superstitious mumbo jumbo, Callahan. Come on, let us go."

"Do you support her presidency?" Enyaw spoke quietly to Scotmax.

"Not particularly, but the population seems satisfied. Listen to the cheering in the streets."

"I'm not asking about them, but about you."

"You don't need to support his presidency. Xocliw killed your begetter, after all."

"She may have killed my begetter, but my partner is Xocliw's offspring and my loyalty is to him."

"Is it? Listen to those cries. It had better be with your partner because his co-begetter is very popular."

"Why her, Scotmax? Why not you or I? She is no more special than we are."

"Be careful, Enyaw. That talk is treasonous."

"Discuss the matter with Nadio, that's all I ask."

"Allecram? I want you to find me a new guard," Xocliw asked her adviser. "I don't trust Enyaw. She is young and full of ideas. I don't like anyone who thinks too much. They are dangerous."

"You don't need to fear her. She is loyal to Oiluj."

"I don't fear her, but she has taken to spending too much time with Scotmax and Scotmax reads too much. She observes everything and sees through our deeds, never smiles, is too restless, and is dangerous. Come away with me and tell me what you think of her."

Xocliw led Allecram away from the group.

"Nadio, can I have a word?" asked Scotmax.

"Yes, what is it?"

"Have you noticed anything strange about Xocliw?"

"You've been with her as much as I have."

"You don't think she has some illness?"

"If anyone is ill, it is us."

"What do you mean by that?"

"Did you know that when they inaugurated Xocliw as President, she first pretended to refuse it?"

"No?"

"She play acted as if she was not worthy and begged the crowds' forgiveness. They lapped it up. Allecram it was who was offering the presidency in a piece of theatre you would never believe."

"But the crowd did?"

"Oh yes, they loved it."

"Scotmax!" said Enyaw, approaching. "We must get to know each other better, come to our apartments to eat."

"Yes, or you to ours."

"Let me know when you are free."

"I will."

Nadio had already begun to walk back to the palace. Yor joined her.

"Is everything okay, Nadio?" he asked.

"We have suffered many trials, Yor. But I was never so worried as I am now."

"Why?"

"I have been having terrible dreams. I think something bad is about to happen."

"We certainly live in strange times and nothing is certain. Ah, here is the entrance to my apartment. Take care, Nadio, don't worry too much."

Yor entered his apartment, leaving Nadio to wait for Scotmax.

"What's wrong Nadio?" she asked as she approached. "What were you talking to my begetter about?"

"Only the strange dreams I've been having."

"You worry too much, Nadio. We have a good life here. We should enjoy it while we can. You look pale, as pale as a thug can look. What will be, will be, Nadio?"

"You know that on the next rotation, the Republic senate is going to ratify Xocliw's presidency?"

"Should that worry me?"

"You wear a weapon at your side, Scotmax?"

"I'm not afraid of Xocliw's tyranny."

"You should be."

"Why should Xocliw be a tyrant? She may think herself a tronqak and the population of the Republic mere cukids, but that makes her no different from any other president."

"You plan and scheme. I know you, Scotmax."

"That's as maybe but..."

"Shhh, someone is coming."

"It's Effeek'o, Nadio, look. Effeek'o, how are you? I haven't seen you since Herse. How are your patients?"

"Well, I hope. And how are you both? Are you well?"

"As well as expected. What brings you to Future?"

"They have invited me as a special adviser to the senate, but between you and me, I had an ulterior motive."

"Oh, yes? And what might that be?"

"The cause for which we all fought on Angetanar. Now is our opportunity. Have you spoken to Enyaw? We must make an alliance."

"I doubt that should be too difficult, but perhaps you should speak with her yourself."

"I will do that."

"Good. Let's catch up later. If you'll excuse me, I need to find Sevan."

Effeek'o, Nadio and Scotmax said their goodbyes and Scotmax went off to find Sevan

"Ah! There you are," she said when she eventually found him. "Can I confide in you?"

"Of course you can."

"I'm worried about Xocliw and what might happen when the senate finally ratifies her presidency."

"What do you mean?"

"I worry it may tempt her to abuse her power, like her co-begotton and her begetter and her co-begetter."

"I see what you mean, quite a lot of family history there. Be careful what you say, though. Look, Enyaw is coming this way and there are others with her."

"I can't see. Do you recognise them?"

"No, can't say as I do. No, wait, I can see now that Nadio is with them, and Effeek'o from Angetenar. Plus some others I don't recognise."

"Hello Scotmax, I hope we are not disturbing you."

"Not at all. I was just visiting my friend, Sevan. You know Sevan?"

"Of course, we have seen each other around the palace."

"Do I know all your friends here?" asked Scotmax.

"Yes, Nadio and Effeek'o, obviously. Do you know Di'Shon and Bernard? They are both senators sympathetic to our cause."

"I am familiar with your work, very pleased to meet you. Are you sure it is safe, meeting like this?"

"Yes, do not worry. Lupercalia preoccupies everyone."

"Ah, yes, the real treasure. That should keep everyone busy for a while. What about my begetter, Yor? Should we include him in our plans?"

"Yes we should," said Nadio.

"Of course," said Effeek'o. "I know he was a staunch supporter of Kirkland, but Matthews' betrayal has turned him against the dynasty. He will be with us, for sure "

"His reputation would lend our cause a great deal of credibility," said Di'Shon.

"I doubt he will join a cause started by others," said Enyaw.

"Especially not if he knows you're involved," agreed Scotmax. "You were our captor."

"Not I, but my begetter," said Enyaw.

"Nobody is to be touched except Xocliw, is that correct?" asked Nadio.

"Good point," said Scotmax. "Allecram is very loyal and may become an obstacle. We should include him in our plans."

"Let us be assassins but not butchers," urged Enyaw. "If only we could kill Xocliw's nature rather than Xocliw herself. Our operation must be clinical. This is not the time for hacks. We need to be considered purgers, not murderers, and as for Allecram, don't worry about him. Without Xocliw he is completely impotent."

CHAPTER 18: BADLANDS

"Enyaw, I am concerned about Allecram and the loyalty he has for Xocliw," said Scotmax.

"Don't worry, Scotmax. What can he do except give his life for his president?"

"He is not easily scared," said Barnard. "Allecram will look back and laugh at this when it is all over. But I think we should not linger longer. It is not wise for us all to be gathered like this for long."

"Our problem is going to be knowing Xocliw's movements. The exact time for the senate's ratification has still not been determined," said Scotmax.

"Don't worry," said Enyaw. "He will not miss the ratification. That will be our opportunity."

"What about Mallik? She hates Xocliw," said Di'Shon.

"Good idea. She likes me. Send her to me and I will convince her."

"It is time to go," said Scotmax. "Go friends and consider yourselves good republicans."

"Be careful to disguise our intention," warned Enyaw. "Go about your business as you would normally."

Everyone left except Enyaw.

"What is this? Sevan? Are you sleeping? Did you hear none of our conversation?"

Sevan let out a loud snore.

"Nevermind, sleep Sevan. Don't trouble your marbles with the concerns of others."

"Enyaw? What are you doing up?" asked Oiluj, seeing her partner arrive back at their apartments.

"I could ask you the same question. You shouldn't be up, my love. You know your constitution is not good."

"Neither is yours, robe up. I hope you are not celebrating the real treasure."

"Lupercalia? You know me better than that, Oiluj."

"Then what have you been doing? You have been very restless lately and yet whenever I ask you what the matter is, you either ignore me or become impatient with me. What is it that troubles you so much? Share it with me. You know a problem shared is a problem halved."

"I'm just not feeling well, that is all."

"Then you should seek help to get better."

"I am my love, I am. Now don't worry your pretty little head about it. Go back to bed and I will be there shortly."

"But if you are really sick? Staying up late will only make it worse. I saw you with some others earlier. What did they want?"

"You need not worry, Oiluj."

"Needn't I? Then tell me. There should be no secrets between us. Am I not your partner?"

"You are my partner and there are no secrets between us."

"If that is true, then you should tell me what is troubling you. I am your partner and Xocliw's offspring. Tell me what is concerning you. I will not share it with anyone."

There was a knock at the door.

"Not now, Oiluj. Who could that be?"

Enyaw opened the door to the apartment.

"Sevan? What are you doing here?"

"I had a visitor after you left. I think he is ill."

Enyaw looked behind Sevan and saw Mallik.

"Mallik? What's wrong? Di'Shon was talking with me about you this very night."

"Good rotation, from one who can barely wish for it."

"If only you were not ill."

"I am not ill, if you can make use of me."

"We have an impressive task, Mallik, if you wish to hear it."

"If you have work for me, I will set aside my sickness."

"I think our work will cure the sickness of many."

"But do we not need to make some sick to make others well?"

"That is true. Let me get ready, and I'll show you our plans."

*

Xocliw and Calpurnio were sleeping in their bed when, suddenly, Calpurnio sat bolt upright.

"Help! They are murdering my partner!"

Xocliw sat upright as well.

"What the fush?" he yelled. "That's the third time tonight."

A guard entered the room, expecting to find an assassin.

"It's okay," said Xocliw. "It's only my partner having another visit to the badlands while she sleeps. Tell High Priest Callahan and see whether he can come up with some remedy."

The guard nodded her understanding and left.

"I may as well get up now," Xocliw grumbled.

"What do you mean?" Calpurnio was shocked. "You shouldn't go anywhere today."

"Why ever not? My enemies only dare conspire in secret. As soon as they see me, their plans dissolve with their will."

"Xocliw? I have been suffering terrible visits to the badlands at night. I dreamt I saw a kharqreik giving birth in the street, the dead were coming back to life, there was a great battle in the clouds which rained debris down on Future. Krarqroins were screaming and the ghosts of the dead were shrieking in the streets."

"Are you saying these are premonitions? What the gods will have will be. Your premonitions could apply to the rest of the galaxy as much as me."

"Premonitions do not appear to warn the death of a beggar, only for presidents."

"Cowards die many times, but the courageous only die once. Death will come when it comes."

There was a knock at the door.

"Come," said Xocliw.

The guard entered.

"Well?"

"The High Priest suggested you should remain in your apartments today."

"Me? What kind of president stays at home through fear? Danger fears me. I am like two kharqreik born on the same rotation. I will leave my apartment today."

"Your confidence confounds your wisdom," Calpurnio pleaded. "Blame my fear for staying home this rotation, not your own. Allecram can go to the senate and say that you are not well. Please!"

Xocliw sighed.

"Very well," she relented. "I will send Allecram and will stay at home if it will bring me peace."

There was another knock on the door. The guard opened it to reveal Enyaw.

"Good rotation, President," said Enyaw. "I have come to take you to the citadel in space for the senate meeting."

"Take my greetings to the senators and tell them I will not attend this rotation."

"Say she is ill," said Calpurnio.

"You would have the president lie? Tell them the president will not come."

"But President?" asked Enyaw. "What should I tell them is the cause?"

"Tell them I will not come. That should be enough to satisfy the senate. But, for your sake, Enyaw, Calpurnio does not want me to go. He has been to the badlands in his sleep and dreamt premonitions which he believes predict my death."

"What were these dreams?"

"I dreamt that Xocliw's statue was so full of holes he became a fountain of life juices," said Calpurnio. "The citizens of the Republic came and washed themselves in the juices."

"I am sure you have misinterpreted the dream. It means that the Republic is going to be refreshed and revived by your presidency."

"You have explained it well, Enyaw." said Xocliw. "Your partnership with Oiluj has made you a genuine friend of the Republic."

"It has. Please listen to a friend of the Republic when she tells you that the senate has agreed to ratify your presidency. If you do not go today, they may change their marbles. If you hide today, will they not say that the president is scared?"

"You see how foolish your dreams seem now, Calpurnio?" said Xocliw. "I am ashamed that I was going to give in to them. I will go to the senate."

There was another knock on the door.

"Come," said Xocliw.

The guard opened the door and Mallik, Di'Shon, Nadio, Scotmax and Bernard were standing outside.

"Good rotation," said Xocliw.

At the same moment, Allecram arrived.

"And Allecram as well, are you only just arriving now from your revelling?"

"Good rotation," said Allecram.

"Let us go to the citadel in space and speak with the senate," said Xocliw. "I will give them a magnificent speech. Come, let us go together."

*

"Ron?" Sevan called the navigational computer as he entered the bridge of the Mastery of the Stars.

"Good morning, Sevan," said Ron. "Nice of one of you to remember I exist. Enjoying your luxury accommodation, are you?"

"It's very nice, yes, thank you. But that's not why I'm here."

"No, I thought not. You probably want me to do something for you, do you?"

"I actually came for a bit of advice."

"Advice? From me? I am honoured."

"Okay, thank you Ron. Now, if you wouldn't mind turning down the sarcasm a bit, I'll tell you what the problem is."

"Fire away."

"I overheard Scotmax and Enyaw and some others talking together. I think they are planning to assassinate President Xocliw. They didn't say it in as many words, but that was the vibe I got."

"And what did you say?"

"Nothing, I pretended to be asleep."

"I see."

"Well, I didn't want to get mixed up in a presidential assassination, not after last time."

"Last time? This would be the third presidential assassination in which they could implicate you."

"Third?"

"Well, there was that awkward business with President Man."

"That was nothing to do with me."

"No, but they accused you of the murder."

"President Chuba accused us of the murder."

"And then you helped President Matthews kill President Ydna and her partner."

"I didn't help. I just happened to be there."

"And now you are conspiring to kill a third."

"I'm not conspiring. I was just in the same place as the conspirators."

"I'm sure the Star Masters will see it that way when it goes to trial."

"What can I do, Ron? We need to stop them."

"Can't you get a message to President Xocliw?"

"If I did, they might discover the message was from me."

"I could send the message from an anonymous account," said Ron.

"You can do that?"

"Of course. What shall I say?"

"Say: President Xocliw, be aware of Enyaw and of Scotmax, Nadio, Di'Shon, Bernard and Mallik. They are conspiring against you."

"Is that it?"

"Do you think I should write more?"

"No, I think that should do it."

"Thanks Ron. Now I'd better go before anyone notices I am missing."

Sevan ran out of the Mastery of the Stars and across the hangar towards the palace shuttles. On the way, he almost ran into Oiluj.

"Where are you going?" Oiluj asked.

"To the citadel in space, to the senate. Are we not late for the ratification?"

"Sevan? Would you do me a favour, please?"

"If I can."

"Look at Enyaw and then come back and tell me if you think he looks ill. What was that noise?"

"I didn't hear anything."

"Listen well, someone is coming."

"I can't hear anything."

High Priest Callahan entered the corridor.

"Good rotation, High Priest, where are you coming from?" asked Oiluj.

"From my own apartments."

"Has President Xocliw left for the senate yet?"

"Not yet. I am on my way to see her now."

"You have some business with her, don't you?"

"Yes, I do."

"Are you aware of any intention of harming her?"

Sevan shuffled awkwardly.

"Not that I know of," said Callahan.

"Enyaw has a request that Xocliw will not grant and it is worrying me."

CHAPTER 19: BLUE FIND

Sevan was troubled. Ron had already sent the message and Sevan was now tormented by the thought that he had been disloyal to Scotmax and Nadio. The other co-conspirators didn't really bother him, but it was the idea that if his message prevented the assassination, it may mean trouble for Scotmax and Nadio, whom he had considered friends.

He had spent a long time trapped in a shuttle with Scotmax and a long time stranded on Pallene with Nadio so he had got to know them both well and now felt he had betrayed them with the anonymous message even though they need never discover it was him who sent it.

He joined High Priest Callahan on a shuttle to the citadel in space and arrived just in time to see President Xocliw arrive.

"Your dire prediction for the rotation has not come true," President Xocliw commented to Callahan as she passed.

"The rotation is not yet over," Callahan warned.

Xocliw was followed by Enyaw, Scotmax, Nadio, Di'Shon, Bernard, Mallik and a host of others.

Xocliw's communicator buzzed.

"It seems I have a message," she said.

"Leave it until later?" said Enyaw.

"Are you sure that is wise?" asked Sevan nervously.

"I am too busy to read it now," said Xocliw.

"You should always check your messages," said Sevan. "You never know."

"Hold your emotions, Sevan. Why are you so keen on messages suddenly?"

Sevan held his tongues.

"The street is no place to read messages," said Scotmax. "We are on the way to the senate."

"Good luck with your enterprise, Scotmax," said a bystander.

"What enterprise?" Scotmax asked.

"Good luck," the bystander repeated and then headed towards Xocliw..

"What did she say?" asked Enyaw.

"She wished me good luck on my enterprise. I think our plan may have been discovered."

"She is heading towards the president."

"If she tells her, I will kill her myself."

"Stay calm. She is not telling her our plan. Look, they are both smiling."

The group entered the senate and took their seats

"Bernard is doing his job," said Enyaw. "Look, he is leading Allecram away. But where is Di'Shon? He should put my motion to the president. Wait, he's doing it now, quick, second the motion."

"Di'Shon? You have your hand raised," said Nadio, attempting to get business underway.

"Are we all ready?" Xocliw interrupted. "What problems does the president and her senate have to solve today?"

"President Xocliw, I have a matter to which I would appreciate your attention," said Enyaw.

"Forget it, Enyaw. Llessur has been banished by decree."

"Am I not allowed to beg for you to repeal the decree?"

"Please consider her petition," said Di'Shon.

"What?" Xocliw was astounded.

"I'm sorry, President Xocliw," said Scotmax. "I too would urge you to consider Enyaw's petition."

"President?" said Nadio.

The senators gathered close to President Xocliw, all expressing their opinions on the matter.

"What is all this?" President Xocliw was becoming annoyed.

"President?" Enyaw asked

"What, Enyaw?"

"Now." said Scotmax.

Scotmax, and then the other conspirators, shot President Xocliw.

"And you, Scotmax?" President Xocliw coughed before collapsing to the floor.

"Liberty! Freedom! Tyranny is dead!" shouted Effeek'o. "Proclaim the news on the streets of Future."

"Go!" said Scotmax. "Declare liberty, freedom and enfranchisement."

"Do not be afraid, senators. We have fulfilled our ambition," said Enyaw.

"Speak, Enyaw," Nadio urged.

"And Scotmax," said Enyaw. "Where is Mallik?"

"He is here," said Effeek'o. "Completely bewildered by this mutiny."

"Stay together," warned Di'Shon. "Beware of Xocliw's allies."

"Don't talk like that, Di'Shon," said Enyaw. "There is nothing to fear. Tell them, Mallik."

"Go Mallik," said Scotmax. "In case the crowd makes you more anxious."

"Good idea. You have nothing to fear," said Enyaw.

Barnard returned.

"Where is Allecram?" asked Scotmax.

"He has fled to his apartments in amazement. There is panic in the citadel as if it were the apocalypse. Ships are leaving for Future, the news is spreading."

"Let us go to the streets of Future and shout peace, freedom and liberty," Enyaw suggested.

"Let us go," Scotmax agreed. "They will celebrate this moment for solar cycles to come."

"And now, Xocliw lies worthless in the shadow of the palace Chuba once occupied."

"And when it is celebrated, they will remember us as the ones who brought liberty to the Republic."

"Shall we go?"

"Yes. You go first, Enyaw. We will follow."

"Wait, look who is coming. It's Allecram's assistant."

"Enyaw, Allecram has sent me here to say that he has requested a safe meeting where you might explain your reasoning for assassinating President Xocliw so that he might better understand and he hopes to support your future endeavours," said the assistant.

"Allecram is smart," said Enyaw. "Tell him to come and see me. He will be safe."

"I will get him," said the assistant as she left.

"We shall surely have Allecram as a friend," said Enyaw.

"You may be right," said Scotmax. "But I am still wary of him."

"Here he comes."

Allecram entered the senate

"Welcome, Allecram," said Enyaw.

"President Xocliw!" said Allecram, staring at the body. "All your conquests have come to this. Goodbye Xocliw."

Allecram turned his attention to the conspirators.

"What are your intentions? Who else's life juices are you going to spill on this rotation? If I am on your list, then this is your best opportunity. Nothing would please me more than to die here beside my president."

"Do not beg for death," said Enyaw. "We mean you no harm. We welcome you, Allecram."

"Your voice will be as strong as ever in the new Republic," said Scotmax.

"But you need to be patient," said Enyaw. "Until we have appeased the citizens. They are currently beside themselves with fear. Then we will explain everything to you."

"I am sure you have your reasons and have acted wisely. Come, Enyaw, let me greet you in the traditional way."

Allecram and Enyaw approached each other and rubbed antennae.

"Next you, Scotmax."

Scotmax took her turn, followed by Di'Shon, Effeek'o, Nadio and Barnard.

"I concede you must see me as a flattering coward," Allecram said once he had finished exchanging greetings. "I was very loyal to Xocliw and if she has gone to the better place and is looking down on me, then I must already be dead to her. For her to see Allecram making peace with her murderers. Please forgive me, Xocliw. I am worthy of the title they give to cowards in the Republic. I am a blue find."

"Allecram," Scotmax attempted to console him.

"I'm sorry, Scotmax."

"You are not a blue find, Allecram. I do not blame you for your loyalty to Xocliw," Scotmax continued. "But what relationship do you intend to have with us? Will you join us or, in the future, will we not be able to rely on you?"

"I am with you, but I would like to know why you considered Xocliw dangerous."

"Don't worry, we had good reason," said Enyaw.

"That is what I wanted to hear. And I would that I may speak at her funeral."

"You shall."

"Enyaw, may I speak with you?" Scotmax took Enyaw aside. "What are you doing? Don't let Allecram speak at Xocliw's funeral. You don't know what he might say. He might move the citizens to revolt."

"Don't worry. I will speak first and give our reasons for the assassination. I will contradict anything he says. The fact we will give Xocliw a proper funeral favours us rather than him."

"I don't know, Enyaw. I don't like it."

"Allecram, you may speak at Xocliw's funeral, but you must not blame us for her death. Simply recount as many outstanding features about her as you can think of. You will speak after me."

"Of course, I would expect no more."

"It is settled then. Guards, have President Xocliw's body prepared for a state funeral."

"What is a blue find?" Sevan asked High Priest Callahan.

"It is the name given to cowards. Pilots too scared to engage in battle would sometimes attempt to desert in their fighters but the fighters never had enough power to reach a safe system so they would nearly always be found floating in space and, starved of oxygen, they would be blue, hence a blue find."

"But I'm the blue side of turquoise."

"Yes, but you are a corporation mining clone, not a Republic fighter pilot. Now, if you'll excuse me, Sevan, I have a funeral to prepare."

Sevan noticed Allecram was standing over Xocliw's body, mumbling something. He edged closer to overhear what Allecram was saying.

"Forgive me for being meek with these butchers. You were the noblest President the Republic has ever had. I wish only bad things for the perpetrators of this evil deed. I venture to prophesy over your dead body. The Republic should be cursed from this rotation forwards. That civil war should blight all corners of the Republic. Destruction and the spilling of life juices shall become so common that co-begetters will merely smile at the sight of their own offspring hacked to pieces in the fortunes of war. Xocliw's spirit will rage with revenge and rising from the worst place cry 'Havoc,' and let slip the dogs of war."

Allecram turned suddenly to face Sevan, causing him to jump and pretend he wasn't trying to eavesdrop on Allecram's mumbling.

"You knew President Matthews, didn't you?" Allecram asked.

"I did," Sevan admitted.

"Did you know she had offspring?"

"I did not."

"Her name is Hours. Xocliw had asked her to come to Future, and she is already in a neighbouring system, Skoll. Her life's in danger. We must get to her first. You are friends with Ay-ttho and Tori."

"That is right."

"The Mastery of the Stars is your ship, is it not?"

"It is."

"And they have not messed you up in this plot to kill Xocliw?"

"They have not. In fact, I attempted to warn the president."

"Good. I have a mission for you and your friends and I will pay well. But first you must attend Xocliw's funeral with me and observe how the citizens receive my speech. This, you will report to Hours. Come, I will explain everything on the way."

*

"What? Have you lost your marbles?" asked Tori, after Sevan had explained the plan.

"He said he would pay very well," said Ay-ttho.

"Have you lost your marbles as well? What about your loyalty to Scotmax?"

"I owe nothing to Scotmax. She still owes me for saving her on Angetenar."

"What about Nadio then?"

"I have a loyalty to Nadio, I'll give you that. But my only loyalty to Scotmax is that Nadio loves her and there is nothing I can do about that. Between you and me, I think Nadio might be better off without her."

"So you will betray her."

"Who said anything about betrayal? All Allecram is asking us to do is to observe the funeral and report those observations to Hours."

"Oh, so you are going to tell Nadio about our mission, are you?"

"Of course not."

"Why not?"

"Because Allecram has asked us expressly not to disclose the mission to anyone."

"And why do you think that is?"

"He said that Hours' life was in danger. Anyway, that's none of our business. We are being paid to do a job, and that is all that matters."

"Is it, Ay-ttho?"

"Listen. Xocliw is dead. That means we are free to relinquish these stupid appointments and return to The Doomed Planet, but we can only do that if we earn some credits and this is the perfect opportunity to do that, hurting no one."

"If you say so."

CHAPTER 20: FOR HOURS TO LIVE

Enyaw and Scotmax arrived at the funeral on Future to find a multitude of citizens demanding answers. They mobbed them as soon as they arrived.

"Give me an opportunity to speak and you shall have your answers," said Enyaw. "Scotmax, go to the other side to speak so that we might divide the crowd. This is becoming dangerous."

Enyaw stood on a wall to address them.

"Those who wish to hear me stay here. Those who wish to hear Scotmax follow him. We will give you the reasons for President Xocliw's death."

There followed a period of confusion while the citizens decided who they wanted to hear speak. When calm had returned, Enyaw prepared to speak.

"Citizens, hear me to the end. I was loyal to President Xocliw, but I was more loyal to the Republic. Had Xocliw lived, she would have enslaved you all, with Xocliw dead, you can all live free. As a friend, I liked Xocliw, when she became president, I rejoiced, when she defeated my begetter, Akpom Chuba, I celebrated with her, yes I celebrated. My loyalty to this Republic and to my partner, Oiluj, is stronger than any loyalty I might have had for my begetter. But Xocliw's ambitions were dangerous and for this reason I combined to kill her. We know that, in our Republic, there is no other way. Since President Man the first, we have been trapped in this violent struggle for power. Who here does not love their Republic. Let them speak if I have offended them. Anyone who does not love the Republic and has been offended, speak now."

There was not a single citizen prepared to risk being branded as someone who didn't love the Republic and so no-one spoke up.

"Therefore, I have offended no-one," Enyaw continued. "Here comes the procession with her body, as is fitting for someone of such importance. I welcome Allecram, who is at her side. Allecram had no part in President Xocliw's death, but he has a part in the New Republic. I shall leave you now with the sentiment that Xocliw died for the good of the Republic and I too shall welcome my death when it comes if it be for the good of the Republic."

"Live, Enyaw, live!" shouted some of her more fanatical supporters.

"Let's carry her to the palace," said one.

"There should be a statue in her honour," shouted another.

"She should be President!" shouted a third.

"She has all of Xocliw's good qualities," said a fourth.

"Let's carry her to the palace," the first supporter suggested again.

"Citizens," Enyaw tried to continue over the shouting.

"Silence! Enyaw is speaking!" shouted the second supporter with a surprisingly loud voice.

"Silence!" the first supporter joined in.

"Good citizens," Enyaw began again. "I will leave you now. Stay to listen to Allecram. Please respect Xocliw's corpse and give her the respect she earned with her earlier deeds. Allecram will tell you of those deeds. Please stay and listen."

Enyaw stepped down from the wall.

"Let us hear Allecram," one of the crowd shouted.

"Allecram, climb on the wall," shouted another.

"For Enyaw's sake, I must address you," said Allecram, climbing up onto the wall.

"What did he say?" asked one of Enyaw's supporters.

"He said for Enyaw's sake he must speak to us."

"He'd better not say anything bad about Enyaw."

"Xocliw was a tyrant," said another in the crowd.

"That's certain," said another. "We are well rid of her."

"Let's hear what Allecram has to say," complained another.

"Citizens," Allecram began.

"Quiet everyone, let us hear him," another frustrated citizen shouted.

"Friends, citizens, members of the Republic, please listen to me. I am here to send Xocliw to the better place, not to praise her. The evil that presidents perpetuate lives on long after they do. The good often go to the better place with them, so let it be with Xocliw. Enyaw has told you that President Xocliw was ambitious. If that was true, then it was a fault that she has paid for dearly. Enyaw is honourable, and it is with her permission that I come to speak with you this rotation. In the war against Enyaw's own begetter, Xocliw captured many enemies which she ransomed to fill the coffers of the Republic. Was this ambitious? When the poor of the Republic cried, Xocliw wept. Was this ambitious? We should make ambition of stronger stuff. Yes, Enyaw said Xocliw was ambitious and Enyaw is honourable. Have you forgotten that when Xocliw was inaugurated as President, she first refused it? She said she was not worthy and begged your forgiveness. Have you forgotten? Is this ambition? Enyaw says she was ambitious and Enyaw is honourable. I do not speak to disprove what she said. I am here only to tell you what I know and that is that you all supported President Xocliw once, and not without reason, so what is it that prevents you from mourning for her now? Bear with me, I need to pause a little."

"There is reason in what he says," said an observer.

"If you think about it, perhaps President Xocliw has been wronged," said another.

"Has she?" said a third. "I tell you this much. Whoever replaces her will be worse."

"She refused the presidency at first. That proves she was not ambitious," a fourth chipped in.

"Look at Allecram, you can see he's upset," said the second.

"There's no-one more noble than Allecram."

"Shhh, he is going to speak again."

"Last rotation, President Xocliw stood for the Republic against the outer regions," Allecram continued. "Now she lies there ready to go to the better place. If I were to stir your marbles to mutiny and rage, I would do Enyaw and Scotmax a very great wrong and you know they are both honourable. I have here President Xocliw's last will and testament, which he left with me for safekeeping, but I will not read it here."

"Read the will!" shouted the crowd. "The will, the will, we will hear the president's will."

"Be patient, I must not read it. Hearing the will of President Xocliw will inflame your marbles and make you mad. You should not know what you inherit from him because if you did, what would come of it?"

Allecram let out a dramatic sigh.

"Traitors! Traitors!" shouted half the crowd.

"The will! The will!" shouted the others.

"Villains, murderers, read the will!" a chant developed.

"If you insist, I shall have to read the will," Allecram conceded.

"Read the will! Read the will!" the chant continued.

"I will read it," said Allecram. "But don't blame me if it upsets you. Look at the President's body there, lying on the hearse. She is wearing the same uniform she wore when she defeated Akpom Chuba, Enyaw's begetter. See how it is stained with her life juices where Scotmax and Enyaw shot her?"

The crowd shouted with rage at their president's assassination.

"Revenge! We want revenge!" shouted the crowd.

"Wait citizens," Allecram pleaded.

"Allecram! Allecram!" another chant developed.

"Citizens," Allecram pleaded again. "Please do not let me stir up your marbles to the point of mutiny. The assassins of Xocliw are honourable. I do not know what reasons they had for the assassination, but, as they are wise and honourable, they will explain their reasons to you. I am not here to change your marbles. Enyaw is a skilled orator, but I am not. You know I am plain and blunt, that I loved our President and that her assassins gave me leave to speak of her. I don't have the power to stir the marbles of citizens, only the ability to speak the truth. I just tell you what you already know and show you his wounded corpse and let the truth speak for me. If Enyaw were I, she would have the words to stir your marbles until you rose in mutiny."

"Mutiny!" shouted the crowd. "Let's get the assassins."

"Wait, citizens," Allecram pleaded. "Let me speak. Let me tell you about the will."

"Read the will! Read the will!" the previous chant resumed.

"To every Republic citizen, President Xocliw leaves seventy-five credits."

"Revenge her death!" someone in the crowd shouted.

"Hear me with patience, citizens. She has left her own grounds and orchards as common land for all citizens to use."

"Send her to the better place," someone else shouted.

The citizens took President Xocliw's corpse and followed the traditional procedures for sending a president to the better place. They processed to the palace gardens where they mounted her mark in a place of honour.

Allecram kept his distance from the proceedings and left the agitated citizens before the end of the ceremony. Instead, he went to seek Sevan, who had observed the speech and the funeral as promised.

"Listen Sevan," Allecram began, once he had found him. "I have done what I can but I fear that Enyaw and Scotmax are in a powerful position and Hours' life is still in danger. For Hours to live, you need to go now to Skoll. Report what you have seen and return with her to Future. Tell no-one except Tori and Ay-ttho about the plan, understand?"

"Understood."

Sevan returned to the Mastery of the Stars where Ay-ttho and Tori were waiting.

The journey to Skoll was just one small jump away. They followed the directions Allecram had given them. Despite its proximity to Future, Skoll appeared relatively undeveloped. In fact, it was practically deserted. The reason for this was its inhospitable atmosphere, and the team had to put on their suits before they could leave the ship. On the surface of Skoll it was raining what Ron described as 'something acidic', but he assured Sevan that it was not strong enough to burn through his suit. This reassured Sevan. But not enough to prevent at least a little anxiety.

Allecram had instructed them to land on a mountainside where there was a small plateau large enough to land the Mastery of the Stars. On the mountain's side was carved a huge stone door, and it was to this point they headed.

Although it appeared to be a door, it was clearly too huge to be of any practical use, and the group searched in vain to find an actual entrance.

"You would think they would have a doorbell somewhere," Sevan said. "Maybe we should have told them we were coming. What if they are out?"

"What if they are out?" Tori scoffed. "Where do you think they've gone? Shopping?"

"The New Republic wants them," said Ay-ttho. "They are obviously in hiding."

"If they were hiding, why would they carve a massive door into a mountain to show everyone where they were hiding?" asked Sevan.

"Because it isn't the entrance?"

They continued to search the mountainside for an actual entrance as Sevan sensed they were being watched. He tried to dismiss his increased uneasiness as paranoia but a noise made all three spin around to discover a large group surrounded them, wearing similar space suits and pointing hand held weapons at the trio.

CHAPTER 21: OFF TO FUTURE

"What do you want?" one of their captors communicated.

"Allecram has sent us here with a message for Hours," said Ay-ttho.

"There is no-one called Hours here. You are mistaken. Now you must leave."

"President Xocliw is dead. Enyaw and Scotmax intend to establish a New Republic. Allecram told us that in order for Hours to live, she must return with us to Future, where Allecram is waiting for her."

"That's exactly the thing you would say if you'd come to kill Hours."

"Ah, so Hours is here," said Sevan.

"I never said that."

"Allecram is creating a desire for mutiny among the citizens," Ay-ttho continued. "In order to capitalise on this, Hours must be on Future. The citizens need to see her."

"And who are you that takes such an interest in the political affairs of the Republic?"

"My name is Ay-ttho. This is Tori, this is Sevan and that is our ship, the Mastery of the Stars."

"The Mastery of the Stars? I know you. Your story is even less probable now. You are friends with Scotmax, you rescued the Swordsmen from Angetenar."

"And this is the Sevan who accompanied President Matthews to Future to kill Ydna and her partner."

"Yes, yes. This is true, the bounty hunter wasn't a bounty hunter. Your exploits are well known here. Very well then, follow me."

The figure turned and walked past the rest of their group towards the mountain side, Ay-ttho, Tori and Sevan followed them into a crevice between the rocks. It was only just large enough for them to squeeze through. At the end, they reached an entrance to an airlock. Although the entrance was small, the airlock itself was large enough to accommodate the entire group. The outside door was closed, vents hissed as the atmosphere was exchanged, and then the inner door opened and it led them through into a large room where the group removed their suits.

Ay-ttho, Tori and Sevan, after checking the atmosphere, removed their helmets and breathed in the cool, if slightly stale, air.

"You must excuse the smell," said their guide. "Our air scrubbers are not what they used to be, and we have had difficulty finding additional parts. You get used to it after a while. Please, leave your suits here. They will be perfectly safe."

They took her at her word and stripped off their suits.

"Please, come with me," she said, leading them into a corridor through what soon became apparent was a large subterranean complex.

Soon, they arrived into a large area which served as a canteen.

"Our provisions are basic. I hope they are to your tastes," she said, directing them to an area where kitchen staff were dolloping ladlefuls of slop onto the trays of underwhelmed workers.

They joined the queue and moments later gathered around a table where they experimented the food.

"It tastes a lot better than it looks," said Sevan.

"I am glad you appreciate our unusual fare," said the guide.

"When can we meet Hours?" asked Ay-ttho.

"You have already met her."

"You?"

The guide nodded.

"What word do you bring from Allercram?" she asked.

Tori and Ay-ttho looked at Sevan, who had a mouthful of slop.

"They have killed President Xocliw," he said when he had swallowed enough to speak. "He was shot by Enyaw and Scotmax and the rest of the conspirators of the New Republic."

"This much you have already told me."

"Allecram told us that your life was in danger. He told us to come here and report to you what happened at the funeral and then take you back to Future."

"And what happened at the funeral?"

"Enyaw spoke first. She said that President Xocliw had been ambitious, and that had been the reason for the assassination. The citizens seemed to support her. But then Allecram got up to speak, and he questioned what

Enyaw had said without really questioning it, but he was planting the seeds of mutiny in the minds of the citizens."

"And?"

"It seemed to work. By the time he had finished speaking, the citizens gave President Xocliw a full funeral with all the ceremony and were demanding revenge on the conspirators."

"Then the time is right. I must leave here and return with you to Future. When the citizens see me, they will see me as the natural successor to Xocliw, just as she succeeded Matthews and Matthews succeeded Kirkland."

Sevan thought it best not to mention Matthews murdering his co-begetter or Kirkland's attempted murder of Akpom Chuba.

"I have a question," said Sevan. "How come we didn't know that Matthews had any offspring until now?"

"She wanted to keep my existence a secret because she knew that the descendants of Akpom Chuba would try to kill me if they knew there was an heir to the dynasty. Enyaw has proved Matthews right, if what Allecram says is correct, and I have no reason to doubt him. As long as the houses of Kirkland and Chuba have descendants, there will be fighting."

"What about the descendants of Man?"

"President Man left no descendants. Once Ozli was killed that left the Republic open to the civil war, it now finds itself in."

Sevan thought about telling Hours that Ozli had named Chuba as his rightful successor, but then thought better of it.

"So, we must prepare for our journey to Future," said Hours. "I will travel in your ship without an escort so as not to raise suspicion. Once our position on Future is established, I will send for the rest of my retinue."

When Hours said she would travel in the Mastery of the Stars, what she actually meant of that she would travel with a large party of others and that she would almost fill the cargo holds with her possessions. Sevan wondered how the Presidential Palace on Future would accommodate such a collection.

While they were preparing, Hours treated the group to sumptuous meals in a huge banqueting hall.

"What is this place?"

"The original President Man designed it as a presidential refuge during the first wars against the outer regions when he was expanding the old

Republic. The refuge contains enough supplies to support a reasonable sized army for several solar cycles. After Man's death, it fell into disuse and Kirkland kept it a secret from Chuba and his descendants."

Suddenly one of Hours' advisors burst into the room.

"My dear Hours," she said in a panic. "They say you are planning to go to Future."

"Let me introduce Doctor Nix," said Hours, without acknowledging the advisor's question. "She likes to keep me safe."

"I think we should move you. Perhaps to a stronghold in the outer regions," said Dr Nix.

"I appreciate your concern, Nix. But this is the perfect opportunity to discover what currency I hold in this new Republic."

"You may lose your life."

"But I may gain the presidency."

Hours turned her attention back to Ay-ttho, Tori, and Sevan.

"So you don't share the same ideals as your colleague Scotmax, then?"

"We just need credits to get home," said Ay-ttho. "Xocliw never paid us, but Allecram had better."

"Well, he holds the purse strings to Xocliw's estate," said Hours.

"Which he's promised to the citizens," said Sevan

"We'll see about that."

"What do you mean?"

"Promises are easily made but less easily fulfilled."

"As long as Allecram fulfils his promise," said Ay-ttho.

"You'll have no problem with Allecram. He is honourable."

"That's what he said about Enyaw and Scotmax," said Sevan. "As he was casting doubt on their words in the marbles of the citizens."

"Don't worry. If you take me to Future, I will ensure that you get the rewards you deserve."

Tori exchanged glances with Ay-ttho and Sevan. He was clearly uncomfortable with Hours' choice of words.

"As soon as your staff has finished loading your cargo, we should be ready to leave," said Ay-ttho.

"Thank you so much for accommodating my keepsakes. I have accumulated such a lot of sentimental memorabilia over the years and I couldn't bear to be parted with any of it."

"We will do our best to ensure it all arrives in perfect condition."

"It is such a thrill for me to be going on the journey in the Mastery of the Stars. I learned so much about it from my co-begetter. Is it true that it has a functional anti-matter drive?"

"I don't like to go into details," said Ay-ttho.

"Why is that?"

"In case the original owner wants to claim it back."

Hours laughed.

"You are a clone after my own marbles," she chortled.

While they were waiting for the Mastery of the Stars to be loaded, Hours took them on a tour of the facility. They passed through a vast hall where, what appeared to be thousands of soldier clones were training.

"Preparing for something?" asked Ay-ttho.

"You can never be too careful," said Hours.

"Where did you get all these clones?" Tori was marvelling at the multitude.

"Barnes."

"Barnes is on your side, then?"

"Barnes is on the side of anyone who can pay him."

"If you have all these troops, why not just take them to Future and take the presidency by force?"

"What would be the point of that? If I was not a popular president, I would waste them all fighting a pointless civil war. Better to take a small contingent, assess the mood of the citizens and then these troops will be much more useful in the future."

Sevan wasn't sure what she meant with the last part, but the prospect of no civil war reassured him.

The facility was huge and by the time Hours had finished showing them around it was already late.

"Let us celebrate this day," said Hours. "To mark the end of this rotation we will have a great festival and as the next rotation arrives we will leave for Future."

She led the group into a hall decorated with lights, where music was being played. In the centre a large group was dancing, their movements were synchronised.

Over the course of the evening, the music changed often, but the dance remained the same, only the speed of the dancing varied with the tempo of the music.

"Do they always dance like that?" Sevan asked Hours.

"How else would they dance?"

"They all do the same moves."

"Of course. How do you dance?"

"My experience of dancing has always been more individual."

"I don't understand."

"You know, everyone doing whatever moves they feel like."

"Why would they want to do that?"

"Individual expression."

"Individual expression? I don't understand."

"Expressing yourself individually. Not being the same as everyone else."

"Why would you not want to be the same as everyone else?"

Sevan let the subject drop and watched the crowd performing the same dance until the next rotation began.

"Let us go friends," Hours announced. "It is time for us to be off to Future and see what our fortune may be."

CHAPTER 22: TO FLY ON SKOLL

Ay-ttho, Tori and Sevan got back into their protective suits, which they had cleaned and serviced for them. They had packed the Mastery of the Stars to the jowls, if it had any jowls, and Ay-ttho was immediately annoyed at the quantity of strangers sharing her personal space which, for her, included the entire ship.

She drew the line at the bridge and ordered all the uninvited occupants to find space elsewhere. Only Hours and Dr Nix could stay.

Sevan marvelled at the size of Hours' retinue. If this was what she considered necessary for a quiet entrance, he couldn't imagine what a full-blown attack would have looked like.

"Incoming ships," Ron warned, as they were just preparing to take off.

"What are they?" asked Ay-ttho.

"They look like mechanical bowmen," said Tori from the weapons chair.

"So, they have already sent my assassins to greet me," said Hours.

"Ron, take off and then give me control," Ay-ttho ordered.

Huge waterfalls of acidic water cascaded off the Mastery of the Stars as it lurched into the air through the torrential rain.

"I don't think they have spotted us yet," said Tori.

"Okay, Ron. Keep us close to the surface until you are certain we are out of range of their scanners."

"The Mastery of the Stars is a large object to go unspotted," Hours commented.

"Not if you are not looking for it. The bowmen are clearly heading for the base. They don't expect anyone to have got here before them, let alone to be leaving with the very thing they desire."

In order to avoid the bowmen's scanners, it was necessary for Ron to navigate directly through the heart of the storm.

"The storm's electrical activity will confuse their scanners," Ay-ttho explained.

"Yes, and it might well fry our circuitry," Tori added.

Sevan didn't like the sound of fried circuitry and remained silent in the corner, Hours having requisitioned his usual seat.

"How long before we are out of scanner range?" Ay-ttho asked.

"Difficult to tell," said Ron. "I am having difficulty hacking their systems. They seem well organised.

"They are the mechanical bowmen, I suppose."

Mechanical Bowmen had been used to assassinate presidents and their supporters ever since the second President Man had killed his own co-begotton. They were renowned as ruthless and rarely failed to eliminate their target. Sevan was eager to evade contact with them and willed the Mastery of the Stars into the storm before they were detected.

"They have landed at the base," said Ron.

"Good," said Hours, "They don't know we have left."

"The ship is taking off again."

"You spoke too soon," Tori complained.

The Mastery of the Stars tipped and rocked as the storm buffeted it. Not being strapped into his usual seat, Sevan held on to whatever he could to stay on his feet.

"This might get bumpy," said Ay-ttho.

"No uxlod, moncur," said Tori, referring to the famous detective of the old Republic, who was famous for solving every case. "Let's just hope our electrics can withstand a direct hit."

"From the bowmen?"

"No, from the electrical storm."

"One of the Bowmen's ships is following us into the storm," said Ron.

"From both," Tori corrected himself. "The storm is interfering with the weapons system. I can't get a lock on the Bowmen's ship."

"Hopefully, the Bowmen are experiencing similar problems."

A missile exploding next to the ship proved that wasn't the case.

"At least it didn't hit us," said Ay-ttho.

"No, I think the storm got it first," said Tori. "But I can get any of our weapons ready. Ron, is there anything you can do?"

"I'm trying," said the computer.

"Ron? How much of this storm is there?"

"We are nearing the centre."

"If anyone has any bright ideas, now would be a great time to share them," said Ay-ttho.

The bridge was silent.

"My sensors detect that the Bowman's ship has locked onto us with its weapons system," said Ron.

"Not the idea I was looking for."

"I don't suppose going to sleep would help?" asked Sevan.

"Not this time."

"My sensors detect they have fired two missiles and they are heading towards us."

"Tori?"

"I'm trying to release the chaff, but nothing is responding."

Ay-ttho swung the ship around towards the most intense looking area of electrical activity.

"We'll get fried," said Tori.

"Slightly preferable to being blown up."

The Mastery of the Stars shuddered under the force of the storm and the lights on the bridge flickered before going out. A moment later, the red emergency lighting came on.

"The Bowman continues to follow us," said Ron.

"Where is he?" asked Ay-ttho.

"I'm sorry," said Ron. "I cannot get an accurate reading, probably the storm."

There was a sudden jolt and Sevan sensed the Mastery of the Stars lost altitude.

"Maintain our course!" shouted Ay-ttho.

"I'll try," said Ron. "But none of the ship's functions appear to be responding. Apart from the warm air hand dryer in the toilets in cargo bay 2."

"Great, I'll warm my hands then, shall I?"

It was then that Sevan realised he could no longer hear the familiar background hum of the engines.

"Are we gliding?" he asked.

"More like plummeting," said Ay-ttho. "Ron, get everything back online as quick as you can. Let me know when you do."

Sevan glanced over at Hours and Nix, who didn't appear to be in the slightest bit perturbed.

"System re-booting now," said Ron.

"How long to impact?"

"Two units."

"Let me know when the system is back."

"Okay, it's just installing some updates."

"What? Now?"

"I'm afraid so. It appears there will be some new flavours in the hot beverage dispenser on level 1."

"Oh great. Shame we won't be able to try them because we'll all be dead! How much longer."

"System reboot, 97%"

There was another large jolt.

"What was that?"

"A Bowman missile glanced off the hull."

"How much longer?"

"98%. It's suggesting I might want to try one of the new hot beverage flavours while I wait."

"How does the beverage machine work if there is no system?"

"I know, ironic, isn't it.?"

"What's it doing now?"

"It's telling me it's getting everything ready for me."

"How long to impact?"

"One unit."

"And the system?"

"99%"

"I knew we shouldn't have installed that cheap system we picked up from the markets on Pandoria."

"It was very cheap," said Tori.

"Ron?"

"Now."

The Mastery of the Stars lurched as the engines cut in, screaming as Ay-ttho pulled out of the dive.

"The Bowman is following," Ron announced.

"He's a stubborn fusher."

The Mastery of the Stars banked steeply as Ay-ttho brought the freighter round to face the Bowman's rapidly approaching ship.

"You're not going back in?" asked Tori.

"Hopefully not. Let's see what marbles this Bowman has."

She fixed the freighter on a collision course with the Bowman and sped up.

"You're mad," said Tori.

"Don't worry, I'll pull out. Ready Ron?"

"I'm afraid the system has stopped responding again."

"What? Why?"

"Optional update of the waste discharge unit on level 4."

"Who installed an optional update?"

"You did."

"What? Why?"

"You said you were tired of pressing buttons."

"Well, let's hope he's not as stubborn as we think."

At the last possible moment, the Bowman veered away. There was a large clunk as the side of his ship collided with the Mastery of the Stars.

"Optional update complete," Ron announced. "The waste discharge unit on level 4 now has added three more smells to its range of deodorants."

"Marvellous. Get us out of here, Ron. Any sign of the Bowmen?"

"He appears to be making an emergency landing."

There was a burst of applause. Sevan realised it was coming from Hours and Nix.

"Excellent. Most stimulating," said Hours. "I knew I would enjoy a journey on the Mastery of the Stars."

Ay-ttho piloted the Mastery of the Stars high into the atmosphere. Through the observation window, Sevan could see the electrical activity in the clouds below. It pleased him to be leaving Skoll.

"How long is the journey to Future?" Hours asked.

"We only have to make one portal jump," explained Ay-ttho. "Assuming the bowmen do not pursue us."

Ay-ttho's fears appeared to be unfounded as they arrived at Future without further molestation. Nobody questioned them as they landed in the hangar of the presidential palace, and nobody attempted to stop Hours' retinue as they unloaded his belongings and transferred them to the presidential apartments. As they did so, Sevan went to find Allecram and brought him to Hours so they could get paid.

*

There was a palace employee called Effeek'o. She was no relation to Effeek'o the medic who conspired with Enyaw and Scotmax to kill Xocliw. She had missed the funeral of Xocliw and planned to pay homage at Xocliw's mark.

On his way, he ran into an angry crowd.

"Who are you?" one of them asked.

"Where are you going?" asked another.

"Where do you live?" asked a third.

"Do you have a partner?" asked a fourth, who was glared at by the rest of the crowd.

"Answer us," said the second.

"Quickly," said the first.

"Wisely," said the second.

"And truthfully," said the third.

"I do not have a partner," said Effeek'o. "And I am going to the President's funeral."

"As a friend or an enemy?"

"A friend."

"Where do you live?"

"I am housed in the palace for now."

"Your name?"

"Effeek'o."

"She's a conspirator," someone shouted.

"I am not Effeek'o the medic, I am Effeek'o the palace servant."

"Tear her to pieces. She's a conspirator."

"I am not Effeek'o the medic. I am Effeek'o the palace servant."

"Her name's Effeek'o, kill her."

The crowd beat Effeek'o the palace servant to death.

"Come on, let's find the other conspirators."

The angry crowd left the lifeless body of Effeek'o the palace servant in the street, and left to hunt the conspirators.

*

Allecram sat in the presidential apartments with Hours and Nix.

"So we are all agreed," said Allecram. "The conspirators must die."

"Your co-begotton, Di-shon must die, Nix," said Hours.

"I agree," said Nix. "As long as Enyaw's co-begotton, Llessur, dies as well."

"She shall die. Don't worry about that," said Allecram. "Leave us, Nix. Make the arrangements."

Nix got up and left.

"Do you trust her?" asked Allecram.

"She is very trustworthy."

"Well, we can at least trust her with these tasks and then, when the war is won, we can set her free."

"She is an old servant, not a tired cateveexea ready for the knackers' yard."

"Like a cateveexea, she needs to be taught to be obedient and perform her tasks well until she is no longer needed anymore."

"Let's not talk of her anymore because we have much to decide."

"Agreed."

CHAPTER 23: ASSAULT ON TITAN

Enyaw was inspecting a platoon of troops she had assembled on Titan with one of her senior officers, Allahyar.

"Is Scotmax on her way?" Enyaw asked.

"She is, she is near," said Allahyar. "Look, here is her servant, Sayyadmanesh."

"Sayyadmanesh? Is Scotmax on her way?"

"She is. She sent me to tell you exactly that."

"Is she bringing the platoons she assembled?"

"Yes, they are arriving now."

"Greetings, Enyaw," Scotmax greeted her when her fleet had landed and she had disembarked. "Show me to my quarters. I need to chat with you."

"Of course, let us go."

"Enyaw, I feel I must challenge you about a matter you are dealing with."

"What is it?"

"The case of Forss and the bribes."

"What of it?"

"You knew I knew Forss and ignored my requests to drop the prosecution."

"You should not try to interfere in a corruption trial."

"Enyaw, at the moment, we have more to worry about than petty bribery."

"Is that because you wish to benefit from your rise to power?"

"You, Enyaw, accuse me of corruption. That's rich."

"We killed Xocliw to rid the Republic of the corruption she fostered. Therefore, we must not ignore even the slightest corruption."

"Do not teach your co-begetter's co-begetter to suck tronqaks eggs. You do not want to make an enemy of me."

"I am not afraid of making an enemy of anyone."

"We are both armed well, with armies at our call. It is not wise to have such a disagreement at this stage."

"I say what I see, Scotmax and I do not shirk from responsibility, not matter the situation."

"You may feel differently when Allecram and Hours arrive with their armies."

"Don't be so eager for them to arrive. The result is not clear cut."

"I'm wondering whether it might be better to be defeated by them than to be victorious with you, Enyaw."

"Stop being so dramatic. Save your anger for the real enemy."

"I didn't come here to be insulted by you."

"That is true. I am sorry. I have been in a bad mood."

"Come here, give me your hand."

"We are on the same side."

"We are."

"What's wrong, Scotmax?"

"Nothing, it's just the way I am."

"And I will try to remember that is the way you are in the future."

"I have never seen you so angry."

"Oh, Scotmax, I am sick with worry."

"Why? Surely you know you are on the side of the right."

"It's not that. Oiluj is dead."

"What?"

"He is dead."

"How are we alive and he is dead?"

"He killed himself."

"No."

"The conspiracy, it seems, was too much for him."

"Oh, my gods."

"We all have to die at some point. Let's speak no more of him. Give me some pish."

Scotmax filled their glasses, and they drank.

"I must say," said Scotmax. "You are taking the news of Oiluj's death better than I would Nadio's."

"Do you think we should attack now?" asked Enyaw, ignoring the question.

"I don't think so."

"Why not?"

"I think it is better for them to find us, then we will fight them while we are rested and they are tired after their journey."

"If we face them now, we deny them the opportunity to bolster their numbers with new recruits."

"Listen Enyaw..."

"You forget our forces are at their maximum. Every rotation that passes, they get stronger."

"If you insist, then we should go to meet them."

"Let us rest now and at the dawn of the next rotation, we leave."

Enyaw slept and dreamt of Xocliw.

*

"Wake up, Sevan," said Tori, shaking him awake in the luxurious bed in his apartment in the palace. "Wake up. We have to go."

"Why? What is it?"

"It's Allecram, Hours and Nix. They're killing senators."

"We're senators, aren't we?"

"Exactly. They even killed Yor."

"Yor? Fushing worst place. We have to go then. Does this mean we won't get paid?"

"What do you think? Hurry, we have to go."

"What about Ay-ttho?"

"She's sleeping. You're going to have to help me move her."

"Oh, fushy!"

Sevan followed Tori to Ay-ttho's room, where Ay-ttho was in a deep slumber in the middle of her bed.

"How are going to move her without waking her up?"

"We'll have to move the entire bed."

"What? It's huge."

"We're both very strong. We're clones."

"Okay, let's give it a go."

One at each end, they slowly lifted the bed. At first the bed wobbled a little at first but they settled on it. Ay-ttho shifted a little, whereupon they froze, but she soon returned to her slumber.

Tori and Sevan edged slowly towards the door. Sevan roughly calculated that the bed would just make its way through the aperture, but it was tight.

Bit by bit the edged towards the door, Tori moving first into the corridor which was thankfully quiet.

They were halfway through the doorway when a noise startled Sevan. He inadvertently flinched, causing the bed to bash against the door frame. This caused Tori to lose his grip and his end of the bed crashed to the floor. Sevan let go as well, and the pair leapt for cover. Tori, out into the corridor behind a strong-looking pillar and Sevan underneath a sideboard with his arms over his antennae.

"What the fushy are you two doing?" Ay-ttho asked.

"We thought you might explode," Tori admitted.

"I should have done. I woke up with my bed being carried out of my room. Why were you trying to steal my bed?"

"We weren't trying to steal your bed," said Tori. "We were trying to steal you. Allecram, Hours and Nix have gone mad. They're killing all the senators. They've even killed Yor. We have to leave."

"Well, what are you waiting for? Let's go."

Tori and Sevan exchanged frustrated glances.

"We're not going via the strange worlds, are we?" asked Sevan, when they were boarding the Mastery of the Stars. "Nothing good ever comes from that route."

"No, it's too obvious," said Ay-ttho. "And too far without a fuel stop. Skoll is out of the question because it is riddled with Hours' supporters. Zistreotov and the Cheng-Huang colony are similarly out of bounds because Enyaw and Scotmax's supporters might blame us for bringing Hours. The Atlas portal has been destroyed and I'm guessing neither of you wants to catapult to Tomorrow."

"No, thanks."

"Then that only leaves Titan and, according to the official records, there's nothing going on there. Very quiet."

"Sounds like our place," said Tori. "Let's look."

*

Allecram, Hours and Nix were on the bridges of their respective command ships of the fleet they had assembled.

"Are you sure they are on Titan?" asked Hours.

"Of course I am," said Allecram. "I know their marbles, what they plan to do."

"We have located the forces of Enyaw and Scotmax," said the ship's computer.

"You approach them from the West, I will approach from the East," said Allecram.

"The forces of Allecram, Hours and Nix are heading this way," said Enyaw.

"Wait," said Scotmax.

"Shall we charge them?" asked Hours.

"No," said Allecram. "We should respond to their first move."

"We wait for the signal," said Hours.

"Let us try to communicate," said Enyaw.

"You love words, don't you, Enyaw?" said Hours, when the communication link was established.

"Good words are better than bad actions, Hours."

"You make good words despite your dangerous actions," said Allecram. "You praised Xocliw, even as you killed her."

"Your actions are unknown, Allecram," said Scotmax. "Let's hope they are better than your words."

"They speak louder than my words."

"Hollow," said Enyaw. "You do well to speak before you try anything."

"It's a shame you didn't take your own advice before killing Xocliw."

"You would be less quick to criticise in front of President Scotmax," said Scotmax.

"This rotation, I am charging my weapons against conspirators and traitors, not presidents."

"The only traitors you be killing are the ones you brought with you."

"I wasn't born to be killed by you, Enyaw."

"You could not die in a more noble way."

"You are not worthy to die in such a way," said Scotmax.

"Hilarious," said Allecram.

"We have talked enough, Allecram," said Hours. "If the traitors dare fight, let them fight."

The connection ended.

"Well, that's that then," said Scotmax. "Did you know that today is the anniversary of my birth? Last night I had a dream that two tronqaks came down and fed from the hands of our troops. Then they flew away and were replaced with thrucols and kerkrids."

"Don't let it worry you," said Enyaw. "I'm sure it means nothing."

"I hope this rotation is not the last we speak together."

"Don't worry, Scotmax. We will speak again."

"And if we lose this battle, will you be willing to be led through the streets of Future?"

"I think not. In case this is our last conference, thank you for everything."

"And I thank you, Enyaw. Good fight."

"And good fight for you."

Enyaw watched the communication link fizzle into nothingness before turning to his ship's computer.

"Do you have a location for Allecram's fleet?"

"Yes I do," said the computer.

"Let's go then. Attack speed."

Scotmax, on the bridge of his own command ship, gave a similar order and their respective fleets hurried to encounter their enemies.

"Enyaw has given the order too early," warned Sayyadmanesh. "The enemy is circling around our flank towards our base."

"Are they firing on our base?" asked Scotmax.

"They are," said Sayyadmanesh.

"Sayyadmanesh, take my fighter and lead the platoon towards that force."

Sayyadmanesh did as he asked him.

"The enemy is surrounding us," Sayyadmanesh reported from the head of the attack formation. "They are..."

He didn't finish his sentence as his ship exploded into pieces as soon as it came within range of the enemies' firepower.

"What a coward I was," Scotmax chastised herself. "Attack!"

Scotmax's fleet charged straight towards the fleet of Allecram. They flew directly into the full force of the weaponry of Allecram's fleet and Scotmax's command ship was the first to fall victim.

"We have Hours on the run," said Enyaw. "Scotmax, give me a report. Scotmax? Why does she not respond?"

"We have lost her ship," Allahyar answered.

"Let us regroup," Enyaw ordered. "What's the damage?"

The ship's computer recounted the list of surviving ships and the much longer list of the ships that had been lost.

"So it is lost," said Enyaw, at last. "Those who wish to flee can flee, but I will not survive this rotation. Thank you, Allahyar."

Enyaw steered the remains of his fleet towards Allecram's command ship and they met them with the same voracious firepower that had consumed Scotmax.

Among the debris, Allecram steered his vessel until he found the crippled ship of Hours and Nix with all aboard alive and well. He transferred them to his own vessel.

At the same moment, emerging from the portal, the Mastery of the Stars materialised into the debris of the battle.

"I'm not sure Titan was a good idea after all," said Sevan.

CHAPTER 24: SPACE LANDING

Ay-ttho attempted to swing the Mastery of the Stars around and re-enter the portal before anyone noticed they were there.

"We've got no reason to run," said Tori. "We've done nothing wrong."

"That all depends on who won this battle," said Ay-ttho. "If it's Scotmax, then she might want to know why we brought her enemy to Future. If it's Allecram, which, judging by the debris it might be, then they might want to finish their task of killing the senators by killing us."

"Either way, the portal seems like the best option," Sevan agreed.

"We have an incoming message," Ron announced.

"Play it over the speaker," said Ay-ttho.

"Identify yourself," the message began. "Do not flee. Resistance is useless. Surrender your vessel in the name of President Hours."

"You were right," said Tori. "What do we do now?"

"I'm not going to surrender our vessel," said Ay-ttho.

"It was nice knowing you both," said Sevan.

"Send a message," Ay-ttho ordered Ron. "This is the ex-Corporation freighter, Mastery of the Stars. We request an audience with President Hours."

"Requests for audiences must be made through the appropriate channels once you are repatriated to Future. Prepare to be boarded."

"Negative. President Hours will want to see us immediately. Tell her it is Ay-ttho, Tori and Sevan of the Mastery of the Stars."

"President Hours is very busy at the moment. You should direct all correspondence through her office on Future, prepare to be boarded."

"This is getting us nowhere," said Tori. "They are charging their cannons."

"Charge ours," said Ay-ttho.

"What? You want to take on a Republic battle cruiser at point blank range?"

"Charge the weapons, Ron," Ay-ttho ordered. "Republic battle cruisers are not designed to engage at close quarters."

"I don't like the sound of this," said Sevan.

Suddenly the power on the Mastery of the Stars went off and the emergency lighting came on.

"You are being held in a restraining beam," said the voice. "Resistance is futile. Prepare to be boarded."

"I don't suppose you feel sleepy?" Tori asked Ay-ttho.

"Not in the slightest."

"So what do we do now?" asked Sevan.

"We prepare to be boarded."

The Republic battle cruiser locked onto to the Mastery of the Stars and fixed a gantry onto its entrance.

Ay-ttho, Tori, and Sevan waited on the bridge for the intruders to arrive.

"Ay-ttho!" Allecram exclaimed as he strolled onto the bridge. "I suppose you've come to get paid, have you? You Corporation security clones are notoriously impatient."

"You see right through me," Ay-ttho lied. "How did the battle go?"

"As you can see, the virtuous side was victorious. It's such a shame that these minor disputes should cause so much bloodshed."

"Like the senators," Tori whispered to Sevan.

"Are you aware of our handiwork?" asked Allecram, overhearing.

"They speak of little else on Future."

"I'm sure they do," Allecram smiled. "Let us hope this brings this recent regrettable spate of blood-letting to an end."

"So, can we get paid?" asked Sevan. "We really must get going."

"Why such a hurry?" asked Allecram. "You must avail yourselves of our hospitality first. There will be great festival to celebrate our victory and we will drink the finest pish in the galaxy."

"Perhaps we could stay for one or two," Sevan conceded. "Just not to be rude."

And so it was that Ay-ttho, Tori, Sevan and the Mastery of the Stars were escorted back to Future by the remains of the fleet commanded by Allecram, Hours and Nix to attend the inauguration of President Hours.

The event was as lavish as Sevan had hoped and he temporarily forgot his burning desire to return to the Doomed Planet to see his aunt and instead lost himself in pish.

Conversations filled with rumours, speculations and predictions surrounded him, but he paid little attention to them and immersed himself in the effects of the fushy and pish. He remembered little of the festival that lasted seven rotations.

When he eventually emerged from the haze, he sensed an atmosphere of uneasiness and foreboding. He couldn't help thinking that they gave him strange looks all the time, but he chalked this up to paranoia.

President Hours had, on their request, relieved them of their responsibilities as senators, but had asked them to stay on the capital planet because she had other plans for them.

The worse part was visiting Nadio and Effeek'o who were being held in prison on charges of conspiracy to murder. How they escaped death during the purge of the senators, Sevan couldn't imagine, but the prospect of getting either of them released seemed bleak.

Sevan was eager to leave, but Ay-ttho and Tori both encouraged him to be patient. They reminded him how difficult it had been when the president had been their enemy and urged him to wait a little longer until they could leave Future with the blessing of its ruler.

And so he waited, a growing sense of uneasiness rising within him. He wanted to buy a ticket on the first transport to The Doomed Planet, but he knew his loyalty lay with Ay-ttho and Tori, who had been there for him when he had needed them most.

"How do you deal with all this?" he asked High Priest Callahan one rotation as they were passing in the corridors.

"What you must remember, Sevan," High Priest Callahan began. "Is that presidents come and go as quickly as solar cycles, sometimes quicker. But the overarching nature of the universe is constant. Presidents cannot escape the nature of things any more than a cukid can escape the clench of a tronkaq."

"So, what is the answer?"

"You must live in the now, Sevan. Be content with what you have and grateful for what you haven't."

"Be grateful for what I haven't?"

"Exactly."

Sevan felt this was of little help, thanked the high priest and went on his way. He wished President Hours would just tell them what it was they had to do for her to be allowed to leave do that they could get on and do it and go.

It felt like the rotation would never arrive until Ay-ttho received a message to take the Mastery of the Stars to rendezvous at a specific location in space. She checked the coordinates several times with Ron, who consistently insisted there was nothing on the charts at that location. So it was with trepidation that she set off together with Tori and Sevan to the rendezvous they had been given.

When they arrived, all they found, as Ron had predicted, was empty space. Several checks persistently confirmed they were at the correct location and so they waited.

And waited.

And waited.

"This is hopeless," said Tori. "No-one is coming. Tori says there is not another ship this side of any portal."

"Be patient," Ay-ttho encouraged.

"Patient for what? It is just another wild crisqix chase."

Sevan felt himself agreeing with Tori, but he didn't want to say so in front of Ay-ttho, who didn't look like she was in the mood for debate.

"Would anyone like a game of Dark Mercenary?" asked Ron.

"No thanks," said Ay-ttho.

"At a time like this?" questioned Tori.

"I do," said Sevan. "Do you still have my character?"

"A ghokvan ate him. Have you forgotten?"

"But he was a level six Threkon."

"Yes, but you only rolled a one on your red mage's summoning spell, remember?"

"Stupid game," Sevan mumbled.

"Look at that!" said Ay-ttho, pointing out of the observation window.

Sevan looked and saw a bright ring, which appeared to be growing. There were light trails leading into the ring, giving the impression that it was sucking matter and light into it.

"Ron! Get us out of here," Ay-ttho shouted.

"Barnes?" Sevan asked.

"I don't know."

The Mastery of the Stars banked at a steep angle, as Ron engaged the engines on full power to swing the ship away from the growing phenomena.

"Current calculations predict we cannot escape it," said Ron.

"Give me everything you've got," Ay-ttho demanded.

"Would firing at it help?" asked Sevan.

"No," said Tori, it would only contribute to its energy.

Sevan had only seen a light like this once before. It was when they had been guests of President Man on the planet of Atlas, where the presidential residence was originally located.

On that occasion, the ring of light had swallowed the planet whole, and no-one had ever seen them since. The Master of the Stars had been lucky to escape the ring of light by following the presidential convoy through a portal which was ultimately also swallowed by the rings.

This time, the ring of light was much closer and none of them knew exactly what would happen to them if it swallowed them up. In the best-case scenario, they would find themselves in another part of the universe. The worst-case scenario was that it would crush them and their ship to a point of singularity.

The way they had explained it to Sevan was that the head of the Corporation, Barnes, had transported objects from one location to another by folding space. This meant that he could move entire planets, which was not possible through a portal.

No-one they knew had survived the process, so they did not know whether it worked or what happened if one was involved in a transfer. In theory Barnes had transferred two planets, The Doomed Planet and Daphnis, to the orbit of Nereid using this very process but, even though Sevan and the others had visited the Doomed Planet since, no-one had explained to them how the process worked or what it felt like to be transferred.

The closest Sevan had been to an explanation was during a meal on Angetenar, when Effeek'o had showed Sevan her napkin, which had a crumb on one edge. Effeek'o folded the napkin and when she unfolded it, the crumb had moved to the opposite edge of the napkin.

"Thus it is theoretically possible to move, even large objects, enormous distances through space," she had explained. "Though, of course, the question about how much energy is required to fold space has yet to be answered. We know how much is required to create a portal but, as you probably know, so far these have been created where relatively little energy was required, in other words, we live around the portals rather than being able to create them where we want."

The ring of light was growing larger and even though the Mastery of the Stars was travelling at full speed, it looked unlikely to escape.

"Cut the engines, Ron," Ay-ttho ordered.

"What?" asked Tori in disbelief.

"We aren't going to outrun it, and I don't want to risk what might happen with the engines on full power once inside."

Ay-ttho was right, the light was already enveloping them. They had no option but to wait, see what happened, and hope for the best.

It was only now that Sevan realised the ring was actually a sphere and the next moment, it had swallowed them.

CHAPTER 25: REVELATION

To Sevan, it appeared they were in a tunnel. Ahead, through an aperture, he could see an empty region of space. The walls of the tunnel appeared to comprise the same view but distorted into a series of rings that became more and more closely packed together, as if he was viewing the universe through a thick lens.

Within a few moments, the distorted light had resolved itself and the crew of the Mastery of the Stars gathered in front of the observation window to examine their new surroundings.

"We are definitely in a different segment," said Ay-ttho.

"Yes, but where?" Tori agreed.

"Navigational plans are recalibrating," said Ron. "This may take some time. However, I have detected an incoming craft. It appears to be the presidential cruiser."

Ay-ttho, Tori, and Sevan exchanged quizzical glances.

Sure enough, the vast presidential cruiser slowly came into view.

"They are requesting we land on the cruiser," said Ron.

"Well, we'd better do what they say then," said Ay-ttho.

Surrounded by the vast emptiness of space, the Mastery of the Stars touched down on the hull of the enormous cruiser. A docking gate extended and secured itself to the exit of their ship.

"They are requesting you to go aboard," said Ron.

"Of course they are."

Ay-ttho, Tori, and Sevan descended through the docking gate into one of the vast corridors. A guard was waiting for them.

"Please follow me," she said.

She led them into a large hall where President Hours, Allecram, and Nix were waiting for them.

"Well, well, well. So it worked." President Hours exclaimed with delight.

"What worked?" asked Ay-ttho, sounding a little aggrieved.

"The experiment. It was a tremendous success and here you are to prove it. I'm relieved. I wouldn't have wanted to come to this stretch of desolate space for nothing."

"What are you talking about?" asked Tori, trying to not sound too rude but failing miserably.

"Why, my dear clone, you and your colleagues have just made history. The Republic has moved substantial matter through folding space without a portal before."

"Well, technically, the process creates a temporary portal," said Nix.

"Yes, yes. It's all about making this region of space a bit more sticky that the other."

"You mean to say that you just used us for an experiment?" asked Ay-ttho.

"Yes, isn't it exciting?"

"And what if it hadn't worked?"

"But it did."

"But it might not have. What would we have done then?"

"Then I think we would have needed to get ourselves some more clones."

"I think what President Hours is trying to say," Allecram interrupted. "Is that you have proved to be an invaluable asset to the Republic and we value your work more than you might imagine. So much so that we would like to contract your services further. Obviously, you will be renumerated very well."

"How well?"

Allecram typed a figure into his communicator and showed it to Ay-ttho, whose antennae straightened slightly. Tori gave her an inquisitive glance, and she whispered something to him. His antennae straightened as well. Sevan offered them both inquisitive glances.

"Later," said Ay-ttho.

Relaxing slightly, she turned back to Allecram.

"What is it you want us to do?"

"As you know, Barnes has had access to this technology for a while and it is important that the Republic has recreated the experiment in order to maintain balance in the galaxy."

"What's your point?"

"Folding space in this way requires an enormous amount of energy. In order for Barnes to have been able to fold space in the way that he has, as frequently as he has, he must have access to an enormous energy source."

"Such as?"

"We are not sure, but we think he might have access to a singularity sphere."

Ay-ttho burst out laughing but soon realised that no one else had joined in. She calmed herself and put on a serious face.

"You've all lost your minds, haven't you? Everyone knows singularity spheres don't exist, they're the stuff of bedtime stories."

"That's what I thought too," said Nix. "Until we received intelligence that not only does such a thing exist, but that Barnes had harnessed the energy of one and was using it to fold space."

"What do you want us to do? Steal it?" Sevan laughed.

No-one else laughed.

"You're not serious," he attempted to clarify.

"You aren't serious, are you?" Ay-ttho checked.

"At this stage, all we want you to do is to confirm the existence of such a device," said Allecram. "We probably don't need to explain how keen the other side is to keep this all a secret. They would go to extreme lengths to prevent knowledge of their operation from being discovered."

"Extreme lengths?" asked Sevan.

"Hence the level of remuneration," Allecram gestured to his communicator.

Ay-ttho and Tori exchanged knowing glances. Sevan stared at them both in frustration.

"It sounds too dangerous for us," he told Allecram. "I think we'll just take the money you owe us and leave. Thank you very much."

"Let's not be too hasty, Sevan," said Ay-ttho. "After all, we are just being asked to confirm the existence of the device, not retrieve it."

"Exactly," Allecram agreed. "If you feel you need to discuss it among yourselves, we'll give you a moment."

"We don't need to discuss it," said Ay-ttho.

"Yes we do," said Sevan.

Allecram, President Hours, and Nix withdrew to allow the group to discuss the offer.

"Have you lost your marbles?" Sevan asked.

Ay-ttho whispered to him the figure Allecram had shown him.

"I see," said Sevan.

"We would never have to work again."

"If we were still alive?"

"Where is your sense of adventure?"

"In the pit of my stomach, where's yours?"

"Come on, Sevan. With this amount of credits you could get everything you always dreamed of."

"I don't know. I dream quite a lot."

"How hard could it be?" asked Tori.

"Very hard. Some might say it's impossible."

"Come on Sevan. What else are you going to do?"

"Live," he sighed. "Do I have a choice?"

"There's the spirit," said Ay-ttho, now let's tell Allecram our decision.

President Hours was in a celebratory mood and had ordered a large banquet to be served, much to Sevan's relief.

"So, have you accepted our offer?" asked Allecram.

"Yes, on one condition."

"What is that?"

"That you release Effeek'o and Nadio."

"I'm afraid that's impossible," said President Hours. "They are enemies of the Republic."

Allecram raised his hand as if to request everyone pause for thought.

"What guarantees would you be able to give us if we released them?" he asked Ay-ttho.

"Release them into our custody. We will be responsible for them. You know they were not the instigators of the conspiracy."

There was a moment's silence while Allecram considered her offer. Without consulting President Hours or Nix, he spoke again.

"Very well. We will release them into your custody on the understanding that you are responsible for their actions."

"Agreed."

To seal the deal, they enjoyed the banquet President Hours had provided them and drank pish late into the rotation.

Sevan didn't remember how he got to bed, but Tori woke him.

"Sevan, come quick, we've been summoned by Allecram."

"What? What time is it?"

"I've no idea. Everything looks the same in space. I could ask Ron."

"No, it doesn't matter. It'll just annoy me if I know how much sleep I haven't had. What about Ay-ttho?"

"I'm not going to wake her. Are you?"

"No, of course not."

Sevan got dressed and followed Tori off the ship to the presidential cruiser.

"Where's Ay-ttho?" Allecram asked when they arrived.

"She's sleeping," said Tori.

"You didn't wake her?"

"No."

"Why not?"

"It's not a good idea."

"Why not?"

"Trust me, you don't want to know. What's all this about, anyway?"

"Nix has gone."

"Gone? Gone where? And why is that a problem?"

"He's been taken."

"Taken? By whom? Where?"

"We think the Corporation noticed our experiments, and they have kidnapped her. We must get to her before Barnes does."

"But if the Corporation has already got her..."

"We've been tracking a ship which is making to leave the segment. We believe they may have Nix."

"Then why don't you go after them? You have the entire Republic force at your disposal."

"That would raise too much suspicion. We want you to track the ship and intercept it if possible."

"It'll cost more."

"Of course, we understand."

"And what about Nadio and Effeek'o?"

"We will have them ready for you on your return."

"Ay-ttho will not be happy about this," said Sevan.

"We'll do it," said Tori.

*

"Have you got a lock on the ship?" Tori asked Ron as the Mastery of the Stars was released from the hull of the presidential cruiser.

"Yes, tracking it now."

"Are you sure Ay-ttho is going to be okay with this?" Sevan asked.

"What does it matter?" said Tori. "She's always going around calling herself the captain. It's time some of us could make some decisions for a change."

By the time Ay-ttho woke up, they were deep into the segment in pursuit of the ship where Dr Nix was suspected to be held.

"Where are we going?" Ay-ttho asked when she arrived on the bridge.

"Tori has accepted a new mission," Sevan explained.

"What new mission?"

"The corporation has captured Dr Nix. We are going to retrieve her," said Tori.

"What? When did this happen?"

"While you were sleeping."

"Why didn't you wake me?"

"Why do you think?"

"Fair point," Ay-ttho glanced at the navigational panels. "So where is this ship and where is it going?"

"Ron is tracking it. It's heading for the far side of the segment."

"Strange. Oh well, breakfast, anyone?"

Ay-ttho left the bridge.

"Well, that went better than expected," said Sevan.

"Yeah," said Tori, almost disappointed.

He stared at the instruments.

"Where are they going?" he wondered aloud.

"By my calculations," answered Ron. "They are heading for the portal to the Gothaehiri system."

"Gothaehiri? Why would they take Dr Nix there?"

"Why would they take her at all?" asked Sevan.

"Well, that's obvious. She's clearly in charge of Hours' and Allecram's research programme into folding space. The Corporation probably wants to find out what she knows. The question is, why would they take her to Gothaehiri to do that?"

"Perhaps that's where the Corporation does their research?"

"I thought they did that on Nereid?"

"Maybe they did until the Republic attacked."

"Then why move their base closer to the capital planet of the Republic? It doesn't make sense. Ron, can you still track them if they go through the portal?"

"That shouldn't be a problem. I have procured access to the Republic's central surveillance system."

"When did you do that?"

"While we were docked on the presidential cruiser, I had a little chat with the central computer."

"You are naughty, Ron, but we like you."

"So, what are we going to do?" asked Sevan

"Ron, is there any risk by following them through the portal?"

"There is always a risk with everything. This is not a popular trading route, so there is not much traffic to hide between, but there's no real reason they should suspect a class 2 Corporation freighter travelling this route."

"Let's go then," said Tori. "Let's follow them in."

CHAPTER 26: TO SAVE NIX

Despite its relative centrality in the Republic, Gothaehiri was an unremarkable, little visited system, mainly because of the similar unremarkableness and lack of resources of its neighbouring systems, Titan and Henneria.

It wasn't a shortcut to anywhere, so people only passed through the Gothaehiri system if they had business on Gothaehiri, and few had a reason for that.

In its rotation, Gothaehiri had been famous for its marine life, which was said to rival that of Pallene, but overfishing had decimated the oceans and industry only existed to make use of the cheap labour force, who were left with few options.

"It's difficult to imagine what reason the Corporation would have for taking Dr Nix to Gothaehiri," said Tori.

By the time they emerged through the portal, it was clear the corporation vessel was heading for the planet that gave Gothaehiri its name. The only planet in the system with conditions hospitable for the likes of Republic and Corporation clones and their owners.

Ron ensured they followed the craft at a discrete distance so as not to arouse the suspicions of their quarry.

Tori felt uneasy about how simple their mission had been so far and he expressed as much to Ay-ttho when she finally returned to the bridge from her extended breakfast.

"Do you think they are trying to lure us in?" she asked. "It's possible."

"Why would they do that?" asked Tori.

"I don't know, but don't you think it's odd that they just board the presidential cruiser and leave with the president's chief scientist, with no one attempting to stop them?"

"It is odd."

"Did it not occur to you to mention it to Allecram?"

"We'd just woken up. I wasn't really thinking straight."

"Obviously."

"Well, what would you have said?"

"I'd have asked a few more questions before agreeing to go on a wild crisqix chase."

"That's all we ever seen to do."

"And we haven't been paid."

"And they haven't delivered Nadio or Effeek'o."

"Yet."

"If they ever do."

"You are such a cynic."

"I'm a cynic? What about you?"

"Can we stop fighting?" asked Sevan. "They restocked and refuelled us, right?"

"Yes."

"Well, I suggest we just cut our losses and go straight back to the Doomed Planet."

"What? Do you know what they are paying us?"

"We haven't seen any of those credits so far. There's no guarantee we ever will."

"Sevan the cynic. I never thought I'd live to see the day."

"There's a lot you don't know about me,"

"I don't think there is."

"We are approaching Gothaehiri," Ron interrupted.

"So what now?" asked Sevan.

"We land close to them but not in the same hangar, then Ron tracks them and informs us of their location via communicator while we pursue them on foot." Ay-ttho surveyed Tori and Sevan. "Unless you have any other ideas?"

"Of course not, Captain," said Tori.

"Very well then. Take us down Ron."

Ron steered the ship through the atmosphere of Gothaehiri to the settlement where the Corporation vessel had landed. It turned out to be quite a ramshackle place, like a spaceport that has seen better, more lucrative rotations, and was now trying to get by on whatever trade it could.

He identified the hangar where the shipped had docked and found another hangar nearby. The same fungal type creatures that they had found on Pandoria operated the hangar. Ay-ttho despised them, but there was no time to find anywhere else.

Ay-ttho communicated to Ron via her communicator while he monitored the spaceport's surveillance systems to see whether any of the crew of the corporation vessel had disembarked. They hadn't.

The group arrived in front of the hangar and found an establishment purportedly selling refreshments, especially beverages, from where they could view the entrance. They took a seat through which they could see the ship through the open doorway. As yet, no-one and nothing had emerged.

"Are you from that corporation ship? The ship that just arrived?" asked the owner of the establishment, a fat thretad, who balanced several cups and containers in his many pink prickly limbs.

"No," said Ay-ttho, hoping the owner would leave them alone.

"But you are corporation security, right?"

"No," said Ay-ttho before thinking better of her answer. "I used to be."

"Oh, I thought, once corporation security, always corporation security. I did not know you could get out."

Ay-ttho focussed on looking out of the window.

"And a mining clone as well. It's rare we get your sort round here."

Ay-ttho was realising their choice of lookout had been a bad idea. If this thretad talked as much as he appeared to, news of their presence would be around the spaceport in no time.

"Let's go," she said to the others.

"But you haven't finished your wobians veal lick," the owner protested.

"It was delicious," said Aythho, leaving some credits on the table.

"Now what?" asked Tori. "We had a good view from there."

"And our business would have been everyone's business by the end of the rotation."

There wasn't a great deal surrounding the hangar except for warehouses, but nowhere the group could sit and observe without raising suspicion.

"What about a roof?" asked Tori.

"If we can get up there," said Ay-ttho.

They walked around the area, but none of the buildings appeared to have external access to the roof.

"How do they get out in the event of a fire?" asked Sevan.

"Something tells me health and safety isn't a priority on Gothaehiri," said Ay-ttho

"Look," said Tori, pointing inside the hangar. "There are gantries on the walls. What if we could get onto one of those?"

"It's possible," said Ay-ttho, checking the hangar for signs of security which seemed to be nonexistent. "Come on."

They entered through a side door in a part of the hangar, which appeared to have the least activity. It was straightforward to climb a ladder onto one of the maintenance gantries and then skirt around the edge of the hangar until they overlooked the corporation ship. Either they hadn't been spotted or no-one was bothered about their presence.

"What do you think they are doing in there?" asked Sevan, gesturing to the ship.

"Your guess is as good as mine," said Ay-ttho.

"Shall we go in and get her?" Tori suggested.

"Let's wait to see if they come out first."

There was no activity around the ship, not even evidence of restocking or refuelling.

"Why here?" asked Sevan.

"They clearly don't ask questions on Gothaehiri."

"Unless they work in the hospitality industry," Tori scoffed.

They waited and watched, but no-one left or entered the ship.

"They could be doing anything in there," said Sevan.

"Agreed," said Tori. "Our brief was to recover Dr Nix. We will not do that if there is nothing left of her. We are going to have to go in."

"Ron, have they connected their ship to the spaceport's central computer?"

"Negative," said Ron. "I cannot access their system."

Ay-ttho sighed.

"We don't know what we are dealing with," she lamented. "How do we get into their ship?"

"We can pose as maintenance workers," Sevan suggested.

Ay-ttho and Tori ignored the suggestion.

"Unless..." Ay-ttho wondered aloud. "Ron, do you think you could establish a communication link?"

"Possibly."

"Maybe we could pose as Republic Revenue and Excise inspectors."

"That's better than my idea?" asked Sevan.

"Yes," said Ay-ttho. "Ron, fabricate a message informing them they are going to be inspected and supply us with fake IDs so that they know to expect us. Let me know when we can go."

Soon afterward, they received the fake IDs on their communicators.

"Dr Slater Regan," Sevan read in disbelief. "Mining commodities expert. What kind of name is that? Who have you got?"

"Major Baxter Nathan," said Tori. "Agent for the Republic/Corporation joint anti-smuggling task force."

"It's better than mine," Sevan grumbled.

"Who have you got?" Tori asked Ay-ttho.

"Colonel Fleming Brandon."

"Why do you get a superior rank to be?" Tori protested.

"All ready," said Ron. "They are expecting you in a matter of units."

The group made their way back down off the gantry and back round to the front of the hangar where they approached the corporation ship unchallenged.

Tori pressed the entrance intercom.

There was a buzz of static, but no voice.

"Republic Revenue and Customs," Tori barked into the intercom. "Random inspection. Open up."

They waited.

Tori buzzed again.

"This is," he checked his communicator. "Major Baxter Nathan of the joint Republic/Corporation anti-smuggling task force. You are required by law to open this door."

Nothing.

Tori and Ay-ttho drew their weapons.

"This is your last chance to open the door before I blow the control panel apart."

The door opened.

Once they were convinced there was no trap immediately inside, the group entered the ship. The door closed behind them.

They proceeded with caution into the ship, which appeared deserted. The layout was like The Mastery of the Stars, so it was simple to find the route to the bridge.

When they arrived, the bridge was deserted and all the instruments were switched off.

"Ron?" Ay-ttho called, using her communicator. "When we were pursuing this ship, did you detect life forms on board this vessel?"

"The distance was too great to detect life forms."

"How about now?"

"I detect three life forms."

"Where are they?"

"On the bridge."

"That's us, you uxlod."

"Affirmative."

"So, apart from us, there are no other life forms on this ship."

"Affirmative."

"Come on, let's go," Ay-ttho said to the others.

They followed her back to the entrance.

"It's locked," she grunted, having pressed several buttons.

"Fushy!" said Sevan.

"Now what?" asked Tori

Ay-ttho blasted the control panel, but the door did not open, even after she spent some time fiddling with the burned wires the blast had exposed.

"They must have flown it remotely," Sevan stated the obvious.

"Allecram must have known," said Tori. "It was a deliberate ruse to strand us here. To get us out of the way."

"Why would they want us out of the way?" asked Ay-ttho. "Why not just kill us?"

"If those are the only two options," said Sevan. "I prefer the stranding."

"It doesn't make sense," said Ay-ttho. "They send us into space, demonstrate space folding to us and then send us on a wild crisqix chase. Why?"

"Maybe they didn't," said Tori. "Maybe the ship was a decoy to make Allecram think Dr Nix had been taken."

"So Dr Nix is still on the presidential cruiser?"

"Along with the corporation agents."

"We need to get back there."

"We need to get off this ship first."

They tried various controls, both at the entrance and at the bridge, but they couldn't get any of the systems to start up. It was almost as if the ship was without power, but they knew that wasn't the case because the life support and lights were still working.

"Now what?" asked Tori.

"Now, we are trapped," said Ay-ttho.

CHAPTER 27: A CALL FROM THE DOOR

Sevan sat down on the floor by the exit door and waited for Ay-ttho or Tori to think of something.

"Ron? Can you access the ship's system and open this door?" Ay-ttho asked.

"Sorry, the ship's system appears to be offline."

"Can't we shout for help?" asked Sevan.

"The door is soundproof."

"I'm hungry," Sevan complained.

"That's it!" said Ay-ttho in a moment of revelation.

"What is?" asked Tori.

"He's hungry! We get Ron to order a delivery from that establishment we went to. When they come to deliver, we can speak with them over the intercom and send them for someone to cut open the door."

"How do we know the intercom works?"

"We don't. But it's the best idea we've got."

"It's the only idea we've got. Ron? We ate some wobians veal lick in a thretan's eating establishment opposite the hangar earlier. Can you identify the establishment?"

"I have located it, yes."

"Do they do delivery?"

"According to their data records, yes."

"Please request a delivery of wobians veal lick to the ship, please."

"Are you hungry?"

"Sevan is."

They waited while Ron contacted the owner. After a while, Ay-ttho's communicator crackled into life.

"Would you like spaorn sustenance sparkles?" asked Ron.

"Spaorn sustenance sparkles?" Ay-ttho asked Sevan.

"Yes, please."

"Yes please, Ron."

"Ask them if they have any Monzuc octo-nutrients."

"Ron?"

"Yes, Ay-ttho?"

"Please ask them if they have any Monzuc octo-nutrient."

"Will do."

They waited longer.

"Ay-ttho?"

"Yes, Ron."

"They don't have Monzuc octo-nutrient but they have tinned Spakruts paste."

"Did you hear that?" Ay-ttho asked Sevan.

"I'm not keen on Spakruts paste. How about Tretet marine mash?"

"How about Tretet marine mash?"

"I'll see."

A few moments passed.

"Large, medium, or small?" asked Ron.

"Wobians veal lick or tretet marine mash?" asked Ay-ttho.

"Both."

Ay-ttho looked at Sevan.

"Large please, oh, and see whether they've got any organic Teraorian nodes."

"For fushy's sake. It's only meant to be to get them to the door."

"Okay, forget the teraorian nodes, then?"

"Ron? Ask them how long it's going to be?"

More time passed.

"They're having to fry a fresh batch of Wobians veal lick and are sending out for the tretet marine mash. It might take some time."

Ay-ttho glared at Sevan.

"Sorry," he smiled sheepishly.

Some time passed and then the intercom buzzed.

"Hello?" Ay-ttho shouted.

"Delivery," a voice crackled through the speaker.

"We can't open the door. Get someone to open the door."

"What? I can't hear you very well."

"That's because I blasted the control panel."

"What did you say? It sounds like someone blasted your control panel."

"I did. You need to get someone to cut open the door."

"Are you paying by credits or vouchers?"

"Er... credits?"

"Was that credits?"

"Yes."

"Or vouchers."

"Credits. Get someone to open the door."

"It might be easier if you opened the door."

"This is pointless."

"Or do you want me to use this delivery hatch?"

"Delivery hatch?"

"It's thirty credits."

"Thirty? That's a ripoff."

"Just leave them in the hatch."

"Where's the?"

They searched the corridor for a hatch.

"Here it is," said Tori, finding a small door in the wall.

"Put the credits in," said Sevan.

"Nevermind the credits," said Ay-ttho. "You are small enough to get in there."

Tori and Ay-ttho pushed Sevan into the hatch, shut the cover and then opened the outer cover. Sevan emerged, much to the amusement of the thretad attempting to deliver Wobians veal lick and tretet marine mash.

"Here you go then," he said, handing Sevan a package. "Thirty credits please."

"Just a unit," said Sevan, leaning back in the hatch. "Can you two fit as well?"

"I might," Ay-ttho shouted back. "But Tori has no chance of getting in."

"Sorry about this," Sevan said to the thretad. "She has the credits. She'll be down in a moment."

"Why don't you use the door?" the thretad asked, puzzled.

"It's broken. Do you know anyone who can cut it?"

"Of course, you should have asked me that in the first place."

"Throw me down thirty credits," Secan shouted up to Ay-ttho. "He's going to get someone to cut open the door."

Ay-ttho threw down some credits and Sevan paid the thretad, who handed over the food.

"I'll be back," said the thretad, going off to find someone.

Sevan sat down on the hangar floor, opened the food package and get stuck in while he watched Ay-ttho struggling to extricate herself from the hatch.

"Comfortable?" she asked once she had freed herself.

Sevan, mouth full of food, nodded and offered her a piece of wobians veal lick.

"No, thank you."

A moment later, the thretad returned with another, more officious looking thetad.

"I understand you locked yourself out of your ship," he said.

"Actually, our colleague is locked in," Ay-ttho clarified.

"Locked in?"

"Yes,"

"How is that possible?"

"That's a good question that's not simple to answer. Do have something to cut open the door?"

"Of course, I just need to see your proof of ownership."

"Is that absolutely necessary?"

"Well, we can hardly go around cutting off doors at random."

"We would hardly be stuck inside someone else's ship, would we?"

The thertad thought about it for a moment.

"Look at me," Ay-ttho persisted. "I am a corporation security clone. This is a corporation freighter. Why would it not be our ship?"

"It's more than my job's worth," the thertad grumbled as he wandered off.

"Is he going to get something?"

Sevan shrugged.

"What's happening?" Tori shouted through the hatch.

"Not much," Ay-ttho admitted. "We are waiting to see whether the thertad that was here is going to get someone to cut open the door or whether we are just sitting here like be'uts placenta wontons."

Suddenly, the engines of the ship started.

"What's happening?" Tori shouted.

"The Engines are starting," said Ay-ttho.

"What should we do?" asked Sevan. "Get back on board?"

"Not likely. We've only just got off."

Sevan and Ay-ttho had to run for cover as the ship lifted into the air.

"I'm going to the bridge," Tori shouted into his communicator.

"Let's get back to the Mastery of the Stars," said Ay-ttho. "Ron? Can you meet us halfway?"

Sevan and Ay-ttho were much less than halfway between the hangars when Ron picked them up. By the time they reached the bridge, the Mastery of the Stars was in pursuit of the corporation ship, which was already leaving the Gothaehirian atmosphere.

They tracked the ship back towards the Titan portal while Tori, unsuccessfully, attempted to override the controls. Contrary to what they had expected, the presidential cruiser was no longer there and the corporation whip did not land on Titan. Instead, it continued towards the portal to Future.

Ay-ttho and Sevan continued to follow in the Mastery of the Stars and Tori continued fiddling with the controls of the corporation ship. They followed it all the way through the Future portal from where it steered towards the citadel in space.

"Try the escape pods again?" Ay-ttho suggested.

"I have. They are all still locked."

Sevan didn't relish the idea of returning to the citadel, but they had little choice. As long as Tori was trapped on the ship, they would have to follow it.

As they approached the citadel, the corporation vessel did not decelerate as Sevan had expected. Instead, it continued on what was quickly looking like an attack run.

Citadel security clearly had the same impression as they launched fighters to intercept the vessel.

It was too late, however, as the corporation ship fired it's missiles at the citadel.

"What the fushy?" Tori exclaimed.

"Tori, try the escape pods again," Ay-ttho shouted. "Try to bypass the system. They're going to shoot you down."

Sevan thought there was no down in space, but he thought it best not to mention that.

Sure enough, by the time the corporation ship had pulled out of its attack run, the Republic fighters were on its tail and had fired.

Having no way to turn on the shields, Tori rushed to bypass the system to operate an escape pod manually.

The ship rocked violently as the Republic missiles found their target.

"What can we do?" asked Sevan. "Should we get involved?"

"I don't want to engage the Republic fighters unless I absolutely have to," said Ay-ttho. "There's no point picking a fight unless it's absolutely necessary."

"But Tori?"

"Let's wait."

The Republic fighters were still tracking the ship and had fired more missiles.

"Hurry, Tori," Ay-ttho urged.

Tori activated the manual controls to open the door to an escape pod. He rushed inside, using the manual controls to close the door behind him, and then fiddled with the control panel to override the automatic settings.

The Republic missiles ripped into the ship's hull and exploded, splitting the ship apart in a shower of burning debris.

Ay-ttho and Sevan watched the exploding ball of fire in horror.

"Look," said Ay-ttho, pointing out the observation window towards the conflagration.

Sevan looked and saw, out of the explosion, an escape pod emerge.

"Let's pick him up."

Ron steered the Mastery of the Stars towards the pod, meanwhile the Republic fighters circled back towards them.

"Incoming communication," Ron announced.

"We advise you to surrender," a voice crackled. "Otherwise, we will be forced to fire."

"Our intentions are peaceful," said Ay-ttho. "I disengaged our weapons system."

"We will escort you to the citadel," said the voice.

"Pick up the pod," Ay-ttho ordered Ron.

Unfortunately, the position of the pod meant Ron had to steer the Mastery of the Stars away from the citadel.

"You will accompany us to the citadel," came the voice. "Or we will fire upon you."

"Hang on a unit," said Ay-ttho. "We have something we have to do first."

"You will follow us immediately."

"How long?" Ay-ttho asked Ron.

"A couple of units. By the way, the fighters are arming their missiles."

The Mastery of the Stars closed in on the escape pod and was opening one of its cargo bay doors just as the fighters launched their missiles.

Ay-ttho steered the ship in such a way that the Mastery of the Stars captured the pod and then began evasive manoeuvres to avoid the incoming missiles.

She swung the freighter around so that it was pointing back towards the fighters just as their missiles impacted on the side of the hull.

Heading back towards the fighters, Ron communicated a message that they would comply and as a result, no more missiles were fired and the Mastery of the Stars sustained only minor damage.

Ron had to deploy a remote welding drone to cut open the escape pod and release Tori.

By the time a Republic patrol ship had docked onto the side of the Mastery of the Stars, Tori was back on the bridge

"That was a close one," he said. "Thanks for picking me up."

"Next time, try not to get trapped on a corporation freighter," said Ay-ttho.

"I'll bear that in mind next time you ask me to board one."

The Republic troops boarded the freighter and took the group into custody.

"We had nothing to do with attacking the citadel," Sevan protested.

"Save it for the judge," snarled a trooper.

"At least we're going to get a trial," said Ay-ttho optimistically.

The troops transferred them to the cells beneath the courtroom on the citadel itself.

"You are very lucky," said their guard. "Usually this court is only used for the most heinous of crimes such as those requiring the death penalty."

Sevan was struggling to share Ay-ttho's optimism.

Ay-ttho, Tori, and Sevan were led into the Citadel's courtroom by armed guards. It did not surprise them to see Allecram, President Hours and Dr Nix sitting waiting for them.

"So obvious when you think about it," said Ay-ttho.

"We have sentenced you to life imprisonment on Aitne," Allecram began. "And we have sentenced you to life imprisonment on Ogenus. On both occasions, you escaped from the Republic's most secure penal facilities. We have therefore decided that we should execute you, so you no longer pose a threat to our society."

CHAPTER 28: THE PLOT THICKENS

"But we received pardons," Tori protested.

"President Hours does not recognise the pardons of past presidents," said Allecram. "Take them away."

The guards led them out of the courtroom and back to the cells, where they sat in glum contemplation.

"What now?" asked Sevan.

"Now we get executed," said Tori.

"You're going to give up now? We've been sentenced to death before."

"I'm tired," said Tori.

"Me too," said Ay-ttho.

"That's a good idea," said Sevan. "Why doesn't Ay-ttho fall asleep?"

"That's not going to work all the time," said Ay-ttho.

"But it might," said Sevan.

They all went to sleep. Sometime later, they all woke up.

"See," said Ay-ttho.

Sevan realised that his friends had given up and that, without their help, he may as well give up, too.

He sat on his bench and thought about his aunt and how it was unlikely now that he would ever get to see her again.

The next rotation, they summoned them to the court.

"Before we execute you, you have one last request," said Allecram. "What is it to be?"

"I would like to visit my aunt on the Doomed Planet," said Sevan speculatively, with no expectation that his request would be granted.

"Very well," said Allecram. "And the others?"

"Wait a unit," said Sevan. "You mean to say that you are actually letting me go to visit my aunt?"

"Yes, why not? If you don't come back, we will simply send the mechanical bowmen."

"In that case," said Ay-ttho. "I would like to visit Ragniethea."

"Ragniethea?" said Tori. "Good choice. I think I would like to visit Bumunerth."

"Clever choices," said Allecram. "But you know that the mechanical bowmen always have their quarry."

Sevan, Ay-ttho and Tori were led away once more.

"That was a brilliant idea to think of your aunt," said Ay-ttho.

"It was an accident," said Sevan.

"A brilliant accident."

"Now what?" asked Sevan.

"They will transport us to our chosen destinations."

"And the mastery of the stars?"

"They will impound it."

"But..."

"One thing at a time, Sevan. We can't do anything about the Mastery if the Stars if we are dead."

The next rotation, Sevan, Ay-ttho and Tori were collected from their cell and taken by separate guards to rockets similar to the type the Republic had used on Syrius when it had intended to send them back to Aitne. On that occasion, they had tampered with the gravity manipulator to allow them to return, but this time, Sevan had no intention of tampering with anything. He wanted to return to the Doomed Planet.

The guards strapped him into his seat and then left, closing the hatch behind them. These penal transporters only contained the barest minimum of life support, and Sevan could only hope that it would get him to his destination.

The rocket had no windows, so he could not see the citadel as they ejected his rocket from it. Nor could he see the rockets of Tori and Ay-ttho heading in different directions.

No doubt Tori and Ay-ttho would attempt to tamper with their rockets, but Sevan just sat tight and waited to arrive.

Every so often, Sevan perceived he was passing through a portal, but other than the strange sensation of jumping between systems, he did not know where he was and lost track of time.

A very bumpy landing, which some might more accurately describe as a crash, indicated his eventual arrival.

He disconnected himself from the life support system, which had kept him alive but had left him very weak. His priority would be to discover where on the Doomed Planet he was and then find his aunt, who was bound to feed him all his favourite treats.

Using most of his remaining strength, Sevan activated the escape hatch and emerged into an environment that did not look at all familiar.

His suit told him the air was breathable, and he emerged into the strange world. It didn't look at all like the Doomed Planet and although he was aware his home planet had some strange places, he couldn't imagine that any of them could be as strange as the place in which he was now standing.

There were plants and grasses, but none of them looked familiar. He surveyed the horizon but could see no settlement or clues as to the best direction to find one. It was pointless to stay on the ship with no supplies. He had survived on the ship's life support so far and now needed to eat something substantial if he were to recover his strength.

He wished the others had chosen the same location as him for their last requests. He imagined they had good reasons for choosing the locations they did, but he had been too shy to ask them when he had the chance. Now they were on the other side of the universe for all he knew.

Sevan shed his suit and set off in a random direction. It wasn't long before he had to seek shade for a rest. Some plants looked like they might bear fruit, but he was too afraid to try it in case it was poisonous.

Despite his fatigue, he forced himself to keep moving and eventually found a river. At first sight, he thought the river was red but, as he drew closer, he realised the redness belonged to a plant that grew profusely on the riverbed and swayed with the current just below the surface.

In between the plants, he occasionally glimpsed a disk like creature swimming. The creature was of a bluer hue, similar to that of the stones on the riverbed, then he realised one side of the creature was blue while the other side was the same shade as the plants.

Occasionally one creature would dart to the bottom where it would kick up a cloud of purple dust which was soon swept away by the current.

Sevan was very thirsty but did not know whether the water was safe to drink. He resisted, but knew he could not do so for long.

He followed the river downstream, imagining he would eventually reach either a settlement or a thoroughfare.

The riverbank was uneven but passable and Sevan resisted the temptation to jump into the clear water even though it looked deliciously cool. Both the red plants and the blue red creatures looked like they might be carnivorous.

When he reached a copse of large plants that cast an area of shade, he took another rest. There was still no evidence of any civilisation. He realised that eventually he would have no choice but to drink the river water and eat the strange fruits.

By the time it was reaching the end of the rotation, Sevan had encountered no signs of dwellings or tracks so, when he reached another copse close to the river, abundant with fruit, he succumbed to his hunger and thirst and gulped down the river water before trying one fruit which had a strong earthy taste and a rubber-like texture which made it very chewy.

Feeling slightly satisfied, Sevan lay down against the stem of one of the large plants and giggled. He did not know what there could be in his current predicament that could be so funny, and yet he could not help giggling uncontrollably.

A sense of euphoria immediately followed the giggling, and he found himself in awe of his surroundings. All the plants and the river and the creatures in the river suddenly felt very different somehow. The colours were all so much more vivid than they had been before and he felt so energised and excited that he got up and continue on his journey, running along the riverbank, jumping over the smaller plants and shrieking with joy.

He hadn't travelled very far like this before he realised that someone or something might hear all the shrieking and he stopped, peering into the twilight, wondering who or what might be watching him.

The more he considered the possibility he was being watched, the more anxious he became until he panicked. He felt overwhelmed by the situation and vomited.

Dizziness and the need to evacuate his waste orifice followed the vomiting. He only undid his waste discharge flap just in time before a torrent of foul smelling diarrhoea gushed out, coating the nearby plants in sticky effluence.

His stomach ached, and he lay down on the ground, slipping into a state of half consciousness in which he dreamt of all the terrible things that had happened to him since the fateful rotation they had chosen him to represent the workers on the concession council on the Doomed Planet which now seemed part of the distant past.

He dreamt he was standing in the observation tower of the concession council building, watching his friend Thertee plunge to his death.

Sevan turned away and stared at the dead bodies of Genzuihines natives. He wanted to get away but was pinned in by snarling Genzuihines beasts on one side and three Alliance guards on the others. The flesh of the guards was burned and peeling. They all had the faces of the head of the corporation, Barnes.

He realised the guards' flesh was burning because everything was on fire. He looked for a way to escape and saw that he was in the Hygeia community on the Doomed Planet.

Sevan saw a doorway. He stumbled through it and found himself on the Mastery of the Stars. All around him in the corridor were strewn the bodies of corporation guards.

A door opened and armed corporation guards rushed through. Sevan turned to run in the opposite direction, but that door opened to reveal more armed corporation guards who raised their weapons to shoot. As they fired, Sevan threw himself to the floor and the laser bolts passed overhead. When silence fell, he raised his head to discover the corridor on either side of him was littered with corporation guards who had shot each other.

The Mastery of the Stars dissolved and Sevan was floating on the prison planet of Aitne, watching the air in his suit escape via a hole in his boot.

As he floated off into space, Aitne became a distant spec and another object came into view. Another planet. It was Future, and it was getting larger. As it approached, Sevan realised he was helpless to prevent himself from falling into its atmosphere.

As he plummeted towards the ground, he saw the buildings of the city planet moving rapidly towards him, or rather, he was moving rapidly towards them.

Sevan braced himself for impact and went crashing through one building and out of the other side before coming to a halt in the adjacent building.

No sooner had he struggled to his feet than he was floored again by a beast that looked like one Ay-ttho had fought on Pandoria.

Sevan scrambled away but tripped over the broken machine of his friend Ozli, who was turning to sludge inside.

He turned away and saw another prisoner from Aitne floating towards him. As they drew close, Sevan could see the dead face of Ay-ttho inside, frozen by the void of space.

Objects which fell from the sky like the fragments of the comet on Angetenar, distracted him.

He ran away but stumbled again, turning to see that he had stumbled over the mutilated bodies of Ydna and Kcocaep.

Sevan had no time to be repulsed by the cadavers. He had to pull off the prisoner's suit because huge boils had developed all over his body and were now bursting.

As his whole body felt like it was exploding, he fell back onto the plants. Through a blurred haze, he could perceive a face staring down at him.

"Where am I?" He asked.

"This is Bumunerth," said the face.

CHAPTER 29: THE LOST ONES

"There are many who have fallen victim to the same mistake," said the face.

The face belonged to a blue furry creature with two horns protruding from its bulbous head. Two small eyes nestled beneath a large monobrow.

"My name is Josh. We are a community of those who were sent by rocket to Aitne but ended up here. We call ourselves the lost ones."

Josh helped Sevan to his feet and led him a little further down the river to the community of lost ones. On the way, Sevan tried to explain what had happened and his desire to return to the Doomed Planet.

"We have lots of broken rockets," said Josh. "But nothing that will fly."

Sevan understood what Josh was referring to when they arrived at the settlement which comprised rockets which had been converted into habitations.

"Soon, we will get help to bring your rocket here, but first, let us get you something to eat. It will help counteract the effects of the gkruts gem you ate. Do you like pre-formed bloons' wontons?"

Sevan explained he did not know what pre-formed bloons' wontons were. They turned out to be a kind of pastry filled with what Sevan later discovered to be the larvae of some kind of insect. Fortunately, he was unaware of this at the time of eating and could therefore enjoy the dish without being distracted by the thought that his food would have otherwise have metamorphosed into a winged creature.

After they had eaten, the community went to the crash site of Sevan's rocket and with surprising rapidity, dismantled it, moved it to the village and reassembled it in a different order so that, by the end, Sevan had a little house complete with a little door and a staircase up to a second floor which he was told was his sleeping area.

The villagers gave Sevan a variety of presents, including blankets and chairs, which helped to make the inside of the rocket more like a home and Sevan was overcome with gratitude to these strangers who did not seem like strangers anymore.

They brought him food and promised that the next day they would initiate him into the ways of the community so that he might provide for himself.

"Did you hear that President Hours has annexed some corporation concessions?" said one villager.

"How do you know that?" asked Sevan.

"They fitted some rockets with tachyon transmitters," Josh explained. "We have adapted them to become receivers so that we can listen in to what is happening around us. We pick up all manner of news that way."

"But why would President Hours want to start another conflict?"

"It acts as a useful distraction from problems within the Republic, if the president can provide the citizens with an external enemy. Barnes is probably compliant."

"Why would Barnes want the Republic to annex his concessions?"

"The corporation and the Republic have collaborated for years to manufacture conflicts to placate the population. I believe the Republic pays Barnes very well for his cooperation."

"I've heard these theories before," said Sevan. "But do you really think there is any truth in them?"

"From what we can gather from the tachyon transmissions, there is a lot of truth."

Sevan thought for a moment.

"Do you know which concessions have been annexed?" he asked the villager.

"I'm not sure of their names, but I think they orbit Nereid."

"Oh no," Sevan slumped down onto one of the recently donated chairs. "I think that's the Doomed planet, my home, and Daphnis."

"Yes, that's what they were called."

"My aunt is there," Sevan said, almost to himself. "I need to get there."

"I'm afraid that's impossible," said Josh. "We have no means to get ourselves off Bumunerth. Landing badly damaged all the rockets and what remained we modified for our dwellings and other purposes."

"There aren't enough parts of a rocket to make a whole one?"

"Even if there were, we don't have the expertise to construct and launch it, sorry."

Sevan looked around at his new home. It wasn't that bad a place to be stranded, but he missed his aunt and he missed his friends. He wondered where Ay-ttho's and Tori's rockets had ended up. If he had landed on Bumunerth, perhaps one of them had made it to the Doomed Planet.

He realised he was likely to spend a long time on Bumunerth, possibly the rest of his life, which might be a long time indeed, given that his genetic programming meant he would not age. He could only be killed if he were to accident or deliberately suffer a fatal injury, which could take a very long time.

"We come from a wide variety of different species," Josh explained. "Our community was not intentional, but we all share a common goal to survive."

Sevan had already experienced the variety of species Josh was referring to. The villagers had constructed Sevan's rocket home specifically to his size. So much so that larger species had to bend down to get through the door while other smaller creatures struggled to reach the door handle.

The villagers realised Sevan was tired and so they left him to himself and promised they would be back early the next rotation to begin his initiation into the ways of the village. He retired immediately to his new bed and dropped into a deep sleep.

A knock on the door woke him. The rotation was still dark and Sevan stumbled to the door, still half asleep.

"Let's go," said Josh, standing on the threshold with a bucket.

"Where are we going?" Sevan asked, following him into the twilight.

"You'll see."

Josh led him to a large barn-like structure in which were tethered several creatures which looked like sereosleodo, but not quite.

"These are jadanirs. They look very much like sereosleodo, don't they? The milk is very similar. "

Sevan had seen sereosleodo on Ogenus and he had to agree they looked very similar.

"Be careful," said Josh. "They can get grumpy. We'll feed them first and then they shouldn't mind you milking them."

"Wait a unit," Sevan protested. "You want me to milk them?"

"Of course. You have to start somewhere."

Sevan only just realised that Josh's bucket was full of dead groqun which he emptied into troughs in front of each jadanir. The beasts began to eagerly wolf down the groqun, crunching the shells noisily.

"The shells help with their eggs," Josh explained. "There is an abundant supply of groqun in the river. I'll make sure you get to try them later."

Sevan wasn't a big fan of crustaceans, but he smiled anyway.

With the bucket now empty, Josh led Sevan round the back of one jadanir, where its juicy tendrils were dangling loosely.

"You just need to suck on the end to get the flow going and then just drop it in the bucket and it will flow until the milk bladder is empty."

"You want me to what?" Sevan was not impressed by Josh's suggestion.

"Suck on it. It doesn't taste bad. Watch."

Josh sucked on the end of a tendril, then dropped it in a bucket where a viscous blue liquid emerged.

"You try," said Josh, licking his lips and offering Sevan a tendril.

Not wanting to upset Josh, who had been so kind to him, Sevan tentatively took hold of one of the slimy tendrils and brought it slowly towards his mouth. Then, with large misgivings, Sevan placed the end of the tendril in his mouth and closed his lips around it.

To his surprise, the sticky tendril tasted of sweet globengi oxo flush and after he sucked, he had to force himself to take the tasty tendril out of his mouth and place it in the bucket where it contributed more creamy blue liquid.

The contents of two milk bladders filled half a bucket and, following two judicious sucks on two more tasty tendrils, within units, the bucket was full.

"I'll take this one back," said Josh, taking the bucket. "You finish the rest."

Sevan looked around. There must have been at least fifteen jadanirs. The task seemed daunting, but he relished the thought of tasting another sixty tendrils.

He had almost finished filling the last bucket when Josh returned with some other villagers of various shapes and sizes.

"I've brought you some help with the buckets," he said.

Josh, Sevan and each of the villagers took a bucket in each hand. For Josh and Sevan, this meant two, but one villager could take seven and others could take three or four.

They carried the buckets to a huge vat and poured the sticky liquid inside. Under the vat was a fire, and a gigantic creature stirred the liquid with a huge spoon. While he was doing this, other villagers were extracting the juice of fruit and storing it in the buckets.

After a while, the gigantic creature shouted some orders which were unintelligible to Sevan. The other villagers quickly extinguished the fire, then passed the buckets of juice to the gigantic creature, who added it to the warm liquid in the vat.

Sevan went with Josh and a couple of villagers to wash the buckets in the river. When they returned, the other villagers were constructing something downhill of the vat. It was like a large wooden scaffold, with cloth at the top and underneath sat a large bucket, almost as large as the vat itself.

The vat pivoted on a large stand and the gigantic creature tipped it so that the liquid poured into the material and then dripped through into the bucket below.

Sevan noticed that the liquid was much lumpier than it had been and the lumps were getting caught in the material. The gigantic creature threw some powder on the mixture and then sat down on the hillside to watch it drip.

"The next stage takes several units," said Josh. "We'll come back later to help mould the jadanir protein. In the meantime, let us break our fast."

Sevan liked the idea of breaking his fast, but he was a little worried about what he would break his fast with. In the end, it turned out to be a yeasty coarse-textured substance with lots of sizeable holes on which Josh showed him how to spread a slightly acidic creamy paste.

"This is jadanir protein," Josh said, spreading it on his own holey substance which he explained they made from baked pulverised plants. "It's called bappir and we use it to make a pleasant drink, which I will share with you later."

After they had eaten, they returned to the hill where the jadanir protein was ready to be shaped and cut into slices. They placed these slices back into the vat in which the gigantic creature had heated some river water. The gigantic creature had large tongs which he used to turn the slices occasionally.

"Let's go," said Josh. "He will do that for a few mega units."

Josh led Sevan back down through the village and out the other side to field after field with long, thin plants.

"This is where we make the Branir," he said.

In one field, a villager was using a type of scythe with long fingers attached to one side to cut down the long plants. As the villager swung the scythe, the fingers caught the plants as it cut them and then deposited them in a pile at the end of the cutting swing. More villagers followed the cutter and tied the plants into bundles which were left in the field.

Josh and Sevan walked on past another field where the bundles were being loaded on to a cart.

They walked further to a large building which looked like they have built it from several rockets. Villagers were stacking bundles inside this construction.

Behind the construction, a bizarre-looking contraption into which villagers were feeding plants. Out of the other end, Sevan could see some kind of dust falling into sacks.

"This will be your job," said Josh.

CHAPTER 30: A KNOCK ON THE DOOR

Josh trained Sevan how to use the machine, warning him to be careful not to get his arms too close to the beaters inside.

"They will tear your arms off," he said.

From that moment, Sevan treated the machine with the utmost respect.

Lunch was more of the branir with jadanir protein and Sevan ate beside the fields with the rest of the villagers.

By the end of the day, Sevan was exhausted and was relieved when Josh told him to wash in the river to prepare for dinner.

He was invited to Josh's house and was pleased to discover that dinner was not more branir with jadanir protein but was a meaty stew which Josh told him was made from an actual jadanir.

Sevan felt sorry for the big dopey beasts but was more hungry than sorry and so ate two bowls.

After dinner, Josh brought him a large jug of liquid, which had a thin tube sticking out of the top.

"We make this from branir," he said, showing Sevan that he should drink by sucking the liquid through the tube.

The liquid was neither sweet nor bitter, and Sevan thought he could soon get used to it. Fortunately, he immediately had to opportunity to get used to it, because no sooner had he finished the first jug than Josh had brought him a second.

By the end of the third, he was getting lightheaded, but he had no time to complain before Josh had presented him with a fourth.

Sevan woke up in his new bed in his new rocket home. He did not know how he got there or how many jugs he had drunk. All that he knew was that his head hurt and his mouth felt like a cukid had emptied it's waste discharge bladder into it.

He realised why he had woken. Someone was knocking on the metal door.

Wearily, he got out of bed, shuffled over to the door, and pulled it open. He almost fell over when he saw Ay-ttho and Tori standing on his threshold. In fact, he did fall over, so Ay-ttho and Tori helped him back to his bed.

"You look terrible," said Tori. "You look like you've drunk six jugs of fermented branir."

"Where in the worst place did you two come from? Did I dream all this?"

Sevan looked around the interior of his rocket home.

"No, this is definitely real," said Ay-ttho, examining the handiwork of the villagers.

"But how did you find me?"

"It was simple, really. I landed on the Doomed Planet, so I stole a ship and went to Ragniethea, where I found Tori, so it made sense that you must be here."

"But out of the entire planet, you found me here? In this village?"

"Well, there aren't any signatures of corporation mining clones anywhere else on the planet."

"Oh, for fushy's sake, what ship did you steal?"

"A Republic special forces scouting vessel."

"For the love of the giant cup, they will be on their way here now."

"That's why we're leaving. Oh, I brought you a surprise."

Ay-ttho beckoned someone from outside. A smaller version of Sevan entered.

"Aunty!"

"You look terrible," said his aunt. "Are you sure you've been eating properly? Do you still feint? You used to feint a lot, he used to feint a lot."

"Thanks, Aunty. You look great too."

"Clean yourself up."

"Yes, Aunty."

Sevan got up and tried unsuccessfully to tidy himself.

As a farewell, Josh broke their fast with a meal made from Jadanir eggs. One egg fed several villagers. It had a soft texture and no strong flavour but required some extent of chewing to get through the yolk.

After the meal, Sevan thanked the villagers, especially Josh, and apologised for having to leave so soon.

"We can give you a lift if you want to get off the planet," Ay-ttho suggested.

"That's very kind of you," said Josh. "But we have established a community here and we like our life. It is better than any of the lives we led before we came here."

"Thanks for going to all the trouble of building my home," said Sevan. "I'm sorry I can't stay to make use if it."

"That's okay. It's always good to have a spare in case we have any unexpected visitors."

"I hate to be the villain," said Tori. "But we really should go. I doubt the Republic is very far behind us and I wouldn't want to lead them here."

They rushed to the special forces scouting vessel as quickly as Sevan's aunt could go, which was frustratingly slow for Tori.

The scouting vessel was a sleek looking grey vessel, unsurprisingly smaller than the Mastery of the Stars. It would easily fit within one of ye freighter's cargo bays. The bridge sat atop a bulbous nose where the surveillance equipment was located. Above the bridge sat a gigantic cannon which Sevan imagined could do a great deal of damage.

Although it was not fitted with an anti-matter drive, Ay-ttho assured Sevan that its gravity manipulator was second to none and it would outmanoeuvre anything else the Republic had with perhaps the exception of the experimental scorpion lizard class which were still in development.

As he approached the entrance, Sevan could see how heavily fortified the vessel was, with gun turrets under the nose and various other weaponry attached to the hull. It was a beautiful vessel, even if it was one of the Republic's weapons of oppression.

Inside, the corridors had grey floors and white walls, typical of Republic military ships.

"I don't know how you expect to keep those walls clean," Sevan's aunt complained. "I hope you don't expect me to do it."

"Of course not," said Sevan before turning to Ay-ttho. "We don't do we?"

"No."

"No, there you go Aunty, you won't need to clean anything."

"You will," Ay-ttho told Sevan.

*

"How did she get my aunt to agree to go with her?" Sevan asked Tori, who was watching him wash down one of the white corridor walls.

"I've no idea. She was already with her when they arrived on Ragniethea to get me."

"Don't get me wrong, I love my aunt and everything. It's just that I didn't expect her to be this annoying."

"From what I gather, the clones in your aunt's container block were keen for Ay-ttho to take her."

"Are you going to help me with this?" Sevan asked, swabbing dirty water over the wall which left it looking more filthy than before.

"What? And take the credit from you when you are doing such a marvellous job. Not a chance. See you later."

As Tori left the corridor, he passed Sevan's aunt coming the other way

"What a mess you are making," she complained as soon as she saw Sevan pasting dirty water over the clean walls. "Can't you do anything right?"

She stormed off up the corridor, leaving Sevan wondering what had just happened. He dumped his brush in the bucket and stomped off to the bridge.

"Why did you have to bring her?" he complained to Ay-ttho.

"I thought you wanted to see her?"

"I did. In her container. Where I could leave her. She's a pain in the waste discharge glands."

"I agree with you there."

"So now we are stuck with her."

"Conditions at the concession are terrible now that the Republic has taken over. The workers are treated no better than slaves."

"What do you mean?"

Ay-ttho explained to Sevan what she had seen during her brief visit to the Doomed Planet. Sevan thought what Ay-ttho was describing was not too different from what he had experienced under the corporation, but thought it was probably better that his aunt was out of the way, even if it meant she was giving him an earful all the time.

"So, what are we going to do now?" he asked Ay-ttho.

"We are going to get the Mastery of the Stars back."

"So, we are going back to the citadel?"

"It seems as good a place to start as any."

Sevan did not like the thought of returning to the citadel, but he had long accepted the fact that he wasn't part of the decision-making process and had learned to just go along with whatever he was told.

"Sevan?" Ay-ttho asked. "If you are a clone, how can you have an aunt?"

"She's not my biological aunt," Sevan explained. "I just called her my aunt because she's always been an aunt-like figure to me. She would complain about the concession and the Corporation turning us all into slaves when I visited her. I thought she was losing her marbles, but she doesn't seem so mad now after everything I've experienced after leaving the Doomed Planet."

"Can you do me a favour?" Ay-ttho asked.

"What's that?"

"Keep your aunt off the bridge."

"Why is that?" said Sevan's aunt, who was coincidentally entering the bridge.

"It's just that the craft isn't very well maintained," said Ay-ttho without skipping a beat. "And we wouldn't want you getting injured by any loose wires or falling panels."

"It looks well maintained to me."

"Yes, I know, it does, doesn't it? It's amazing how deceptive appearances can be."

Sevan convinced his aunt to return to her quarters and show him her collection of miniature cukid models which she had had the foresight to pack when Ay-ttho had collected her.

"Do you have a plan?" Tori asked Ay-ttho when he entered the bridge later.

"I've been trying to get hold of Ron via the communicator, but he's not responding. They must have deactivated him. Would you mind monitoring things here while I have a look around the ship?"

"Not at all."

Ay-ttho was away for many units but eventually returned carrying a bundle of clothes.

"What the fushy have you got there?" asked Tori.

"I have a plan."

Meanwhile, in the crew sleeping quarters, in the captain's quarters to be exact, where Sevan's aunt had made herself at home, she was almost halfway through showing Sevan her collection of miniature cukid models which he had seen several times before.

"Sevan, please come to the bridge, alone," Ay-ttho's voice sounded over the tannoy.

"I am sorry, Aunty," he said. "I have to go. You'll have to show me the rest of your collection another time."

"You never show an interest in my hobbies," she complained.

Sevan, who had just spent many units looking at the collection, which he had already seen many times before, decided it was best not to pursue the matter and left.

"Put these on," said Ay-ttho when Sevan entered the bridge. She thrust a pile of clothes into his hands.

"What's this?"

"It's amazing what they've got on this ship. If you go into the storage area, they've got all kinds of stuff. And wait until you see this."

Ay-ttho flicked some switches. Sevan did not perceive any discernible change in anything.

"Isn't that amazing?" Tori enthused.

"What just happened?" Sevan asked.

"It's a cloaking device."

"But I can still see us."

"Of course you can. It cloaks us from those outside the ship."

"But I heard that ships with cloaking devices still show up on scanners."

"Only if they are looking for us. If they don't scan, they won't pick us up."

"But what if they routinely scan?"

"You have to put a damper on everything, don't you? You're as bad as your aunt. Get changed. We'll be at the Citadel soon."

"The citadel? But aren't they just going to arrest us again?"

"That's what the costumes are for."

"You mean you just expect to walk in there?"

"Why not?"

"Er... because they are going to arrest us?"

"Not if I dress us as someone else, silly."

Yet again, this rotation, Sevan decided it was pointless to argue, so he went off a

and prepared for their arrival at the citadel in space.

CHAPTER 31: THE GRAND EXPERIMENT

"Explain to us again," Sevan asked Ay-ttho, as they walked towards the exit of the vessel. "What is our job? What are we supposed to do?"

"This is the last time, Sevan," Ay-ttho sighed with impatience. "We are senators. You represent the mining colonies. I represent the corporation security clones and Tori is the representative for Republic security clones."

"But what are we supposed to do?"

"You do nothing. Just follow our lead."

"Oi, you lot!" Tori shouted at a group of guards gathered by the entrance to the hangar. "Come here and guard this ship."

"He's taking his role seriously, isn't he?" Sevan whispered to Ay-ttho.

"Are you on holiday?" Tori continued. "What are you doing hanging around there? Come here and do your job?"

"Coming," one of the shocked guards replied without questioning Tori's authority.

"Then where are your supervisors? What are you doing lounging around here when you should be on duty?"

"Sorry," said another guard.

"Sorry? That's not good enough. I should have you sent to Aitne."

"Sorry."

"Stop talking and guard the ship."

"Yes, Sir. I imagine you are here for the great experiment, are you?."

"The Great Experiment?" Ay-ttho blurted out. "That is confidential. Tell me everything you know about the great experiment."

"Everyone in the citadel knows about it. It's the research programme into folding space. The Republic is finally going to emerge from under the thumb of the corporation."

"Guard the ship!" shouted Tori.

The guards went away without protest.

"Should we have asked them about the Mastery of the Stars?" Ay-ttho asked Tori.

"Why would senators be asking about a captured corporation freighter? It might have blown our cover."

"It would take a lot to blow our cover with that bunch of uxclods."

"Let's go."

*

Hours was walking with Allecram and Dr Nix.

"The great experiment will go ahead as planned."

"President Hours, I must urge caution. Our intelligence suggests this is not a time to take risks."

"You and your superstitious mumbo jumbo, Allecram. Also, I want you to find me an additional guard. I don't trust mine. They were here when Xocliw was president. They are dangerous."

"You don't need to fear them. They are loyal to you."

"I don't fear them, but they spent too much time with Xocliw."

Hours led Allecram away from Nix.

"Have you noticed anything strange about Nix?"

"You've been with her as much as I have."

"You don't think she has some illness?"

"No, why?"

"I have been having terrible dreams. I think something bad is about to happen."

"We certainly live in strange times and nothing is certain. Ah, here is the entrance to my apartment. Take care, President, don't worry too much."

Allecram entered his apartment, leaving Hours to wait for Nix.

"What's wrong my President?" she asked as she approached. "What were you talking to Allecram about?"

"Only the strange dreams I've been having."

"You worry too much. The experiment will be a success. "

"Shhh, someone is coming."

"It's Callahan, look. High Priest, how are you? I haven't seen you since the inauguration. How are your followers?"

"Well, I hope. And how are you? Are you well?"

"As well as expected. What brings you to the citadel?"

"They have invited me as a special adviser to the senate, but between you and me, I had an ulterior motive."

"Oh, yes? And what might that be?"

"I wanted to see this great experiment. Can you get me a good seat?"

"I doubt that should be too difficult."

"Thank you."

"Let's catch up later. If you'll excuse me, Nix and I need to finish the preparations."

*

Ay-ttho, Tori and Sevan seemed to have no problems walking around the corridors of the citadel unchallenged. Until they met a tall, rather officious looking official.

"Good rotation, Senators," he said. "I gather you are here for the great experiment."

"Correct," said Tori, using his best senator voice.

"Please come this way. The presentation is about to start."

The official turned on his heels and led the group of pretend senators to a large, dimly lit auditorium covered in an impressive transparent dome which provided an incredible view of the firmament of stars above.

He led them to a row of seats besides groups of genuine senators, all looking up through the observation window at the dark universe beyond.

"Beloved Senators," a voice rang around the arena.

Sevan recognised the voice. It belonged to President Hours, who suddenly became illuminated on a plinth at the front of the auditorium.

"For too long, we have been at the mercy of the corporation," the president continued. "They have used their superior technology to blackmail us into accepting their demands. But this rotation, all this is about to change. This rotation you are about to witness the fruits of the Republic's extensive research into the precise art of folding space."

The auditorium, bursting with senators and other very important guests, burst into raptures of applause.

"Please enjoy the show." President Hours left the plinth, and the auditorium darkened, giving an even better view of the galaxy outside.

Looking up through the observation windows, Sevan saw a bright ring which appeared to be growing. There were light trails leading into the rings, giving the impression that it was sucking matter and light into it. He had seen this vision before, when he had been on the old presidential planet of Atlas. On that occasion, it was Atlas that had either been destroyed or had been transported to, only the giant cup knows, where.

"They are going to fold the citadel," Ay-ttho said, getting to her feet and leaving.

Nearby senators, overhearing Ay-ttho's words, panicked.

As Tori and Sevan followed Ay-ttho out of the auditorium, word was spreading rapidly throughout the auditorium about what was happening and the senators got up out of their seats.

Ay-ttho and the others ran through the corridors towards the hangar where they found the scouting vessel waiting where they had left it. Sevan's aunt stood at the top of the entrance ramp.

"Where have you been?" she complained. "Why did you leave me here all by myself?"

"Let's go inside," said Sevan. "We have to leave now."

"Why? We've only just left here. I want to look around."

"That's not possible, Aunty. They are folding space around us."

"What nonsense. Let me go."

Sevan's aunt struggled to make her was down the ramp past Sevan.

"Get her in here," Tori shouted back to them.

"Sorry about this, Aunty."

Sevan bent down, picked up his aunt, and threw her over his shoulder.

"What are you doing? Put me down, you little uxclod."

"I'm afraid I can't do that," said Sevan. "We have to leave now."

As he deposited her in the entrance corridor, the doors shut behind them. By the time Sevan reached the bridge, Ay-ttho was steering the vessel out of the hangar doors and into space. Through the observation windows, he could see the giant ring in the sky around which a giant cloud had formed.

There was a column of ships following them out of the citadel. Hundreds of ships racing to escape the expanding rings were not without danger, and several ships collided with each other, causing a trail of debris behind them.

Ay-ttho steered the vessel towards the nearest portal and increased the engines to full power. The expanding light curved and was now enveloping the citadel, but it was still expanding and perhaps soon it would envelop the scouting vessel, too.

As he had on his escape from Atlas, Sevan glanced backwards and forwards, trying to guess which would happen first, their arrival at the portal or being swallowed by the rings. The difference was too small and trying to work it out was hurting his marbles, so he gave up trying to guess and went back to his seat, resigned to accept whatever fate befell them, yet again.

Sevan no longer had to look behind to see the rings of light, they were almost alongside. He could see the portal getting bigger as they drew closer, but would they arrive in time?

The gravity manipulator was at full strength, but they were being held back by the pull of the folding space. Sevan felt they were losing the race and yet the portal was just up ahead, not much further, and they would be there.

Light faded, but Sevan knew it was not going away as the rings were passing light speed; the fold was almost complete.

Sevan fainted.

When Sevan opened his eyes, his vision was blurred and only slowly revealed his surroundings. He realised he was still on the bridge of the scouting vessel. He saw Ay-ttho and Tori. They had survived, but where were they? Another place in space? Another place in time? He looked out of the observation window and saw, stretching out behind them, a column of spacecraft and, behind them, the citadel.

He ran over to the window and looked ahead. The portal had gone.

"Where are we?" he asked.

"Who knows," said Ay-ttho.

"We have to go back to the citadel," said Tori.

"Why?" Sevan asked.

"The instruments on this vessel cannot tell us where we are. Maybe there is better technology there."

In order to return, they had to weave their way through the column of ships that had fled the citadel, some of which had collided with each other and had left a considerable amount of debris. Other ships were also attempting to return to the citadel, and it took some time to find a space to dock.

When they finally disembarked, the hangar was in chaos, with senators and their crews running in all directions.

Ay-ttho, Tori, and Sevan struggled through the crowds, trying to find the control centre. When they arrived, they found the entrance blocked by a crowd of senators and a line of guards, preventing anyone from entering the control room. They struggled to get to the front of the crowd.

"Let us in," Ay-ttho demanded when she reached the front.

"I'm sorry, my orders are to let no-one in," said the guard.

"We need to know where we are. If you let us in, my colleague Tori can use the instruments to tell us where we are."

"You are welcome to try," said a voice from behind the guard where the door was opening. "But I think you will get the same results as our best operatives who have been working on this very problem."

"And what do they say?"

"According to the readings, we are in no known part of the universe."

"What?"

"You and your colleague are welcome to try, but I doubt you will arrive at any other conclusion. Let them in."

The guards permitted Ay-ttho, Tori, and Sevan to pass into the huge control room. Tori went straight to the navigation equipment and, after several frantic moments, he sat back in his chair and sighed.

"Well?" asked Ay-ttho.

"According to all the charts," said Tori. "This place should not exist."

CHAPTER 32: WHAT NOW?

"What do you mean? Doesn't exist?" asked Ay-ttho.

"According to all the charts in the citadel's navigational system, we are not on any of them," said Tori

"So, where are we, then?"

"Somewhere else."

Ay-ttho sighed. It was not the news she had hoped for.

Sevan slumped into a vacant chair. He couldn't imagine what he would tell his aunt.

"What do you mean? Somewhere else?" she demanded when he eventually picked up the courage to tell her.

"That's what Tori said, Aunty. We are somewhere else."

"Well, this is a fine bunch of friends you've got, isn't it? You always found it difficult to find decent friends. Didn't I tell you they would wind up getting you into trouble one of these rotations? And there you are."

Sevan knew it was pointless pursuing any kind of counterargument. He simply helped himself to a piece of fruit from the fruit bowl.

"Who said you could have one of those?" his aunt snapped.

"Sorry," he said, placing the fruit back in the bowl, and then he realised there was a bowl of fruit on the ship. Sevan had never seen a bowl of fruit on a ship before.

"Where did they come from?" he asked.

"Probably from the hollow hogweed tree. That's where hollow hogweed fruit usually comes from."

"No, what I mean is, how did they get on the ship?"

"I imagine someone brought it on."

"Yes, but who?"

"I don't know, probably the nice people you stole the ship from."

"Republic scouts? Fruit?"

Sevan decided he should report his discovery to Ay-ttho.

"So, what?" she said.

"Why would Republic scouts eat fruit?"

"For the vitamins?"

"When have you ever seen fruit on a Republic vessel?"

"So, what's your point?"

"Why is there fruit on a Republic Scouting vessel?"

"Sevan, we have too much to worry about besides your fruit."

"But it's not my fruit. That's the point."

"Sevan, I'm busy."

Ay-ttho walked off. Sevan explored the ship to see whether it had more fruit.

He wandered around and found the stores that Ay-ttho had mentioned. There were many costumes and props and an impressive collection of weaponry, but no fruit.

Past the storeroom, all he found were the waste discharge units, so he doubled back.

On the way back, opposite the storeroom, he found another door he hadn't noticed before which led to a room filled with blocks which, on closer inspection, appeared to be carbon. It was then he realised that each block of carbon contained a creature or a thing. He decided to find Ay-ttho or Tori and headed back toward the bridge.

However, on the way, he passed through the common room and saw that, on a table, there sat a piece of fruit he was certain hadn't been there before.

He headed straight for the bridge, but before he got there, he met Ay-ttho and Sevan coming the other way.

"Stay here and make sure your aunt doesn't get into any trouble," she said as she passed.

"Where are you going?"

"There is a meeting in the citadel to decide what to do. We didn't think you would be interested."

They were right, but Sevan still felt it would have been nice to have been asked. He thought about going to his aunt's room again, but then thought better of it.

Instead, he sat in the common room and stared at the piece of fruit on the table as if he was willing it to speak and tell him the answer to all his questions.

He was still sat contemplating the fruit when Tori and Ay-ttho returned from the meeting.

"There are creatures imprisoned in blocks of carbon in the cargo bay," he blurted out in case he lost another opportunity to share his news.

"I know," said Ay-ttho.

"You know?"

"Yes, they are probably prisoners being transported somewhere."

"What are we going to do with them?"

"Nothing."

This reply did not satisfy Sevan.

"And look at all this fruit that's popping up all over the place. Where in the worst place is that all coming from?"

"Oh, sorry, that's me," said Tori, picking up the fruit and taking a bite out of it. "There was a trader in the citadel, so I got some."

The two major dilemmas in Sevan's life were now solved. He wasn't sure what to do with himself. His driving ambition to return to the Doomed Planet was no longer necessary, and he felt at a bit of a loss without a purpose.

"What happened at the meeting?" he asked.

"They think they might know where we are," said Ay-ttho.

"Oh yes? And where's that?"

"Near a system called Kale. They wanted volunteers to test their theory."

"How?"

"By going to Kale or ..."

"Or what?"

"Or falling off the edge of the universe."

"Ha ha, only a bunch of idiots would volunteer for that mission."

Ay-ttho and Tori were silent.

"We are that bunch of idiots aren't we?" Sevan realised.

"Get ready," said Ay-ttho. "We are going on a journey."

"What is at the edge of the universe?" Sevan asked Tori later when they were already underway.

"There is no edge to the universe," said Tori. "Space spreads out infinitely in all directions. Galaxies fill all the space through-out the entire infinite universe."

"But I've heard stories..."

"The Universe has an edge," Ay-ttho interrupted. "Not in space, but in time. We don't know whether the space folding has sent us to a different time and space. We could be 25 billion years in the past."

"What makes you say that?"

"The cosmic background is hotter. They are trying to calculate the period now."

"So you mean, not only are we in a different place, we are in a different time?"

"He's quick, isn't he?" Ay-ttho joked to Tori

"So, can we fall off the edge of the universe?"

"Well..."

"No," said Tori.

"I wouldn't be so sure," said Ay-ttho. "First, you are assuming the universe is infinite. What if it's not? What if, at the edge of the universe, we find another universe, a multiverse?"

"And if we don't?" then we cease to exist.

"It's academic," said Tori. "The universe is expanding too fast to reach the edge."

"In this ship, maybe," said Ay-ttho. "But what about the Mastery of the Stars' anti-matter drive?"

"We don't have the Mastery of the Stars."

"Which is why we need to find her."

"So, which way is Kale?"

"Hopefully it's this way," Ay-ttho programmed some coordinates into the navigation computer. "Either that or it's the edge of the universe."

"I thought you said this ship wasn't fast enough to reach the edge of the universe?"

"That's true."

"Is there a portal?"

"I don't know."

"How long is it going to take?"

"I don't know."

"So, why are we going?"

"Because they are paying us."

"But if we are 25 billion years in the past, there'll be nothing to spend it on."

"We'll just have to get back to the future, then."

"To Future?"

"No, to the future."

"Oh."

The conversation was clearly going nowhere, and Ay-ttho tried to ignore Sevan. The bridge was considerably smaller than the bridge on the Mastery of the Stars and Sevan felt uncomfortable, so he went to his own quarters.

There were four rooms on the vessel. His aunt had the nicest. It had probably been the captain's quarters. Ay-ttho and Tori had their own rooms, which had most likely been designed for officers, and Sevan had a bed in a bunk room, which was presumably where the rest of the crew had slept.

He didn't mind. There was plenty of space, and he was used to sleeping in a small bed. He missed the Mastery of the Stars, however. His room there had become a home from home and he felt violated every time someone had captured the Mastery of the Stars and he perceived that there had been other individuals snooping around his possessions. He owned nothing of value. It was just the thought that someone or something else had been touching his stuff.

Sevan wondered how long it was going to take to reach Kale and, assuming it was going to be a long time, lay down on his bed and closed his eyes.

CHAPTER 33: SENT TO KALE

Sevan opened his eyes. He didn't know how long he had slept for. At first, he wasn't really sure where he was, but he soon realised he was in the crew quarters of the Republic scout vessel that Ay-ttho had stolen on the Doomed Planet.

He wondered how far they had travelled and how much further they had to go before they arrived on Kale. According to the experts on the citadel, Kale was the nearest system to wherever the president's great space folding experiment had deposited them.

At least they had some idea of where they were in space, even if they weren't sure where they were in time. Although, of course, even Sevan knew that if they were at a different point in time, then Kale probably wouldn't be where they expected it to be.

He felt he should probably see how everyone was, especially his aunt, who would have a complaint or two. When he emerged from his room, he found Ay-ttho, Tori, and his aunt laughing and joking in the common room. The joviality ceased as soon as they saw Sevan.

"Are you okay?" asked Tori. "You've been asleep for a long time."

"What about Kale?" Sevan asked.

"What about it?"

"Are we getting closer?"

"Oh, we're definitely getting closer," said Ay-ttho.

"Any idea when we will arrive?"

"Your guess is as good as ours. We've turned on the proximity sensor alarms, so we should get a warning when we are approaching the system."

"What are we going to do on Kale?"

Ay-ttho considered the question beneath her, so Tori answered.

"We are going to confirm exactly when and where we are and see whether there is any way to get back to our own place and time."

As if on cue, the proximity alarm sounded.

"There you are," said Ay-ttho. "We are approaching Kale now. According to these charts, the only habitable planet in the Kale system is Chaldene."

"I thought they always named systems after their habitable planets," said Sevan.

"Usually, but not always," said Tori. "In this case, Kale is the star and Chaldene is the planet."

"How long will it take us to get to Chaldene?"

"Not long."

"Are you in a hurry?" asked Ay-ttho. "Is there somewhere you need to be?"

"No, but..."

Sevan bit his tongues but couldn't suppress his curiosity for long.

"What is on Chaldene?"

"We are about to find out," said Ay-ttho.

"I already have it within scanner range," said Tori. "There doesn't appear to be any sign of life. We may have had a wasted journey."

Sevan's hearts sank. He was going to be trapped in deep space with his aunt forever.

"No, wait. There is something there. Very feint. Must be a tiny community, perhaps even just one individual."

"What can one individual do?" Sevan complained

"You never know," said Ay-ttho. "It might be God."

"I thought you said the giant cup doesn't exist?"

"It doesn't. I never said God doesn't exist, though."

"Does it?"

"I don't know. Let's find out."

Ay-ttho steered the vessel towards the signal on Chaldene and they waited with expectation.

What they found was a relatively large complex, with hangars and buildings which had all manner of technology attached to the roofs.

They landed at the entrance to a hangar and waited for Tori to finish scanning the site for signs of life.

"The signal is coming from that building over there," he said, pointing to the largest block. "Looks like it's only one individual."

"Let's go out and have a look," said Ay-ttho, double checking the atmosphere was not harmful.

They descended from the vessel and began walking towards the building. They were about halfway between the two when a shot ricocheted off the ground beside them.

"Don't come any further," someone shouted from a window. "The Republic has no business here. Get back on your ship and leave."

"We are not Republic troops," Ay-ttho shouted back.

"You look like you are Republic troops."

"He used to be a Republic security clone, I'll give you that. But we are corporation clones. I stole this ship on The Doomed Planet."

"Uxclod! A Republic scouting vessel does not have the range to travel that far. You must have a battle cruiser nearby."

"We came from the citadel."

"More uxclod! The citadel is in orbit around Future, again, much too far for a Republic scouting vessel."

"The Republic has discovered how to fold space. They deposited the citadel relatively close to here."

There was a long silence.

"What do you think he's doing?" Sevan asked after a while.

"I think he's thinking," said Tori

"What are you doing?" Ay-ttho shouted.

"I'm thinking."

"What are you thinking about?"

"The Republic does not have the technology to fold space."

"It does now."

There followed another long silence.

"What do you want?" the individual asked at last.

"We want to find out how to get back to the Republic. We are not even sure what time this is."

"So you are from the Republic."

"Yes, we are from the Republic, but we are not from the Republic, if you know what I mean."

Another long pause.

"You may proceed, but leave any weapons you have on the ground beside you first."

Tori and Ay-ttho removed their hand held weapons and placed them on the ground. Sevan did not carry a weapon. He was always worried it might go off accidentally.

"What about your weapon?"

"I don't carry one," Sevan explained. "I'm always worried it might go off accidentally."

"Very well. You may proceed."

They trudged towards the building and when they reached the entrance, they saw a figure in the entrance, pointing a weapon at them. He had a bulbous head, a long beard, and wore a long cloak.

"What do you want?" he asked.

"We already told you," said Ay-ttho. "We are here because the Republic folded the surrounding space against our will. We want to get back to our own place and time. What time is this?"

"It's now."

"But it is always now."

"Exactly."

Ay-ttho sighed. This wasn't how she had hoped the exchange would develop.

"You had better come in."

They climbed the steps to a large reception hall.

"Who are you?" Tori asked.

"Some call me the Hermit of Chaldene, others that knew me a long time ago called me Witt. You may call me what you wish. It doesn't really matter. Follow me."

Witt led them through the vast entrance hall to a side room littered with equipment in various states of disrepair. In the middle sat an assortment of chairs. Witt invited them to sit down.

"What is this place?" Ay-ttho asked.

"It's an old corporation research station. I and my team were researching the multiverse but after the incident they closed the station."

"The incident?"

"I lost the rest of my team while conducting an experiment at the edge of the universe."

"So, the universe has an edge?"

"Of course it does."

"So we could have fallen off the edge of the universe?" asked Sevan.

"Don't be silly. The universe is expanding at speeds way faster than the potential of that little scouting vessel of yours. You would need an anti-matter drive in something the size of a freighter to catch the edge of the universe."

Tori, Ay-ttho and Sevan all glanced at each other.

"Doesn't the Mastery of the Stars have an anti-matter drive?" said Sevan.

Tori and Ay-ttho gave him a hard stare.

"You have an anti-matter drive?" asked Witt with sudden excitement.

"We had," Ay-ttho corrected. "That is why we are trying to get back to the Republic. To find it."

"Well, why didn't you say that in the first place?"

"You can help us get back?"

"Of course I can. Folding space is easy. All you need is an enormous source of energy and we have an enormous source of energy right there."

He pointed outside at the star of Kale, which was sending beams of dusty light through the dirty windows.

"We'll need to make some modifications to that vessel of yours, but it shouldn't be too difficult."

Witt rested back in his chair.

"I will do it on one condition."

"What's that?" asked Ay-ttho.

"That after you find your ship, we use it to recover my colleagues."

"Where are your colleagues?"

"That's not important."

"It might be."

"It's not."

Ay-ttho thought about it for a moment. She looked at Tori, who shrugged. Then she looked at Sevan, who was looking at her in expectation.

"Okay, we'll do it," she said.

"Excellent," said Witt, who leapt to his feet. "We must start straight away. Come with me I'll…"

Witt could not finish his sentence because of an ear-splitting shrieking noise which was being emitted from a control panel in the room's corner.

Witt took a small device from his pocket and pressed a button. The shrieking stopped with a beep.

"What in the worst place was that?" Ay-ttho asked.

"It was the perimeter alarm. Is there someone else on your ship?"

"Aunty!" Sevan exclaimed.

Witt was already halfway to the door with his weapon in hand.

"She's harmless," Sevan shouted after him.

By the time Sevan, Tori and Ay-ttho reached the hallway, Witt was already coming back inside.

"I thought you said she was harmless," he complained.

Not far behind him was the diminutive figure of Sevan's aunt, who was marching towards them. She was clearly annoyed and Sevan braced himself for the impending onslaught.

"What are you doing abandoning me?" she launched into a tirade. "What if I had been eaten by tronqaks? You have no sense of responsibility. That's your trouble."

"I don't think there are troqaks here," Sevan tried to defend himself. "There aren't, are there?"

"There are actually," said Witt. "They brought them here to hunt the cukids, which were out of control. They brought the cukids here as a food source for the staff on the base but, with no natural predator, they ran amok."

"Good to see you, Sevan's aunt," said Ay-ttho, who still hadn't bothered to learn her name. "You were resting, so we thought it best not to wake you from your beauty sleep."

"Is that meant to be funny?" she snapped. "What are we doing here, anyway?"

"This is Witt. He is going to help us get back to the Republic."

"Why would we want to do that? You should see the mess they made on The Doomed Planet."

"I did. I was there, remember? Witt is going to help us get our ship back, the Mastery of the Stars. You will like it. It's much more comfortable than the scouting vessel."

"That's easy."

"So, what do we have to do?" Ay-ttho asked Witt.

"First, we have to equip your ship with extra heat shields."

"Heat shields? Why? We didn't detect much heat on any of the occasions we've witnessed folding space."

"How many have you witnessed?"

"There was the time that Barnes destroyed Atlas, then the Republic experimented on us and then the citadel was transported here, so, three. But on none of those occasions, did we need extra heat shields?"

"You will now."

"Why?"

"See that star?"

"Yes?"

"We'll fly into it."

CHAPTER 34: SUDDEN DESTRUCTION

"What? Have you lost your marbles?" Ay-ttho was astonished. "You mean it, don't you?"

"With any luck, you won't actually fly into the star," said Witt. "The energy exchangers should hopefully have harvested enough energy by then to fold space."

"And if they haven't?"

"Then you will fly into the star."

"And die?"

"Obviously."

"Ay-ttho? How much do we really need the Mastery of the Stars? I mean, this scouting vessel isn't too bad, and this planet seems okay. We've been to much worse places."

Ay-ttho observed Sevan, but she was deep in her own thoughts.

"Oh, no, you must go," said Witt. "And I will come with you. That's how much faith I have in this technology."

Ay-ttho looked at him for a long time and then sighed.

"We'll think about it," she said at last. "But, so as not to lose time while we consider your proposals, what preparations do we need to make?"

"No, you must decide now," Witt protested.

"Those are our terms. Take them or leave them."

"Oh, and we have to go to the Citadel first and rescue the others," Sevan added.

"There are others?"

"Yes, but there's no need to worry about them," said Ay-ttho.

"You're just going to leave them?" asked Sevan.

"Of course. Sevan, the senators in that Citadel, are the worst scum in the Republic. You've been a Senator. You know what they're like."

"But what about all the support staff that work in the citadel?"

"That's their problem."

"But that's not ethical."

"Sevan, I'm getting the Mastery of the Stars back. Besides, they won't fit in the scouting vessel."

"But there are bigger ships in the citadel."

"But we are modifying the scouting vessel."

"We could modify one of their ships," Witt suggested.

"For the last time," Ay-ttho shouted. "I am not taking any senators. We can report where they are when we reach the Republic.

It was Witt's turn to stare at Ay-ttho and he could tell from her expression that she was in no mood to negotiate.

"Alright, I'll show you what we need to do. But we will need to travel to another station which is set in the middle of that mountain range over there. There is nowhere to land your ship, so we will have to go by foot."

"Can't we use a winch?"

"Unfortunately, no, the winds are too strong up there. It's not safe to lower anyone, and the equipment would get damaged if we tried to winch it out."

"Are we going to carry it out?"

"We don't need to. Follow me. I have some trolleys fitted with gravity manipulators we can use. I use them for moving heavy objects."

Witt led them to a large shed near the hangar, which was piled high with equipment of all shapes and sizes. Littered around the space were several trolleys, some empty but others loaded with equipment. Ay-ttho, Tori and Sevan set about moving the equipment while Witt moved them out of the shed using a remote device. Sevan's aunt watched and supervised by offering the occasional critical comment.

"I don't think we should fly into any stars," Sevan confided to Tori as they began transporting the trolleys towards the mountains.

They perched his aunt on top of a trolley in a comfortable chair, having refused to stay on the ship in case tronqaks ate her.

The journey wound over the plain and into the foothills before they reached rocky cliffs which towered above them on either side of the trail.

"What a place to build a base," Tori muttered to himself.

"The base was hidden," said Witt. "Our research facility was a decoy, so they wouldn't search for the real base. We stored most of the useful equipment here."

"It doesn't seem very windy," said Ay-ttho.

"No, the gorges sheltered us, but if you tried to climb on top of the cliffs, you would surely be swept to your death."

"Wouldn't we be better off just staying here?" Sevan whispered to Tori.

Tori ignored Sevan. He knew there was little point in engaging in a debate in the presence of Witt. Much better to wait until they were alone with Ay-ttho.

Tori wasn't convinced that staying was a good idea, either. He didn't relish the thought of spending the rest of his days on Chaldene with Witt.

They loaded the trolleys with equipment as directed by Witt and set off back to the research facility to begin work on the scouting vessel.

They slept and ate on the vessel and Witt replenished their stocks from the vast basement underneath the facility.

"I just don't understand why Barnes or Hours or anyone else would be bothered about you," Witt said during one meal after Sevan and the others had recounted virtually their entire life stories

Sevan wasn't sure whether to feel insulted or flattered.

"That's what puzzles me too," Ay-ttho agreed. "Why bother to put us through all these trials? If they really wanted to execute us, they could have done it a long time ago."

"Unless they are just incompetent," said Witt.

They worked long and hard to make the scouting vessel ready for the journey that Sevan wasn't sure they should take and, despite his constant reminders, no discussion had taken place between them about whether they would actually go.

The closer the vessel reached to completion, the more confident Witt became they had accepted his plan. Every so often, Ay-ttho would make a comment that left him in no doubt that she considered the matter to be unresolved.

"These supplies will make the journey so comfortable," he might enthuse.

"That's if we go," she would remind him.

Then, one night, when the ship had virtually reached completion, a series of enormous explosions woke Sevan.

He rushed to the bridge, where he found Tori staring through the observation window at the research facility, which was engulfed in flames.

"Witt!" Sevan exclaimed.

"What's all this fuss?" said his aunt, entering the bridge. "Oh, my."

Tori and Sevan rushed out to see whether there was anything they could do, but the heat from the conflagration was so great, they couldn't get anywhere near the building.

The three of them sat on the steps of the scouting vessel and watched the flames. Eventually, Ay-ttho joined them.

"What happened?" she asked.

"No idea," said Tori. "There were some explosions and then...this."

"Witt?"

Tori shrugged.

Ay-ttho sat down with them.

The flames had died down substantially, but there was still a considerable amount of the building on fire when Witt approached them.

"Witt! You're alive!" Sevan exclaimed. "Thank the Giant Cup."

"What happened?" asked Ay-ttho.

Witt shrugged, sitting down beside them.

"I couldn't sleep, so I went for a walk. There were some explosions, and I returned to find this."

"But what caused it?" Sevan asked.

"Your guess is as good as mine. There wasn't anything in the research facility that would cause explosions of that magnitude. My guess is that someone started the explosions deliberately."

"But who would want to destroy the research facility?" asked Tori. "It's in the middle of nowhere."

"There are lots of individuals opposed to the facility. Our research into the multiverse was very controversial, which is why they shut us down. If someone discovered that I had stayed here to continue the work, they might have wanted to do something about it, I suppose."

"But who?"

"The Republic for one. They rely on their citizens having no alternative. If they found out that in another universe did things differently, they might want to change things here."

"And are they?"

"What?"

"Done differently in another universe?"

"I've no idea. I haven't been able to contact my colleagues who crossed over."

"They might be dead."

"They might be, but my instruments have detected signs of tachyon transmissions, so I think they are still alive."

"Or whatever ate them is playing with their transmitter," said Sevan. They ignored him.

"Now what?" asked Tori.

"We can't stay here," said Witt. "All my supplies have been destroyed and I'm not very good at hunting tronqaks. Our only option is to fold space."

"Is the ship ready?"

"Not quite, but I have enough equipment here to finish the work."

"Can't we just return using the ship's gravity manipulators?" asked Sevan

"We could, but by the time we arrived, I would have certainly died of old age. If we arrived at all, we would undoubtedly run out of fuel first."

"So, how did you get here?"

"By folding space."

"Of course," said Ay-ttho. "I guess there's nothing for it then. We have to fly into the star. Whoever destroyed the facility could still be here. We should be careful."

It took several rotations to finish the work, by which time the supplies they had stored on the scouting vessel were running low. It had limited storage compared to the Mastery of the Stars and was not designed for long journeys with large crews.

Finally, they were ready to leave. They took one last look at the smouldering remains and assumed that whoever was interested in destroying the facility had no desire to kill them, otherwise they would have been dead by now.

"All ready?" Witt asked.

"The important question is, are you ready?" asked Ay-ttho

"As ready as I'll ever be."

"Then let's go."

The heavily modified scouting vessel took off into the atmosphere. Extra heat shields meant that they no longer had a view through the observation window and had to rely on monitors for a view of the space which surrounded them.

A view of their destination, the star, Kale, soon filled the empty screen.

"Let's go," said Ay-ttho.

The ship shuddered as the gravity manipulators reached full power and the vessel hurtled towards the burning ball of flame.

Witt was busy scrutinising a panel of instruments he had installed on the bridge.

"Now we are out of the atmosphere, we can harvest much more energy," he said.

"How much energy will we consume?" asked Sevan

"Technically, you consume no energy when you bend spacetime. All matter bends the surrounding spacetime without cost. So if you already have enough matter in place to bend spacetime sufficiently to cause your one unit object to move one unit, then the cost is zero."

Sevan didn't really understand what he was talking about.

"Then why do we need to fly into this star?"

"All we need is an initial investment in work. The only way we can bend spacetime is by introducing a second massive object, so we just need to compensate for the energy wasted on gravitational waves."

"Hence the gravity manipulators."

"Exactly."

Sevan was pleased that he sounded like he knew what he was talking about, but really, he was none the wiser.

"Gravity is the word we used to describe curved space," Witt continued, perceiving Sevan's confusion. "Don't think of curved space as simply 'no longer flat', also consider that it includes a gravitational gradient that will cause matter to move across that gradient. As an example, the planet of Chaldene bends the surrounding space, with a vertical gravitational gradient, causing the surrounding things to speed up towards it."

Sevan looked no more enlightened.

"When we talk about the consumption of energy," Witt persisted. "We really mean transfer of energy from one state or form to another, because energy can't be destroyed. We only need the amount of energy to move this ship. How fast we want it to accelerate dictates the amount of energy.

According to the Jean equation, we probably use the same amount of energy moving from one place to another that we would use travelling there conventionally, but it takes a lot less time."

Witt could see his explanation was having little effect on Sevan's understanding, so he went back to staring at his instruments.

"This is it!" he announced dramatically. "Brace yourselves. We are about to fold spacetime."

On the monitors, Sevan could see the star getting closer. He could feel the bridge getting hotter

"Why isn't anything happening?" he asked.

"Any unit now," said Witt.

A couple of units passed and still nothing happened. Sevan felt himself perspiring.

The sound of the gravity manipulators straining on full power was almost unbearable, and then it happened. A pin prick on the monitor at first and then the familiar image Sevan had seen on the other occasions space had folded around him. The pin prick grew, swallowing the star ahead of them, the light distorted all around. The view ahead was no longer of the star but of another place in space and possibly in time. Soon the light surrounded them and then faded as they passed the speed of light. A moment later, they were in empty space.

CHAPTER 35: THE CAMP AT MOONCIRCLE LAKE

"Where are we?" asked Ay-ttho.

"And when are we?" asked Witt.

"It looks like we are somewhere in the Future system," said Tori.

"Good," said Witt. "It looks like, as I had hoped, we have reversed the same fold made by the Republic. They stretched tight the fabric of spacetime and it's possible that, as it folded, it left a kind of cosmic crease."

"They were a band on the Doomed Planet," said Sevan. "The Cosmic Creases."

"So, where is this freighter of yours?" asked Witt.

"Good question," said Ay-ttho. "We have some friends we need to collect too."

"There wasn't any talk of friends."

"It's something we have to do."

"Where are they?"

"I suspect they are on Future."

"But we can't just land on Future in this vessel. We will be arrested straight away."

"Exactly. We just need to get close enough to establish a strong tachyon transmission. Future has a moon. We can land there while I contact some friends on Future."

Tori navigated the vessel into the shadow of the moon to avoid detection by Republic scanners. And landed by the side of Mooncircle Lake. Rather than being an actual body of water, Mooncircle Lake was an enormous crater, which had been given, like many other craters on the satellite, an aquatic name. There was some water on the moon left over from its collision with Future aeons before, but this was trapped in tiny beads of volcanically cooked glass and not good for drinking.

Witt had filled the ship with many gadgets from the research facility, which perhaps accounted for his not being particularly upset when it burned to the ground. Sevan imagined he had already filled the scouting vessel with everything of use in the research facility.

"So, what do we do first?" asked Tori. "Find Nadio and Effeeko, or the Mastery of the Stars?"

"Good question," said Ay-ttho. "We are fairly sure that Effeeko and Nadio are here. We don't know where the Mastery of the Stars is, so I suggest we find our friends first. In getting them, we might find information which might lead us to our ship."

Ay-ttho went to the communications terminal and began preparing transmissions. Sevan contented himself with watching Witt work.

"Your aunt's strange, isn't she?" he said.

"Well, what's normal?" Sevan asked

"True, but there is something about your aunt I just can't place my staff on."

"Do you really think there is a multiverse?"

"I don't think, Sevan, I know there is. My colleagues are there and what you are searching for might be there too."

"I'm not searching for anything."

"Aren't you?"

Sevan didn't know what Witt was talking about, so did what he usually did in these situations, which was to remain silent.

"I got in touch with D'Heli and Alyr," said Ay-ttho.

"D'Heli and Alyr?" asked Sevan. "Those names sound familiar."

"I'm not surprised. They led you to Pelou on your first visit to Future. They are part of a resistance network. I kept in touch with them after Pelou and Daxu defected to Barnes."

"Defected is a little strong, isn't it?"

"Is it? Anyway, they are going to bring a shuttle here and smuggle us onto Future."

"All of us?"

"Why not? There are only four of us. We'll need everyone if Nadio and Effeeko are in a poor state."

Sevan didn't want to think about it.

"Have any of you heard of a walking phantom?" asked Witt.

"The only time I heard that phrase was from the looters on Daphnis. They used it to refer to Barnes. Why?"

"I've been scanning Tachyon transmissions for mentions of the Mastery of the Stars," he said. "Something came up in the Nereid system. Apparently, a walking phantom has it."

"I'm glad all this equipment has some use," said Tori.

"Why would Barnes have the Mastery of the Stars?" asked Sevan

"It was a corporation freighter," said Ay-ttho. "Maybe the Republic just returned it."

"Does he know it has an anti-matter drive?" asked Witt.

"Barnes knows everything," said Tori. "Or seems to."

"Then it's possible the corporation's research is advanced as mine. You said that Barnes is already folding space?"

"Yes, before the Republic."

"Then it's possible he is already aware of the multiverse and that he needs an anti-matter drive to reach it. What's wrong Ay-ttho?"

Ay-ttho appeared to have drifted off into some kind of trance. She snapped out of it

"Yes, sorry. I was just remembering something Brabin said."

"What did he say?"

"It wasn't so much what he said as what he did."

"What did he do?"

"Nevermind. It's not important now. Let's get ready. D'Heli and Alyr will be here soon. But you should know that the Republic has anti-matter. Brabin was storing it for them."

"Then there is no time to waste. The Republic is probably already building their own ship to reach the multiverse."

"How is it possible?" asked Tori.

"First, you must fold space and time to get as close to the edge of the universe as possible. It's easier to do this by going back in time when the universe was smaller. Then you simply have to travel faster than the universe is expanding to break through to the next universe."

"And this is what your colleagues did?"

"Exactly."

"And how do you get back?"

"Again, you simply travel faster than the expansion of that universe and break back through."

"And what if that universe is expanding faster than the maximum speed of your ship?"

"Then you have problems."

"What did Brabin do?" Tori asked Ay-ttho when they were away from Witt.

"You remember, he gave us the anti-matter cylinders on Lenguicarro?"

"Yes?"

"When he gave them to me, he said it was the work of Cronos. He told me to use the anti-matter to do excellent work and leave me criminal past behind."

"You don't believe in Chronos."

"What do you mean? We know Chronos and the other Star Masters exist."

"What I mean is that you don't follow his cult. Why would you worry about the words of a Saturnian high priest?"

"Because maybe this isn't a coincidence. Maybe we should go to the multiverse."

"You're serious, aren't you?"

"I'm not sure what I think at the moment. Let's find Nadio and Effeeko and then go to Nereid and get the ship."

"What is this?" Ay-ttho asked when D'Heli and Alyr arrived in the smallest shuttle she had ever seen.

"Nice to see you too," said D'Heli. "We had to pretend we were amateur geologists coming to collect samples from Mooncircle Lake. The rocks are our alibi for the additional weight when we return."

"Smart thinking. Let's get loaded up, shall we?"

They loaded a substantial quantity of weapons and then tried to explain to Sevan's aunt what was happening before boarding the shuttle.

"Sounds like a silly idea to me," she said. "And what happens to me when you lot get yourselves killed?"

Sevan tried to assure her that wasn't going to happen, but it was difficult because he wasn't sure himself.

"What's the plan, then?" asked Tori after they finally boarded the shuttle.

"D'Heli and Alyr are going to take us close to the presidential palace where we will pretend we are tourists," said Ay-ttho.

"I've got a terrible feeling of déjà vu," said Sevan.

"We will use our knowledge of the palace to sneak in and find the detention centre."

"And if they aren't there?"

"Then we will persuade a detention officer to access the system and find out where they are."

"How about your communicator?"

"I've already tried it. There is no sign of the Mastery of the Stars here. I guess it probably is on Daphnis or somewhere in the Nereid system."

"What in the worst place is that?" Tori yelled. "Something ran over my feet."

"Relax," said Alyr. "That's only Shots, our pet cukid."

"You have a pet cukid? Isn't that unsanitary?"

"She's very well trained."

"Even só, doesn't she chew the wires?"

"Occasionally, but we tell her not to."

"I'm sure that helps."

"We are ready to leave," said D'Heli, closing the doors. "Next stop Future."

D'Heli landed the craft in one of the tourist hangars near the presidential palace. The border patrol seemed satisfied with their excuse for the additional weight and, although the tourist hangars were more expensive, it helped with their cover.

Ay-ttho, Tori, Sevan and Witt descended from the shuttle, leaving D'Heli and Alyr inside to look after it and the cukid which they had to hold to prevent it from escaping through the opening doors.

"Naughty, Fulanu," said Alyr.

"Your cukid is called Fulanu?"

"Yes. We have two more at home called Beltrano and Ciclano."

"Don't they fight?"

"Sometimes. But mainly the play eat and sleep."

"And evacuate their waste produce orifices," added D'Heli.

"Yes, but they are trained to go in their waste produce container."

"You have a cukid waste product container in your home?" asked Ay-ttho with disgust

"Yes, but we clean it regularly."

Ay-ttho shook her head as she finished concealing weapons about her person before descending from the shuttle. Tori, Sevan and Witt, with similarly ensconced weapons, followed her.

Being very familiar with the layout of the palace, it was very easy for them to find a poorly guarded side door and make their way through the labyrinth of corridors to the detention centre far below the presidential apartments.

They avoided contact with guards or staff until they were close to the detention centre entrance, where the security was, unsurprisingly, more strict.

As en ex-Republic security clone, Tori drew his weapon and pointed it at Ay-ttho, Sevan and Witt to pretend he had arrested them and was bringing them into custody.

"Three to check in," he said as they approached the detention centre reception.

"If not been told of any to check in," said the guard.

"Why doesn't that surprise me," said Tori. "Those uxclods upstairs would forget their own antennae if they weren't attached."

The guard chuckled in agreement.

"Do me a favour," said Tori. "I'm up to my antennae in transfers. Let me take these three through, and I'll make sure personally that the codes are sent to you before the end of the rotation."

"I'm afraid that's more than my job's worth. You are welcome to wait here with them until the codes come through."

"I can't do that. I've got a collection from Aitne. If I don't leave now, I won't make it and you know what that bunch on Aitne are like if you're even a unit late."

The guard chortled again. He clearly knew what Tori was talking about.

"I sympathise," he said. "I really do, but they're really tightening up on protocols here since Hours took charge. What have they done, anyway?"

"You don't recognise them? These two are Ay-ttho and Sevan, who collaborated with the traitor, Scotmax. And this is professor Witt, the leading scientist in the world of space folding and multiverses."

"Don't let Dr Nix hear you say that," said the guard, glancing nervously at a security camera.

"You have two other traitors, don't you?" asked Ay-ttho. "Nadio and Effeeko?"

"We did. They've been transferred out of here."

"Where to?"

"You know I'm not allowed to share classified information."

The guard stared at Tori. Tori stared back at the guard. Then the guard burst out laughing and so Tori joined in.

"They've been taken to the Nereid system."

"Nereid?"

"I know, unconventional."

"You know, I've just realised there's something I need to do. I'll take these prisoners and be out of your way."

"Are you sure? I doubt those codes will take long to arrive."

"No, it's fine. I'll come back later."

"Okay, suit yourself."

"Thank you, bye."

Tori led the others back out into the corridor.

"Well, that settles it then," said Ay-ttho. "We are going to Nereid."

CHAPTER 36: A WALKING PHANTOM

The group rushed back to the shuttle and then back to Mooncircle Lake, where Sevan's aunt was demanding to know what had taken them so long.

"Where are we going now?" she asked, seeing them hastily preparing the scouting vessel for launch.

"Nereid," Sevan answered.

"Nereid? Where in the worst place is that?"

"It's where the Doomed Planet is."

"You're taking me back to that uxclod hole."

"Not exactly."

"Then what are you doing?"

"We think that both our friends and our ship are on Daphnis."

"But Daphnis isn't near the Doomed Planet."

"It is now."

"Sometimes you make no sense, Sevan. I'm going for a quick nap. When I come back, I expect you to be making sense. Is that understood?"

"Yes, aunty."

While Sevan's aunty retired to the best quarters on the ship, everyone else said goodbye to D'Heli and Alyr, thanked them for their help and, on their insistence, also said goodbye to Fulanu, the cukid, who appeared oblivious to them.

Moments later, they were on their way. Now that the Atlas portal had been destroyed, the journey to Nereid was not as straightforward, but they went via the Aitne system, despite the horrible memories it held for everyone except Witt, who was completely immersed in the study of his instruments.

Passing through the old Daphnis system with no Daphnis was strange for Sevan, but he knew they were only one jump from Nereid where Barnes had moved the planet.

Nereid was a system of mixed emotions for Sevan. It was there that he had made friends with Ozli, but that also reminded him that Ozli had died. It was also the new location of his home planet, the Doomed Planet, but that also increasingly held less significance for him. His life continued to draw him away from his past to a new life to which he had already become accustomed. The presence of his aunt had removed the overwhelming desire to return, and he now felt at a loss as to what he should be doing. He felt he was simply a passenger in life and was becoming less and less satisfied with it.

As they approached Nereid, the first thing that came into view was the vast sphere which contained the Doomed Planet, Daphnis, and their moons. They approached the sphere with trepidation, hoping that they would not become a victim of its in-built defences.

If rumours were true, then the mining concessions on the planets had been requisitioned by the Republic, so a Republic scouting vessel should have no problem passing the security checks. The only problem was that the scouting vessel they were flying was stolen. Sure enough, no longer had they entered the sphere than they received a communication.

"Scout ship Sentinel. We list your status as stolen. Please proceed to the military hangar at the concession on The Doomed Planet."

"We are a Republic security detail returning the vessel, but we have a passenger to deliver to Daphnis first," Tori responded.

"Negative. You are to proceed to the military hangar on the concession on the Doomed Planet."

"We can't do that. We have a delivery to make on Daphnis first."

"Negative. You are to proceed to the military hangar on the concession on the Doomed Planet. Failure to comply will result in punitive measures."

"What do they mean by punitive measures?" asked Sevan.

"Probably missiles," said Ay-ttho, who continued to steer the ship towards Daphnis.

"You have failed to comply with our instructions," continued the communication. "Therefore, you will be escorted."

"Two fighters have launched from the Doomed Planet," said Tori

"We'll be on Daphnis before they reach us," said Ay-ttho. "We will hide in the spacecraft graveyard where the looters live."

"How are we going to communicate with the looters?" asked Sevan. "We relied on what's his face last time."

"I assume you mean the professor. And the answer is, I don't know. We'll find a way."

"You know the professor?" asked Witt.

"Knew. He was killed."

"My goodness, what a tragedy! He was such a clever linguist."

"You knew him?"

"Of course. We worked together in his camp on Daphnis on a prototype vibration communicator. I think I've got it here somewhere."

"Are you serious? Are we talking about the same professor?"

"Of course, 'I had a name but I don't wish to use it anymore,'" Witt said, mimicking the voice of the professor.

"That's the guy," said Ay-ttho. "Did you know him? He said the corporation gave him his name."

"Yes, that much I don't know very much about. He never wanted to talk about it. But I learned a lot about his work and I'm sure I have that prototype. Wait a unit, I'll be back in a..."

Witt wandered off, looking for the prototype in one of the many boxes that were stacked along the corridors of the ship.

"They are gaining on us," said Tori.

"Don't worry," said Ay-ttho.

The scouting vessel was already descending into the Daphnisian atmosphere. As they descended through the atmosphere, Sevan glimpsed the surface of the planet. It was as desolate as he remembered. Soon they were flying over the desert, littered with the broken hulls of freighters, shuttles, frigates, and many other ships.

Ay-ttho brought the scouting vessel down in between the wrecks and shut off the power. Before long, the Republic fighters had entered the atmosphere and we're scouring the wrecks for signs of life. Occasionally, they would fire a bolt into a pile of debris, no doubt triggered by pillagers.

Within the scouting vessel, they could hear the Republic fighters drawing closer and then the first laser bolt struck the hull. The ship shook and loose machinery fell from their mountings.

"Without power, we have no shields," said Ay-ttho. "We are sitting cukids."

Ay-ttho went to reboot the power, but nothing happened.

"They've disabled our power," she said. "Lucky uxclods. We'll have to evacuate."

Ay-ttho opened the doors, and they fled into a nearby wreck. Laser bolts rained down all around them.

"My instruments," Witt panicked, but Tori held him to prevent him from re-entering the ship.

The Republic fighters landed on the outskirts of the scrapyard.

"Get ready," said Ay-ttho, unholstering her weapon.

Through the gaps in the wrecks, they could see the Republic troopers descending from their vessels.

"There are a lot of them," said Ay-ttho.

The ground vibrated, much to the consternation of the Republic troopers who soon found themselves surrounded by a hoard of green eight-legged creatures with tails that held an assortment of weapons looted from Corporation and Republic ships.

"Looters!" said Ay-ttho.

Within moments, the looters had made quick work of the troopers and inspected the fighters.

Witt rushed back into the scouting vessel to inspect his instruments. Meanwhile, the looters, losing interest in the fighters, advanced on Ay-ttho and the rest of the group

The ground vibrated with the thunderous chatter of the drum tissue stretched over their thoraxes.

Witt returned with a device very similar in construction to the device the professor had used to communicate with the looters during their last visit.

"They say they remember the last time you came," said Witt.

"Tell them we heard rumours of a walking phantom and we wanted to know whether it was the same walking phantom they saw the last time we came."

The machine vibrated, and the looters vibrated in response.

"They say they haven't seen walking dead, but they have seen bombers and they saw the boats you used last time. Remember, this was only a prototype translator."

"They must be talking about the Mastery of the Stars," said Ay-ttho. "Ask them where they saw it?"

Witt transmitted the question, then translated the answer.

"They say it landed on concessions, whatever that means."

"It landed in the concession. Well, we have to get it then. Ask them if they have heard of any prisoners called Nadio or Effeeko."

Witt translated again.

"They say they never heard of anyone with this name, but prisoner transports came and went in and out of the concessions."

"Thank them for their help. We must go to the concession then."

"They say you're welcome. But we can't go in the scouting vessel. It has no power."

"We'll have to take a fighter then. Please ask the looters if they are okay with that."

"Yes, they are okay with that," said Witt, once he had translated their answer. "Alright, let me get my instruments."

"No time. You'll have to leave them here."

"What? I can't."

"Ask the looters to look after them."

Witt sent the message, translated the reply and then look puzzled.

"What's wrong?" asked Ay-ttho, impatient to get moving.

"They just said 'of course we'. They didn't say will or won't."

Witt tried again and then looked more satisfied.

"They said they are happy," he said.

Unfortunately, Witt had told the looters there were some tools on the ship and would they like to look at them? Rather than keep an eye on his equipment, the looters understood they had invited them to play with it.

Satisfied they had understood him, Witt went with the others, but as they were boarding, the looters tried to communicate something.

"They are asking if we are going to get a Republic soldier."

"Tell them we are going to rescue our ship and our friends."

A moment's translation later.

"They are asking if we want to torture the soldiers."

"Tell them no thank you, we are just going to get our friends."

"Now there are asking if we want to be friends with a soldier."

"Witt? Are you sure your translation box works properly?"

"I think they agree," said Witt. "Let's go."

They boarded the Republic fighter and headed toward the concession. The city was still on the horizon when the communications panel buzzed into life with a message.

"XR 220? What is your destination?"

"We request permission to land at the concession."

"Please state your authorisation number."

"An engagement with a stolen scouting vessel damaged our information. We seek landing permission for urgent repairs."

"One moment."

The group exchanged glances while they waited for a reply.

"Permission granted. Land at the maintenance hangar in sector B."

"Our navigation is down," said Ay-ttho. "Handing over remote access."

"What?" said Tori. "Have you lost your Marbles?"

"I don't know the way to the maintenance hangar in sector B."

"We don't want to be in any hangar, surrounded by Republic troops. Set her down in the street."

"Good point."

"XR 220, awaiting permission for remote control."

"Negative, negative. Instruments were damaged. Making emergency landing."

Ay-ttho found a quiet street near the perimeter wall and touched down.

"Quick, let's run for it," she said, opening the doors.

Sevan followed them out into the dusty streets of the Daphnis concession.

"Now we are in the qindrul's belly," he said.

CHAPTER 37: THE ENEMY REVEALED

"What's a Qindrul?" asked Witt.

"It's folklore from the Doomed Planet," Ay-ttho explained. "Keane was a star traveller considered so unlucky that his fellow travellers threw him off their ship where he was swallowed by the mythical qindrul beast that was attacking them. The clones on the Doomed Planet use the phrase 'in the belly of the qindrul' to explain when they are really in trouble."

"I see, a bit like: in the khaurkrin's nest."

"Exactly."

Ay-ttho led them through some side streets. They could hear Republic soldiers heading towards the fighter along the primary thoroughfare.

"So, where should we look for Nadio and Effeeko?" asked Tori

"I guess they'll be in the detention centre," said Ay-ttho. "If we'd landed in a hangar, we might have found the Mastery of the Stars and used it to blow the side off the detention centre."

"Why didn't you use the fighter to blow the side off the detention centre?"

"It's too late to come up with these ideas now."

"Where is the detention centre?"

"Good question."

Ay-ttho picked up a rock and threw it through the window of a nearby establishment. Alarms immediately sounded.

"What the fushy are you doing?" asked Tori.

"Getting arrested," said Ay-ttho. "Then they'll take us to the detention centre."

"I won't be arrested."

"Fine, take my weapons, you lot hide and then follow where they take me."

"You have lost your Marbles."

Tori took the weapons and then ran after Sevan and Witt, who had already found a hiding place.

They heard the Republic troops arrive and Ay-ttho surrender without a fight. Then, as they led Ay-ttho away, Tori, Sevan and Witt followed at a discreet distance.

All was going fine until the end of the street when the troopers loaded Ay-ttho into a transporter and sped off into the traffic.

Tori flagged down a hover cab, and they all jumped in.

"Follow that transporter," said Tori, pointing to the fast disappearing vehicle.

"Have you lost your Marbles?" asked the hover cab driver. "You aren't on your entertainment implant bow, you know."

"I'll make it work your while."

The driver thought about it for a moment.

"How much worth my while?"

Tori offered a handful of credits. The driver took them and floored the throttle, sending Tori, Sevan and Witt to the back of the cab with the force of the acceleration.

"Quite a gravity manipulator you have on this thing," Tori commented, seeing the transporter coming back within view.

"I made some modifications," the driver said proudly.

They followed the transporter until it disappeared into a walled compound.

"What is this place?" Tori asked as he paid the driver.

"You don't want to know."

"No, I do. I really want to know."

"No, you don't."

"Yes, I do. That's why I'm asking you."

"Oh, alright then. They call it the keep. It was the corporation's stronghold in the old days. Now the Republic uses it as their centre of operations."

"Do they keep prisoners there?"

"Oh, yes. Many go in but much fewer come out. At least not by their own means, if you know what I mean. I guess that's why they call it the keep, because they keep everything inside."

"Yes, thank you. Any ideas how to get in?"

The driver laughed.

"You don't want to go in there."

"Yes, I do."

"No, you don't."

"I do. My friend is in there."

"Oh dear, I am sorry."

"So, have you any idea how to get in?"

"No, sorry. Commit a crime maybe?"

"Thank you," Tori said without feeling as he watched the hover car drive away.

The wall was large, certainly too large to scale.

"Any ideas?" he asked Witt and Sevan.

Sevan looked blank. Witt was contemplative.

"We could commit a crime," said Sevan.

"Thank you. Witt, do you have any ideas that doesn't involve committing a crime?"

Witt thought hard and long.

"No," he said at last.

"Right then. What crime shall we commit?"

"It needs to be one series enough to be sent to the keep," said Witt.

"But Ay-ttho was brought here for throwing a rock through a window," said Sevan.

"They probably brought her here because they worked out who she was," said Tori.

"There's your answer then," said Witt. "They will probably work out who we are."

"Then all we need to do is knock on the door," said Sevan.

Tori looked at Sevan in disbelief, then at Witt and then back at Sevan.

"You are both serious, aren't you?" he said.

"Why not," said Witt. "The worst that could happen is that they turn us away."

"Or kill us," said Tori.

"Don't worry, Sevan," said Witt. "They aren't going to kill us."

Tori wanted to respond, but didn't. Instead, the three walked to the entrance, through which the transporter containing Ay-ttho had driven.

It was an enormous gate forged out of metal. They couldn't see any bell to ring and no obvious place to knock. So Tori took his weapon and bashed it against the metal as hard as he could.

To their amazement, the doors opened, and they could walk through to some kind of holding area. The gates shut behind them and they were trapped.

"Leave your weapons here," a voice instructed them via a tannoy.

They did as they were asked and left their weapons on the ground. The gate in front of them opened, and they walked into the compound, leaving their weapons behind.

Further into the compound, they could see Ay-ttho. She was talking to someone who was obscured by a row of guards.

"You are going to love this," Ay-ttho said to them as they approached.

As they got closer and rounded the guards, they could see who Ay-ttho was talking to.

"Aunty!" Sevan exclaimed. "They got you too."

Sevan's aunt laughed a hysterical laugh he had never heard from her before. He looked inquiringly at Ay-ttho, then Tori and finally Witt. Wondering why he didn't get the joke

"They didn't get me," Sevan's aunt said, when she had finally stopped laughing. "I am they."

"What do you mean?"

"I got you. Oh, nevermind. Someone explain it to him later. "

"Explain what?"

"I don't think your aunt is your aunt," said Witt.

"If course I'm not his aunt. We're clones. How could I be his aunt?"

"I always thought it was a symbolic thing," said Sevan.

"Of course not," the clone, who used to be his aunt, said.

"Then who are you?"

"Who I am is not important. You should ask why I am."

"Why are you, then?"

"I am because you have to be trained."

"Me?"

"You have to be trained to fulfil the role for which we created you."

"What?"

"They assigned me to ensure you reached the lottery in which they selected you to be the workers' representative. Unfortunately, you were kidnapped by the other side."

"Is this true?" Sevan looked at Ay-ttho.

"Not exactly."

"Yes, Ay-ttho, not exactly. We restored your training frequently, Sevan."

"When?"

"We sent you to Pandoria."

"You sent us to Pandoria?" Tori scoffed.

"What else would you do when you realised the Doomed Planet was missing?"

"I don't believe it."

"Then we brought you to Nereid. We've done that a few times now."

"Uxclod!" said Ay-ttho.

"It doesn't matter whether you believe me," Sevan's ex-aunt continued. "The point is, Sevan's training has been progressing, and he is now ready to take the next step."

"Which is?"

"To travel into the multiverse."

"Forget it," said Ay-ttho.

"I expect you would quite like to see your ship again."

"And Nadio and Effeeko. Where are they?"

"Waiting on your ship. I will take you to them, if you would like. We have been making some modifications to your ship, so it is not quite ready for you to leave yet."

"What have you done to my ship?"

"Oh, I think you'll be quite pleased with our upgrades."

They followed Sevan's ex-aunt across the compound to a large hanger, in which stood the Mastery of the Stars, surrounded by a small army of workers.

"Get them off my ship," Ay-ttho barked.

"Your ship? Have you never considered how easy it was for you to steal that freighter?"

"I don't remember it being that easy," said Sevan.

"Only because you were flying. And how about the anti-matter drive? Do you not think it a little coincidental you could get exactly what you needed?"

"I stole the parts and Brabin gave me the anti-matter."

"Very convenient."

"We are not going to the multiverse."

"Let us be the judge of that. Would you like to see inside?"

Sevan's ex-aunt led them into the ship, where more workers were fitting assorted devices to the interior of the corridors.

"What in the worst place are you doing?"

"It was explained to me, but to be honest, science is not my strong point. I'd like to re-acquaint you with someone who knows a lot about this stuff, though."

As they entered the bridge, Ay-ttho, Tori, and Sevan froze. In the centre was the head of the corporation and Sevan's creator, Barnes, chatting with his own creator, Daxu.

"Sevan! Ay-ttho! So glad to see you again," said Daxu, striding over. "And your Republic friend..."

"Tori," said Tori.

"Yes, that's right. I see you have brought a new friend. Who might this be?"

"Witt," said Witt. "Pleased to meet you."

"Not *the* Witt? Of the barrier of Witt?"

"The same. Are you familiar with my work?"

"Familiar? We are right this moment equipping this ship to traverse the barrier."

"May I see?"

"Of course, come this way."

Daxu and Witt were now lost in conversation as Daxu began the tour, leaving Ay-ttho, Sevan and Tori alone with Barnes.

"Well, well, well," he said. "What a pleasure. We must stop bumping into each other like this."

"I want to see Nadio and Effeeko," said Ay-ttho.

"Of course you do. Where are they, Ron?"

"They are in the officers' mess," replied the navigation computer, who was so much more than a navigation computer.

"Thank you, Ron," said Ay-ttho, turning on her heels and leaving the bridge.

Tori and Sevan followed her, all the while throwing nervous glances back at a grinning Barnes.

When they arrived in the mess, they found Nadio and Effeeko chatting to none other than Pelou Furle, an acquaintance Sevan had met on Future who had led him to Barnes' creator, Daxu.

"Ay-ttho!" Nadio leapt up as soon as he saw her.

"You are so big now," said Ay-ttho.

"It's good to see you all," said Effeeko.

"Have they been treating you well?" asked Tori.

"Yes, we can't complain."

"Do you remember me?" asked Pelou Furle.

"Of course," said Sevan. "The last time I saw you was just before Barnes tried to kill us."

"Are you sure?" Pelou looked confused.

"Yes, he folded space and sent Atlas to the Giant Cup only knows where."

"Oh, Atlas is safe and well. He just moved it to annoy President Man."

"Can you explain something to me please, Pelou?"

"I'll try."

"I thought the Republic had taken over the concessions."

"Only Nereid and the Doomed Planet. Barnes wouldn't let them have Daphnis."

"Why not?"

"You'll see soon enough."

"I don't like surprises."

"Okay, let's just say that Barnes has some equipment here that he doesn't want the Republic to know about."

"But they are right next door."

"Exactly, who would be stupid enough to keep something this important right under their noses?"

"What is it?"

"Be patient."

"I can't."

"Okay, he has a white hole."

"Impossible," said Tori.

"Why?"

"Because white holes give out energy. Where is all that energy?"

"That's the clever thing," said Pelou. "He is using the energy to fold space and they expel the excess energy into the area of the fold."

Sevan was lost.

"What do you mean 'the area of the fold'?"

"Barnes uses the energy he needs to move one bit of space to another, right?"

"Right. So we expel the excess energy where the space has been moved to, not here."

"Clever."

"Isn't it?"

"So he has a massive source of power that is invisible to detection."

"Exactly."

"But what could he do with that?"

"Anything he wants."

CHAPTER 38: THE BARRIER OF WITT

"This is fantastic," said Witt, striding into the mess, followed by a very pleased looking Daxu. "We are going to cross the barrier into the multiverse."

"Hang on a gods damned unit," said Ay-ttho. "Who is we?"

"We," he said, gesticulating to those present at the table. "This ship is equipped and ready to go. It's very exciting."

"No-one is taking this ship to no multiverse. It's my ship, and it stays here."

"I thought it was our ship," said Tori.

"Whatever," said Ay-ttho. "It's not going to no multiverse."

"Any multiiverse," said Witt.

"What?"

"It's: not going to *any* multiverse."

"Good. I'm glad we agree."

"No, you said *no* multiverse. It's *any* multiverse."

"I don't care what multiverse it is. My ship's not going."

"Our ship," said Tori.

"Our ship."

Ay-ttho stormed out of the mess. Tori, Daxu, and Pelou ran after her, leaving Sevan and Witt alone at the table. Witt sat down.

"Why do you want to go to the multiverse?" Sevan asked him.

"My friends are there."

"But even before that, you wanted to go."

"Are you not curious about what lies beyond our universe?"

"Yes, but I don't want to go there."

"We can't find out if we can't go."

"If the gods wanted us to leave the universe, they would have made it easier."

"Would they? Tell me what you know about gods, Sevan."

"Not much. I know there are a lot. They have hundreds of statues to them on Herse."

Witt laughed loudly and for a long time.

"What's so funny?"

"I'm sorry, it's just that to me the idea that gods can be depicted as statues is ridiculous. The gods exist in all forms."

"So you believe in gods, then?"

"Not in the sense the Herseans do. Sevan, Daxu told me a great deal about the work that he and Barnes have been doing. You are an integral part of that work."

"Me?"

"Your entire life has been preparing for this moment. It won't be easy, but if anyone can do it, you can."

"Do what?"

"The coming rotations will be challenging, Sevan. You should get some rest and I'll tell you all about it."

Sevan was feeling weary, so he said goodbye to Witt and tried to find the others. According to Ron, Ay-ttho and Tori had already retired to their quarters, so Sevan decided he would too. He wasn't comfortable about so many clones working on the ship while he slept, but he locked his door, lay down on his familiar bunk, closed his eyes, and drifted off to sleep.

A great commotion and a loud squeaking noise awoke him. He got up and went to the bridge to find out what was going on.

On the bridge, he found an angry looking Ay-ttho together with Tori, who was looking concerned and Witt, who was looking very smug.

"Ron? Why can't we turn around?"

"The ship has been hard wired on its present course."

"Impossible!" Ay-ttho shouted.

"What happened?" Sevan asked Tori, quietly.

"While we were sleeping, Witt set the ship on a course for the edge of the universe."

"How?"

"Barnes and his cronies have tampered with Ron so that we can't change our flight path. They've already folded space so that we are pretty close to the edge already."

"What's that noise?"

"The antimatter drive. It's on full power."

"How long can it hold like this?"

"I think we are about to find out."

"This is madness," Ay-ttho continued. "We can't cross into another universe. You're going to kill us all."

"You are thinking only in terms of the dimensions with which you are familiar," Witt tried to explain. "Higher dimensional branes overlap in a three-dimensional subspace, and that overlap is what we experience as reality."

"What are you talking about?" Ay-ttho snapped irritably.

"Scientists always assumed that the universe was flat. But we discovered that there was a slight positive curvature which was within the margin of error of the cosmologists' measurements and therefore realised the universe is finite. But the problem is that the universe is constantly getting bigger. At the largest scales, its expansion pulls galaxies apart faster than the light can travel between them. I called the boundary past which light coming from our region of spacetime can never travel, the Barrier. We can pass this barrier with the anti matter drive by travelling many times faster than light. We achieve it by altering the topology of spacetime by folding space."

"I wish I'd never asked. Nevertheless, we don't want to go."

"It's too late for that. Space has already been folded. We are already at the edge of the universe. We will pass through the barrier any unit now."

"Oh my Giant Cup," said Sevan.

"My team located a black hole large enough to travel through," Witt continued.

"We are going to be crushed to nothing."

"No, Sevan. This one is large enough so that when we pass through the event horizon, it will feel no more than passing your hand through the flame of a candle."

"I tried that once and burnt myself."

"Passing through the black hole is only the first hurdle, then we must find my colleagues and then we will need to locate a large enough black hole to return. Barnes and Daxu think their white hole is large enough."

"And if it isn't?"

"It will crush us to nothing."

"Oh, my."

"We are approaching a black hole," said Ron.

"Ron? You've finally decided to speak to us," Ay-ttho complained. "Now turn the ship around."

"I'm afraid my navigation abilities have been disabled. And even if they weren't, we have passed the point of no return already."

"What we are going into is a bubble universe that quickly expanded and moved away from our own," Witt explained. "It should only take a unit to cross the barrier."

The ship warmed and then cooled almost as quickly.

"I have regained control of my systems," said Ron.

"Thank the Giant Cup," said Sevan.

"We are being spewed out into this parallel universe," Witt explained.

He rushed excitedly to his apparatus and began fiddling with knobs, buttons, and dials.

"It's working!" he exclaimed. "Ron? Can you link to my apparatus? You should be able to track my colleagues."

"Setting course now," Ron confirmed.

Witt looked extremely satisfied, some might say, smug.

"At least we're not dead," said Sevan.

"How do you know we're not?" said Ay-ttho.

"You think we might have passed into the Better Place?"

"Or the Worst."

Sevan wasn't so relieved at having survived the black and white holes.

"Relax," said Tori. "They just invented the Good and Worst places so that you wouldn't complain about the unnecessary drudgery of your actual existence."

"Unnecessary?"

"Of course. Who benefited from all that mining you helped with on The Doomed Planet?"

"We all did."

"That's what they told you, but actually you were working for the profit of the corporation and the Republic. Your own welfare wasn't a consideration."

"What about Binge?"

"The Binge festival was the one rotation in the entire solar cycle where you could do what you wanted and they drugged you with fushy. It was a distraction to stop you from rising against your oppression. That is why I joined the resistance."

"You are a member of the resistance?"

"You are a member of the resistance."

"But we were senators."

"The revolution works in mysterious ways."

"You're sounding like Scotmax."

Ay-ttho motioned for Sevan to be quiet because, with perfect timing, Nadio and Effeeko chose that precise moment to enter the bridge.

"What was that about Scotmax?" Nadio asked.

"We were saying how much we miss her," Tori lied.

"Where are we?" asked Effeeko.

"You tell them," Ay-ttho told Tori

"At least the laws of physics appear to be the same," said Witt, checking his instruments.

"Why wouldn't they be?" Effeeko inquired.

"Effeeko," Tori began. "I think you'd better sit down."

After he had completed his explanation, Tori led Effeeko and Nadio to their quarters, where they could rest while they recovered from the shock.

Meanwhile, Ron followed the course provided by the instruments of Witt, who continued to check them methodically.

"There is a slight problem," said Ron after a while. "Although I can follow the virtual beacon that Witt's instruments are providing, I have no navigation charts for this universe."

"Obviously."

"Which is going to make it exceedingly difficult to find Barnes' black hole but also, my navigation charts for the universe we have just left appear to have been wiped, so even if we could traverse Barnes' black hole and return to our universe, we would be lost."

"When did you last see the charts?" Ay-ttho asked, as if Ron might have simply misplaced them.

"I had them before we entered the black hole."

"Black holes shoot out jets of electro-magnetic radiation," said Witt. "It's possible that some of this energy has disrupted Ron's storage."

"Great. So, even if we can get back, we probably can't get back."

"Unless my colleagues have a copy of the charts," said Witt.

"What are the chances of that?"

"I'm sure they would have charts on their ship."

"If that's the case, then why haven't they already returned themselves?"

"I guess we'll have to ask them when we meet them," said Witt. "We are nearing their system now. I'm trying to send them a tachyon transmission."

Ay-ttho checked on Effeeko and Nadio, who were recovering well from their shock.

"I bet you're regretting the rotation you got messed up with us?" Ay-ttho asked Effeeko.

"If I hadn't I wouldn't be alive now. I would have died in a meteor shower on Angetenar."

"That's true."

"And I would have been a slave on Sicheoyama," said Nadio.

"I suppose neither of those is as good as being lost in another universe."

Back on the bridge, Witt took a break from his instruments and turned to Sevan.

"Are you ready?" he asked.

"Ready for what?"

"Your challenges."

"What challenges?"

"Your aunt didn't tell you?"

"Tell me what?"

"Oh, nothing, nevermind."

"You can't do that."

"What?"

"Tell me I must prepare for some challenges and then not tell me what they are."

"It's nothing really, don't worry, I shouldn't have said anything."

"Obviously."

"Don't worry, Sevan. You can find all the answers you need within."

"Don't get all philosophical on me."

"No, really, Sevan. I don't know much more than that. Your aunt said that you would have to overcome some challenges and that the answers are inside of you. I just assumed she had told you what they were. I'm sure everything will become clear."

This was the last thing Sevan needed. As if being stuck in another universe wasn't bad enough, now he would have to face challenges and search within himself. He went for a lay down.

"What was all that about?" asked Tori, seeing Sevan skulk off the bridge.

"Nothing. I think he's homesick."

"I'm not sure he knows where home is."

"I think he's pretty sure it's not in this universe."

"Sorry to interrupt you," said Ron. "We are approaching the planet from where the signal is emanating."

"Great," said Witt. "Take us straight there."

CHAPTER 39: SILVER ASSASSINS

"The signal appears to be coming from a moon," said Ron, as the Mastery of the Stars orbited a brown and blue planet.

In the distance, the system's only star looked small, the moon cold and desolate.

"The moon appears to be just a large rock," said Ron. "I can't detect anything else on the surface. The signal appears to be coming from beneath the crust.

By the time Ron had landed the freighter on the barren surface, Ay-ttho, Nadio, Effeeko, and Sevan had all returned to the bridge.

"This is as close as I can get to the signal," Ron explained.

"What's it like out there?" Ay-ttho asked.

"There is a small amount of gravity, but the air is not breathable. If you are going outside, you will have to wear suits."

"Can you transmit the signal locator to my communicator?"

"I can."

"Let's get suited up then."

It took some time for the group to help each other get into the full suits. What little atmosphere there was sodium and potassium. It was practically a vacuum.

They descended from the freighter with their weighted boots onto the dusty rock of the surface.

"This way," said Ay-ttho, via their communicators.

They followed her slowly as the lack of gravity made any movement clumsy. Soon, they were descending the side of a crater and, once on the crater floor, they could see that the walls of the crater were peppered with caves, it reminded Sevan of the crater on Nereid at the foot of Waterfall where they had met his friend Ozli. This made him feel sad, since Ozli had died, but he continued to follow the others as best he could, given the limits of low gravity.

Ay-ttho followed the signal into a cave and they soon reached a door. It appeared to be hermetically sealed. There was certainly no sign of any controls. In the event, it didn't matter because the door opened of its own accord and so they ventured through.

They appeared to have entered an airlock because, no sooner had the doors shut behind them than there was a hiss of air and the doors in front of them opened.

"This is fantastic," said Witt. "A bubble universe with the same rules as ours. A slight variation both ways, and this wouldn't exist."

The door had opened to reveal the interior of an underground bunker. It was filled with enormous creatures with elongated necks and beaked heads. Their arms, which reached as far as the floor, had something sticking out of them and we're connected to their legs by some kind of web which Sevan realised was feathered.

They were clearly working and cooperating, but no sounds could be heard.

"Telepathy?" Tori whispered to Witt.

"Unlikely. More likely, they are communicating on a frequency outside of our audible range."

A few of the creatures had watched the door open and now approached them. They had long, thin legs and feet that ended in claws. Sevan realised that not only were they covered in small hairs but the hairs were changing colour ever so slightly. Their heads were enormous and their jaws toothless, and they had giant crests with irregular blooms of colour.

One creature was carrying a box, suddenly the box spoke.

"We are waiting for you," said the box.

"Good," said Witt. "We have come to find some of my friends."

"People know," it said.

"May we see them?"

"Yes. Proposal is youth."

The group looked at each other in confusion.

"I suspect they are using the box to translate," said Witt. "It's probably not perfect. We should be careful we understand them."

"Yes. Sounds good," said the box. "Your friend had a terrible accident. We can explain everything."

"Can you take us to them?" asked Witt.

"He us," said the box, and the creatures looked concerned.

"Please, would you take us to my friends?"

"Because we try to inform you. Your friends are here. A terrible accident happened and I'm not here anymore. You can try the explanation, but the instructions remain."

"Are they okay?"

"This is very strict. They don't work very well. I thought it would be good to show you the way."

"Please take us to them."

"Thank you very much," said the box, and the creatures led them into the bunker.

The group followed the creatures through the complex, which smelt badly of throns. Sevan hated throns. He had tried them once on Pallene, but thought they were disgusting.

Eventually they reached a room which particularly excited Witt because it contained some equipment that he recognised as belonging to his friends.

"Where are they? Are they here?"

"I do not think so. Like I said, there was an accident, but it's not here. But your instructions are on the table."

Witt rushed to the table and examined the apparatus there.

"They have tried to cross back through the barrier," he read. "But these... I'm sorry, I don't know what to call you."

The creatures listened with interest but did not respond.

"What are your names?" Witt persisted.

"My name is Marcus, he is Force, and she is Eves," said the creature with the box.

"Pleased to meet you," Witt then turned back to the group of his fellow travellers. "They must have attempted to recross the barrier, but it sounds like there must have been some kind of accident. We need to find out where they are."

"We can take you to them."

"Thank you."

"It's ten million. Follow me, please," said Marcus, before leaving the room.

The others exchanged confused glances and then followed.

"We don't have to pay, do we?" asked Sevan.

"I hope not," said Tori. "I don't know what the currency is in this universe, but I know we've got none of it."

"It's okay. We don't want your money. We just want to help you," said Marcus through the box.

Sevan made a mental note to be careful about what he said.

"Let's talk about ourselves along the way," said Marcus. "Your friends call us silver assassins and say we are a lot like the so-called mechanical archers in your universe."

"The mechanical bowmen," Witt whispered.

"Machine gun," Marcus continued. "We play the role of space police, helping those in need and defending Whitehall's border with the rest of the universe. To bring our friends back to your universe, we had to use what is called a song of time. Singing about everything in the universe and listening to this song, we found a universe black hole big enough for them to pass through. Unfortunately, the nature of the black hole changed, and I had to cancel my mission. It injured your friend in the rescue process. We take them to a facility where they can be treated."

"What is Whitehall? Is it the name of this universe?" asked Witt.

"White holes are the opposite of black holes. It releases energy into the universe. You came to our universe through the White Hole. There is no name in our universe. We call it the universe. What is the name of your universe?"

"Ah, white holes, not Whitehall," Witt realised. "Our universe does not have a name either. Perhaps we should give it one."

"The name doesn't matter. The situation is the same if you give them a name. But please tell me about this person." the creature gesticulated towards Sevan. "He's not special, right?"

"That's right. He's not special," Ay-ttho laughed.

"It's weird because we feel good with him."

Ay-ttho laughed even more.

"You can keep him," she laughed.

"We thought."

Sevan suddenly looked worried.

"There is a prophecy that one day an outstanding leader will come and live as our ruler and give them everything they need. Here your friends remind us of many of these prophecies."

"I hope they don't mean you," Ay-ttho joked with Sevan.

"In fact, we are talking about him."

Ay-ttho had to try hard to suppress her laugh.

They followed the creatures as best they could, although their suits were cumbersome.

They led them to an observation deck with an impressive view of the blue-green planet the moon was orbiting.

"We need to get you there," said Marcus. "You can take it to the next rocket that goes."

"When is that?" asked Witt.

"There is this incarnation. I'll take it right away."

The creatures led them from the observation deck down to a hanger where a rocket was being prepared for launch. Sevan noticed there were any creatures who appeared to be guarding both the rocket and the facility.

"There's a lot of security, isn't there?" he commented to Witt.

"Yes, there have been some terrorist attacks recently, and this is the second flight to Earth since the last time," Marcus replied, overhearing.

Sevan marvelled at how good Marcus's hearing was, but he was more concerned with the fact there might be another terrorist attack.

"Why are there terrorist attacks?" he asked.

"It left a powerful impression on us."

Sevan was sure the attacks left a big impression. He wasn't satisfied with the answer, but he didn't feel he had the energy to probe further.

Marcus led them inside, but all the seats were much too large for them. Marcus tried to strap them all in one seat but it was too much of a squeeze, so he strapped Witt Sevan and Effeeko into one seat while strapping Ay-ttho, Nadio and Tori into another.

Then Marcus, Force, and Eve sat in other seats while the pilot and copilot made the pre-flight checks.

Sevan could hear steam hissing and metal groaning. He wasn't convinced this rocket ride was a good idea, but there wasn't a lot he felt he could do about it. There were no windows where Sevan was sitting and he could barely see through the observation windows in front of the pilot and co-pilot because they were so huge.

He felt the rumble of the main engines, then the rocket lurched forward for a moment before tilting back upright. There was a deafening roar, and he felt the rocket shake and shudder. As the rocket accelerated, he felt an immense pressure. This was something completely different from his experience of space flight so far, which had been solely via gravity manipulators and anti-matter drives.

The whole thing was over as abruptly as it began. The roar stopped, the shuddering stopped, and it's dead quiet. All Sevan could hear were the cooling fans from some of the equipment gently whirring in the background. Everything around him was eerily, perfectly still.

He didn't have long to enjoy the silence, however, as soon afterwards he heard a bang and felt a jolt and then smelt an interesting odour

"What in the worst place has happened?" Sevan asked.

"Don't worry," said Witt. "We are entering the atmosphere of the planet. The smell is just the ablative material burning off."

"What?"

"It's a technique we haven't needed to use for solar cycles but, basically, they cover the spacecraft with ablative material that burns away slowly in a controlled manner so the gases can remove heat from the spacecraft. The remaining solid material insulates the spacecraft from the heat."

Sevan wished he hadn't asked.

"Oh, yes," Witt continued. "Our own space program used similar techniques in the early rotations. I expect these creatures haven't been using reusable spacecraft for long."

"There is another type?"

"Yes, long ago, spacecraft used to be destroyed every time they landed. They crashed."

"Are we going to crash?" Sevan was exceedingly concerned.

"Yes," said the creature.

CHAPTER 40: A SONG OF TIME

"There are many games to use to pass the time. Tell us about your game," Marcus said.

"What game?" Sevan asked. "This is no time to talk about games. We are about to crash."

"Caution? It is not normal. We're Just Enlandona Art Mospera."

Sevan looked at Witt. Witt shrugged.

"Why didn't we just use the Mastery of the Stars? It would have been much easier," said Sevan.

"I know," said Ay-ttho. "They would have fitted into one of the cargo bays."

"What? And miss out on this fantastic experience, to fly on a ship designed by species from another universe."

"You say there are stars?" asked the creature. "Your friends will talk about them. Are you on board? Look?"

"Yes, lovely," said Sevan, although he couldn't see the stars. Only the pilot and co-pilot had a view through the observation windows.

"Does that mean yes? Can I contact my colleagues to participate?"

"Do what you want," Sevan tried to shrug, but the straps impeded his movement.

"Thank you very much. Take necessary action immediately. I'm about to land, so it's a good idea to get ready now."

Sevan braced himself.

The landing wasn't as bad as Sevan had expected. It was certainly better than the time they had crash landed the rocket on Sirius.

There was a long wait while the pilot and co-pilot appeared to go through a series of checks.

Marcus gave his box a tap, as if it was malfunctioning.

"Wait for the gas to go out," the box said.

"I think he is referring to the toxic fumes that surrounded the craft on entry," said Witt. "Before gravity manipulators, this was a common problem."

"I'm glad you know your ancient history and your science."

"I want to know more about this gravity processor," said Marcus.

"I will tell you all that I can," Witt agreed.

Marcus looked offended and went quiet. Sevan wondered what the translator box had done with Witt's sentence.

The door of the craft opened and Marcus helped them unstrap themselves from their seats. They led them into a complex.

The atmosphere of the planet was suitable for them and so they climbed out of them and left them with Marcus.

"I'm sorry again. My colleague and I need to pass some tests," the box translated. "This allows other organisers to take you to your friends. You don't have to listen to my words for the time being."

"Thank you very much," said Witt.

"It's ten million," said Marcus, who then turned to leave.

"Do they want us to pay them?" Sevan asked Witt.

"I don't know. Ten million what?"

"You don't have to pay us. Bring it to your friends," said another creature, who beckoned them to follow him or her.

They followed the creature through the complex to an exit on the other side. When they reached the outside of the complex, it led them to what might be best described as baskets.

"Please add to cart," said the creature.

They looked at each other, wondering what the creature meant.

"I think they want us to get in the basket," said Witt

"And yes," said the creature.

Witt and Sevan clambered into one. Ay-ttho and Tori into a second, and Effeeko and Nadio into a third.

No sooner had they climbed into the baskets than three of the creatures unfurled huge wings, which they flapped, raising themselves up into the air. With their large clawed feet, they grasped onto a basket each and lifted them high into the air.

As soon as they were in the air, Sevan could see ocean covered most of the planet with many islands punctuating the surface of the water.

The creatures landed the baskets in a clearing on a forested island. At the edge of the clearing, they could see the wreckage of a ship, presumably belonging to Witt's friends.

In the air, Sevan saw a different type of creature flying. It had wings attached to long hind legs and smaller front legs, plus a huge thin tail.

On the edge of the forest, he saw a couple of other creatures. One was red and black striped and walked on four legs, while the other was green and walked on large hind legs. Both had formidable tails.

They led Sevan and the others through the forest until they arrived at a cliff face. They followed the cliff around until they arrived at a series of well-built wooden platforms lined with grass or leaves. On one platform, Sevan could see a group of individuals that looked like Witt. They were covered entirely, apart from their eyes and mouths with some type of cloth which was oozing with a liquid or paste.

"Pirate?" Witt asked.

"Witt?" a weak voice responded. "They told me you had made it."

"What happened?"

"To return to our universe, we need to find a black hole large enough, right?"

"Right."

"In order to locate that black hole, we needed to use what the khalgoins call the song of time."

"The khalgoins?"

"The creatures who brought you here. That is what we have named their species."

"Okay, sorry, tell me about the song of time."

"Similar to our own science, they understand that the smallest particles in the universe vibrate. They see these vibrations as a kind of music and by listening carefully they can extrapolate the form of the universe, not only through space but through time."

"Fantastic."

"Unfortunately, it is. The predictions are not accurate enough to find a path back to our own universe. There is a way I know there is, but our ship is now damaged beyond repair, as are we. How is your ship?"

"It still flies, but unfortunately, like you, all our navigation data was wiped during the passage between the black and white holes."

"There may be another way. Who have you brought with you?"

"This is Ay-ttho. We came on her ship."

Both Tori and Sevan thought about protesting, but both independently concluded that the moment was inappropriate.

"Effeeko is a medical doctor from Angetenar."

"Angetenar? I used to explore the caves there."

"Unfortunately, an asteroid shower destroyed everything," said Effeeko.

"That is unfortunate."

"This is Nadio," Witt continued.

"A Thug!"

"This is Tori, ex-Republic security clone. And Sevan..."

"It's him!" Pirate attempted to sit up to get a better look.

Everyone turned to look at Tori.

"No, him," said Witt, pointing towards Sevan. "The answer is within him."

The exertion was too much, and Pirate collapsed into a stupor.

"I think Sevan also has an answer," said one of the khalgoins that had led them there. "May he live with us as a prophet and give us an answer."

"You're welcome to him," said Ay-ttho.

"Ten million?" asked the khalgoin.

"Okay. Ten million what?"

"I don't know. Please say. That's your idea."

"Do you have credits?"

"What is a credit?"

"Credits are what we use for money."

"What is money?"

"You don't have money? How do you buy or sell things?"

"What are you buying?"

"What are you selling?"

"What to sell."

"I don't know. I don't know what you've got." Ay-ttho turned to the others. "Is there anything you want to swap for Sevan?"

"I am here, you know," Sevan protested.

"I will give you anything," said the khalgoin. "You can take whatever you want."

"We can take whatever we want," Ay-ttho repeated. "What would you like?"

"You are not swapping me for anything," Sevan protested again.

Ay-ttho shrugged.

"Don't worry about the third time," said the khalgoin. "You are well taken care of here. You can get whatever you want."

"See," said Sevan. "You'll live like a King."

"What did he mean? The third time?"

There was a pause, during which the khalgoin began shaking the translating box.

"Perhaps it's not working," Witt suggested.

While they had been talking, Effeeko and Nadio had been examining Witt's friends.

"They are badly burned," Effeeko announced. "These coverings seem to be whatever they use to treat burns."

"Will they work?" asked Witt.

"I don't know. We'll have to hope so."

"What is a King? Are you okay? Then we must live as one," said the translation box. The khalgoin stopped shaking it.

"A king is a ruler of a monarchy," said Ay-ttho. "We have a republic, so we have a president."

"I don't know what a kingdom, republic or president is."

"How do you govern yourselves?" asked Witt.

"Please take care of me."

"Maybe they don't have a leader," suggested Tori. "Maybe that's why they want Sevan."

"Why choose Sevan?" asked Ay-ttho.

"Why not?" Sevan protested yet again.

"Who is Saipan?" asked the khalgoin.

The group exchanged glances.

"Forget it," said Pirate, who had regained consciousness. "The translation box doesn't work properly. Be very careful about what you say and even more careful not to misunderstand."

"That makes sense," said Witt.

"They want Sevan to stay and be their guru. It would fulfil a prophecy of theirs. Sevan would be treated very well. Like a King, in fact. But you need Sev..."

It became too difficult for Pirate to speak and he slumped back into unconsciousness.

"What he said was a fact," said the khalgoin. "We treat Saipan very well. Let me show you our intentions."

"Okay then," said Ay-ttho. "Show us."

"I'll stay here with my friends," said Witt.

"Me too," said Effeeko.

"And me," said Nadio.

"Just us three," said Ay-ttho, turning to Tori and Sevan. "We will go with you."

They were led back to the baskets and flown back to the island on which they had landed. The khalgoin led them back through the complex until they arrived at an enormous palace. Everything inside was huge to match the size of the khalgoin, but then they arrived at an area in which everything was smaller. In fact, the furniture, fixtures and fittings were all the perfect size for Sevan, Ay-ttho and Tori.

"Do you like it?" asked the khalgoin.

"Yes," said Sevan. "I like it very much."

The khalgoin motioned for Sevan to follow him to a cupboard and gestured that Sevan should open it. When he did, Sevan discovered they crammed it with bottles of what he seriously hoped was Pish.

He took out a bottle and saw there was a table next to the cupboard with glasses. Wasting no time, he opened a bottle and poured the ruby contents into a glass.

"Oh, my Giant Cup!" he exclaimed once he had taken a sip. "That is the best pish I have ever tasted."

"Is your name pish?" asked the khalgoin. "Your friend taught us how to do this. This is our first attempt."

"For your first time, this is pretty amazing."

"Thank you, I like you."

"Ay-ttho, are you there?" buzzed Ay-ttho's communicator.

"Effeeko?" Ay-ttho answered. "What is it?"

"Pirate came round again. He knows how we can get back. Come back and make sure you bring Sevan."

"Okay, why? What is it?"

Effeeko's answer was lost in a wave of static.

"Come on, Sevan, we've seen enough," said Ay-ttho.

"I'm not sure I have. I think I'd like to see more."

He took another large gulp of the pish and slumped down in a large armchair that was so comfortable they could have specifically moulded it for his body.

"You go, I'll stay here for a while," he said.

"Effeeko wants us to go back."

"You go. You can tell me what he says later."

"Effeeko? Can you hear me?" Ay-ttho shouted into her communicator

"Ay-ttho? Yes, can you hear me?"

"Yes. Sevan is reluctant to come back with us. Can you tell us more about why he might be important?"

"The key to getting back home is within Sevan."

"What do you mean?"

"He is a biological star chart. They have embedded the route home within him. We cannot get home without him."

"Did you hear that, Sevan? Come with us, otherwise none of us can get back."

Sevan took another sip of pish.

CHAPTER 41: THE PIRATE

"Why should I go?" asked Sevan. "Everyone treats me like rubbish and then as soon as I find someone who appreciates me, you want me to leave."

"You have to come. We can't get home without you."

"How did this star chart get inside me? Can't you just take it out?"

"Did you hear that, Effeeko?" Ay-ttho asked her communicator.

"Yes, I did. Apparently, that's not an option. Ron has been modified to interface with Sevan, but he cannot download the data. We must connect Sevan to Ron all the time."

"You hear that Sevan? There's no option. Come with us."

"Why do you want to go back, anyway? To be chased around the Republic? We're not welcome there, we're welcome here."

"You've only been here five units. You've no idea what this place is like."

Sevan finished the pish in his glass, then poured himself another, filling it up to the brim.

"Come on, Sevan. We don't want to stay here. We didn't want to come here."

Sevan downed the entire glass in one go.

Ay-ttho and Tori watched him impatiently.

"Well?" asked Tori.

Sevan placed his empty glass on a small table.

"You don't understand. They used me," he said.

"They used us all," said Ay-ttho.

"Even my aunt isn't my aunt any more."

"She never was, Sevan. Look, I understand you feel betrayed, but you haven't been betrayed by us. If our friendship means anything, you will help us get back to our own universe."

Sevan poured himself another drink.

"Come on, Sevan," Tori pleaded. "This desire you always had to get back to your aunt has always been holding you back. Now you can pursue your dreams. You can do whatever you want."

"I don't have any dreams."

"Perhaps it's time to get some."

"How about living here and being revered by the khalgoin? That seems like a pretty wonderful dream to me."

"Come on, Tori. This is pointless. Let's go," said Ay-ttho, turning to leave.

Tori looked at Sevan with disappointment and then turned to follow Ay-ttho. Sevan watched them go and then helped himself to another glass of pish.

The apartments the khalgoin had provided him with were spectacularly luxurious. They made the presidential palace on Future look positively ordinary.

Sevan took soothing baths, ate delicious meals, and slept in the most comfortable bed he had ever enjoyed.

The khalgoin asked him questions, which made him feel very important, and he tried to answer as best he could.

"How does the gravity manipulator work?" they asked.

"I really don't know. You would be better off asking Witt about that."

"Who is Bertel?"

"I don't know. Who is Bertel?"

"I'm not thinking about anything. Who is Bethel?"

"I don't know Bethel either."

"Bethel?"

Sevan shrugged. The khalgoin gave up. The translator box was obviously not working as well as it needed. They left Sevan alone, and he helped himself to more pish.

He soon got bored with his new life of luxury and soon he was missing his friends.

"Where have my friends gone? Have they gone back to see Pirate?" he asked the khalgoin.

"A friend of mine? Do you mean friends? Yes, they come back to find other friends."

"I would like to see them."

"Please confirm."

"I would definitely like to see my friends."

But the khalgoin was already leaving and was beckoning for Sevan to follow.

*

"Did you miss us?" Ay-ttho asked as she saw Sevan approaching the makeshift hospital where Pirate and the others were recuperating.

"Don't flatter yourself," Sevan retorted, but he knew Ay-ttho was correct.

"So, are you coming with us?" asked Tori.

"Let me speak with Pirate."

Sevan found Pirate sitting up in his bed, chatting with Effeeko and Witt.

"You look better."

"I feel better. Effeeko is a miracle worker. Are you coming with us? You know we can't leave without you."

"Why is that?"

"Well, we could download the contents of your marbles. It would only take up around 5 petabytes, but unfortunately, the way they have designed Ron's interface doesn't allow for download."

"Why not?"

"I don't know. It's almost as if Barnes thought you might want to stay and wanted to prevent you. Probably to prevent it from falling into the possession of the khalgoin."

"Barnes?"

"Didn't Effeeko tell you? This was all organiser by Barnes. I contacted him by shooting tachyon transmissions through a black hole."

"Can you contact him now?"

"No, they damaged the transmitter in the accident."

"The Mastery of the Stars has a transmitter."

"Exactly. But we have to get to it. We also need to use the khalgoin song of time to find a suitable black hole."

"So, what are you waiting for?"

"First, we needed you to agree to come with us. Then we need to get to the Mastery of the Stars, which won't be easy."

"Why?"

"The khalgoin don't want us to leave. The accident was caused because they sabotaged our mission. We have been trying to keep as much as possible secret from them."

"What's the plan, then?"

"They consider you to be special. You must convince them to take us all to the Mastery of the Stars."

"What about the song of time?"

"Their instruments are all on the research base on the same moon. We just have to get there."

"Alright, I'll see what I can do."

Sevan approached one of the khalgoin that had returned him to the island.

"I would like you to take me and my friends to the Mastery of the Stars. There are some things I need to get," he said.

"Please tell me when you want to go."

"As soon as possible."

"Get your basket ready."

"What basket? Do you mean you will get the baskets ready?"

"Yes, the cart will be moved to the launch location."

Sevan told the others to prepare themselves.

The khalgoin moved Witt's friends into their beds and placed each in a flying basket of their own. They divided Sevan and the others between a couple of other baskets and they began once more the spectacular journey from the island to the launch site.

Once they arrived, the khalgoin gave them their space suits back and climbed into them. Witt's friends were installed in a hermetically sealed medical pod which, although designed for one khalgoin, was easily modified to accommodate the three patients.

They struggled again into the seats which had been designed for the khalgoin. Because of the angle of the ship, Sevan and the others were practically laying on their backs.

When the engines started, the entire ship shook and Sevan worried once again that it might fall apart. It felt like a kick in his waste discharge region when the rocket shot into the air. Certainly not as smooth as the Mastery of the Stars.

During the launch, the rocket seemed to decelerate and then re-accelerate.

"What was that?" Sevan asked Witt, who was strapped in next to him.

"Probably nothing to worry about. I think they are just avoiding over stressing the ship. You do that when you are not using a gravity manipulator."

"Probably?"

The landing was equally uncomfortable and before long, they were transporting Witt's friends across the dusty surface of the moon to the Mastery of the Stars, where Effeeko installed them in the sick bay.

"I need to come with you to the moon base so we can use the song of time to locate a suitable exit point," said Pirate. "Meanwhile, show me to the tachyon transmitter and I will try to get in touch with Barnes."

Outside the ship, Sevan communicated Pirate's message to the khalgoin.

"My friends wish to return to their universe. They wish to use the song of time to find a route back."

"Everything is fine during your stay. Please let me know when you're ready. Let me hear the song of time," came the reply.

"Okay, I will get them," said Sevan.

He returned to the bridge to find Pirate and Witt fiddling with the Tachyon transmitter.

"We were firing the transmissions through a black hole," Pirate was saying. "I think that's what we need to do to make contact. We need to find the black hole first."

"They said we can use the song of time," said Sevan. "They're ready when we are."

"Good, let's go," said Witt.

Pirate was in a patient hover chair from the sick bay. The rest of them followed him out of the ship to where the khalgoin were waiting.

The khalgoin led them into the base where the khalgoin they knew as Marcus met them.

"Nice to see you again, my friend," he said through the box. "I know Sevan is here to fulfil his prophecy, but I'm taking you to Song of Time to find your ticket home again."

"Thank you very much," said Pirate. "I think I know where we might have made the mistake last time."

"I'm simulating and I'm pretty close to the resolution limit," said Marcus. "Some simulations and theoretical analyses agreed that the chord network reaches a scale range where the ratio $\gamma = \xi / t$ remains almost constant."

"What is the constant?" asked Pirate.

"On days when radiation and matter predominated, it was 0.3 and 0.55, respectively."

"It's possible that gravitational radiation is much less efficient than we thought," Pirate mused. "Maybe the loops are smaller."

Sevan, Ay-ttho and Tori exchanged confused glances.

"The kink angle decreases, slowly, because of the effect of stretching," said Witt.

"The scale in question is close to the resolution limit, making it difficult to get information about this in a simulation," said Marcus.

"What does all this mean?" asked Sevan.

"To reduce the number of dimensions to the four we observe, the remaining six or seven dimensions are compacted, curled up to a small size, for example forming a loop of small radius," said Witt.

Sevan shrugged. Pirate sighed with impatience.

"All constituents of the universe are rooted in what we call baxters," he explained as if he was talking to a newly birthed offspring. "This applies to all the particles, so we cannot see beyond our baxter, but it does not apply to Nathan particles, which correspond to closed chord loops. This means that gravity can leak away from our baxter, giving rise to observable deviations from Nathian gravity on large scales."

Sevan decided not to ask any more. Pirate turned his attention back to Marcus.

"I'm worried that any period of inflation would have diluted the numbers of pre-existing chords to an unobservable level," he said. "Only chords formed after or at the end of inflation could be observationally relevant."

"We solved this problem," said Marcus. "Four-dimensional physical spacetime metrics are adjusted by factors that depend on their location in interior space."

"So you first fix the moduli by hand?"

"Okay, we also developed an equation to explain the additional stream storage requirements," Marcus replied. "Examining the collisions of these chords revealed that the same kinematic constraints as the Southern Goto string collisions also apply here."

They arrived in a vast control room.

"This is where they monitor the song of time," Pirate explained.

"The basic principle," Witt continued. "Is that the universe comprises music. By analysis the melodies of a particular space or time, we can predict the melodies of other spaces and times and therefore identify where there might be a black hole suitable for our needs."

Witt approached Sevan and spoke more quietly.

"Barnes has loaded the music of our universe into your Marbles. That's why the khalgoin want you to stay. Extracting the music of our universe fulfils their prophecy."

"What? How do they intend to extract it?"

"Shh, I don't know. But don't worry, we don't intend to let them get a hold of your marbles."

"Now is the time for us to do business," said Marcus. "You have full access to music from that era. Now you need to grab Sevan and extract the music from his accounts."

Another khalgoin grasped Sevan and lifted him from the ground.

CHAPTER 42: THE END OF THE WORLD

As the Khalgoin carried Sevan from the room, Ay-ttho and Tori went to stop them, but several more khalgoin prevented them from getting close.

"We have to stop them," said Tori.

"If we did, they would not let us access the song of time which we need to return to our own universe."

"So, what do you intend to do?"

"I intend to analyse the song of time and find a way out of this place."

"But Sevan?" Tori protested.

"He'll have to manage as best he can until we are finished here."

The khalgoin had taken Sevan to a room and strapped him into a chair which had obviously been designed for him because it was his size, not khalgoin size. He tested the straps but knew it was pointless to struggle.

Next to him was an apparatus with cables and terminals that looked remarkably like the weapons system on the Mastery of the Stars.

They confirmed his fears when the khalgoin attached the terminals to his antennae. They were going to extract the data from his marbles.

It wasn't long before they had attached all the terminals and the khalgoin turned their attention to a machine by Sevan's side, covered with dials and screens.

Through a window, Sevan could see into the control room. He could see Pirate and Witt focussing on the instruments. Then he saw Tori and Ay-ttho staring back at him.

Khalgoin, all holding weapons, surrounded them.

"We have to get him out of there," said Tori.

"Wait," said Pirate. "Not until I have the data."

"How long will that take?" asked Ay-ttho.

"At the moment we are scanning the chord tensions, then we need to identify a region which matches the conditions consistent with a black hole leading to a corresponding white hole."

"I see, but how long will it take?"

"We have to be patient."

Tori was finding it very difficult to be patient, as was Sevan, who could hear the khalgoin starting up the machine.

"I'm going over there," said Tori

"No," said Pirate. "Without this data, we cannot do anything. Wait."

"We are measuring ten dimensions," Witt explained. "We need the note and volume of each one spread over a universal scale. It can't be done in five units."

"No," said Pirate. "But we can record all the data and analyse it on the ship."

"How are we going to do that? We don't have a storage device large enough."

"Yes we do," said Pirate, pointing toward Sevan.

"I don't follow you."

"I imagine the machine they have connected to Sevan is connected to the same network we are accessing, right?"

"It might be."

"Then all we have to do is hack into the system and get it to blow instead of suck."

"You mean upload the data from this universe rather than allow them to download the data from our universe?"

"Exactly."

"But do his marbles have enough capacity?"

"I guess we are about to find out."

"And what if they don't?" asked Tori.

"Then we may lose your friend."

"You can't do this," Ay-ttho protested.

"If they suck his marbles dry, you'll lose him, anyway. I've already accessed the machine and have reversed the dials, so they'll think they are downloading data when actually we are uploading data. I'm going to begin the transfer now."

Ay-ttho and Tori watched in horror as Sevan appeared to fall into a trance.

"But he needs his marbles to live," said Tori. "You can't fill them with other stuff."

"It's not a problem," said Pirate. "To accommodate the new data, his marbles should just jettison data it doesn't need."

"You mean he's going to forget things?"

"Yes, but probably unimportant things. Don't forget that Barnes designed him for this mission. His marbles are designed to receive a large capacity of data."

"He never struck me as having a large capacity," Ay-ttho mused.

"He probably won't forget things straight away. The new ones will gradually replace unrequited memories."

Ay-ttho and Tori continued to observe Sevan, who was looking a little distressed.

"The data transfer is proceeding well," Pirate confirmed.

The Khalgoin began fiddling with the dials on the machine into which the terminals on Sevan's antennae we're connected.

"I think they've worked out that something is wrong," said Tori.

Sevan seemed oblivious to what was going on around him.

"It's okay," said Pirate. "I've disabled their controls. They can't interrupt the transfer."

The khalgoin looked towards the control room.

"They suspect something," said Tori.

"Not long now," said Pirate.

"We need to be ready," said Ay-ttho, observing the surrounding khalgoin and, in particular, the weapons they were holding. Tori also observed the situation in the room.

The khalgoin attending Sevan were becoming more animated and returned to the control room.

"Come on, we have to go," said Tori.

"Almost there," said Pirate.

"What did you do with the machine?" said the box.

The khalgoin surrounding them made a move. In unison, Ay-ttho and Tori relieved the nearest khalgoin to each of them of their weapons and then used the weapons to shoot the other weapon carrying khalgoin.

"It's done," said Pirate.

Ay-ttho and Tori ran straight towards the room where Sevan was being held, causing the advancing khalgoin to turn around and flee. Despite being significantly large than Tori and Ay-ttho, the Khalgoin feared the weapon welding clones.

The khalgoin kept out of their way as Tori ran to the room where Sevan was being held.

They could hear banging noises in the closed doors of the control room.

"What's happening?" Witt asked.

"I've locked the doors," said Pirate. "They're trying to break in."

"What happens when they do?"

"Hopefully they won't."

Tori and Ay-ttho carefully removed the terminals from Sevan's antennae. Sevan was unresponsive, and they had to support him to lead him out of the room

Supporting Sevan with one arm each and brandishing their weapons with the other, Tori and Ay-ttho returned to the control room.

"What now?" asked Witt.

"I have an idea," said Ay-ttho. "Open the doors."

As Pirate opened the doors, Ay-ttho took Sevan from Tori, secured him with one arm and pointed the weapon to his head.

"Escort us safely to our ship or I will blow his head off," she said as the khalgoin rushed in.

They halted immediately.

"I understand what you're saying," said the khalgoin they knew as Marcus. "Lets do this. Don't hurt him."

Holding her weapon at Sevan's head the whole time, Ay-ttho led the group out of the control centre with Tori covering them from the rear.

The khalgoin let them pass, though pointed their weapons at them the whole time.

It was slow progress but, eventually, they reached the Mastery of the Stars. As soon as they were within the ship, Ay-ttho ordered Ron to close the doors and take off. She handed Sevan to Tori and Effeeko, who took him to the sick bay while she, Pirate and Witt went to the bridge.

As they departed from the khalgoin moon, they could see the Khalgoin rockets being launched to pursue them.

"Do you have terminals in the sick bay?" asked Pirate. "We must give Ron access to Sevan in order to calculate the correct way to fold space to arrive at a suitable black hole."

"Head for the nearest star, Ron," said Witt. "We will need its energy to fold space."

Ron communicated the requirements to Tori and Effeeko in the sick bay. After making Sevan comfortable, they carefully attached terminals to his antennae.

"There is a lot of data here," said Ron. "It may take some time to calculate."

"Well, hurry," said Ay-ttho. "I don't know how, but those rockets are catching us and, according to the scanners, they are armed."

"I will do my best," said Ron. "But you should realise that rushing the calculations could lead to errors which could be catastrophic."

"Just do it as quick as you can," said Ay-ttho.

Before long, the khalgoin rockets had almost caught them and had fired.

"Why are they catching us?" said Ay-ttho. "Is there something wrong with the anti-matter drive?"

"I'm busy right now," said Ron.

"Okay, don't worry," she pulled out her communicator. "Tori? Check out the anti-matter drive. Find out why we are going so slow."

Moments later, Tori responded.

"I think the khalgoin have been on the ship. Some components are missing, but I think I can fix it."

"Hurry."

"We are very close to the point where we can capture sufficient energy from the star," said Witt.

"Ron?"

"I have completed initial calculations and am just checking the results."

"Tori?"

"Yes, it's not a problem. They didn't do much damage. You should be able to fold space."

The ship rocked as the khalgoin weapons found their target.

"Ron?"

"Just double checking the calculations."

"There's no time. Fold space now."

"But..."

"Fold space!"

Within moments, the light outside the observation windows had distorted. Ay-ttho could see the ring begin to envelope not just them and the pursuing rockets but the khalgoin planet as well.

"Ron, it's taking the entire planet with us."

"I was about to explain that I was having difficulty with elements of the calculations."

"What will happen, Witt?"

"There should be enough energy from the star to move us and the planet. We might have to get too close to comfort to make it work, but I think the issue is more where the fold will leave us."

"What do you mean?"

"Ron should have calculated for the fold to deliver us next to the event horizon of the black hole. But if the fold is moving a larger object, I can't be sure exactly where the fold will deposit us or the planet."

The ring enlarged and Ay-ttho could see they were slowly being enveloped. The closer they got to the star, the hotter the ship became.

"Can the shields protect us?" Ay-ttho asked.

"For now, yes," said Witt. "But I don't know how much longer they will be effective?"

"How long will the folding take?"

"Until there is enough energy to move us and the planet."

"How long is that?"

Witt shrugged. Sparks flew out of one of the control panels.

"The temperature has exceeded safe operating levels," Ron warned.

"Just a little more," said Witt, staring at his instruments that were also sparking.

Ay-ttho gazed out of the observation window, willing the fold to complete. He could see their destination appearing through the ring, and then it was all over. All was silent. The temperature fell. Ahead of them, Ay-ttho could see the khalgoin planet that had been behind them.

"What happened?" asked Ay-ttho. "Where is the black hole?"

"It is on the other side of the khalgoin planet," Witt explained. "We have been deposited exactly where Ron had calculated, just beyond the event horizon. But because of folding space, our position in relation to the Khalgoin planet has been reversed."

"Which means?"

"Which means they have been deposited on the other side of the event horizon."

"You mean they are being sucked into the black hole?"

"I'm afraid so."

"Is there anything we can do?"

"Not without sacrificing ourselves."

"But it's a whole species."

"There's nothing we can do."

"Nothing?"

"Nothing."

As Ay-ttho watched, the khalgoin planet slowly fade.

"What is happening?" she asked.

"It is simply disappearing into the black hole."

"What will happen to it?"

"Not sure. I asked Ron to identify a black hole large enough for us to survive. I'm not sure if it is large enough for an entire planet to go through unharmed."

"So, what do we do now?"

"First," said Pirate. "We should use the tachyon transmitter to contact Barnes."

CHAPTER 43: HOMEWARD BOUND

Ay-ttho watched the khalgoin planet slowly disappear until she could see it no more. Then she left Pirate and Witt to set up the tachyon transmitter while she went to see Sevan.

When she arrived in the sick bay, Sevan was not so much unconscious anymore but more in some kind of stupor, as if he was having some kind of nightmare.

"How is he?" Ay-ttho asked.

"Still unresponsive," said Effeeko.

Tori arrived back from fixing the anti-matter drive.

"Wash your hands before you come into my sick bay," said Effeeko.

"I have washed my hands."

"Could have fooled me."

"He's waking up," Ay-ttho interrupted.

"No," said Effeeko. "He's been like this for a while."

"Where am I?" said Sevan.

"Oh," Effeeko relented. "He didn't do that before."

"You are on the Mastery of the Stars," Ay-ttho told Sevan.

"The what?"

"Our ship."

"Ship?"

"It's his memory," said Tori. "Pirate has wiped his memory."

"Who's Pirate?" asked Sevan.

"Do you know who I am?"

Sevan shook his head.

"How about me?" asked Ay-ttho

Sevan thought about it for a moment and then shook his head. Effeeko moved forward.

"If he doesn't remember us, he won't remember you," said Ay-ttho.

"You're the doctor," Sevan said to Effeeko.

Effeeko smiled at Ay-ttho, who frowned.

"What do you remember?" Tori asked.

Sevan considered the question.

"I know where we are."

"Where are we?"

"We are at the centre of what they call the Milky Way."

"Milky Way? What kind of name for a star system is that?"

"How do you know?" asked Effeeko.

"I can see the stars out of the window. I know where I am."

"Do you know who you are?"

Sevan thought again, then shook his head.

"Do you know why you are here?"

"Is it because I know places?"

"You could say that."

"I did say that."

"Pirate and Witt have contacted Barnes on the tachyon transmitter," Ron announced.

"I'll be right there," said Ay-ttho. "Sevan? Do you think you can come with me?"

Sevan ignored her.

"Sevan?"

"Oh, sorry. Do you mean me?" Sevan apologised.

"Yes. Do you think you can come with me to the Bridge?"

"Where is it?"

"It's not far."

"Okay, sure."

Ay-ttho led Sevan to the bridge. Along the way, he marvelled at every sight he encountered along the corridors.

"Where is it?" asked Sevan when they arrived.

"Where's what?"

"The bridge."

"This is the bridge."

"I can't see a bridge."

"This control room. We call it the bridge."

"Why?"

"This is Witt, and this is Pirate," said Ay-ttho, ignoring Sevan's question.

"Hello Sevan," said Witt. "How are you feeling?"

"I'm not sure. I feel very confused."

"That's to be expected," said Pirate. "Your marbles are full."

"My marbles?"

"Come and sit here," said Witt. "We have someone you should talk to."

"He's here," said Pirate, to a screen on which Sevan could make out the flickering image of someone who looked remarkably like himself, except he was wearing a hooded robe.

"Hello Sevan," said the figure. "My name is Barnes. I am your creator, your begetter, if you like. I have Daxu with me. He created me, so the entire family is here."

Barnes laughed a laugh that left Sevan feeling uncomfortable.

"You are coming home," said Barnes. "Witt will connect you to the terminals so that when you arrive back in this universe, you can find your way home. You have fulfilled you purpose."

"My purpose?"

"The purpose for which Barnes created you. You are a biological map of our own universe and you have made it possible to recover the crew that went before you. You should be very proud."

"Should I?"

"Of course. Your mission has been a success. You are going to deliver your colleagues back where they belong."

Sevan didn't feel very proud.

"I will meet you here when you arrive," Barnes continued. "You shall live in luxury as a hero."

"That's nice."

"See you soon, Sevan."

The image flickered and disappeared.

"What was all that about?" Sevan asked.

"Don't worry," said Witt. "Everything will probably come back to you with time. Let's connect you to the terminals and then we can get out of here."

"Well done," Tori said to Ay-ttho.

"For not saying anything to Barnes. I know you wanted to."

"It was difficult to resist."

Witt and Pirate connected Sevan to the terminals, and Ron read the data.

"Are we ready?" asked Pirate. "Ready to enter the black hole? Ron."

"I am ready," said Ron. "By the time we reach the other side, I should have analysed enough of the data to calculate our position in our universe."

"Are you sure this is going to work?" asked Tori. "You saw what happened to their planet."

"Their planet had too great a mass to fit through," said Witt. "If our calculations are correct, this ship should be able to pass through, just like we did before."

"Should?" Tori was not convinced.

"Crossing the event horizon," said Ron.

"No going back now," said Pirate.

"I don't like him," Tori whispered to Ay-ttho.

Sevan, under the influence of Ron's probing, had slipped back into a stupor. He was oblivious to the noise of the gravity manipulators being pushed to the limit by the anti-matter drive on full power.

The ship warmed and then cooled almost as quickly, and then the gravity manipulators fell silent as Ron disengaged the drive and began his calculations as to their location.

"One thing is certain," said Witt. "We are not on Daphnis. So whatever white hole we came through was not the one Barnes and Daxu found."

"Not necessarily," said Ron. "It is entirely possible we passed through the white hole and then straight through the fold where they are diverting the excess energy. But I consider it unlikely. I am calculating our location now."

"Ron? I have a question," said Ay-ttho. "Barnes has loaded a star chart of the known universe into Sevan's marbles, right?"

"That is correct."

"Am I right in saying that the entire universe has not been mapped and that if we are at the opposite side of the universe to the Republic, then we might be in an unmapped area?"

"You are correct, yes."

"But the chances of that are very slim," Witt protested. "And we can just keep folding space until we arrive at an area that has been charted."

"That might be dangerous," said Pirate. "If we don't know where we are, there is a risk we could fold straight into a planet or a star."

"That is also correct," said Ron.

"Whose side are you on?" Witt complained to Pirate.

"It's not a question of sides," said Ay-ttho. "It is a question of not being stranded."

"I have completed my calculations," Ron announced. "and can't find this location on any of the charts. Despite modelling the constellations to calculate our position, I could not find any matching patterns."

"But that's impossible," said Witt. "You can scan a megaparsec."

"That is correct," said Ron. "However, the universe is currently estimated to be over 3000 giga parsecs and the star charts I can access via Sevan map only a tiny fraction of that area."

"I knew it," said Tori. "I knew this would happen. Now what? We can't fold."

"My scan has so far identified 55 potentially habitable exoplanets," said Ron. "Might I suggest we start with these? Correction, I have identified 97 potentially habitable exoplanets. The nearest is ten parsecs away."

"That's all very well, but unless you know otherwise, I doubt these systems are linked by portals in which case, even with an anti-matter drive Witt and Pirate will be dead before we get there and the rest of us will have probably killed each other through boredom."

"No problem," said Witt. "If Ron already has a megaparsec diameter scan, then we can use that to fold to one edge, then he can scan again. We can move half a megaparsec at a time."

"Might I suggest we fold to an exoplanet?" said Pirate. "If we find civilisation, they might have star charts."

"I hate to pour waste discharge on your anti-matter drive, Pirate," said Witt. "But the Republic survey calculated one technologically advanced civilization for every trillion planets."

"Whatever."

"That's only around ten in this entire galaxy."

"Wherever this galaxy is," Tori added.

"If we don't have any better plans, then I suggest I prepare to fold space as soon as Ron has made the calculations," said Witt. "Ron, head for the nearest star."

Pirate began removing the terminals from Sevan's antennae.

"Let's give him a break," he said.

Ay-ttho and Tori helped Sevan back to the sick bay where he fell asleep.

It wasn't long before Witt's apparatus was ready and Ron had brought the ship close enough to the nearest star for them to fold space. Within moments, the procedure was completed and the Mastery of the Stars was in orbit around a planet, which Ron scanned for signs of civilization.

"In areas of woodland and grass, I can detect evidence of settlements," Ron announced. "However, there is no evidence of technology."

"What are we looking at?" asked Ay-ttho, entering the bridge.

"Pre-civilization," said Witt. "How are we doing for provisions?"

"There are plenty in the cargo holds."

"No need to hang around then. Ron? Head for the nearest star."

"I have begun a scan of the next 500 kiloparsecs," said Ron. "I will locate a habitable exoplanet as far as possible."

"Excellent."

This process repeated itself time after time, with Ron identifying planets at varying stages of habitability.

"I can detect communities scattered across the planet," said Ron after scanning the latest location. "No examples of proto-urban settlements, however."

"It's the nearest we've got so far," said Witt. "Do you want to have a look?"

"Why would we waste units and risk injury with some primitive weapon? Let's go."

The search continued, just under 500 kiloparsecs at a time, but on each occasion, even if there was evidence of early civilization, there was no evidence of technology.

"How long is this going to take?" Tori complained.

"As long as it takes," said Witt. "Until Ron finds a recognisable sector of the universe or we find a civilised society with star charts."

"Of course the problem," Pirate began. "Is that Ron's half megaparsecs scan is photon based? It takes these photons around 3 million FSCs to travel that distance. In that time, its own star could have swallowed a habitable planet."

"What's an FSC?" asked Sevan, who had entered the bridge unnoticed.

"Sevan? How are you?" said Ay-ttho.

"I feel better, thank you. What's happening?"

"Pirate was just arguing that our method of seeking possible civilisations is flawed," said Witt. "But I'm afraid he is exaggerating."

"An FSC is a Future Solar Cycle, a standard unit of time used in the Republic," Pirate explained.

"But it doesn't change our odds of finding a technological society?" said Witt.

"There could've anything between a thousand and a hundred million civilisations in an average sized galaxy. That means we would have to visit a thousand planets before we found civilization."

"We've already got close."

"To civilization, not to a technologically advanced society."

"You sound like a broken entertainment implant, Pirate. With folding, we are crossing hundreds of galaxies. It's only a matter of time before Ron recognised something."

"At this rate, it will take six million folds to cross the universe. Sevan's star chart only covers a hundredth of the universe, even at the most optimistic estimates. We could be looking at a million and a half folds. It could take hundreds of FSCs to find the Republic."

"When did you suddenly become a pessimist?"

"I became a realist. We are lost."

CHAPTER 44: DOOMED TO VICTORY

"There is a flaw in your argument," Witt told Pirate. "We can't have folded more than 1,500 giga parsecs from the Republic."

"That could still take decades and you think our equipment will last that long?"

"Our food certainly won't," said Ay-ttho.

"Neither will Witt nor Pirate," Tori chuckled.

"We could go into suspended animation," said Witt.

"Do you think I'm going to sit here looking for planets while you sleep?" Tori complained.

"We can all go into suspended animation until Ron finds a suitable planet," Ay-ttho suggested.

Effeeko agreed his patients would probably benefit from suspended animation and so the patients and the seven healthy crew installed themselves in the barely used suspended animation units, and Ron took control of the mission.

It took 15 FNCs and over ten and a half thousand folds before Ron found a planet with a civilisation that had any mechanisation at all and roughly the same period again before he found evidence of industrialisation. Unfortunately, they appeared to be engaged in a globe-wide war.

After the crew had been in almost fifty FNCs of suspended animation, Ron found a planet that had been destroyed, presumably by weaponry that had been created as soon as the primitive species understood the most basic of the laws of physics.

After sixty-five FNCs of suspended animation, Ron found a planet on which the inhabitants had developed a system of primitive space flight, although this was clear to Ron that they could not travel much further than their own star system and had therefore not yet discovered portals and would not have star charts beyond their own observations which would certainly be inferior to Ron's own observational capacity and therefore he left them alone.

Fifteen FNCs later, Ron discovered a system in which they had colonised several planets, but there was still no evidence of interstellar capabilities. In all this time, Ron could not locate their correct position in relation to the Republic, and so he continued.

It wasn't until eighty-five FNCs had passed since the crew entered suspended animation that Ron found evidence of a civilisation capable of interstellar travel. There was evidence of gravity manipulation and ships clearly designed to travel through portals. He began reviving the crew.

All the crew were reanimated successfully except for one of Effeeko's patients, who was considered to have died very early in the journey.

"How long were we suspended for?" Ay-ttho asked Ron.

"Eighty-five FNCs."

"Barnes will think we are dead for sure," Tori laughed. "How far did we travel?"

"Over 300 giga parsecs."

"That's ridiculous," said Witt. "You should have encountered the Republic by now."

"Depends whether we were travelling towards it or away," said Ron. "We've probably only travelled across ten percent of the universe."

"You said we could have been 1,500 giga parsecs away from the Republic," said Pirate.

"At this rate it could take us..." Tori struggled with the maths

"Another 500 FSCs to reach the Republic," Pirate helped.

"Not unless this civilization has a star chart which includes portions of our star chart," said Witt.

"I love your optimism," said Pirate.

"We are about to find out," said Ron. "They have scanned us."

"What do we do?" asked Sevan.

"Hey Sevan, how are you feeling?" asked Ay-ttho. "Any of those memories returned yet?"

"I remember being put into suspended animation, but nothing before that."

"Oh, dear."

"I am receiving a transmission," said Ron. "I can't decipher it. Their ships are approaching. I detect weapon type systems are activated."

"We should activate our weapons system."

"Steady on, Tori," said Witt. "Given that we are not responding to their signal, they have every right to consider that we might be hostile. I would suggest that the last thing we want to do is activate our weapons system."

Several gunships approached, and Ron received several messages he could not decipher. He sent some back to show willing but held little hope that they would successfully translate them.

A larger ship approached and swallowed the Mastery of the Stars into its hull. The Mastery of the Stars, once moored within the alien ship's hold, was sprayed with a liquid.

"I think they are attempting to decontaminate us," said Witt. "Let's suit up."

They secured Effeeko, Nadio and the patients in the sick bay and then climbed into the full space suits, making sure they removed the weapons first. Then they opened the entrance hatch and slowly descended the ramp into the hold of the alien ship. There was no sign of the aliens themselves, so the group moved clear of the Mastery of the Stars into an empty area of the hold and waited.

The sprinkler system started up again, and they doused them in the same liquid that had bathed the Mastery of the Stars.

"It's a good job we wore our suits," said Tori

Unintelligible noise suddenly filled the hold. It sounded like they were being given instructions, but they could not understand what they were being asked to do.

A window opened and Sevan's hearts skipped several beats because the creatures which were on the other side were so close in appearance to the khalgoin, he thought they might have caught up with them and would be extremely upset that their planet had been deposited in a black hole.

A moment later, he realised they were not the khalgoin. They were smaller and had fur and a tail, but we're otherwise very similar to the khalgoin in appearance.

Next to the khalgoin-like creatures appeared a different type of creature. They weren't entirely different from Sevan himself except that they had no antennae and their feet seemed extraordinarily large. They wore a tight fitting suit, had gigantic eyes and the mouth and nose extended into an almost beak like shape.

They started making the same kind if noises the group had heard earlier. It was a kind of chatter made up of chirps, trills, hoots, clucks and whistles. To Sevan, it was completely unintelligible.

"We come from a place we call the Republic," said Witt.

The creatures stared.

In the meantime, Ron was attempting to communicate with the alien ship using a series of languages that scientists in the Republic had developed specifically for communicating with alien civilisations.

Next to the window, a door opened in the hold's side to a separate anti-chamber which also had an observation window for the creatures who were observing the group amongst much chattering, chirping and hooting. They entered the anti-chamber, and the door closed behind them.

Witt was attempting to aid the process by giving a running commentary, pointing and naming each individual in turn.

"Let's remove our helmets," Ay-ttho suggested, having already identified breathable air.

"No," said Witt. "In the same way that they are protecting themselves again unknown bacteria or viruses we may carry, we need to protect ourselves against theirs."

On a screen, a symbol appeared, and a creature was pointing to themselves.

"That's obviously the symbol they use to represent themselves," said Witt.

The symbol was replaced by another and the creature began pointing to the khalgoin like being

"And that symbol must represent them."

Then the two symbols appeared, one above each other and next to them were two other symbols. The creature was pointing to the fur of the khalgoin-like creature and then pointing to their own smooth skin.

"They are showing us the symbols that represent their differences," said Witt. "I think they are trying to teach us their language."

"This could take some time," said Tori.

The next symbol to be displayed was a new one altogether, and the creature was pointing to towards the group.

"That must be us."

Another symbol appeared, and the creature pointed to their ship. Then these two symbols appeared next to each other, with a space in the middle that was soon replaced by a third symbol. The creature began pointing to the Mastery of the Stars.

"I think these three symbols mean we came to this ship in the Mastery of the Stars."

"Why don't they tell us something we don't already know?" asked Tori

"Because they are teaching us their language. They need to use things they can be clear we understand. Are you getting all this, Ron?"

"Yes," said Ron via the communicator. "I am working with the alien ship's system to create a new language we can both understand. I will let you know when we have achieved anything useful."

Three more symbols appeared and one of the khalgoin-like creatures jumped up and down on the spot.

"That middle symbol I recognised," said Witt. "It is the symbol for that... this is no good. We are going to have to name them. What shall we call that creature?"

"How about vrequx?" Ay-ttho suggested.

"Fine, vrequx it is. So this sequence must say the vrequx is jumping."

The three symbols were now replaced with seven symbols, and the vrequx was pretending to be tired.

"Where did they get this one from?" Tori scoffed.

"I recognise the symbols for vrequx and jumping...and that one must be the...so, it's something the vrequx is jumping something something something, and one of them must be tired."

"When the vrequx jumps, he gets tired," Pirate suggested.

"Yes, that's brilliant," Witt agreed. "That must be it."

Next eight symbols appeared, and the vrequx laid down and pretended to sleep.

"Okay, we have the vrequx something jump something something something something something. One of the something's must be sleep."

"The vrequx has jumped and gone to sleep?" Pirate suggested.

"Could be."

Then seven symbols appeared, and the vrequx pretended to wake up.

"Something something sleep the vrequx something something. And it's something to do with waking up."

"After he sleeps, the vrequx wakes up," said Pirate.

"You are good at this."

Seven more symbols appeared.

"Something, then that's the symbol for us, something tired, something, us, something sleep."

"I think they're asking us if we want to sleep," said Pirate.

Witt attempted miming sleep and no but the creature didn't seem interested.

Ten symbols appeared.

"The vrequx something sleep something, the something something something tired."

"No idea," said Pirate. "Maybe it's something about not being tired because he slept?'

"Not sure. Why are they so keen that we sleep?"

Eight more symbols appeared.

"Something, us, something, tired, us, something, sleep. They just keep talking about sleep. How do we tell them we don't want to sleep?"

Witt attempted miming this too, but received a similarly uninterested reaction.

"I think they are just trying to give us examples of their sentence structure," said Pirate. "They have given us examples of symbols that represent objects, difference, cause and clauses. If we can find the right symbols, we can communicate what we need. Let's start by showing them our words, which are equivalent to their symbols. Ron? Can you project their symbols with the corresponding words, please?"

And so began the process. First, Ron showed the aliens the words they thought best represented the symbols. Then he projected images to ask for the relevant symbols. He projected their own star chart and, to everyone's delight, the aliens could identify a portion of the star chart and connected it with their own. Ron tried to communicate that they intended to return to their own galaxy.

"I'm not going," said Sevan.

CHAPTER 45: BLITZKREIG AND DOOMSDAY

"What do you mean, you're not going back?" Ay-ttho asked Sevan.

"There's nothing for me in the Republic. I've been used and now I'm going to return to what?"

"But you can't stay here."

"Why not?"

"You don't speak the same language. You don't even know whether the bacteria and viruses in this galaxy will kill you."

"Why is that a problem suddenly? It wasn't a problem when we met the khalgoin."

"He has a point," said Tori. "We have been very relaxed with our protocols until now."

"What are you going to eat?" asked Ay-ttho.

"I'm sure they have food."

"Sevan, we are your friends. You might not remember it, but we've been through a lot together."

"Just to train me to go to the khalgoin from what I've been told."

"It's not like that. Tori and I were not in on the conspiracy. I promise."

Sevan was silent.

"Look," Ay-ttho persisted. "Come with us now and I promise, if you don't like the Republic, I will bring you back here myself."

"How?"

"Witt will fold space for us, won't you Witt?"

Witt looked surprised.

"Of course he will. You have my promise. I'll make sure he does."

Sevan sighed.

"Where are we going, then?" asked Tori

"It makes sense to go back to Daphnis, where Barnes's operation was."

"Where it was 85 FSCs ago."

"Barnes will still be alive. He has the same genetics as you."

"Yes, but a lot can happen in 85 FSCs."

"Let's tell them we would like to go back to our ship," said Witt. "Ron? Can you help with that?"

"Of course, I have developed a new language with their ship computer and we can converse in a basic way. There is one slight problem, however. Their computer is saying that they want us to stay to be studied further."

"Please communicate that we cannot stay but will send others to facilitate a process of mutual learning."

"They say that is not satisfactory, that we are not their guests but their subjects."

"So they will not open the door?"

"They will not."

"Please tell them to open the door before we make them open the door," said Ay-ttho.

"They aren't going to open the door."

"Ron? I want you to blast the door and the observation room," said Ay-ttho. "Everyone to the back of the room."

There were two enormous explosions as a hole was blown through the door and the observation room was destroyed. As soon as debris stopped falling, Tori led the group through the hole into the hold, which was filled with smoke. They ran to the Mastery of the Stars, up the ramp and through the doors that Ron was already shutting.

The smoke that filled the hold had barely cleared when Ron turned the Mastery of the Star's cannons on the entrance to the hold. Two blasts created a hole large enough and, before the aliens had time to react, Ron was flying the Mastery of the Stars through the gap.

"Head for the nearest star," said Witt as he ran onto the bridge.

The alien ships had already responded and we're turning towards the Mastery of the Stars. Some had already fired but had not yet had time to target effectively.

Ron used the full power of the anti-matter drive to head for the nearest star and their pace was faster than the alien fighters that clearly hadn't yet developed an equivalent technology.

"How long to the nearest star?" Witt asked.

"I'm calculating," said Ron.

"Have you had time to process their star chart?"

"I am processing the data now. I should have calculated the parameters to fold to Daphnis by the time we have enough energy."

The Mastery of the Stars had already put enough distance between them and the alien fighters for them to be outside of weapons range and they showed no signs of closing

"I have successfully concluded the calculations," said Ron.

"Have you checked them?" asked Witt.

"Yes."

"Double checked them?"

"Yes."

"So we won't be taking anyone or anything with us?"

"No."

"Good. How close are we to having enough energy?"

"Very close."

Folding was becoming commonplace for the crew. Ay-ttho wished she could see the looks on the faces of the alien fighter pilots as they watched the Mastery of the Stars disappear.

When they emerged into orbit around Nereid, the first thing they noticed was that the energy/defence sphere which had surrounded Daphnis and The Doomed Planet was now in ruins.

"What's happened?" asked Witt.

"Alot can happen in 85 FNCs," said Tori.

"What should we do now?"

"Ron? Can you give us any idea about what is happening on the surface?" asked Ay-ttho.

"Comparing the surface structures with my records, it would appear that there has been a lot of destruction."

"Let's check The Doomed Planet."

"It's very much a similar story, I'm afraid. There are inhabitants and evidence of commerce, but the concession is only a shadow of its former self."

"What now?" asked Tori. "Should we see if we can find Barnes?"

"What about the tachyon transmitter?" Pirate suggested.

"Good idea," said Witt. "I'll help you set it up."

In an office in the presidential palace on Future, a communicator buzzed. The occupant of the office had long expected this moment and picked it up.

"Hello? Is that Barnes?"

"No, I don't think Barnes can come to the communicator right now. Please leave a message?"

"Who is this?"

"Fine. Please leave a message?"

Witt disconnected the call.

"I didn't like the sound of that," he said.

"Ron? Can you give us a list of species you can identify on Daphnis?"

"Running the scan now. Shall I inform you of each species as soon as I identify them?"

"Yes, please."

"Corporation mining clones, Corporation security clones, Republic clones, Future indigenous, Thugs, Looters, Pillagers, Khalgoin..."

"Wait a unit," said Witt. "Did you say Khalgoin?"

"Yes, there are quite a lot of them."

"But that's impossible."

"Not necessarily," said Pirate. "Perhaps their planet remained intact?"

"Even if it did, they lacked the technology to fold space. How did they get here so quickly?"

"Perhaps they set off in a different direction than us?"

"Or," Effeeko began. "The Republic finished their ship, and the khalgoin used it to return to this universe."

"Their planet was destroyed."

"But not their moon."

"Even if they came back on a Republic ship," said Witt. "They wouldn't have a star map for this universe."

"No, but perhaps they got lucky and came through Barnes' white hole."

"In which case, it would have spewed them out wherever Barnes was dumping the energy."

"Which I would bet was not a million parsecs from here."

"Either way," said Tori. "They are here. Now, what are we going to do?"

"I suggest you decide quickly," said Ron. "There are several Republic fighters approaching us at speed."

"What should we do?" asked Tori.

"We don't know where we might be safe," said Ay-ttho.

"We have to decide quickly," said Witt.

"I suggest we go somewhere they are unlikely to look for us where we can lie low until we can work out a little better what is going on," Pirate suggested.

"Angetenar," Ay-ttho said at once.

"Angetenar?" Nadio and Effeeko exclaimed in unison.

"Given that an asteroid storm destroyed it, I doubt anyone will look there."

"Ron? Make the calculations," said Witt. "Head to the nearest star."

"That phrase is getting a bit irritating," Ay-ttho whispered to Tori.

"I know what you mean."

Ay-ttho noticed that Sevan was quietly sobbing.

"What's wrong?" she asked.

"I have nowhere to go to," she said.

"None of us have."

"So, what are we supposed to do?"

"I don't know. Find somewhere where we can be happy. Somewhere where we're not wanted for experiments or slaves or convicts. Let's try to find somewhere where we can all settle down and put all these adventures behind us. I know Tori feels the same."

"It's true, I do," said Tori. "We have been used and I think we deserve a break."

"But what will we do?" asked Sevan.

"I don't know," Ay-ttho admitted. "Perhaps we could join a commune like the one on Sonvaenope."

"Where is Sonvaenope?"

"I'm sure we can ask Witt to jump there."

"We don't know whether anything survives on Sonvaenope," said Tori.

"Shut up Tori," said Ay-ttho. "We'll find somewhere."

The Republic fighters were no match for the Mastery of the Stars' anti-matter drive and they made it close enough to the star to fold space and, soon enough, they were in orbit around Angetenar.

"Where to now?" asked Witt.

"We should go to the caverns," said Ay-ttho. "We once found survivors there. It's probably our best bet."

As the Mastery of the Stars approached the surface of the planet, Ay-ttho was amazed at how much vegetation there was, even in areas that had been barren.

"This used to look like a wasteland," she said.

"I imagine nutrient rich ash covered the entire area, which has helped to promote regrowth which has been unhindered by the interference of Angetenarians," said Witt.

The dusty plain which led up to the caverns was now covered in woodland, so much so that there was no space to land, even on what had been the rocky entrance to the caverns. Ron had to steer the ship into the cavern entrance and land it inside.

"This is fantastic," said Ay-ttho. "It's so beautiful."

"It's amazing isn't what planets can do when left to their own devices."

"That's all very nice," said Tori. "But does anyone have a plan?"

"The plan is to hide here and not get caught," said Ay-ttho.

"For the rest of our lives?"

"I could live here for the rest of my life."

"Well, I couldn't."

"You don't have to stay."

"Then I need to take the ship."

"Fine, just leave me some stuff. I can look after myself. Where are you going to go?"

"I don't know yet. I'll have to think about it."

"If you go," said Effeeko. "I'll have to come with you. My patients need the sick bay."

"And I need my instruments," said Witt.

"I don't want to stay," said Pirate.

"Nadio?" Ay-ttho asked.

"I think I'll stay with Effeeko, sorry."

Ay-ttho turned to look at Sevan. Sevan shrugged.

"Fine. I'll stay here by myself then."

Ay-ttho stormed off the bridge.

"Leave her," said Tori. "She'll get over it."

"Even if she doesn't," said Witt. "It is sensible to wait here until we have a better idea of what is going on. I'll see what I can find with the tachyon transmitter."

Ay-ttho left the ship and went for a wander through the forest. She found a rock on which she could sit and look across the plain to the ruins of the city still poking above the forest canopy.

She considered walking down to the city to see what might be left, but knew she had all the time in the universe to do that, so she just sat and stared towards the horizon.

Sevan broke her almost meditative state, stumbling through the undergrowth.

"What is it?" Ay-ttho grumbled.

"It's Witt," said Sevan breathlessly. "He's made contact. They're on their way."

CHAPTER 46: THE SACRIFICE

"Who is?" asked Ay-ttho.

"D'Heli and Alyr."

"They're still alive?"

"Yes, and they're here on Angetenar."

"What?"

"They were in the caverns to meet us at the ship. Are you coming?"

"Sure."

Ay-ttho followed Sevan back to the Mastery of the Stars and when they arrived, D'Heli and Alyr were already there. They were in the officers' mess, giving a potted history of the Republic over the last 85 FNCs.

"You haven't missed much," said D'Heli. "When the zoxans arrived..."

"Who are the zoxans?" asked Ay-ttho.

"That's what they called the khalgoin," Witt explained.

"They just destroyed everything they encountered," said D'Heli. "They caught both the Republic and the Corporation by surprise and both underestimated the zoxans' abilities and determination. Within only a few FSCs, they had swept through the entire Republic and had installed themselves everywhere, creating a dictatorship that plunged the citizens into slavery."

"The Republic was always a dictatorship," said Ay-ttho.

"Yes, but the citizens weren't treated as slaves."

"The clones were," said Tori.

"Of course, you make a good point. However, that is the situation we find ourselves in at the moment. A few of us escaped here."

"What is life like here in the caves?" asked Ay-ttho.

"We survive. The vegetation provides us with fruit and vegetables. We can cultivate grains and even make our own pleasure drink. It's not quite fishy, but it's better than nothing."

"May I try some, please?" asked Sevan.

"No animals?" asked Witt.

"No, they were wiped out by the meteor shower or died shortly afterwards when the vegetation died off. There are some species but nothing large. We could have brought livestock with us, but we left in a bit of a rush."

"You have enough knowledge of food growing, though." said Ay-ttho.

"Do you remember back in the days of the first President Man? There was an attempt to completely automate food production."

"Kind of."

"They constructed droids and sent them to all corners of the Republic to increase food production."

"I'm surprised they didn't create farming clones," Tori scoffed.

"We've got a droid," D'Heli continued. "He knows everything about food production and survival. He's become our leader, more or less, because he tells us what we need to do. We call him the Electric Man because he's our president."

"And the khalgoin don't come here?" asked Ay-ttho.

"The khalgoin?"

"Sorry, the..."

"Zoxans," Witt helped.

"I'm sure they have scanned the planet," said D'Heli. "But we are too deep in the caverns to be picked up."

"That's true," said Pirate. "Ron didn't pick up anything. How long have you been here?"

"A long time. Occasionally, we send out a scout ship, but unfortunately, they don't always come back."

"I still don't understand," said Witt. "How they overcame both the Republic and the Corporation. We saw their technology. It was inferior to anything in the Republic."

"It is a mystery," D'Heli agreed. "Some say the Corporation or the Republic, or both, were betrayed from within."

"What about the scorpion lizards?" asked Ay-ttho. "They looked unbeatable."

"But they were beaten. Remember, the scorpion lizards were just prototypes, and the Republic had few of them. Let me introduce you to our community. Carry what you can. We can come back for Effeeko and his patients."

Nadio elected to stay and assist Effeeko, but the others collected as much as they could carry and then followed D'Heli and Alyr deeper into the cavern.

They hadn't travelled far into the cavern before they saw some of the many buildings which had been constructed from wood, using the natural shape of the cavern and resulting in spectacular designs. They had set round wooden doors into the rock, below similar shaped windows.

The cavern was lit by lights set into the rock at regular intervals.

"They run off cold fusion," said D'Heli. "A basic technology, but it suits our needs."

They passed through a set of iron gates and the walls narrowed until it opened out into a vast underground cavern which stretched upwards and downwards as far as they could see. Lights dotted the walls of the cavern. Each light was a dwelling with a door and windows linked to the other dwellings by narrow paths cut into the rock.

"I'll take you somewhere where you can relax and freshen up," said D'Heli. "Then we'll get you something to eat and afterwards you can meet the Electric Man."

D'Heli led them through one of the rounded doorways into a smaller cave filled with wooden furniture. Platforms had been constructed to create mezzanine levels, and they had painted the rock white.

The cold fusion lights meant the rooms were not at all dim and D'Heli showed them around the bedrooms, kitchen, dining area and common room.

"You may rest here," he said. "There will be someone along later with some food."

Sevan immediately collapsed onto a bed. It wasn't that he was tired; he had just lost all motivation. Ay-ttho went to sit by him.

"How are you feeling?" she asked.

"Terrible."

"That's understandable. You've been through a lot."

"Have I? I wouldn't know."

"You must believe me that Tori and I had no involvement in this. They used us as much as you."

"I don't blame you, but at least you remember life before the khalgoin."

"To be honest, you're not missing much. You have spent most of your waking life as a Corporation mining clone until they picked you as the workers' representative. Then you were the chief council member, but they didn't like you, so you ended up wandering around the Republic with us."

"Doing what?"

"Originally we were just trying to get back to the Doomed Planet, but that proved to be quite difficult and in the end we seemed to just run from one enemy to another. That's how we ended up with the khalgoin and you know the rest."

"There must be more to it than that."

"There is quite a lot. But it would take a long time to tell you everything."

"Apparently, time is something I have lots of."

While Ay-ttho was telling Sevan his life story, the food arrived. It comprised Gurengi algae crisps, Lurirans space-beetle and Globbon octo-nuts with a topping of Daregs beetle dust. It wasn't the most appealing meal they had ever seen, but it was welcome and they ate it all.

"We have supplies in the Mastery of the Stars," said Tori. "If you can round up some help, we can transfer it into the caverns."

"Thank you. We have a central storage area we use to pool our resources."

"Use the galley on the Mastery of the Stars as well, if you wish."

"That's very kind of you. I think we are going to need to move your ship into a deeper cavern. If a patrol ship passes, they are bound to pick it up on their scanners. I have a location in mind and then we can leave the supplies on the ship. It will be more secure than our central storeroom."

Tori and D'Heli left to move the ship.

"I'll come with you," said Witt. "I would like to fetch some instruments to continue my studies."

On the way, Tori recounted their adventure to the khalgoin universe in more detail, answering as many of D'Heli's questions as he could

They left Ay-ttho, Sevan and Pirate in the underground dwelling to rest.

"You must have residents that require treatment," Effeeko said when D'Heli arrived on the ship. "We can use the Mastery of the Stars' sick bay as a clinic and I can treat your community as best I can."

"That is very kind of you," said D'Heli. "We have healers who make medicines from whatever they can find in the forest, but the resources you have here will be a significant improvement."

"I wouldn't want to tread on anyone's claws."

"Not at all. They will welcome the help."

D'Heli helped Ron navigate the ship out of the cavern to another cavern further down the huge gorge which was now covered in forest. This cavern was much larger than the first, and Ron could fly the ship deep inside the mountain until D'Heli showed where he should land. He had chosen a flat stretch with smaller tunnels leading off from the side. It was through these tunnels that he showed them the route back to the settlement where they had been accommodated.

"This apartment is great," said Tori. "But we can sleep on the ship. We don't want anyone to make sacrifices on our behalf."

"It's not a sacrifice," said D'Heli. "This was my apartment, but it is too big for me now. I have moved in with Alyr."

"I feel bad now. You must have your home back. We can sleep on the ship. It's not a problem."

"No, I insist. This place has too many memories. I was looking for an excuse to move, so you are doing me a favour."

Tori wondered what memories D'Heli was trying to escape but didn't want to pry and, as D'Heli didn't volunteer more information, he let the matter rest.

Witt had carried an armful of equipment from the Mastery of the Stars and began setting it up in the common room. Pirate joined him to observe the procedure.

Ay-tho and Sevan rested, having not yet fully recovered from the effects of suspended animation.

"Do you mind if I wander around the settlement?" Tori asked D'Heli.

"Of course not. I'll give you a tour."

D'Heli led Tori along the trail which led around the sides of the cavern. There were many residents coming and going. Some working together to drag timber, others carrying baskets filled with fruit or insects. The size of the community impressed Tori.

"Do you think there are communities like this in other parts of the Republic?" he asked.

"We don't know. If there are, we haven't found any yet. Like I said, we occasionally send out scouting vessels, but our resources are very limited."

"Would you like us to go on a scouting mission for you?"

"That sounds like an excellent idea. Let's ask the Electric Man."

"Does he decide everything?"

"He has to. We rely on his knowledge to survive."

CHAPTER 47: THE ELECTRIC MAN

Sevan woke up suddenly in a cold sweat, having had another nightmare, but at least he had got some sleep, which was becoming increasingly difficult. He did not know how long he had slept for and at first and wasn't really sure where he was, but he soon realised he was in D'Heli's apartment in the caverns of Angetenar.

What they were going to do now? Would they end up living on Angetenar for the foreseeable future? According to D'Heli, the rest of the Republic was living in servitude to the khalgoin.

At least they had somewhere they could hide from the khalgoin, even if they did not know how long their exile would be. He wished he'd never left the concession on the Doomed Planet and he also realised that he could never go back to that life.

He felt he should probably see how everyone was, especially Ay-ttho, who had spent a lot of time describing to Sevan the life he had forgotten.

When Seven emerged, he found Ay-ttho, Tori, Witt and Pirate in the common room.

"Are you okay?" asked Tori. "You've been asleep for a long time."

"What are we going to do?" Sevan asked.

"About what?"

"Are we going to stay here?"

"You are free to stay," said Ay-ttho. "Tori has offered our services as a scout ship to see whether we can find other communities like this one."

"When would we leave?"

"Your guess is as good as ours. We've got to speak to the Electric Man first. Apparently, he's in charge. We haven't discussed it with Effeeko or Nadio either."

"What about the khalgoin?"

Ay-ttho considered the question beneath her, so Tori answered.

"We are obviously going to avoid them."

As if on cue, D'Heli entered.

"Good, you are all here," he said. "The Electric Man has agreed to see you. I have already sent someone to fetch Effeeko and Nadio. They will meet us there."

"I thought Effeeko and Nadio were unaware of the plan," said Sevan.

"They are," said Tori. "We will have to speak to them quickly before the meeting."

"And if they don't like the idea?"

"That's a real possibility. They don't have to come with us if they don't want to."

"We are not in a hurry?" said Ay-ttho. "If they want to spend some time here before we go, that's fine. Next question?"

Sevan bit his tongues, he knew Ay-ttho detested lots of questions couldn't suppress his curiosity for long.

"Where are you planning to go?"

"We'll have to discuss that."

"Sonvaenope seems the obvious starting point," said Tori. "There was only a small community there. Perhaps the khalgoin have ignored it."

"Our scout ships have already been to Sonvaenope," said D'Heli. "There was nothing there."

Sevan's hearts sank. He was going to be wandering around the universe forever.

"No, wait. There is something there," said Witt, staring at his equipment. "Very feint. Must be a tiny community, perhaps even just one individual."

"What use is one individual?" Sevan complained

"Don't forget, I was alone on Chaldene when you found me."

"Yes, and if we hadn't I would still have my memory. "

"But you would be stuck in deep space."

"Why?"

"Because you didn't know how to fold space."

D'heli led them to the offices of the Electric Man, where they waited with expectation.

What they found was a relatively large reception hall with wooden furniture and decorations. They took seats and waited until the Electric Man was ready for them.

"His office is in there," said D'Heli pointing to a large wooden door.

"The Electric Man will see you now," said a guard, leading them to the doorway.

They passed through the doorway into a vast, luxuriously fitted office.

"Don't come any further," a distinctly electronic voice ordered.. "What is your business here? How do we know the zoxans have not sent you to spy on us?"

"We are not zoxan spies," Ay-ttho answered.

"You look like you are zoxan spies."

"He used to be a Republic security clone," said Ay-ttho. "We are corporation clones. He is an Angetenarian, he is a Thug, and they are indigenous Futurians. We have been to the universe the zoxans came from. We were in suspended animation for 85 FNCs and when we woke up, the zoxans had taken over the Republic."

"A Corporation freighter cannot travel to another universe."

"We know how to fold space,"

"Even if you did, there is the barrier of Witt to consider."

"We found a black hole which led to a white hole in their universe. We returned the same way," said Witt.

"And who might you be?"

"I am Professor Witt."

There was a long silence.

"What do you think he's doing?" Sevan asked after a while.

"I think he's thinking," said Tori

"What are you doing?" Ay-ttho asked

"I'm thinking."

"What are you thinking about?"

"You story seems unbelievable."

"I know, but it's true."

There followed another long silence.

"What do you want?" the Electric Man asked at last.

"We have nowhere to go. We thought we might make ourselves useful. Perhaps a scout ship. Witt has identified a signal on Sonvaenope."

"When have already sent a scout ship to Sonvaenope, it was deserted."

"Perhaps someone or something has landed there since."

Another long pause.

"Please enter. You may be seated."

They proceeded further into the office and sat on luxurious wooden chairs. The Electric Man looked like a more upmarket version of the electronic waiters that had served Sevan when he was chief council member back on the Doomed Planet.

"What do you want from me?" he asked.

"We already told you," said Ay-ttho. "We have nowhere to go and nothing to do, so we thought we might as well make ourselves useful and try to find other communities hiding from the khalgoin, sorry, I mean zoxans. "

"If the zoxans can't find them, what makes you think you can?"

"The technology on the Mastery of the Stars is far superior to anything the kho... zoxans have."

"You forget that when they took control of the Republic, they also took control of our technology. For example, they now have a fleet of fully functioning scorpion lizards and have improved on the prototype."

Ay-ttho sighed. This wasn't how she had hoped the conversation would develop. "Please tell us something about yourself?"

"I'm sure D'heli has told you all you need to know, but some call me the Electric Man, others that knew me a long time ago know that my job was increasing food production around the Republic. You may call me what you wish. It doesn't really matter. So you could pass the edge of the universe?"

"And return," said Witt.

"You have an anti-matter drive?" asked the Electric Man.

"We do," said Ay-ttho.

Witt sat in his chair.

"I will support your desire to work as a scout ship on one condition."

"What's that?" asked Ay-ttho.

"That you leave your colleagues here with enough medical equipment to treat this community. Where are your colleagues?"

Ay-ttho thought about it for a moment. She looked at Tori, who shrugged. Then she looked at Sevan, who was looking at her in expectation.

"We haven't had time to discuss our plan with them," she said.

"Excellent," said the Electric Man, standing up. "We must start straight away. Come with me I'll..."

He couldn't finish his sentence because the guard led two more visitors into the room.

"Nadio!" Sevan exclaimed. "Effeeko!"

Effeeko was already halfway into the room before he spoke.

"You started without us," he observed.

Not far behind him was the large furry figure of Nadio marching towards them. He was clearly annoyed and Sevan braced himself for the impending onslaught.

"What are you doing starting without us?" he launched into a tirade. "You always abandon us on that ship and make decisions without us."

"I asked you if you wanted to come," Ay-ttho tried to defend herself. "We haven't made any decisions, but we have something to discuss with you."

"I thought we had," said the Electric Man. "They will stay here and establish a hospital while you go scouting for other settlements."

"Good to see you involving us in decisions again," said Nadio.

"We are involving you now," Ay-ttho snapped.

"Why would we want to go scouting? You've seen the mess they made on The Doomed Planet and Daphnis."

"I did. I was there, remember?"

"So, what's so difficult to understand?"

"What else do we have to do?" Ay-ttho asked.

"The community here needs our help."

"That's why we were going to suggest that you and Effeeko stay here."

"You want to get rid of me?"

"Of course not. But you said yourself that you wanted to help."

"And you don't?"

"I do, which is why I suggested scouting. It's more use than staying here."

"Your friend is right," the Electric Man told Nadio. "Your skills are incalculable to us here, whereas Ay-ttho can serve us best by trying to find other communities like ours."

Nadio wasn't happy, but he kept his feelings to himself. Ay-ttho thanked the Electric Man and promised that he would work with Effeeko to transfer the sick bay into the community.

"What if we get sick?" asked Sevan.

"We won't have Effeeko even if we do," reasoned Ay-ttho.

"But Ron can look after us."

"Don't worry, we are leaving enough emergency facilities for the five of us."

"Five?"

"Yes, Witt and Pirate will come with us."

"Really?"

"Really."

Once most of the sick bay, plus Effeeko's patients, had been transferred into the community, the Mastery of the Stars was ready to leave. They restocked it with a reasonable quantity of provisions and Witt overhauled the gravity manipulators and heat shields that had taken a battering over the previous 85 FSCs.

"Ready to go?" Ay-ttho asked Sevan.

"I'm not sure that I am."

"Come on, it's going to be like the old rotations again."

"I don't remember the old rotations."

"Then it'll be a fresh experience for you."

"I don't remember everything, but every so often I get like a... I'm not sure how to explain it... like flashbacks."

"Maybe your memory is coming back. I think this trip will be good for you. You've been very distant recently."

"I've been avoiding everyone. Everything irritates me and I'm worried I might snap at any moment and start shouting at someone."

"You probably deserve a bit of shouting, given what you've been through."

"It's not just that. I'm afraid to go to sleep."

"Why?"

"I've been having terrible dreams so I just end up laying awake."

"Let's see Effeeko."

"No, I just want to stop talking about it. Leave me alone, I'm going to find some pish."

Ay-ttho watched Sevan walk away. She was worried about him. He had been through a lot and hadn't asked for any of it. She followed him to his quarters and once she was satisfied that he was just going to bed; she went to the bridge where she found Tori, Witt and Pirate waiting for her.

"Where's Sevan?" asked Tori.

"He's in his room. Is everything ready?"

"Yes, just waiting for you."

"Okay, give me a unit. I just want to say goodbye to Nadio and Effeeko. You coming?"

"You know I hate goodbyes."

"I'll be right back."

Ay-ttho descended from the ship and found Nadio and Effeeko waiting for her on the edge of the cavern.

"All ready?" asked Effeeko.

"Yes, I think so. Did you get everything you wanted?"

"Yes, thank you? Don't forget, if you need any advice, I'm always at the end of a tachyon transmitter."

"Thanks. I'll try not to send too many messages. I don't want to tell the khalgoin where you are."

"You mean the zoxans."

"Whatever."

She looked at Nadio, who didn't look happy.

"I'll be back," she told him.

"You'd better be."

"I will."

Ay-ttho, overcome with emotion, turned, re-entered the ship and, without looking behind, closed the door.

She took a moment to compose herself and then headed back to the bridge where the others were still waiting.

"Head to the nearest star," she said.

THE END

The crew will be back in Book Four - *Surviving the Zoxans*

*

Enjoy this book? You can make a big difference.

Reviews are the most powerful tools in my arsenal for getting attention for my books. Much as I'd like to, I don't have the financial muscle of a large publisher. I can't take out full-page ads in the newspaper or put posters on the subway.

(Not yet anyway)

But I have something much more powerful and effective than that, and it's something those publishers would kill to get their hands on.

A committed and loyal bunch of readers.

Honest reviews of my books help bring them to other readers' attention.

If you've enjoyed this book, I would be very grateful if you could spend just five minutes leaving a review (it can be as short as you like).

Thank you very much.

To find the link to where you can review the book, simply scan this QR code:

Get a free and exclusive bonus epilogue to End of the Universe, only available here.

Building a relationship with my readers is the very best thing about writing. I occasionally send newsletters with details on new releases, special offers, and other bits of news relating to my novels.

If you sign up to the mailing list, I'll send you an exclusive epilogue to *End of the Universe.*

You can get the epilogue, for free, at:https://dl.bookfunnel.com/yjmjxv8im4

Not ready to leave Sevan and the team yet?

Read the first chapters of Surviving the Zoxans

CHAPTER 1: THE STAKES GET HIGHER

Sevan's marbles were still sore when he was awoken by the ship's alarm. He dragged himself out of his bunk and up to the bridge where he could see Sonvaenope large in the observation windows and it was clear someone on the surface was shooting at them.

"What's happening?" he asked.

"We are being shot at," said Ay-ttho

"No uxlod, Moncur," said Sevan, referring to the famous detective of the entertainment implant series of the old Republic, who was famous for solving every case. "Have they done much damage?"

"None," said Tori. "Their weapon isn't powerful. Ron is transmitting 'we come in peace' messages."

"As long as we don't come in pieces," Sevan joked, but nobody laughed.

"This is the same location we left the colony of Angetenarians all that time ago," Tori observed.

Sevan thought that would save money in set building if they ever made the story of their lives into a series for an entertainment implant.

Ron landed the ship on the outskirts and, even before the engines had shut down, a large crowd had gathered.

"Oh, my Giant Cup!" Ay-ttho exclaimed as she watched the crowd part to let through an individual, clearly of some importance.

"What is it?" asked Sevan.

"Sgniwef!"

"Sgniwef of Ao-Jun?" asked Tori. "But surely that's impossible. We have been in suspended animation for ages. She must be dead by now."

"The Ao-jun live long lives," Ay-ttho explained. "That is Sgniwef. I would bet Sevan's marbles on it."

"Not the Sgniwef of the Zistreotovean war?" asked Pirate.

"The same."

"I wonder if she is still with Luap?"

Ay-ttho descended from the ship and approached Sgniwef, whom, she considered, had not aged considerably.

Sevan thought the entertainment implant series of their lives was looking very viable if they could re-use characters.

"It has been a very long time, Sgniwef. I think the last time I saw you, Matthews was president," said Ay-ttho

"Who is it that claims to know me from such times past?" Sgniwef asked.

"My name is Ay-ttho San An Wan. This is Tori, Sevan, Pirate and Witt. And this is our ship, the Mastery of the Stars."

"Sevan? Didn't he help Matthews kill Kirkland?"

"I didn't help so much as tagged along."

"You should also remember Matthews exiled us, and we fought against her."

"Yes, I recollect something of that sort. What brings you here to Sonvaenope?"

"We detected your signal from Angetenar. You should be careful because if we can detect you, the khalgoin might also and your gun will be no match against them."

"First, who are these khalgoin of whom you speak? And second, what you experienced were only warning shots. Our true arsenal is much more powerful."

"Glad to hear it. I'm sorry, I believe you call the khalgoin, zoxans."

"Oh yes, the zoxans. We have successfully hidden from the zoxans for many FSCs, but we have heard of new dangers of zoxans helping one tribe of old Republicans against another. The Ao-jun are now nomadic, like nearly all non-zoxans who are not enslaved. How do we know you are not in league with the zoxans?"

"I ask to trust us and take my word for it."

"That is easier said than done. However, the Ao-jun are hospitable. Therefore, I invite you to stay with us at our settlement for as long as you need and trust that you do not bring the zoxan forces with you."

"We are very grateful for your trust and promise that we will not betray it. There is one thing I don't understand. Our scanners showed a tiny settlement, but your settlement is large."

"We have been using radiation masking to hide us. You shouldn't have been able to detect us at all. We must be vulnerable to the zoxans."

"I don't think so. The scanners on the Mastery of the Stars are very good, far advanced than anything the zoxans have, I would imagine."

"Let's hope you are right."

Sgniwef led them into the settlement and into a large hall which looked like they must use it as a meeting place.

"This is Luap, my partner," said Sgniwef, gesturing to where Luap was sitting.

"So that is Luap," Witt whispered. "I thought the face that launched a thousand ships would have been nicer."

"Oh, I don't know," whispered Pirate. "I think time has been very kind to her."

"Luap will throw a party in your honour," said Sgniwef. "You must forgive me. I have business I must attend to and must leave, but I will return. In the meantime, I will leave you in the capable claws of my partner."

"Lucky us," Pirate whispered.

Sgniwef left the hall and left the visitors wondering what to do next.

"You must forgive my partner," said Luap. "He is always very busy. Please take a seat."

The visitors took seats and Luap ordered food and drinks to be brought. Pirate stared at Luap and realised that Luap was staring back at him. Luap approached Pirate.

"Where are you from?" he asked. "Who is your family?"

Luap found Pirate beautiful and Pirate realised this instantly.

"My name is Pirate and my origins are of no consequence."

"May I confess I find myself attracted to you?"

"You may, and may I confess I share the same feelings for you?"

Immediately, Pirate thought about how he might capture Luap and take him away from Sgniwef.

"Would you like to come and see our ship?" Pirate asked.

"I would like that very much," said Luap. "But first you must eat and drink. There is much to celebrate when we meet fellow refugees."

They served the visitors food, the likes of which they had not tasted for many FSCs. They also served them drinks which Sevan did not recognise as either fushy or pish but were very agreeable and left him with the same pleasant sensation.

The hall became populated with what Sevan imagined must have been the leading figures in the settlement. They mingled with the visitors and asked them many questions about how they arrived on Sonvaenope and how they had escaped the zoxans.

The visitors had similar questions of their own, and the hall was alive with conversation. Pirate monopolised Luap, asking her many questions about her life and making many boasts about his.

He suspected she was not happy with Sgniwef, but he could not draw her on the topic, nor would she make any comment related to the period surrounding the Zistreotovean war during which they supposedly kidnapped her and took her to Zistreotov. Pirate supposed the entire episode must have been too traumatic for her.

"From where do you come?" Luap asked Pirate.

"I am originally from Future," he said. "But I spent most of my career on a planet called Chaldene in the Kale system."

"I've never heard of it."

"It's a long way from here, near the edge of the universe. We were experimenting with the possibility of crossing the barrier of Witt into parallel universes. My friend over there is the very Witt who gave the barrier of Witt its name."

Pirate gesticulated towards Witt, who appeared to be delivering a lecture on the science of white holes to a rapt audience.

"You are far more attractive than he is," said Luap.

"That's easy. Look at the shape of his head."

"That's not what I meant."

"I know, I'm sorry. I was only joking. We were successful in crossing to a parallel universe, but we became trapped there and Witt had to come and rescue us. I was burned badly. Here you can see some of my scars."

Luap marvelled at Pirate, whom he considered to be fiercely beautiful. He liked him, not just for his looks, but also because he seemed knowledgeable.

"They say the zoxans came from another universe."

"So I've heard."

Pirate could sense Luap's feelings for him, but it hardly mattered because Luap soon made matters clear.

"I like you very much Pirate," he said. "Do you feel the same about me?"

Pirate admitted he did, and the two left the gathering unnoticed.

*

"You have much that would benefit our own community," Witt told Sgniwef when she returned to the settlement. "And I dare say that we have much that would benefit you. I suggest we use the Mastery of the Stars to shuttle between the two communities to facilitate a trade between us, assuming that Ay-ttho is agreeable to such a suggestion."

"At least we would do something useful," said Ay-ttho.

"I agree," said Sgniwef. "Such a trade would be beneficial to both communities. Let us discuss your initial requirements and then we can load your ship with whatever we can spare of the things you desire."

The gathering had soon agreed on a list and Sgniwef ordered that they deliver the required produce to the Mastery of the Stars.

Once they had loaded everything, they prepared to leave.

"I'm sorry that Luap is not here to bid you farewell," said Sgniwef. "Something very important must have come up to detain him elsewhere because I know he has enjoyed your visit immensely and would certainly want to have said goodbye."

"Until next time," said Witt. "I have the list of produce you require and will do my utmost to return with the goods as soon as possible."

A sizable crowd had gathered to wave goodbye to the freighter as it took off, and Sevan felt that perhaps this new life playing trade between the two settlements might not be so bad after all.

"Should we head to the star and fold?" asked Ay-tho.

"I think it might be better if we use the conventional portals," said Witt. "I have been inspecting the mechanisms and I think it's better if we don't attempt to fold space until I've performed some maintenance."

"What if the khalgoin are guarding the portals?" asked Tori.

"Ron?" asked Ay-tho. "Please do a scan and see whether there are any ships at the portal."

"There are no ships on this side of the portal. However, my scanners cannot see through the portal, so there is a possibility that there might be ships on the other side."

"We can't risk it," said Ay-ttho. "We have to fold space."

"I can't guarantee the mechanism will remain stable," Witt warned. "If the field collapses, the ship will be destroyed. There may be khalgoin on the other side of the portal, but we stand a greater chance of survival with them than we do if the field collapses."

"Very well," Ay-ttho sighed. "Ron? Head for the Angetenar portal."

As they emerged from the portal, the khalgoin were waiting for them. Ay-ttho toyed with the idea of trying to outrun them, but she knew that wherever they ran, the khalgoin would be waiting.

Instead, she asked Ron to cut the engines and waited while the Khalgoin ship drew alongside them.

Pirate, whom they hadn't seen for most of the journey, arrived on the bridge.

"What's happening?" he asked.

"Where have you been?" asked Witt. "And... what the uxclod?"

Behind Pirate, he noticed Luap.

"What's he doing here?"

"He came along for the ride."

"Have you lost your marbles?" asked Tori. "Have you been living under a rock? Do you not remember what Sgniwef did last time someone ran off with Luap?"

"What happened?"

"Have you heard of the Zistreotovean war?"

"Oh, that."

"Oh that? They annihilated Zistreotov. It had been the most popular gambling venue in the Republic and they reduced it to rubble. What do you think she's going to do when she discovers you've kidnapped Luap?"

"I didn't kidnap him. He came of his own free will."

"I don't think Sgniwef will see it that way. She didn't last time."

"What are we going to do?" asked Sevan.

"We have to take him back," said Tori.

"I think the khalgoin might have different ideas," said Ay-ttho as the khalgoin ship locked onto the side of the Mastery of the Stars

CHAPTER 2: CHANGE OF PLAN

"You will never be separated from the one you love and who loves you," Pirate told Luap as they sat in his quarters, waiting to be boarded by the khalgoin. "Now I have given my hearts to you, and love for you has inflamed me. I am entirely devoted to you. A faithful lover, I will be with you throughout my whole life. Of this, you may be certain. Although I have brought you from Sonvaenope, a more beautiful and more rich life you will find on Angetenar where all will be according to your pleasure. All that you would wish, I will wish, and so too all that you will command."

"But are we going to Angetenar?" asked Luap. "We appear to have been captured by the zoxans."

"Mere details," Pirate reassured her.

There was a loud metallic clunk, and the ship rocked slightly as the zoxans attached a boarding platform to the freighter.

"They better not have damaged the paintwork," Ay-ttho complained from the bridge where she was waiting with Tori, Witt and Sevan.

The zoxans opened the door and a loud tannoy relayed their instructions, which echoed through the corridors of the freighter.

"Everyone must exit the ship through the front door. Don't carry guns."

"At least their system of translation has got better," commented Witt.

Ay-ttho, Tori, Sevan and Witt met Pirate and Luap by the exit and they all traversed the gantry leading to the zoxan ship together.

The gantry led to a door which opened automatically before them and then closed automatically once they had all passed through.

They had entered a room with a row of chairs.

"Please stay seated," came an announcement over a tannoy.

"I might have been wrong about the translations," Witt admitted.

They sat in the chairs and a frosted window in front of them unfrosted, revealing a group of zoxans.

"Where did you travel from?" a translated voice asked via the tannoy.

The six exchanged glances.

"We have come from the outer regions," said Ay-ttho.

"Where in the outer region?"

"We were travelling for a long time in suspended animation from another region of the universe."

"Don't lie. We know you came from a network of systems they called the Republic. You are a Republic and Corporate Security Clone, a Corporate Mining Clone, two Futurists and Ao Jr."

Their perception impressed Sevan.

"We can help each other," they continued. "You can help us find the traitor colony, and we make sure the rest of your life is comfortable."

"I don't know of any traitor colony. We have been searching for others of our own kind, but have been unsuccessful."

"You came from the Sonvaenope portal, so look there."

"We came through the Sonvaenope portal exactly because we found no-one there. If we had found anyone, we would have stayed there."

"And you go to Angetenar. Let's go together and see what we can find."

"There is no point. We already scanned Angetenar and there was nothing there. We can show you the results if you like."

"So we have a choice. Herse or Sicheoyama. Or is Ao Jun apparently with you, and Ao Jun is your destiny?"

"No destination. We are simply wandering, visiting a system at a time."

"We are in love and we wish to become partners," Pirate announced.

The others turned to him in surprise at the sudden outburst.

"How wonderful for you!" exclaimed the zoxan. "If you agree to help us, we will provide you with a wonderful ceremony and a beautiful apartment."

"Yeah, why not?" said Pirate. "We'll help you find the traitors."

The others were shocked by Pirate's collaboration.

"Please tell me where they are."

"Oh, I don't know where they are. But I will help you look."

The zoxan, although not completely satisfied, seemed to be content with the deal. Another door opened, and they escorted the group into the ship.

The zoxans formally partnered Luap and Pirate, the next rotation. Luap and Pirate, who had agreed to help the Zoxans, were given extraordinary material privilege. They gave them the "Moldavite Chamber", a magnificent room resplendent with olive-coloured gems which decorate huge pillars, fine mirrors, and animated sculptures. Its pallasite walls permitted those within the chamber to see what was happening outside, but no one outside could see those inside. The Moldavite Chamber signalled Pirate's and Luap's worth to the Zoxans. In return Pirate and Luap held discussion with the khalgoin, who quizzed them about the probable location of traitors. The others could not be sure what they discussed in these meetings, as Luap and Pirate ceased to mix with the others.

The khalgoin had decided to first visit Herse and headed towards the portal.

"At least we'll find out if there are other colonies," said Ay-ttho.

*

On Sonvaenope, Sgniwef was furious when she discovered Luap was missing. All the feelings of rage she had experienced at the outset of the Zistreotovean war came flooding back to her.

She summoned Kram, Nala, Eporhtwol, and Divad, all veterans of the Zistreotovean war, as well as Ozan, Tufan, Tetteh, Pelkan and Phoenix, younger and enthusiastic fighter pilots that had quickly risen through the ranks to command their own destroyers. Then there were Antilochus, Ajax, Nestor, and Oscar, who, although not in command of their own destroyers, were formidable pilots.

"It has happened again," she told them. "After all this time, someone has again kidnapped him. This time by that freighter from Angetenar. We must go after them and show no mercy."

They prepared their ships and were soon on their way to the Angetenar portal.

When the fleet had passed through the portal. Nala called Sgniwef to report what he had detected on his scanners.

"I located the Mastery of the Stars," he announced. "Unfortunately, it is attached to a zoxan scout ship. They are heading for the Herse portal."

"Let's catch them before they reach the portal," Sgniwef suggested. "We don't know how many zoxans might be on the other side."

*

"Ay-ttho?" Ron whispered into her communicator. "I have detected a fleet of Ao-jun destroyers arriving this side of the Sonvaenope portal. They are heading this way."

"Thanks," Ay-ttho whispered back. "Keep me updated."

Judging by the sudden increase in activity, the zoxans had also spotted the Ao-jun, but despite the scout ship heading full speed for the Herse portal, it was considerably slower than the Ao-jun destroyers and it was carrying the Mastery of the Stars.

"They'd be better off using the Mastery of the Stars engines," Ay-ttho commented to Tori as she received regular updates from Ron on the Ao-jun pursuit.

"I am already within weapons range," Nala reported to Sgniwef.

"Be careful," Sgniwef warned. "You may try to disable their engines, but it's likely Luap is on board, so we must do nothing that might endanger her."

The Zoxan ship was well within range of Nala's weapons system long before the Ao-jun were in range of theirs and so Nala fired. The Zoxan ship rocked with the blasts.

"How did the khalgoin ever take over the Republic?" Ay-ttho wondered aloud as the group dived for cover under a table. Loose equipment was already falling from the walls and ceiling around them.

"D'Heli told me they captured the scorpion lizards and modified them for their own use," Witt explained. "Unlike the prototypes, these ships were invincible."

"Where are they now?"

"Nobody knows."

"Well, I don't think much of their scout ships," said Ay-ttho as it shook with another blast.

"I wouldn't worry. I think we'll be safe enough. Sgniwef won't risk anything happening to Luap. They are probably just trying to disable the ship."

"We're almost at the portal, according to Ron."

"Quickly, don't let them get through the portal," Sgniwef shouted to her fleet.

By this time, the Zoxans had shot back, but their weapons were no match for the Ao-jun armour.

Nala managed a shot which disabled the scout ship's engine, but the vessel was still floating in the portal's direction.

"You must not let them enter!" Sgniwef yelled.

The Ao-jun fleet tried to circle the scout ship but couldn't do so without being sucked into the portal themselves. Sgniwef tried to activate the tractor beam on her destroyer, but it was too late. She watched helplessly as the khalgoin ship slipped into the portal and out of sight.

"We must follow them," said Sgniwef.

"But we don't know how many zoxans will be on the other side," cautioned Eporhtwol.

"There might not be any."

"Do you really want to take that risk?"

"For Luap? Of course."

The Zoxan ship slipped into the portal, followed, not long afterwards, by the Ao-Jun fleet.

When they all emerged on the other side, the Zoxan continued to fire on the fleet, who withdrew to beyond weapons range to contemplate their next move.

"We can't do anything that would endanger the life of Luap," Sgniwef repeated. "Their ship is disabled. They can't go anywhere and there are clearly no other Zoxan ships in this system."

"That's true," agreed Eporhtwol. "But we can't get close to them either. Those Zoxan cannons would rip even our destroyers apart if we got anywhere near."

"So we need to disable their weapons system. How are we going to do that?"

"Why don't we suggest a summit? We can send a delegation on board and once there, we can sabotage their systems."

"Do you think they are going to allow us on their ship?"

"It doesn't matter. We can meet by shuttle. We can hack into their systems via the system on the shuttle."

*

On the Zoxan ship, Sevan, Ay-ttho, Tori and Witt emerged from their hiding places once the fighting had stopped. They could see the khalgoin busy organising something.

The room in which they were being kept had an observation window and through it they could see a Zoxan shuttle launch.

They watched it appear to get smaller and smaller as it travelled away, and then it stopped, little more than a speck. Soon it was joined by another speck.

"They must be having a parley," said Witt.

"What's a parley?" Sevan asked.

"They are meeting to discuss how to resolve their differences."

There was a bright light from the location of the specs, and it soon became clear that there had been an explosion.

"Or not," said Ay-ttho.

The lights flickered.

"What's happening?" asked Tori

"I don't know," said Witt. "But the Khalgoin look like they are panicking."

Sure enough, a moment later, a Zoxan entered the room.

"We must use your ship to escape," he said.

"Okay," Ay-ttho didn't want to argue. "Let's go."

When they got to the entrance to the ship, they found the Zoxans already struggling to get on board and make their way to the more spacious cargo decks.

"What's going on?" asked Ay-ttho.

"To be honest, we're a little panicked," he answered. "Now that Ao Jun has disabled the engine and weapon system, what do you think?"

"I think we should get out of here. You must release our ship."

"Yes, my colleague has set up a system to allow you to unlock your ship's engine."

"Good."

Ay-ttho and the others tried to board amongst the Zoxans, who were way too big to negotiate the corridors of the Mastery of the Stars without difficulty. Luap and Pirate were fetched and loaded on board as well.

"You won't get a fancy apartment here, you know," Ay-ttho warned them.

Once everyone was all aboard, a Zoxan operated a remote device which released the bolts holding the Mastery of Stars in place and it floated free.

"They'll pay for that paintwork," Ay-ttho complained.

Through the observation window, they could see the Ao-jun fleet approaching.

Ron started the engines, and the freighter picked up speed, but the Ao-jun were already at full speed and continued to catch them. Nala's ship was soon within range and fired.

"What was that?" asked Tori as the freighter rocked from a hit to the hull.

"That," said Ay-ttho, pointing to a monitor. "Belongs to Nala. It was Llehctim's old ship, the most advanced weaponry in the Republic, until they built the scorpion lizards. He killed Enaud, who was the last one stupid enough to kidnap Luap."

Sevan noticed that Luap, who was becoming emotional at the mention of Enaud, left the bridge in a hurry, followed by Pirate.

Meanwhile, although the Mastery of the Stars was rapidly gathering speed, Nala was still scoring direct hits.

"Where are we going?" asked Tori.

"Head for the star, Ron," said Ay-ttho. "We'll fold."

"No!" Witt shouted. "You'll kill us all."

"We'll die here if we don't."

Not ready to leave Sevan and the team?

Get Book Four in the Mastery of the Stars series

Surviving the Zoxans

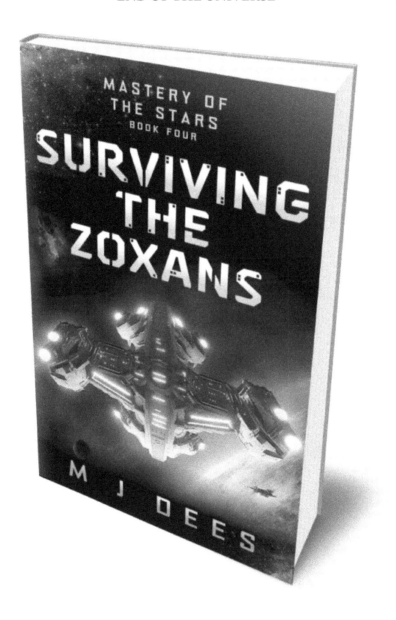

Pre-order now[1]

ABOUT THE AUTHOR

M J Dees is the author of eight novels ranging from psychological thrillers, to dystopia, to historical, to humorous fiction, and the Mastery of the Stars sci-fi novella series. He makes his online home at mjdees.com[1].You can connect with M J on Twitter at @mjdeeswriter[2], on Facebook at facebook.com/mjdeeswriter[3] and send him an email at mj@mjdees.com if the mood strikes you.

---

1. http://www.mjdees.com/

2. http://www.twitter.com/mjdeeswriter

3. http://www.facebook.com/mjdeeswriter

ALSO BY M J DEES

The Astonishing Anniversaries of James and David: Part One

How do you know if you have achieved success? No matter how successful he becomes, James doesn't feel happy. Meanwhile, his twin brother, David, seems content regardless of the dreadful life-threatening events which afflict him year after year. The Astonishing Anniversaries of James and David is as much a nostalgic romp through the 70s, 80s and 90s England as it is a shocking and occasionally tragic comedy.

Get it now[1]

Fred & Leah

At a time of war, soldiers are not always the only casualties.

On September 3rd, 1939, Fred knew he would have no choice but to go to France and fight. However, when he found himself among the thousands of men stranded after the Dunkirk evacuation, he did not know whether he would see his wife, Leah, and his two children again.

It leaves Leah trying to raise her two children by herself, but even she can't stop the bombs from falling on her street.

M J Dees' fourth novel and his first historical novel, Fred and Leah, is based on a real-life love story of two people whose lives were irrevocably altered by war.

Get it now[1]

Albert & Marie

What would you do if you were convinced you were going to die?

Swept up in the frenzy of patriotism, Albert volunteers to serve his king and country.

They shipped him off to the trenches of France along with almost every able-bodied man that he knew, leaving his estranged wife and his child behind.

Convinced he will die a horrible death, he seeks comfort in the arms of Marie, a local French woman who gives him hope his last days might become bearable.

Unfortunately, to do so would mean committing bigamy and he is caught between love and the law.

<u>Get it now</u>[1]

---

1.   https://buy.bookfunnel.com/y99ybm832n

DEDICATION

To Marize, Raya and Absolem, for their constant interference, us, and the universe.

ACKNOWLEDGEMENTS

I am indebted to my Beta Reading Team and my Advance Review Team.

COPYRIGHT

Ingram Content Group UK Ltd.
Milton Keynes UK
UKHW040753030723
424469UK00001B/143